Storm Over The Morning Calm

Storm Over the Morning Calm

A Novel by
Jerry Gibbs

Jerry Gibbs

WINDSOR HOUSE
PUBLISHING GROUP INC.

Windsor House Publishing Group
Austin, Texas

Storm Over the Morning Calm

A Novel by Jerry Gibbs

This is a work of fiction. All similarities to other than known
events and historical figures are unintended and coincidental.

Printing History
First Edition November, 1998

ISBN: 1-881636-28-3
Library of Congress Card Number: 98-060400

For information address: Windsor House Publishing Group, Inc.,
11901 Hobby Horse Court, Suite 1516, Austin, Texas 78758.

The name "Windsor House" and the logo are trademarks belonging to
Windsor House Publishing Group, Inc.

PRINTED IN THE UNITED STATES OF AMERICA
10 9 8 7 6 5 4 3 2 1

PREFACE

Korea was in its day the cultural mentor of both China and Japan. Its location made it a traditional road of war between these two nations. Korea remained a Chinese vassal state until 1895 when Japan shattered the antique armies of China. After war with Russia ending in 1905, Japan extended its hegemony over Korea until the end of World War II.

Korea has been known over history as Koguryo, Shilla and Parhee, Koryo, and Choson. The present name of Korea is derived from Koryo.

It has been called at times as "The Hermit Kingdom," for its desire to be left alone, the "Bandit Kingdom," for its continuing resistance to foreign oppression, and the "Land of the Morning Calm," for its weather. Korea is a land of terrain extremes and weather extremes. Because of its location on a peninsula between the Yellow Sea and the Japanese Sea with the accompanying morning temperature inversion patterns, mornings are almost always calm resulting in the name.

The Koreans are a hardy race who have never accepted foreign domination. They are hard working and intelligent. They are a race to be admired.

Prologue

The alarm clock went off at 0530 beside the bed of Lieutenant General Peter Goodwin, Commanding General of the U.S. Army 11th Corps in Frankfurt, Germany, formerly the Federal Republic of Germany. At this time of the year and at this latitude it was pitch dark and would remain so for another two hours. Pete Goodwin turned off the alarm, turned on the light, and examined the answering machine on his telephone. He had been in command of the Corps for almost three years and had established certain procedures for how he was to be notified of significant events. If it was really important, General Goodwin was to be called immediately. If it was not that important but something that he should not be blind-sided on by the press, the message was to be left on his answering machine. The machine was not blinking.

Pete got out of bed and took the first of his two morning showers. The first shower was a brief hot one to loosen the muscles before his morning exercises. He then proceeded to do 10 minutes of stretching exercises followed by 30 minutes on his exercise bike. He preferred jogging, but the doctors had told him that because of the traumatic arthritis in both knees he should not jog. At his most recent annual physical he had been given a clean bill of health except for the knees that had been damaged by many parachute jumps and by playing football five years too many. He was lucky that the 11th Corps had a holistic orthopedic surgeon who believed in cutting only as a last resort. A year ago, Pete had a definite limp. Not anymore. The surgeon had recommended arch supports, 1,600 units of Ibuprofen a day, and no jogging. It worked.

Pete had been in the Army over forty years, longer than most, but that was because his promotions had come later than for his contemporaries. He had passed his sixtieth birthday, but still was only ten pounds over his West Point weight. He was six feet tall, with a full head of brown hair graying around the edges. He was told that he looked closer to fifty. He felt closer to fifty.

After the exercises and his second shower, Pete changed into the battle-field fatigues that had been laid out for him by his orderly. These clothes were really an improvement over the old fatigue uniform of the past which

1

needed to be tailored, starched, and changed every day. They looked good and it was a violation of Army regulations to tailor them or starch them. It was like the policy to paint vehicles in camouflage colors instead of Army Green. There was no incentive now to spend time in painting vehicles that could be better spent in maintaining them. These were two very smart ideas. Not only were the troops and vehicles less visible in combat, but much time and effort were saved the elimination of meaningless tasks.

At 0705 Pete went downstairs to breakfast. Over the years this time had been worked out as the most convenient for Pete and his personal staff. A Lieutenant General commanding a Corps, unlike a staff officer, is authorized a personal staff. The intent is to maximize the time and effort that the General can devote to the troops and the mission. Pete was authorized a Commissioned Officer Aide-De-Camp, a driver, and an orderly. Waiting for him at the breakfast table were his Aide, Captain Alexandra Parker, known as Sandy, and his driver, Master Sergeant Rock Kowslowski. His orderly was ready to serve breakfast to the three of them. Pete had decided on this morning procedure about a year ago, when Captain Parker had been selected to be his Aide. It was the duty of the Aide and driver to get him to the office and to his appointments on time. Sandy, his Aide, and Rock, his driver, lived alone and had to eat breakfast somewhere. The arrangement worked out wonderfully and saved everyone time.

This was not entirely altruistic on Pete's part. Pete's wife had died four years ago, before he took over the Corps. He now lived alone. The villa that had been furnished to him by the German government was far more than he needed and quite lonely. He would have preferred a more humble residence, but protocol dictated that he have the best residence in the Corps, as well as a place to hold formal functions. One of the problems with these functions was that they required a hostess, normally the General's wife. Pete had solved this by asking if the wives of the senior officers on his staff would be willing to be his official hostesses on a rotating basis. Surprisingly, they were most enthusiastic, and the competition was fierce. Each woman strived to produce a better function than the others. It was humorous, in a way to observe.

As Pete entered the kitchen, both Sandy and Rock arose from the table where they were drinking coffee. Pete gestured for them to remain seated and took his seat. One of the nice things about this arrangement was that they could have their morning briefing in a comfortable setting.

"OK," said Pete, as he drank his orange juice, "anything happen last night that I need to know about?"

"General," said Sandy. "I checked with the Secretary of the General Staff this morning and things in 11th Corps are pretty benign. Nothing on the message board indicates any problems in the international arena other than Korea. We had the normal number of accidents and bar fights but nobody was killed. All in all, a good night. You have an eight o'clock with the Chief of Staff and at ten o'clock you are scheduled for your press conference. The speeches for these are in the folder right next to you."

Sandy was referring to the speeches that Pete was to make in the next several days pertaining to the inactivation of the 11th Corps in Germany and his own retirement. This was the price of success. The cold war was over and the United States had won. The decision makers in Washington had decided that the U.S. no longer needed two U.S. Army Corps in Europe. One would be adequate.

"Is there anything in these speeches that we haven't gone over before?" asked General Goodwin. "No sir," replied Captain Parker, "These drafts were originally written by you, edited by your staff, approved by the Pentagon, and wordsmithed by about everybody possible. They may not be everlasting prose, but they are certainly safe, whatever that means."

"I guess that's good enough," said Goodwin, "Nobody ever remembers a eulogy anyway."

Breakfast was served and the conversation died down. Pete caught himself gazing at Sandy Parker and thinking to himself that this was one fine woman. Not only was she a great Aide but she was very attractive. Pete tried continuously, but unsuccessfully, to dismiss these thoughts since an intimate relationship could really complicate things.

Sandy Parker worked very hard at looking good, unlike some of her West Point classmates who had let themselves go to pot. She remembered the label 'Hudson Hip Disease' used at West Point for describing female cadets who ate too much and did not exercise. Sandy was tall at 5'10" weighed 135 and ran four miles a day. she usually tied up her long red hair in a bun. At thirty-one, she was still told that she had the best legs in the Corps. She was also very smart.

Pete decided to get his mind on something else and asked Rock how his son Pete was doing.

Rock took a minute to respond. He had named his son after then Major Goodwin when he was his driver during the Vietnam War – how long ago – 20 years?. The fact of the matter was that Rock's son, Pete, would not have been accepted into West Point without General Goodwin's help. "General, Pete is doing well. He and your son, Stephen, are probably both going Infantry at branch drawing next week. Any thoughts on that ?"

"You know, Rock, you are very diplomatic," Goodwin responded. "We both know that your son is doing just great at West Point, star man, letter man, and all the rest, and that Stephen is your typical C student. But what the Hell, my record at West Point was as about as mediocre as possible. One of these two will make it big, and one won't. That's the nature of this business. I probably never told you this, but my getting into West Point was a total accident. By every definition, in those days, I would have been classified as poor white trash. The fact that I ended up with three stars has as much to do with luck as anything else. The next time you talk to Pete, you tell him how proud I am of him and to do his best to beat Stephen's butt. You know, of course, I'm going to tell Stephen the same thing."

Rock continued, "I checked with counterintelligence this morning and they said that as far as they could tell there is no threat of terrorism today. All seems to be calm. I thought we might take the green route to the Corps headquarters. I know how much you enjoy that route, even though it does take a few more minutes."

General Goodwin's staff car pulled up in front of the 11th Dreadnought Corps Headquarters at exactly 0800. This was as it should be. Any earlier and the honor guard would not be ready. This would especially irritate the German members of the honor guard who sincerely believed that "promptness is the courtesy of Kings."

After the ritual salutes, band playing, and flag raisings, General Goodwin gratefully escaped to the quiet of his office. The first person to meet him was his secretary, the legendary Brigitte. Pete wondered if anyone knew how old this lady really was. But who cares, he thought. She is a patriot, a friend, and trustful woman.

"Brigitte, I would very much like a cup of coffee."

"General," the old woman replied, "we have been doing this for three years. It is ready for you on your desk."

"Thank you, Brigitte, never mind me . . ., force of habit, I guess. Will you please tell the Chief that I'm ready to see him now?"

U.S. Army Colonel, Reuben Tanaka, had been at his desk since six o'clock. This was the primary duty of a chief of staff – to make sure the staff was working together and in response to the guidance of the boss. He and General Goodwin had been working together for about two years, and they could practically read one another's mind. Rube knew that the General would be preoccupied today, and therefore wanted a short meeting. General Goodwin probably didn't want to be bothered with details, Rube thought. Telling him that everything was on track would be sufficient. This gave Rube a little time for reverie. Where else in the world could a Japanese Jew be tolerated, he asked himself, much less be successful? Maybe if we pull this one off I might even get my star.

"Good morning, General," said Tanaka. "As I think you already know, it was a quiet night in 11th Corps and I don't think we are going to get any rockets from the Seventh Imperial Army in Heidelberg or from the puzzle palace in Washington." Tanaka was using the typical pejorative terms for higher headquarters. "I have reviewed the plans for the deactivation and everything is on track. Everyone has agreed to the timeline and, wonder of all wonders, we have actually received the fund citations to do the necessary work. And now let's turn to your speech."

Just at that moment, the General's red phone rang and the indicator said Flash Override. My God, Goodwin thought to himself, I've only seen Flash Override twice in my life and both times were in Korea. He picked up the phone and the operator came on the line immediately.

"Stand by for Green Six, sir."

Pete wondered what Brian would be up to at this time of the morning. Brian Hampton was the Army Chief of Staff and an old friend of Goodwin's. Pete checked his watch to see what time it was in Washington. Eight minus six equates out to two AM.

"Hampton here. Is that you, Pete?"

"Roger, Chief, this is Pete. What gives?"

"Pete," said Hampton, "I need you in Washington immediately. I know what you have on your schedule today, but it must be canceled. Rube has worked for me in the past and he can handle it. I'll agree to whatever cover and deception plan he comes up with. I have arranged a Special Air Mission VC 135 to pick you up at Frankfurt International. Bring a fresh set of greens and civvies. You are going to be talking with many important people. What's more, you can't tell anyone what is going on. Trust me on this one."

"OK, Brian, you know I trust you. Will do. But what is this is all about?"

"Well, Pete," said Hampton, "I really shouldn't, but I owe you." There was a long silence.

"Korea," Hampton finally admitted. "It's Korea."

*   *   *

It had been a hectic ten hours. Rock was instructed by Pete to go to the General's quarters and pack a bag for an indefinite time, including clothes for an ambiguous set of occasions. Fortunately, Rock had done this many times before and was pretty good at it. Sandy was told to go home and get her clothes. General Goodwin wondered what Brian was going to think when he show up with his Aide, but wasn't told to come alone. Goodwin believed that Sandy had earned the right for some high level visibility. Besides that, he needed her help and advice. He knew that Sandy had a good head on her shoulders and was straight forward as opposed to other idiot aides Pete had in the past who told him only what they thought he wanted to hear.

Reuben Tanaka took the news with his usual stoicism. "General, I don't see much of a problem. We have kept this very low key up until now, and so far there has not been an awful lot of press interest. I think I will just blame your cancellations on the staff. They will understand. I'll explain that you were called to Water Reed Hospital for your retirement physical. Do you have any idea what this is all about?"

General Goodwin thought about it for a moment. "Rube, this is in confidence, just for your ears only, but the Chief said Korea. I know we both read the intelligence briefs every day, but trouble's brewing. I've had two tours in Korea in the past, which is more than the careerists who always avoided Korea as a backwater. Maybe they want my opinion."

"General," replied Rube, "my guess is it's more than that. If it is , please count me in. I want to be the first Japanese Jew to wear a star."

Goodwin thought for a minute. "Well, Rube, you might be right. Perhaps you'd like to know something about being promoted to three stars that very few know. By law, if you get promoted to three-star general, you are authorized another five years of active duty, which is really bad personnel management. The Army wants you to have only one duty assignment as Lieutenant General to keep the upward mobility flowing. So, in order to be appointed to three stars, once you have been selected, you must sign an undated request for retirement. If you get selected for four stars, great, if not, thank you and goodbye. I'm really not ready to hang it up, so let's see how this plays. For now, I gotta go."

The staff car with Pete and Sandy exceeded the speed limit on the way to the airport, although that was really a contradiction in terms in Germany.

"General," asked Master Sergeant Kowslowski, "If there is something going on, let me help. I think there might be one more war left in this old war horse. Besides, if our kids are going to be involved, I want you in charge and you need me."

The VC 135 lifted off right at 2000 local as scheduled. Brian must have had a lot of clout to pull this off. From conversation with the crew chief, General Goodwin ascertained that this was the personal bird of the Commander in Chief of U.S. Air Forces in Europe. Goodwin bet that CINCUSAFE was not amused.

Pete sat back in his seat as the plane lifted off. He turned to Sandy, who was seated next to him, "I wonder if we have a frustrated fighter pilot at the controls? I have never been comfortable when someone I don't know is flying. I think anyone who pilots an airplane should first prove they know how to fly gliders. That is pure aviation. I am very glad that they require every graduate of the Air Force Academy to have demonstrated proficiency in gliders. I learned to fly gliders in Italy and ended up being an instructor pilot. I was always amazed at how many of these Air Force and Navy zoomies didn't have the slightest conception of coordinated flight. They all thought that the answer to any problem was to add a little power. What do you do if you don't have that kind of throttle? Oh well, there is nothing much I can do about it now except pray."

Sandy smiled and agreed.

As the plane leveled off, the cabin steward appeared. "Sir, I am Airman First Class Newton and I will be your cabin attendant for this flight. I have been told that you are to be considered a Very Important Person and that CINCUSAFE sends his regards and wishes you good luck and Godspeed."

"Well," thought Goodwin. "This trip may not be all that bad, after all."

"General," said Newton, "The Pilot in Command asked me to tell you that we have clearance all the way into Andrews, and that because of the favorable winds we should be on the ground at about 2200 Washington time. She wishes you a good trip and invites you to come up to the cabin. She knows your reputation as a glider instructor."

"She?" queried Goodwin.

"Yes sir. Captain Powell has been flying for CINCUSAFE for over a year. She has been selected to go to F-15 transition training and then to Edwards to become a test pilot."

"Airman Newton," asked Sandy, "Would that by any chance be Elizabeth Powell?"

"Yes Ma'am. That's her name."

"General, could I go forward?" asked Sandy. "I think she is a West Point classmate of mine, and, as I recall, she was the all time klutz of the Western world in plebe gymnastics. No coordination whatsoever."

"Go ahead, Sandy, you sure know how to make me feel better."

Captain Parker made her way up to the flight deck. The overhead lights were off and about all that could be seen was the glow of the instruments and the lights of Northern Europe stretching out beneath the plane. What a beautiful sight, thought Sandy.

"Beth, is that you? Are you really the Pilot in Command of this plane?"

"You bet your sweet ass, Sandy, " replied Beth Powell. "What are you doing here ?"

"My boss, General Goodwin, has been called to Washington for something that so far he has not told me about. He'll tell me at the appropriate time, I'm sure. He's a nice guy and has always played it straight with me. But, if this is as important as I think it is, I guess I'm honored to have been asked to come along."

"Well, Sandy," Beth agreed, "I think you are right about the importance.

When CINCUSAFE got a call at nine this morning from the Chairman of The Joint Chiefs of Staff, He canceled our previously scheduled flight to Ankara and told me to fully cooperate. I have never had such ease in getting flight plans approved and clearance to Washington. Normally, that takes hours, sometimes even days. This time, when I made the request, I got an immediate approval. So, is there anything I can do to help?"

"Beth, The General gets nervous when he is not doing the flying or doesn't know the pilot. I think he has a lot on his mind. Why don't I go back and have him come up to the cabin to meet you. We can do girl talk later. I always meant to ask you what happened to that beautiful First Classman you stole from me."

"Hah," answered Beth. "That's the best favor I ever did for you. He might have been absolutely beautiful in the uniform, but after graduation, he flunked out of jump school and ranger school, got boarded out of the Army, and then disappeared off the face of the earth."

Sandy laughed, walked back to the main cabin and sat down. "General," she said, " I don't think you have anything to worry about. This lady pilot is good. She'd like you to come forward to meet you."

"OK, Sandy," General Goodwin said, "I'll do that. But when I return, I need to talk to you. I have a lot on my mind and it always helps to be able to bounce thoughts off someone with good judgment. Be prepared, I'm going to lay a lot on you," Pete chuckled, "figuratively speaking ,of course."

Sandy smiled contentedly. The sexual tension between them had been growing for months. General Goodwin's wife had died four years ago. Sandy had divorced her husband two years ago. Both were lonely people. Sandy wondered where this relationship was heading. Sandy questioned its potential. She doubted it would work . . . or would it?

General Goodwin made his way up to the front cabin. On his way, he wondered whether he had gone too far this time. "Well, this is not the right time to dwell on that, it is just going to get in the way. But, on the other hand, it's not going to go away either. Let's try to suppress it and be professional. There are more important issues at stake, or are there?"

"Evening, Captain, may I have permission to come aboard?" asked Goodwin.

"Permission granted, sir," responded Beth. "It's a pleasure to have you. My copilot needs a pit stop anyway. Why don't you take the right seat."

Goodwin knew the drill. Without being asked, he fastened the seat and shoulder harnesses and placed the oxygen mask on his forehead so that it could be pulled down at an instant's notice. This action received an approving glance from Beth.

"Beautiful night, General, everything is absolutely nominal," said Beth.

"Our numbers in the inertial navigation system are right on and have been verified." Goodwin knew this remark reflected the pilot's concern over the disaster of Korean Air Lines Flight 007 in which the pilot punched the wrong numbers, flew over Soviet airspace and was shot down. "Besides, we have the most modern version of NAVSTAR GPS available and I can tell within 15 meters exactly where we are. Right now, we are exactly where we should be. This is a good thing tonight, because the forecasters tell us that we are going to have a super Northern Lights show. Although a beautiful thing to watch, it wreaks havoc with magnetic navigation systems. Sandy told me about your concern with coordinated flight. Let me assure you that our automatic navigation system has been programmed for coordinated flight. When I turn it off in preparation for landing and start flying manually, you might want to come up again and check me out. It might make you feel better to know that I got my Silver badge in soaring at Black Forest Glidercamp last summer."

"I give up, Captain. I see that you and Sandy have been conspiring against me. I think I'll go back to the passenger's compartment and be a good little boy."

"Korea," Goodwin said to Sandy after he returned. "That's what this is all about."

General Goodwin and Sandy had made themselves comfortable in the conference room of the VC 135, which definitely beats flying coach. Airman Newton, after asking them if there was anything they might want, had brought them a bottle of mediocre chardonnay and an ash tray, and then disappeared.

Goodwin took out a cigarette and turned to Sandy, "I have been trying to quit smoking for years and have been fairly successful at it. I don't smoke in the office, I really don't crave a cigarette when I am under tension, or anything like that. But I do smoke when I have to engage in reflective thought. This is one of those times. I hope you don't mind."

"General, I don't mind at all. As a matter of fact, I think I'll join you. I am a closet smoker, too." Sandy took a cigarette and lit it.

"Sandy," asked the General, "What do you know about Korea?"

"Probably less than I should," admitted Sandy, "they didn't teach us anything about it that amounted to a hill of beans in military history at West Point. It was almost as if it paled into insignificance when compared to Napoleon's wars, Jackson's valley campaigns, World War II, and, for that matter, Vietnam."

"You have got that right," agreed Goodwin. "We always seem doomed to learn the wrong lessons. Korea was the right war, at the right time, for the right reasons. Vietnam, on the other hand, was the wrong war, at the wrong time, for the wrong reasons. And yet, how many people think that way?

"Let me tell you why I think they are calling me back to Washington. One more time the decision makers there have ignored Korea. Now, they're wishing they hadn't. I have a reputation for understanding Korea. This is not the first time I have been asked to pull the chestnuts out of the fire there. Whether they just want my advice or want me to actually do something, I guess we will find out tomorrow. I must admit that I am eager for one more shot. I'm not ready for retirement. Except for these two lousy knees, the docs tell me that I'm in perfect condition, although they don't understand why, considering the way I have abused my body over the years. I hope this doesn't sound too selfish, but if someone has to do something, it might as well be me." Goodwin takes a drag from his cigarette, leans back. Sandy relaxes.

"A little necessary background is in order. Korea, both North and South, was subjugated by one empire or another, usually China, for over two thousand years. It became known as The Hermit Kingdom by some and The Bandit Kingdom by others. Because of these circumstances, the people of Korea became crafty, smart, resilient, stoic, and strong. Maybe what you'd call Darwinism at work – adapt or perish. At the end of World War II, Korea was not at the top of the international agenda. As almost an afterthought, the United Nations decided to temporarily divide Korea at the 38th latitude line, later to be called the 38th parallel. Let the Soviet Union administer the northern half and the British administer the southern half and later have plebiscites. But that is when it all started to come unglued. The Soviets had no intention of turning over any territory, Korea, Eastern Europe, or anywhere else to anyone. They considered these territories as the spoils of war and, because of their fear resulting from centuries of invasion, were in the process of establishing a Cordon Sanitaire around their boundaries.

"At the same time, the Brits opted out. They were so exhausted after the war that they simply could not take on any responsibilities other than Palestine and Cyprus. By default, the U.S. was asked to take over what, by that time, was being called South Korea. At least we did something smart then. The U.S. requested that this be designated a United Nations responsibility and that the U.S. be the agent. This turned out to be extremely advantageous in 1950.

"Between 1946 and 1950, the Soviet Union poured a lot of money and material into North Korea with the intent of dominating the peninsula, and by force, if necessary. During the same years, the United States had allowed its forces in the far East including Korea and Japan, to completely deteriorate. Divisions existed in name only. They were lucky to have the combat power of a regiment, if that."

Pete explained how in late June, 1950, the North Koreans, with their Soviet advisors, attacked. In less than two months they had occupied most of South Korea except for a small bridgehead around the southeastern port city of Pusan. General Douglas MacArthur had been given command of what was called United Nations Forces, Korea.– fancy name but very few forces. He scraped up everything he could find and managed to hold the bridgehead. By using economy of force strategies, MacArthur was able to put together an amphibious invasion force that unexpectedly attacked the port city of Inchon on the west coast of Korea, about halfway up the peninsula. This completely took the North Koreans by surprise. They panicked and fell apart. Within several months MacArthur had gone over to the offensive and was on his way to the Manchurian border at the Yalu river. At that time he was predicting complete victory and stated that he would have the troops home by Christmas. He did not count on the Chinese reaction. On a cold night in November several Chinese Field Armies attacked across the Manchurian border. Again, it was a very close thing. MacArthur's Eighth Army and 10th Corps almost collapsed. Over three years, the battle raged up and down the peninsula. But finally, the war ended and *where* the war ended is very important to understanding the next forty years.

"There is a natural defensive line between the north and south portions of Korea," Goodwin told Sandy. "The western half of this line follows the Imjin Gang river, about twenty to thirty miles south of the 38th parallel. It then bends to the northeast and is anchored on the ridgelines of some high and rugged mountains, all twenty or thirty miles north of the 38th parallel. Sort of like a big S lying on its side, horizontally bisected by the 38th parallel. The reason that this was so important is that the 38th parallel was totally artificial from any military perspective. It gave the North Koreans a unique advantage in 1950 that they would never have again. Unfortunately, the success of the 1950 invasion had a negative affect on military planning for over twenty years. American and South Korean planners had drawn the wrong conclusions. They had committed the worst kind of military sin. By misreading the lessons of history, they had presented their enemy with a military advantage."

Sandy was intrigued.

"As in any military analysis," Goodwin continued, "the first thing to consider is the terrain. The Korean Peninsula extends southward from the north eastern section of the vast Asian continent, spanning 1,000 kilometers north to south. It shares most of its northern border with China and touches Russia. Seventy percent of the country is mountainous. The T'aebaek mountains run the full length of the east coast where the tides of the Sea of Japan have carved out sheer cliffs. The western slopes are quite gentle, forming plains. There are many rivers with the most important ones from a tactical point of view being the Han-gang, which flows through Seoul, and its major tributary, the Imjin.

"If you study the history of Korea, you will read about seven or eight invasions, some going north and some going south. In every case but one, the direction of attack, or the avenue of approach, as tacticians prefer to call it, has been along the Kaesong – Munson approach and has occurred during winter. If you look at the map, the reason becomes obvious, at least to me. The eastern half of the country is extremely mountainous with all the advantages going to the defender. The western half is quite flat and easy to transit except for the Imjin-Gang. Kaesong is on the northern side of the river and Munson is on the south. Because of the climate, this river freezes over solid for about four months a year. The Imjin is no longer a barrier as long as your troops are hardy enough to fight in the winter, and Lord knows, if there is anything true to be said about the Koreans, they are hardy.

"Also, if you look at the map a little further to the east of Kaesong-Munson, you will see the Chorwan valley – a really tough piece of terrain. The 38th parallel puts most of the tough going behind you, creating what is otherwise known as a free shot. This is the route the North Koreans took in 1950. But if you then look at where the war ended in 1953, at what came to be called the Demilitarized Zone, you find exactly the opposite. The whole Chorwan valley is in South Korean hands. This has now become a very tough baby. If you then look at the other approach, the Kaesong-Munson approach, the logic is exactly reversed. All these brilliant planners based their war plans on a repeat of a Chorwan attack. They had their forces in exactly the wrong place. I believe, although there is no way in the world that I can prove it, that my change in the defense strategy of South Korea might have actually avoided World War III."

"Sounds like Korea is a beautiful place with the mountains and valleys," Sandy said.

"Oh, yes, and Korea is a land of extreme temperatures, hot in the summer, cold in the winter. Because it is surrounded by water, it almost always has temperature inversions in the morning, resulting in very calm mornings. It is known as the Land of the Morning Calm."

BOOK 1

THE PAST

Chapter One

K orea," thought First Lieutenant Peter Goodwin, recently of the 82nd Airborne Division, to himself. "Why in the world are they sending me there?"

The year was 1953.

The Northwest Orient Stratocruiser had taken off from Idlewild Airport in New York, stopped in Minneapolis, stopped again in Seattle, and, according to the pilot, was going to stop again at the last island in the Aleutian chain, called Shemya. Goodwin got out the map from the receptacle on the seat in front of him to see if he could find Shemya. Holy smokes, Goodwin thought to himself, that is a mighty small place in the middle of nowhere and in December, it's awfully dark and cold. He hoped the pilot could find Shemya, after telling the passengers that the plane had passed the point of no return. Not enough fuel to return to Seattle. It was either find Shemya or take a bath in a very cold Bering Sea. How reassuring.

The Stratocruiser started to descend and let down the landing gear. Goodwin looked out the window and saw nothing but snow rushing by the plane. The plane then made what pilots refer to as a positive landing. That is, fly it right into the runway without flaring. After bouncing a few times, the plane came to a stop. At that time it was expected that the plane would taxi to the operations building. That did not happen. The pilot came on the intercom and announced that because of a crash earlier that night there was debris on the runway. Therefore, a bus would come to pick up the passengers and transport them to the operations building. Unfortunately, this would cause about five hours delay because they would have to wait until daylight to check for debris on the runway before taking off for Tokyo. (A few months later, Goodwin found out that this happened on every flight into Shemya. The long delay gave the stewardesses time to pick up a little pocket money, since there were no women assigned to Shemya.)

The bus arrived and took the passengers and crew to the operations building.

Goodwin proceeded to get into a conversation with the NCO in Charge of the passenger terminal. "Too bad, Lieutenant, that you won't be here for our going away ceremony tomorrow," said the NCO.

"What's that?" responded Goodwin.

"Well," said the NCO, "the tour on this Godforsaken place is for one year. Sergeant Smith is going home tomorrow. All of us walk up the north end of the island, pick up a rock, carry it to the south side and throw it into the ocean. We figure that, given enough time, we can move this frigging place to Hawaii."

Eventually, the Stratocruiser took off for Haneda Airport in Tokyo. The pilot announced that it was going to be a long and uneventful flight and the passengers might want to get a rest. Pete Goodwin noticed that the stews looked a little weary.

This long flight gave Pete time to reflect on the last two years. About six months before graduation from West Point, he had met Mary Lou. Pete had been getting tired of the very enjoyable, but meaningless, lifestyle of New York City. Lovely ladies, sexually talented, a million laughs, but something was missing. One night, at the Astor Hotel bar, he had noticed this magnificent blond sitting with what looked to be her parents. One thing about the West Point curriculum was that it taught you to seize the initiative. Pete had gone over to speak with the father.

"Excuse me, sir," Pete had said, "I know that I am probably out of line, but I couldn't take my eyes off of your daughter. I am sure you will tell me to go away, and I probably deserve it. I am a West Point cadet and I hope you will introduce me to your daughter. Even if you do not, I had to try, because I never would have forgiven myself for not knowing what might have been."

"Sit down, son," the father had said. "That has got to be the biggest line of bull shit I have ever heard. My daughter is driving me crazy. This is my daughter, Mary Lou, but watch out – she has left a trail of broken hearts several miles long. I have a suspicion that you two might be cut from the same bolt of cloth. And your name, please?"

"Sir," responded Pete. "My name is Pete Goodwin and I am a first classman at West Point. That means that I will graduate this coming June."

"Mary Lou," the father had said, "this is Pete. Do you want to talk with him or do you want him to go away?"

"Let him stay, daddy, this sounds interesting."

That was the beginning of a wonderful, but ill-fated love affair. Mary Lou was a Phi Beta Kappa student at Columbia University, had been selected by a campus organization as America's Prettiest Coed, was sexually liberated, and had a mind of her own. Pete saw her as the first real feminist. Mary Lou loved visiting West Point. She loved the parades, the pageantry, the cadet dances, everything about it. Every weekend, she would drive up to the Point in the brand new red Chevrolet her indulgent father had given to her, since in those days cadets were not allowed to have cars. Sometimes she would stay at the Hotel Thayer at West Point, sometimes they would go down to New York City, and sometimes they would just drive around the beautiful Hudson valley until they found a place to spend the night.

Unfortunately, the relationship had to end. West Point was an artificial environment not reflecting the real world. After graduation, Pete was assigned first to Fort Sill for basic Field Artillery training, then to Fort Benning for jump school, and then to Fort Bragg to the 82nd Airborne Division. Although Mary Lou visited frequently, she didn't like what she saw – substandard living and not much money. This was not the kind of life she was looking forward to. She and Pete would have dinner at the homes of Pete's married classmates and she was appalled at how they lived. When Pete's orders to Korea came down, it was the last straw. Pete would be gone for 16 months and Mary Lou finally laid down the ultimatum. Choose the Army or her.

Pete chose the Army and that was it. Intellectually, Pete knew he made the right choice. Eventually, either he would destroy her or she would destroy him. Rationalizing, however, didn't alleviate the hurt. The next morning, Mary Lou drove Pete to Idlewild Airport in that same red convertible, and it was over.

The Stratocruiser landed at Haneda without event. Pete and the other soldiers on board were taken by bus to Grant barracks on the outskirts of Tokyo. They were told by the officer in charge that they would go by train to the port of Sasebo in the next couple of days. From there, they would go by ship to Korea. They were further told to stay out of trouble. The Japs smile a lot at Americans, they were told, and will try to sell you anything, but deep down, they hate your guts.

That night Pete wandered around Tokyo. The advice was correct. You could get a hotel room for two dollars, a beer for a quarter, a girl for the night for the price of a meal, and yet you could sense the hostility. One night in Tokyo was enough for Pete. Three days later, he boarded the train for Sasebo. The trip took over eight hours. This was a beautiful country Pete thought. The coastline looked a lot like the Big Sur country of California. There was no obvious evidence that Japan had ever been bombed.

Sasebo was another thing entirely. This was a typical sea port town with a large U.S. Navy presence. It was one big brothel and Pete couldn't wait to leave. Some soldiers had managed to be there for over two weeks. All it took was a little bribe to the NCO in charge who made out the manifests. After all, the time in Sasebo counted against the 16 month Korean tour of duty. Pete, however, went to the NCO and told him that he wanted the first available transportation to Korea. The NCO was delighted. This meant that he could bump somebody else and pick up another few bucks.

That night, Pete boarded the U.S.S. Sea Serpent, which was known to the crew as "The Snake." The ship was a worn out bucket of bolts. It was probably used for this run because it couldn't survive on the open sea. The next morning, the ship sailed into Pusan harbor. Pete was grateful that the sea had been calm. As the ship got closer, the ravages of war became readily apparent. There didn't seem to be a single building standing that was not damaged and there were hulks all over the harbor. Pete thought it interesting how a person can study military history all his or her life, but nothing really prepares one for the aftermath of a war.

The captain from the Transportation Corps met the troops at the dock. He gathered them together to give them the standard briefing. "Men," said the Captain, "Welcome to Korea. You have landed at the Port of Pusan. As soon as we get your orders straight and receive instructions from the Eighth Army in Yong Dong Po, you will be processed to your final destinations. For most of you this means a long train ride to the north, but that will come later. Pusan Reception Station can not be described as a first class hotel. You will be billeted in squad tents with outdoor latrines. The mess hall is a converted cannery factory. You might notice a barbed wire fence and armed guards. This is for your protection. Although the armistice has been signed, the war is still officially on and will be for another seven months. There are a lot of bad guys wandering around out there. Some are cut off North Korean troops, some are South Korean deserters, and some are well organized bandits. Let there be no doubt, these people will kill you for a pack of cigarettes. Stay in the compound and follow instructions if you want to stay alive. If you don't believe me, we had had three fatalities in the last week – men who thought they might go downtown and visit the bar girls. This really is Indian country. This definitely is not Sasebo. Now, if you line up over there underneath the signs indicating the first letter of your last name, we will start your process-ing. One more time, please believe me. *Pay attention.* One other thing. There is a group here in Korea called 'Slicky Boys,' These guys are the world's best thieves. It is really unbelievable how sly they are. Sleep with all your valuables inside your pants and inside your sleeping bag. If you don't, I guarantee they will be gone in the morning."

Pusan Reception Station was really the pits. It was exactly as described by the captain who gave the briefing. Pete could not wait to leave. Two days later, the orders came down. He was to take a train to Yong Dong Po just outside of Seoul, the capitol, for further processing. He was told that he was going to be assigned to a Field Artillery Battalion in I Corps Artillery, but that the precise battalion would not be decided on until the processing at Yong Dong Po.

The next morning Pete and several hundred other soldiers boarded "The Orient Express," a whimsical label, at best. Pete believed the relic to be fifty years old at least. It had wooden seats, some missing. Pete noticed that the heat came from a woodburning stove at the end of the car, which he thought might explain some of the missing seats. Also, some of the windows were missing and patched up with cardboard and masking tape. Fortunately, at Pusan they had been issued winter gear. The supply sergeant had told them that this gear was ugly, ungainly, and heavy. About the only saving grace was that it kept you warm, a fact that they would soon learn to appreciate. Pete was already starting to appreciate the gear. The temperature outside was below freezing and it was supposed to get below zero by the time they got to Yong Dong Po, eight hours away.

Pete gazed out the window. Fortunately, he had a window that still had its glass, minimizing the cold draft. The countryside was devastated. Although most of the landscape was rice paddy, whenever the train came to a village, there was nothing to be seen that did not show the ravages of war. Pete could not see even a single building that was not damaged in one way or another. But, he noticed something else. There were no beggars, no people standing around doing nothing. Everyone that he could see was working. The women, who the troops called called "mamasans," all seemed to have a baby strapped to their back. They were working at hard labor tasks, like rebuilding roads. The men, who likewise were called "pappasans," were carrying the materials on "A-Frames." The A-Frame was an ingenious device. It consisted of several pieces of wood put together in the shape of an A and strapped to the back. When the wearer leaned forward, all the weight went to the shoulders. When the wearer leaned back, the weight was transferred to the two poles that just cleared the ground when walking. Pete learned that these pappasans could carry their bodyweight on these A-Frames all day long. The most significant thing Pete observed on the trip, however, was how hard-working everyone was. The Koreans were diligently going about the business of rebuilding their country, and without complaint.

The Orient Express pulled into Yong Dong Po at 1400 hours. Here the reception for Pete was entirely different. At all of the previous stops, Pete was just another face in the crowd waiting his turn to be processed. This time, a Sergeant walked up and down the line asking for Lieutenant Goodwin.

"That's me," responded Goodwin.

"Great, sir," said the NCO, "I don't know who you are, but I have orders to get you on the 1600 train north to Yonson. Please follow me."

The next two hours were a blur. It is amazing how fast the Army bureaucracy can function when it has to. By 1500 the necessary paperwork was completed and Goodwin was in a Jeep headed for the north side of Seoul. The rail tracks between the south and north sides of Seoul had been heavily damaged during the war and had not yet been repaired. Again, as Pete was driven through Seoul, he noticed that the buildings he could see were all damaged, but that everyone was working to rebuild them. The Jeep pulled up to what might have been a railroad station in the past. The sergeant hurried Pete to the first car of the train and told the MP in charge that this was his last passenger. The train pulled out immediately. Pete was impressed. Nobody ever held a train for him before.

The train headed north and made multiple stops. Pete learned that this train had the nickname "The Nowhere Local." At each stop the MP would call off a few names and people would get off. As it got dark and cold Pete realized that there were only four people on the train: himself, the MP and two PFC's who looked as scared as he felt.

"Yonson," announced the MP, "Last stop, everybody off. We have got to back up this wreck over five miles before we can turn it around. If you don't already know, there are train robbers out here."

Pete and PFCs Hawkins and Barnes got off the the train, which immediately started backing up. There was nobody around. The place looked like the face of the moon. At that point, Pete realized that, in the haste of the day, nobody had issued him a weapon or ammunition. Pete didn't know what to do. Although he was taught at West Point to improvise, he was flat out of ideas.

Suddenly headlights from a truck appeared down the road. It seemed an eternity, but the Army three quarter ton truck finally got there.

"Lieutenant Goodwin, is that you?" asked the driver. "Sorry I was not here to meet you, but we had a bandit roadblock down the road a piece and the MPs have just now opened the road."

"Welcome to our little piece of Korea."

Chapter Two

What's your name, soldier?" Goodwin asked the driver.

"Specialist 4th class Rinaldi," responded the driver.

"I know this sounds silly, but where am I and where are we going? Things got so hectic at the Yong Dong Po repple depple (Armyspeak for Replacement Depot) that they never told me anything."

"Sir," said Rinaldi. "You have just gotten off the train at Yonson, the last stop on the Nowhere Local. You are, right now, about ten miles north of the 38th parallel and we have about five more miles north to go until we get to the 150th Field Artillery Battalion. Our battalion is the furthermost north U.S. unit in Korea. The battalion commander tells us that that is something which we should be very proud of. In all candor, it scares the hell out of me. I have been instructed to take you straight to the hootch (Armyspeak for living quarters, derived from the Korean word *Hootchie Wa*) of Colonel Castle, the battalion commander. He said that he needs to speak with you immediately."

Goodwin thought about that for a minute. For over a week, there had been no urgency whatsoever and nobody seemed to care who he was nor where he was going. Now, all of a sudden, things had changed.

"OK, Rinaldi, let's go. I assume Hawkins and Barnes are going with us."

"Yes sir, they can just get in the back of the truck."

"Well," answered Goodwin, "it's awfully cold out here. Why don't we just throw our gear in the back of the truck and the four of us squeeze in up front. From what I remember about the three quarter ton truck, it has a very good heater."

"Sir, Eighth Army regulations are quite specific. Only three people in the front of the truck."

Goodwin knew that this was a test designed to measure his leadership skills in the battalion. By tomorrow, everyone in the battalion would know how he handled it.

"I tell you what, Specialist Rinaldi, I won't tell anyone if you don't. I have an approved driver's license for this kind of truck and if regulations scare you, I will drive and you can ride in the back of the truck."

Rinaldi answered quickly. He understood what was going on. "Sir, I'm sure that we can all fit into the front of the truck. Why don't we get started?"

Barnes and Hawkins had been watching this byplay with detached amusement. Of course, they didn't want to ride in the back of a very cold truck, but, much more important, they wanted to see what this lieutenant was made of. He had passed the first test.

The truck pulled away from the station. Rinaldi asked Goodwin if he knew how to use a "grease gun," army slang for the caliber .45 automatic weapon, which had a firing rate of 500 rounds a minute.

"You bet, Rinaldi, I qualified on this thing at Camp Buckner during my yearling summer. Why?"

"Lieutenant," said Rinaldi, "We have trouble on this road quite often. If something happens, I will need your help. There is a grease gun on the floor right in front of you. It is locked and loaded. You might know that these old, three quarter ton trucks have a windshield that can be raised instantly. The latch on your side is already open. If something happens, I will release the latch on my side and the window will fly up. At that time you fire at anything that moves. We have found that the Gooks around here fire on us at any convenient opportunity, but don't want a serious fight. Trust me on this one. I usually drive right through it."

Pete was wondering how many surprises were in store for him. He sure didn't learn about *this* at West Point.

Fortunately, the trip to the 150th Field Artillery Battalion was uneventful. About all that Goodwin saw were many abandoned villages. He asked Rinaldi where all the people were. Rinaldi told him that they were presently twenty miles north of the no-farming line, and that the South Korean government had decided that, for the time being, because of the unsettled conditions, civilians would not be allowed north of the town of Uijongbu, about twenty miles to the south. The idea was that that anyone specifically unaccounted for was hostile and could be fired upon. That didn't stop the bad guys, but at least you didn't have to go through a long process to defend yourself.

"OK," said Pete, "that makes sense, but what about the "slicky boys" I have heard so much about?"

Rinaldi laughed out loud at that one. "Lieutenant, we don't have a slicky boy problem – at least not now. About a mile south of our battalion is the Turkish Brigade. They don't mess around. A few months ago, a slicky boy tried to infiltrate the Turkish compound. They executed him on the spot, cut off his head, and displayed it on a pole in front of their headquarters. No more problem. Unfortunately, the Turkish Brigade is going home in a few months. After that we'll probably have a problem again."

Pete again started to wonder just how complete his West Point education had been.

The three quarter ton truck finally made its way through the front gate of the 150th Field Artillery Battalion compound. Rinaldi told the lieutenant that they were going straight to the hootch of the battalion commander where he would get something to eat.

"That's great, Rinaldi, I'm starving. But what about Barnes and Hawkins here? They haven't eaten either."

Rinaldi hesitated. "Lieutenant," he said impatiently. "That is the second time tonight you have pulled my chain. I promise you that I will make sure that they get properly fed and bedded down."

"Fair enough, Rinaldi. I'll hold you to that."

The truck pulled up in front of the commander's hootch. It was what is referred to as an arctic shelter. Goodwin had not seen one of these since winter maneuvers in Camp Drum last year. The whole thing came in a big box. The box came apart and became the floor of the shelter. Inside the box were seven curved ribs that formed the roof and sides. Also inside the box were a number of insulated strips that fit over the ribs and completed the structure. The whole thing was quite warm and cozy.

Goodwin parked his gear outside and knocked on the door. "Come in," responded Lieutenant Colonel Thomas Castle, commander of the 150th Field Artillery Battalion.

"Lieutenant Goodwin reporting as ordered, sir," said Pete, using the protocol that he had been taught at West Point.

"Come in quickly, Lieutenant, it's cold out there. And bring your gear with you. It might freeze rock solid, and though we don't have a big slicky boy problem here, it just might be gone when you leave," replied Colonel Castle. "Join me by the tent stove. Have you ever seen one of these before?"

"Yes sir," said Pete. "We used them at Camp Drum, New York, last winter when the Army decided that the 82nd should be trained in winter operations. That was a real experience, since almost no one in the Division had ever seen snow before. The Division was composed of southern whites and inner city blacks. But we got through it and ended up being pretty good. From what I remember, these things put out a lot of heat, but are very dangerous."

"Right on, Lieutenant, there have been more soldiers killed in Eighth Army in the last four months from tent stove accidents than all other causes combined. The Commanding General is furious. If anyone has a tent stove accident these days, he is history. The policy in this battalion is that all tent stoves must be constantly observed. If you want it on at night, you must have a duty roster of people that stay awake. But enough of that. I owe you an explanation as to why I had you hustled through Yong Dong Po. The simple fact of the matter is that the Battery Commander of C Battery committed suicide yesterday. I needed a new Battery Commander, and given the circumstances of the situation, I didn't have anyone in the battalion I thought could do the job.

"The best way I can explain why I selected you is to tell you about our mission, which as you will see is somewhat unique. But first, I want to know a little bit about you. I have a friend at the replacement Depot in Yong Dong Po. He saw your file before you got there. He noticed a few things out of the ordinary. Check me if I am wrong. You are a graduate of West Point, served a tour with the 82nd Airborne Division, a paratrooper, and a Ranger. You must admit that that is unusual for an artilleryman. Tell me how it came about."

"Sir," responded Goodwin, "Upon graduation, I selected Airborne because I needed the extra 110 dollars a month to make my car payments. When I arrived at the 82nd, I found that I had made the right choice for the wrong reason. That Division is good. They are extremely proud of their heritage. Their attitude was that they could do anything, no matter how difficult. I learned a lot and enjoyed it immensely. During January and February of last year, the Division, as I mentioned, was sent to Camp Drum for winter maneuvers. I was assigned full time as an artillery forward observer with the 505th Parachute Infantry Regiment. It was there that I first ran into Army Rangers. They were a cut above the average. I decided that, if given the opportunity I would like to see if I could do that. That summer the Division received a huge enlisted levy for Korea and suddenly had a bad officer-to-enlisted-man ratio. The officers were driving the few remaining troops crazy looking for something meaningful for them to do. I then applied for Ranger School. Division was delighted, one fewer officer that they didn't have to worry about. Three months later, I graduated and went back to the Division until November, when I received my orders to Korea."

"One other thing sir. I have never enjoyed jumping out of perfectly good airplanes. I guess I am something like Maxwell Taylor, who was the commander of the 101st Airborne. He said that he hated jumping out of airplanes, but loved being around people who did."

"Goodwin," asked Colonel Castle, "are there any other Artillery Airborne Rangers around?"

"Not that I know of. I am told that there are some who were Airborne Rangers when they were in the infantry, then later transferred to the artillery, but I am probably the first to do it this way."

"OK, now let's talk about our mission. When I am finished I think you will understand why I was interested in your background," said Castle.

Chapter Three

Forgive me," said Castle, "I know that you have not eaten since this morning. I've something here for you. That's one good thing about a tent stove – you can cook on it. I'm afraid that your gourmet meal is going to be fried spam and dehydrated potatoes. The refrigerator ship that brings in food supplies broke down off Okinawa. We are existing off emergency rations. About all I can say is that while this is your first meal of this kind, we've been eating like this for a week. I can, however offer you a drink. I have a bottle of good scotch. Go ahead and eat and drink while I tell you about the mission and the situation."

"Great, sir," responded Pete, "I could really use that drink and I am hungry enough to eat the south end of a northbound mule."

Pete believed Castle to be a real gentleman and detected his regret at not being able to offer him a better reception.

Pete took a sip of his drink and tried the food. it was not all that bad. It was hot and obviously had a few extra spices added, none of which he could identify.

"Ok, Goodwin, let's get on with it. By the way do you mind if I call you Pete? You can call me Colonel, or sir." Castle made an old Army joke.

With a mouth full of food, Pete nodded.

"Look at the map," said Castle. "The first thing to notice is the Demilitarized Zone. This is where the war ended. It is about a mile wide and is intended to keep us and the North Koreans separated until elections are held. My guess is that it is going to be here for a long time, since I don't think the North Koreans have any intention of having free elections. They know that they would lose. Now see where the 150th is located? We are right up here close to the DMZ (using Armyspeak for the Demilitarized Zone). We are the furthermost north Allied unit. All the infantry and armor units are south of us. There is a reason for this. By its nature, an artillery battalion can make itself fairly comfortable even in a combat configuration. Infantry and armor can't. The infantry and armor have been withdrawn to holding areas, although they do send out patrols and man outposts along the DMZ.

"If the North Koreans attack, the infantry and the armor need time to deploy to their combat positions. That's where we come in and the reason that we are located where we are. The 150th is equipped with the 240 millimeter howitzer. We have six of them. This old gun is a relic of the Italian campaign of World War II. It was developed specifically for bunker busting. It has a range of over 25,000 yards and fires a projectile weighing over 365 pounds. It is quite accurate. As an artilleryman, I am sure that you know that artillery weapons design is more of an art than a science. The 240 is less accurate than the 8 inch howitzer, but much more accurate than the 155 mm howitzer. On the other hand, it is relatively immobile. That is the price you pay for the explosive power of the projectile. Each howitzer weighs 32 tons. The only way it can be moved is by breaking it down into two parts and lifting each of the pieces by a crane onto a ponderous carriage. Under ideal conditions, this takes about two hours.

"Because of the accuracy, range, and explosive power of of the 240, our mission is simple. If war begins, we are to stay here and fire all our ammunition at choke points such as road junctions, bridges, and mountain passes. When our ammunition is exhausted, we are to disable the guns and get out the best way we can. For this reason we have double our normal basic load of ammunition. There will be no resupply. That is why I asked for you. The mission for your battery will be first that of artillery and when your ammunition is totally expended, you turn into infantry. I emphasize, when your ammunition is expended. There will obviously be a temptation to move out early. We don't move out until the ammunition is gone. That is our mission. We do not expect to stop them, but hope to delay them, disrupt them, and buy time.

"There is a history behind this. In the early years of the war, this was a 105 mm howitzer battalion in direct support of the 24th Infantry Regiment. Under attack the regiment broke and ran. The 150th did not. They fired until all their ammunition was gone and then extricated most of the howitzers. The 24th was dropped from the rolls of the active Army. The 150th received a Presidential Unit Citation.

"Now, the obvious question is how we get out of here at that time. If we get lucky we ride out on trucks. I don't think that will happen. With all the North Koreans wandering around out there, some of whom are probably designated to stay behind, I believe we will have to fight our way out.

"I think we have talked long enough tonight. Breakfast is in the officer's mess about fifty yards just off to your right. It starts at 0600. You will be billeted with Lieutenant Noonan, our communications officer. Your hootch is down to your left. He is expecting you. I think you will like him. He is a good Commo and always seems to have the right joke at the right time. As you will soon find out, a good sense of humor goes a long way out here.

"One last thing, I don't know why your predecessor killed himself.

There were no signs to give me any indication that he was troubled. We have an Article 32 investigation going on and maybe we will find out." Pete later learned that the officer had gotten a "Dear John" in the mail.

"That was quite extraordinary," thought Pete to himself as he carried his gear to his hootch. "He didn't have to do that. I'll have to remember how important that kind of treatment is. The guy has already got my loyalty."

Pete made his way to the hootch that had a sign on the door "Lt. Noonan." He noticed that the other name on the door had been recently painted over. He wondered what the right protocol was. He decided to knock.

"Who is it?" came a voice from inside.

"Lieutenant Pete Goodwin. I have been told by the battalion commander that this is where I will be billeted."

"Just a second, " came the voice from inside. "I have to unbolt the door." The door opened and Lieutenant Jim Noonan, known to everyone as "Noonie," stepped forward. "Sorry about that," said Noonan, "you will find out pretty soon that it helps to be careful in this place. Come on inside. I have been looking forward to meeting you. We need fresh blood, if you will pardon the expression."

Upon entering, the first thing Pete noticed was a .45 caliber pistol lying on a table with a clip in it. Whether the clip was loaded or whether there was a round in the chamber, he would never know, but he was glad he had knocked.

"Put your gear over there," said Noonie. "That will be your bunk. Before you ask, that was not the bunk of Captain Hollester, who killed himself yesterday. His bunk was in another hootch. That bunk belonged to the old S-4 who went home last week. We still have not received a replacement and the battalion commander has given me the additional duty of S-4 until we get one. Can I get you something to drink or eat?"

"I've already had a plate of spam and potatoes in the battalion commander's quarters, but I'm still a little hungry. What have you got?"

"How about a real hamburger? One of my additional duties is battalion scrounger. I have a real advantage. We have three 20 ton cranes in the battalion for digging spade pits for the howitzers and assembling them. One of these can dig a latrine in about 20 minutes, dig a well in a couple of hours, and dig a ditch around a perimeter in an afternoon, work that normally takes many weeks by hand. Needless to say, we scroungers are in great demand and we don't come cheap. We have lots of plywood, paint, and all the other things it takes to make life tolerable here. You will see that we have electric lights in the battalion. These are not in our Table of Organization and Equipment. I got the generators from the engineers, the engines from the

Brits, and the cable from the Signal Corps, sometimes for rental of the cranes, and sometimes for things I got from rental of the cranes. For example, the Brits will give almost anything for dry cereal. I got the dry cereal from the infantry and so on.The hamburger meat came from the Corps Artillery Commander's mess and the buns from a local bakery that I get flour for. The onions are free."

"I'd like one very much," said Pete, "I am almost afraid to ask , but would you have a beer to go with the hamburger, by any chance?"

"Sure, what brand do you want ? I think I've got them all."

Pete and Noonie talked for two hours and Pete started to feel very sleepy. It had been a long day. "Noonie," said Pete, "I think I'm about ready to call it a day. What do we do about the tent stove?"

"Ah," said Noonie, "I see you have already gotten Colonel Castle's briefing on that. We turn it off when we go to bed. We have about a half hour before things get quite cold. You might notice that we have army cots, mattresses, and arctic sleeping bags. None of these is authorized on our Table of Organization and Equipment. However, a little horse trading enabled me to get them. We have them for all the troops of the battalion and they are most appreciated. It means we sleep warm.

"Something else I bet the Colonel didn't tell you. Even though we are 20 miles above the no-farming line, we have a bunch of Korean houseboys. They do our laundry, shine our boots, and take care of our hootches. For this service you will be asked to pay a grand sum of ten dollars a month. Our houseboy, Kim, will come in at 5 o'clock and light the stove. He will also put water on the stove so that when you get up there will be water for shaving and washing. Showers are another thing. We do those in the evening before supper. Tomorrow, I will show you another example of ingenuity. We and the troops have hot showers and nobody else does. We have lots of visitors who ask if they can take a shower. Of course we always say yes, but we extract a price. Now let's turn in."

As Pete drifted off to sleep, he thought to himself. "Hey, I might have lucked into something good. We have a battalion commander who cares, a mission that is important and tangible, and, from what I have observed, soldiers who are going to make the best of a difficult situation without feeling sorry for themselves." Pete was looking forward to what tomorrow would bring as he drifted into sleep.

Chapter Four

At about five-thirty in the morning, Pete was awakened by a stirring in the hootch. Before he could check it out, he first had to find the opening in the arctic sleeping bag. During the night, he had rolled over and was face down to the small opening. When he finally found the opening, he observed a figure moving around. As soon as he sat upright, he saw a smiling face. The face looked at him and said, "Good morning, sir, I am Kim. I am your houseboy. Welcome to Korea. The stove is starting to warm up and the water for your shave is about ready."

Goodwin wondered what time Kim had gotten up and where he slept.

Noonie and Pete walked down to the officer's mess. "Pete," said Noonie, "Watch your rear end. You are the first West Pointer that has ever been assigned to this battalion. Most of the senior officers earned their battlefield commissions in World War II. They are not bad people, but they are suspicious. You are going to have to earn their trust. They don't understand why the Colonel brought in an outsider rather that giving one of them the command of C Battery. I won't tell you who is who. I think you will figure that out quickly. Also be careful where you sit. Pecking order is very important. You will see the same thing at the movie tonight. The more senior you are, the closer you sit to the screen. I would suggest that you take your lead from the battalion commander on this. He understands and will probably tell you what to do."

They entered the mess and sure enough, the room quieted down. Some of the officers looked at Pete and gave him a friendly wave. Others remained very still and quiet. Colonel Castle looked up and said, "Lieutenant Goodwin, why don't you take a seat over there," indicating a seat about halfway down the tables, roughly in proportion to Goodwin's rank among the officers. "Let me introduce you. Gentlemen, this is Lieutenant Goodwin. He has been assigned to us by Eighth Army. I have decided to give him command of C battery. Rather than telling you about him, I have arranged a schedule for him to come talk to you. And now, Let's have breakfast. We have a full day's work ahead of us."

Pete understood exactly what had just happened. Colonel Castle had told everyone that the matter of who would command C Battery was over. But

Pete knew he would have to earn the command all by himself and he thought that was fair.

Pete took his designated seat and glanced around. While the building was an old quonset hut originally designed during World War II, it was quite well appointed. There was a nice looking bar over in the corner that looked like it was made of mahogany. There was a fireplace at the far end that was lighted and going strong. The seats were at tables that had tablecloths with comfortable chairs and artificial flowers. Pete could see what Noonie was talking about, and wondered how many other units lived this way.

Breakfast was served on china. The silverware was definitely not Army issue. Pete was asked by the Korean waiter how he liked his eggs. He told the waiter scrambled and expected powdered eggs. But when his plate arrived, it consisted of fried spam, two well-cooked fresh scrambled eggs, toast and fresh butter. Pete was to find out later that Noonie had been able to solve all the problems of rations except bacon and ham, but he was working on that.

After breakfast, the Colonel asked Pete to accompany him to his head-quarters. As they walked, Pete wondered how many other surprises this day would bring. He also realized that the spam and dehydrated potatoes last night were part of his orientation. Better food was available.

"Come on in," said Castle, "I think we covered most of of what I wanted to tell you last night. There is more we need to talk about. But that can wait. Lieutenant Worth, the executive officer of C Battery will be here in a few minutes. He will escort you. C Battery is an interesting outfit. Many of the troops are draftees from the upper Midwest. Others are from the deep south. I understand that the 82nd has not yet been integrated in accordance with the President's order. We have been, and after a lot of initial misgivings, it has worked out just fine. Two of your officers are good and two are bums. I'll let you figure out who is what. Captain Hollester, the guy who took his life yesterday, was never very popular, so you don't have that to contend with that. On the other hand, the troops need a sense of purpose. They need to be convinced that they have a meaningful mission and that they have a reasonable chance of coming out alive. I see that Worth has just arrived. I have you scheduled to spend the morning in C Battery to get acquainted, and to spend the afternoon with the staff. Good luck."

Pete and Lieutenant Worth left battalion headquarters together. Worth asked Pete, "Sir, what do you want to see?"

"Well, Lieutenant, is this the first time you have broken in a new battery commander?"

"Yes sir, I am new at this. They didn't teach us how to do this at ROTC or at Fort Sill."

"OK," said Pete, thinking to himself that West Point also had not taught him what to do. "Let's go to the Command Post. First, I want you to assemble the officers and senior NCOs in the mess hall. Also, unless there is some overriding reason to the contrary, give the troops a training holiday this morning. That will take you a few minutes. While it is being arranged, I want to take a walk around the battery compound so that I can get a preliminary feel for the place."

"Yes Sir," Worth replied and then departed.

Pete's walk around the compound revealed both good and bad. The troops seemed to be reasonably well taken care of, but security was lousy. A decent Ranger patrol could get in easily, Pete thought, and destroy the place. And although Pete had not talked to anyone yet, he could detect a feeling of complacency.

When Lieutenant Worth rejoined Pete, they walked to the mess hall. Pete knew that what happened next was very important and anticipated the reaction of the troops when he entered.

As they entered, Lieutenant Worth, yelled out, "Attention." That was the first good sign. But then Pete noticed that some leaped immediately to a good position of attention, while others sort of slouched up. Pete noticed and remembered each face, thanks to his photographic mind. Though he didn't know any of their names, he would correlate names and faces later.

"Gentlemen," said Pete. "Please be seated."

"My name is Pete Goodwin. I have been selected to be the battery commander of C Battery. I have been told very good things about C Battery. I am honored to be allowed to serve with you. Let me start off by telling you about myself. I graduated from West Point two years ago. I went to the Artillery school at Fort Sill, jump school, and Ranger school. I spent a year in the 82nd Airborne Division as a forward observer and as a battery executive officer. That's about it. What is more important is you. You have been in Korea for a long time. I have not. Therefore, I have much to learn. So, I am not here to lecture to you, I am here to learn from you. But, I must tell you a few things that are important to me. First, we have a mission. No matter what else, everything we do must be directed towards accomplishing that. Second, within that mission, it is my responsibility to do whatever is necessary to keep you alive. And third, I must do whatever it takes to make life as comfortable as possible in these difficult circumstances. What I am asking you today is to tell me what I need to know. Today is free. I promise you that whatever is said today stops here. Now, tell me what I need to know."

For what seemed to be an eternity, the room was silent. Finally, a hand was raised in the rear. "Sir, I am corporal Belcher and I am the supply sergeant. Why are we here?"

Pete was ready for that one. He had asked himself the same question. "I will give you the answer that General Ridgway, the commander who replaced General MacArthur, gave me. We are here because the properly constituted government of the United States said we were to be here. But that needs elaboration. Why does the government want us here? It has been decided that the defense of South Korea is important to the United States. They feel that we must stop communism before it takes over the world. This is really the first test. If we do well here, it will probably deter aggression elsewhere. Also, they feel that, given the opportunity, South Korea will develop into a great nation." Although Pete didn't believe that at the time, but it turned out to be true.

The next several questions were predictable. They all centered around living conditions and Pete's response was to ask for time to look into them.

Then came the tough question. "Sir, if this war starts up again, what are our chances of getting out alive?"

Pete answered, "Great question! I see that as the reason they sent me here. I have much work to do, but let me tell you how I see it. First, we must be able to fire our ammunition at the designated targets. I will be checking out our ability over the next several days. Second, we must have good plans for getting out of here if and when the time comes. That will be one of my primary concerns. And third, in order to do so, we must be in the best of physical condition. Lieutenant Worth, we will start a vigorous PT program tomorrow morning which will include a run. I will lead." The groan from the room was barely audible, but not quite. The meeting was over.

Pete asked Worth and the First Sergeant to accompany him back to the orderly room, which was the name for Pete's headquarters. Pete had several questions.

"How often do we fire the weapons?" asked Pete. The silence was embarrassing. Finally Worth responded.

"Sir we have not fired them since we moved here three months ago. The reason is that because of our proximity to the DMZ, our direction of fire, and our minimum range, in order to fire we would have to land in the DMZ. Also we are told that firing the weapons would give away our position."

Pete was stunned. He thought to himself how negative this was to an artilleryman. "How do we know how good our maintenance is? How do we know how accurate our fire would be?" The questions just kept coming. "Is there anywhere we can fire?"

"Yes sir," replied the First Sergeant, since he knew what Pete was concerned about. "We could move the howitzers about 5 miles south of here and fire into Bullseye impact area. We haven't done it in the past, since the mission didn't include moving."

"Worth," said Pete, "I want a plan at 0800 tomorrow morning as to how we can move these babies and fire once a week. Are you up to it?"

"Yes sir," replied Worth, though at that time he had not the slightest idea how to do it.

"OK, next, what are our plans for getting out of here when the time comes?"

Again a silence. "Sir, we assumed that battalion headquarters would tell us what to do."

"I guess that is an area that I'm pretty good in," said Goodwin. "Tomorrow at 0800, I want some good terrain maps on my desk. I also want the two best woodsmen in the battery. Ask around, I know they are here.

"That's enough for today. You can be sure I will have more questions. PT at 0600 tomorrow. I expect everyone there, even those with sick slips. The only exceptions will be the duty mess crew and one man in the orderly room. I will check your rosters. Any questions? Very well, get cracking."

Worth and the First Sergeant watched Goodwin leave. "You know, lieutenant, I think we got ourselves a real BC," said the First Sergeant, using the artillery expression for Battery Commander.

Chapter Five

Pete ate lunch at the officer's mess. He came to the conclusion that on one hand this was a great place to eat, while on the other, it was not the real world. He decided to make effective immediately, the rule that at least one officer of C Battery would eat every meal with the troops. He knew the officers would not be happy. They ate better at the officer's mess. He turned to Worth to issue the instructions. Pete told Worth that he would be on the roster and for Worth to have the arrangements in effect starting with supper tonight. Worth started to object, but fell quiet. He knew Pete was right.

After lunch, Pete followed the schedule that had been established by Colonel Castle. His first stop was in the office of the Battalion Executive Officer.

The Exec was old enough to be Pete's father. He had been an enlisted man in World War II, had received a battlefield commission, had gone into the Army reserves, and had been recalled to active duty for service in Korea. He had paid his dues. He represented the best of the citizen soldier, who usually harbored a suspicion of the regular army. He was wise enough and experienced enough to withhold judgment. "Some Ring-Knockers" were good and some were not, using the term was one that most non-West Pointers used when referring to graduates of the Military Academy. He seemed to have the right credentials.

"Good afternoon, sir," said Pete. "Thank you for see seeing me. I have been briefed by the Battalion Commander on the mission. I believe that I understand it and what needs to be done, but I certainly would welcome any advice you might have for me." The Exec simply nodded.

The rest of the afternoon fell into a pattern. Each of the officers that Pete met with was polite and said basically the same thing. Prove to us that you can accomplish this difficult mission. We will help in any way that we can, but the ball is in your court.

Implicit in these conversations was the "newby" or "newcomer" suspicion. Pete knew he had to walk a fine line. He would be supported in making changes as long as he did not openly criticize past practices. Fair enough.

At about 1700, Pete returned to his hootch. Noonie was waiting for him. Pete was exhausted. He had been interrogated by experts and was still feeling the effects of a long trip and time change. "Noonie, you wouldn't by any chance have a dry martini in your treasure trove, would you?"

"Coming right up," said Noonie. "I already have them ready. Here you are," he said. "I anticipated what kind of day you would have. For whatever it is worth, I am told that you had a good day. Especially among the officers and NCOs of C Battery. There is a lot of grumbling about your officer's mess schedule, and about your PT program, but they know you're right. Everyone is intrigued about your request for two woodsmen. They wonder what you are up to. There are no secrets in the battalion. News travels fast. As soon as you finish your drink, I think you might want to take a shower. C'mon, I'll show you the eighth wonder of the world."

Pete and Noonie walked down the hill to the shower. Noonie explained. "A shower needs three basic elements. The first, obviously, is water. One of the nice things about this battalion is that we have cranes for both lifting and digging. Using our crane we dug a well. The water table around here is about twenty feet down. Once the hole is dug and water is flowing, we put in a pipe and fill in the hole with rocks. Second, you need to lift the water up to the shower. As you know, the standard water trailer in the Army has a hand pump. I was able to get a few of these. That gets the water to the top of the shower. Next, you have to heat the water. The Army has something called immersion heaters that are used to boil water for field mess halls. Again we have a few extra. The rig works pretty well. One of the rules is that before you use the shower, you must pump the handpump 100 times. This keeps the barrels on top full and hot for the next person." Noonie chuckled to himself. "I'll tell you a funny story. The NCO's of B Battery thought that they might tap off some of the heat to the NCO latrine and devised a jury-rig. It worked great for a couple of days, but one night the latrine caught on fire. We all have fond memories of the First Sergeant of B Battery running down the street yelling Fire! Fire! with his pants aflame down around his ankles."

The shower was great. The water was hot, although it did smell funny. But, Pete was not complaining. Given the conditions, it had to be about the most refreshing shower he had ever taken. He was beginning to realize just how important things that most people take for granted really are. In this battalion they had electric lights and hot showers. Nobody else did. Pete wondered whether the troops appreciated these conveniences and considered it one of his duties to ensure that the troops realize how much was being done for them, considering the difficult circumstances.

Supper in the officer's mess was subdued. Most of the officers that Pete had met during the day made a point of coming up and talking to him. Some did not. Dinner was quite good. The main dish was pheasant. It seems that pheasant abounded in this area, even after the war. Noonie had obtained a couple of shotguns and organized hunting parties. This guy was good and Pete wondered what company was going to be lucky enough to have him as CEO several years from now. The meal was accompanied by a very good Australian white wine.

After dinner, the mess was reconfigured for a movie. The mess officer announced that the movie for tonight would be an old Humphrey Bogart film. This time the groans were audible, but nobody left. After all, where else was there to go? During the movie Pete noticed that the audience knew all the words and said them out loud. This was part of the enjoyment. About halfway through the flick, Pete gave up and went back to the hootch. PT was at 0600 and he needed to be at his best.

At 0600 Pete was standing in front of the orderly room. The troops of C Battery were being assembled. It was easy to see that things were not all that well organized. He had ascertained that there were 114 troops in the battery according to the Morning Report. By a quick visual count Pete could see only about 70. Pete knew his orders had not been carried out. He would have a serious meeting with the First Sergeant and the Exec later, not wanting to embarrass them in front of the troops.

"Good Morning, gentlemen," Pete greeted the troops, "I am Lieutenant Goodwin and I have been appointed the Battery Commander of C Battery. We are going to have a rigorous PT program in C battery. The reason is simple. If the worst should happen, we are going to have to walk out of here. If you are in good condition, you will make it. And if you are not, you will probably die along the side of the road. I will lead PT for the first week. After that, a roster will be established. Every one of you is going to lead PT sooner or later. We will start out by doing four repetitions of the Army daily dozen. We will then run a half mile. This is not much, but I can see that some of you are not in the best of shape. Within a month, we will be doing 12 repetitions and running 2 miles. For those of you who have sick slips, I have asked the battalion surgeon to do a reevaluation. For today, you will stay out here until we are finished and do deep breathing exercises."

As expected, it was a disaster. The troops were in worse shape than Pete had anticipated. But, at least he made his point.

After the run, Pete asked the Exec and the First Sergeant to join him in the orderly room. "Where were all the troops?" Pete asked. "Did I not make myself clear yesterday? Tomorrow I expect them all here. No excuses. Any questions?" There were none.

"Now let's have breakfast. I will eat with the troops." The Exec and the First Sergeant exchanged a glance. The former BC had never eaten breakfast in the battery mess hall. The food was terrible. It was poorly cooked and cold. "Who is the mess officer?" asked Pete.

"We don't have one," replied the Exec.

"Worth, I want you to select a mess officer immediately, and I mean right now. Until further notice, he is to eat all of his meals in the battery mess. No exceptions. The officer's mess is off limits to him until I decide otherwise. I will hold him personally responsible for the quality of the food. If he needs help, tell him to come see me. And now, I'm going for a run. I will see you at 0800 for our scheduled meeting." Pete was already thinking about asking Noonie for help.

Earlier, Pete had noticed a hill that overlooked the battalion. He wondered if there was a way to get to the top. He ran out of the front gate of the battalion, which elicited a puzzled look from the gate guards, and soon found a path that seemed to lead to the top of the hill. The view from the top was breathtaking. To the north and northwest he could see all the way to the DMZ and the Imjin Gang. To the south he could see the entire battalion area and about twenty miles farther. That was the good news. The bad news was that he could find no evidence of anyone being up there before. From this crest, Pete thought, the enemy could destroy the entire battalion with a couple of mortars. As soon as the troops were in decent shape, he would bring them up there. After enjoying the view, Pete jogged back to orderly room for his meeting. On the way, he couldn't help but wonder how well this meeting would go. So far, it had not been a good day.

Pete arrived at the orderly room at exactly 0800. The officers and NCOs were waiting for him. "Good sign," thought Pete. "At least people are starting to respond."

"OK, Gentlemen," said Pete, "Let's talk about firing the howitzers first. Worth, I asked you to devise a plan. What do you have?"

"Sir, we have not moved the howitzers or fired them for over three months. We are out of practice. Just simply moving them is difficult and dangerous. I would suggest that we first practice moving them. I don't believe you have ever seen this done. It is quite remarkable. While that is going on, I will scout out a viable firing site so that we can fire into Bullseye range. Once that is completed, we will have to survey the coordinates of the site and dig the firing positions. In order to fire the 240, you must dig a big recoil pit to take up the force generated by the propellant. If you don't, the howitzer will literally flip over backwards. Sir, I know how to do this. I promise you that I can have this battery moving and firing properly in less than a month. I am looking forward to it. Nobody ever seemed interested before."

"Great," said Pete. "When do we get started?"

"Today. We are going to disassemble and reassemble one howitzer starting at 0900. I would appreciate it if you would stay away. It probably won't go too well the first time. I will keep at it until we get it right. I think the troops want to prove to you that they are capable, but they need practice."

"Approved. Let me know when I can watch. Now, let's talk about the two woodsmen I asked about. I guess you need an explanation on that. It could happen that we may have to get out of here under difficult conditions. I want to be sure that we can. Have you found them for me?"

"Yes sir." replied the First Sergeant. "I think you already know them. They're waiting outside. Do you want to see them now?"

Barnes and Hawkins, the two PFC's that came to the battalion on the same train with Pete, walked in the door.

"Well," said Pete, "this is a pleasant surprise. I didn't expect to see you two again so soon. What happened?"

Barnes spoke first. "Sir, two nights ago you took care of us. In case you are interested, Rinaldi arranged for us to get a meal and decent beds. I don't think he wanted to cross you again. When we processed through battalion, we requested to be assigned to your battery. Last night the first sergeant asked for volunteers who knew a little about woodsmanship. Hawkins and I grew up together in Wisconsin. From the age of thirteen, we have always competed to get the first deer of the season. Why do you want us?"

"Sit down, I think you are going to like this. The mission of this battery is, if the war starts, to fire all of our ammunition. We are then to disable the howitzers and get out the best way we can. There seem to be no plans for doing so, much less training and rehearsal. I want you two to learn this area like the back of your hands. Then I want you to devise different ways to get out of here. Once we have agreed that you have good plans, you will lead the battery out in training runs. Quite simply, I want the troops to feel certain that they will get out, so that they will remain by their guns until the ammunition is exhausted. If they are not certain, they may cut and run. One last point. There are a lot of minefields around here. Some are marked and some are not. Make sure you check with the engineers before you go wandering around in the boonies. Any questions?" No one spoke. "How about reporting back to me in about a week. If you need any assistance, come see me immediately. Thank you." As the two men turned to go, Pete remembered, "Oh, one other thing. I learned last night that there are plenty of pheasants around here. I have arranged for you to have a couple of shotguns with plenty of number six and number eight shot. This will give you a good cover, and I think the troops will also enjoy having something other than Army rations."

Pete was already starting to feel better. This day was now going well. He thought he would take a walk around the battery area and look things over. Management by walking around was the expression. The first stop was the mess hall, where breakfast had been a disaster. Second Lieutenant Smithers, who had just been appointed the mess officer, was screaming at the mess sergeant and the cooks incoherently."

"At ease," ordered Pete, "What's going on? Why don't you and the mess sergeant join me for a cup of coffee? It's been a long morning already."

Smithers had made the typical error of leadership. He did not understand the problem and concluded that the right course of action was to chew out everybody in sight. The mess sergeant gave Pete a look of gratitude. After the coffee was served, Pete asked the mess sergeant why breakfast had not been very good.

"Sir, our rations have not been coming in as they should. Also, my cooks all had guard duty last night. They were tired before they even got here. In order to prepare a decent meal, the cooks need to be here at least an hour before serving time. They came off guard duty at 0600. Also, we mess personnel have to do our own KP. The BC before you did not allow a KP roster."

Pete took a risk. "I hear you. If I can get you good rations, get the cooks off guard duty, and some Korean laborers to do the KP, can you feed the troops the way they deserve? However, you and your cooks will still do PT."

"Yes, sir," replied Smithers and the mess sergeant simultaneously.

Pete left, knowing that he really needed Noonie now. When he presented Noonie with the problem, the response was immediate. "No sweat, I can do it today, but I will need the loan of one of your cranes this afternoon. I have some serious horsetrading to do."

Supper that night at the C battery mess was a triumph. The meal consisted of pheasant, New Zealand beef, and fresh potatoes. Pete had also instituted the sale of beer at the evening meal, something that was totally in violation of army regulations, but had been going on for years at the 82nd. The Korean mess attendants were ecstatic.

Not only did the Koreans have a job, but they could also steal just enough to feed their families.

Chapter Six

T he next few months went by very quickly. Worth had made good on his promise to have the battery moving and firing properly. This did not make the staff officers at I Corps Artillery headquarters happy, however. Every time one of the 240 mm rounds of the 150th battalion landed in the Bullseye artillery impact area, they had to shut down the range for five minutes. The smoke and debris made observation of any other fire adjustments impossible. The forward observers of C Battery took somewhat of a perverse pleasure in this.

During the same time, Pete's PT program began to pay off. They were up to 12 repetitions of the Army "daily dozen" exercise program and running two miles rather easily. One morning, Pete changed the routine and ran them up the hill overlooking the battalion area. It was time to make a point. Pete had arranged for the mess sergeant to arrive before the troops, and had hot coffee waiting for them. Pete showed the men of C Battery where the DMZ and the enemy were. He then showed them the terrain to the south, where they would have to fight their way out in the event it was necessary. They were impressed. Nobody had ever explained this to them before. Pete introduced Barnes and Hawkins, and explained what they had been up to besides hunting pheasant, venison, and wild boar. He explained that PT was going to change a bit. Now they were going to practice possible escape routes. This time there was not an audible groan. Pete sensed positive anticipation. The troops loved it. They were actually looking forward to a change in their monotonous routine. They had come to believe in themselves and wanted a new challenge.

That night Pete ran a very basic course in land navigation. Part of the course taught how to use a compass, part taught how to use the stars, and part focused on dead reckoning. The troops got hopelessly lost, but had a blast. They had learned that under Pete an honest mistake was never questioned. Pete gathered them together in the mess hall afterwards and opened the beer bar.

"OK," said Pete, "you see how difficult that was. Suppose it was real and there were North Koreans out to get you. Most of you would not have made it home. Tomorrow morning during PT we are going to start going over the different ways out until you know them by heart. When I think you have got that, we are going to do it again at night. In the meantime, we will have training courses every night in night operations. If you know how to fight at night and your opponent does not, you have a huge advantage. Believe it or not, the night can be your friend. Untrained soldiers, no matter where they come from, are usually scared of the night. Trained soldiers welcome the night." Pete noticed by the mens' faces that this was going to take some convincing.

Pete also knew that creating confidence in night operations was going to take some time. He recalled how hard it was in ranger school when they had very well trained instructors and everyone was a volunteer and a parachutist. That night he walked the battery back up the same hill they had been to the day before. But this time they went slowly. They stopped every few minutes to listen and observe. The troops were amazed at how far sound carries at night and how hard it is to determine where the sound is coming from. Pete also demonstrated how to see at night. He explained how most people don't realize that you can see much better if you don't look directly at the object of your attention. For whatever reason, peripheral vision is much better than direct vision in limited light. When the men got to the top of the hill, Pete showed them how damaging bright lights, such as those around the battalion compound, were to night vision. Finally, he pointed out the stars, and showed how to determine direction from them. Most people have heard of the North Star, Pete told them, but many don't have the slightest idea how to find it. He demonstrated the various ways.

This was enough for one night, but Pete had another surprise in store for the men. He instructed them to find their way back to batallion compound in groups of five, and had them select their own leaders. Barnes and Hawkins waited for them. During this exercise, the men realized that in a real North Korean ambush, most of them would not have made it. At beer call that night however the troops good naturedly cried "foul." Pete observed that this was going to turn into a friendly competition.

Pete took the troops back to the hill again the next night, but this time he had a different demonstration planned. He told the troops to look down the path they had just come up. Soon, they heard someone approaching with the clanking of Army gear, including the mess kit, the canteen, the bayonet, and the stacking swivel of the rifle. It was so obvious. Anyone could do it. And then, shortly thereafter, they clearly saw Hawkin's face. Piece of cake. At that time, Barnes threw down an M-80 grenade simulator in front of the troops. When it went off they all hit the dirt, and to their credit, Barnes had come up the hill at exactly the same time as Hawkins, but he had all of his gear taped down so it wouldn't rattle, wore camouflage paint on this face and hands, and stayed to the side of the path instead of the middle. They neither saw nor heard him.

After that, it got easier. Barnes and Hawkins guided the troops down the various routes during the daylight until they learned them. It was now time to integrate the night training with the route training. The troops did just great. But Pete took a precaution. He knew that the Turkish Brigade was located south of the battalion and informed the Turks what was happening. The Turks were delighted and wanted to play. Though Pete's battery never got as good as the Turks, he gained their respect.

One night, a patrol reported in late. Pete started to worry. About that time, the phone rang and it was the Turkish adjutant on the line. He suggested that Pete bring a truck and pick up some very drunk soldiers. It seems that Pete's patrol and a Turkish patrol had a real contest. The Turks invited Pete's guys in for a drink of raki, the Turkish version of pernod. It was no contest. Beer does not prepare anyone for raki and the Turks were very amused. Pete never said a word. He thought about PT the next morning and smiled.

By early summer things had become routine. The battery could shoot, move, and communicate as well as light artillery. They had complete confidence in themselves as artillerymen. What's more, they knew that if push came to shove, they would be able to get out, no matter how difficult it was. They were even asked to go to other units and teach others their skills. During an exercise of the Second Infantry Division, the battery was asked to play the part of North Korean insurgents. They cleaned their clocks, simply because they owned the night.

Pete was looking for another challenge. Noonie had gone home because his 16 month tour in Korea was over. Wonder of all wonders, Lieutenant Smithers had been selected to replace Noonie and, if anything, was more successful as the battalion scrounge.

Pete decided that athletics might be the answer. Although the troops were in excellent shape, they were not necessarily athletic achievers yet. Over the next few months of training, they won the I Corps flag football tournament and basketball tournament. Pete was disappointed that they didn't win the softball tournament, but he never found a pitcher. During the final playoff game in the football tournament, he was injured on a clean play on the defensive end. The troops cheered madly as he was carried off. He questioned the reason for the cheers, but not too hard.

But, all good things come to an end. In November, the powers that were, decided that it was time to draw down U.S. forces in Korea. The 150th was scheduled for deactivation from the active Army. Fortunately, because of its record, it was to be immediately reactivated in the Utah National Guard, where they had originated during World War II. The heritage would be continued.

At the final ceremony, Pete gave a speech that he would give again several decades later at 11th Corps. "Men, it is time for us to go. I have never been more proud of my friends than I am today. C Battery will continue and, I expect, will be heard from again. Let us reflect on what we have accomplished. We proved to the world that we could take on any challenge. We did the best thing possible. We won without having to fight a war, and with casualties. The other side gave up, because they did not want to take us on. They knew we would have kicked their butts.

"And now for the good news. For those of you who are draftees or National Guardsmen called to active duty, you will go home early. Those of us in the regular Army, will be reassigned and finish out our tour of duty. There is a message there somewhere. But, please remember, no matter what the mission, no matter how difficult it seemed at the time, you won. Dismissed."

First Lieutenant Pete Goodwin, U.S. Army, had been assigned to the Civil Affairs section of the Eighth Army in Seoul for the remaining four months of his tour of duty. Of all the jobs available, this was his last choice. But, as it turned out, it was one of the best things that ever happened to him. During these four months, Pete learned much about Korea – knowledge that, at the time, he did not realize would serve him well in later years. He learned that the Koreans, technically the South Koreans, were indefatigable. They were mission-oriented and would not allow anything to stand in their way to nationhood. Korea was a dictatorship, no doubt, but a dictatorship by consent. If the government decided that a road had to be built in an area, the Korean leaders would simply tell the villagers in that location to get out their hand tools and do it. And they would.

Pete also got a chance to observe the South Korean army. It was fair to say that they had not performed too well during the war. They were neither properly trained nor equipped. But, Pete detected a total dedication for improvement. Twenty years later, Pete would find out that this dedication had paid off.

Four months later, Pete had been reassigned to the 82nd Airborne. At least this time it was a direct Pan American flight into Los Angeles, without a stop at Shemya.

Chapter Seven

The VC 135 droned on through the night sky. Pete and Sandy had been invited up to the pilot's compartment to watch the aurora borealis. It was spectacular. But Sandy noticed that Pete's attention, although polite, was quite perfunctory. He still had a lot on his mind. He wanted to talk some more. As an aide, Sandy had learned how to be a good listener. She fully understood her role as an aide and suggested that they return to the passenger compartment. This action got a bemused glance from Beth. Beth had misinterpreted the signals.

After they had returned to their seats, Pete remembered, "Well Sandy, that was my first tour of duty in Korea. I learned that Korea really was important in the overall scheme of things and that the Koreans, with our help, could indeed become a strong nation and our most significant ally in that part of the world. Altruism aside, supporting South Korea in 1953 and later was in our best interest. After that tour, my life was on the fast track. Master's degree in mathematics, teacher at West Point, general's aide, Vietnam, Pentagon, battalion and brigade command and the Army War College. Then, in 1973, I was called to the Military Personnel Center to discuss my next assignment. I had been selected to go to Korea to be the Chief of Staff of the First Combined Field Army. I was a colonel at the time and the position called for a brigadier general. Obviously, that was an offer I could not refuse, although I did not relish being separated from my family. I was told that there were some problems with the North Koreans, but nothing serious. Boy, were they wrong about that."

Pete continued, "This time the trip to Korea was quite pleasant. I flew commercial all the way and the plane was practically empty. There was no opportunity for the stews to do anything except take care of the passengers. We landed at Kimpo airport in Seoul at two in the afternoon, where I was met by the Commanding General's aide and driver. They had already arranged for my passport and customs clearance and my baggage showed up immediately. I cleared the airport in less than 10 minutes. Quite a difference from my previous arrival. The trip to Field Army headquarters at Camp Red Cloud in Uijongbu took about an hour, which included going right through the middle of Seoul. The route consisted, for the most part, of American style superhighways. There was absolutely no evidence of war damage in Seoul. As a matter of fact, there was no evidence of war damage anywhere. As we traveled north the country became less urban – intentional on the part of the government because of war potential. I could not help but notice forests where, twenty years ago, the area was barren. I found out that in 1955 the government decided to reforest the country and gave every village an area of responsibility. End of problem. In essence, the physical difference between South Korea in 1953 and 1973 was astonishing. I didn't even see any mommasans and pappasans. They were now driving pick-up trucks.

"On the trip to Uijongbu, the general's aide attempted to fill me in on what I was getting in to. He first described the commanding general. He told me that Lieutenant General Pace was probably the last of a dying breed. He definitely was not the Harvard Business School type. He was an old cavalry soldier who had been one of Patton's favorites during World War II. He was adored by the South Koreans and cautiously respected by the American higher chain of command. He did not fit the present conventional mode. He had the habit of playing the dumb old country boy role, though he was actually very brilliant and could be articulate when he wanted to be. He detested phonies and was expert at identifying them. The aide told me that I was the third Chief of Staff in the last six months. General Pace had fired the last two. He further told me that when Pace called you a "midget," you were in trouble, but if he called you a "rattleass," you were in good shape." Sandy laughed at this. "Finally, he told me that the reason I had been selected was that General Pace was a good friend of retired Colonel Castle, who was my battalion commander 20 years ago in Korea, and that Castle had recommended me. He did not tell me what General Pace was looking for in a Chief of Staff. He thought I should find that out for myself.

"The aide told me that General Pace was at Eighth Army that afternoon. And that he actually spent most of his time out of the headquarters with the troops during the day. He didn't like to be burdened with paperwork that would restrict his ability to get out of the headquarters. He was asked to take care of me and get me settled. He said that cocktail hour at the Commanding General's mess started promptly at 1830 with dinner at 1900. All officers were expected to be there and if you weren't you had better have a very good reason. 'Take your lead from the general,' the aide warned me. 'Do not discuss business unless he initiates it. Be prepared for the unexpected. He likes to test people. If he asks you a question and you don't know the answer, say so. I have never heard him ask a question that he did not already know the answer to. Dress is casual - sport shirt and slacks. We used to wear a coat and tie but he changed that several months ago. Remember, the general has two personalities: the public one and the private one. Don't confuse the two.'"

The staff car pulled up to a row of quonset huts in which the senior staff officers were billeted. Two officers were assigned to each. From the outside they looked rather plain and austere. Pete was met at the door by a Korean houseboy by the name of Chan who took his baggage and ushered him inside. What a contrast to the outside! The inside looked like an upper class hotel suite- private bedroom and bath, air conditioning, shared living room, well appointed, with a refrigerator and stocked bar. About the only thing that was missing was a television. Chan fixed Pete a drink and told him to relax while he did the unpacking and pressed his clothes. Chan pointed to a box in the bedroom to be used for dirty laundry. Pete was going to get used to being spoiled. The hootch was always clean, the laundry was always done on time, and his boots and shoes were always polished. Uijongbu also had a resident tailor that would come to the hootch on a moment's notice to alter his clothes or make him new ones.

At just after 1700 hours Colonel Rich Benson, U.S. Army, came into the hootch. He knocked on the door to Pete's room and was told to come in.

"Hi," said Rich, "I guess we are going to share this hootch for a while. As I expect you've been told, the previous life expectancy of the Chief of Staff around here has not been very long. Why don't we go into the living room and have a drink. What would you like?"

"A dry martini on the rocks seems appropriate," said Pete. "But only one. General Pace's aide warned me that I might get tested tonight."

"If you aren't, that will be a first around here," responded Rich. "That seems to be one of the general's favorite indoor sports. I really don't sense any malice, he just likes to size people up early on. But you will notice that he only tests American officers. He treats the Korean officers with the utmost of courtesy and respect. How familiar are you with the composition of the Field Army and the headquarters?"

"Not very," replied Pete, "I would appreciate anything you can tell me."

"OK, the short course. The First Combined Field Army has 12 divisions, 11 Korean and one U.S., plus the usual assortment of support troops, mostly Korean. The headquarters itself is strictly a tactical headquarters. Logistics are handled for us by the Korean Support Command and by the U.S. Eighth Army in Seoul. We have about 30 U.S. officers and about 70 Korean officers. The rule is if the boss is an American then his deputy is Korean. Our Deputy Commanding General is Korean and your Deputy Chief of Staff is Korean. The G-3 and G-2 are Korean, the G-1 and G-4 are American. I am the Deputy G-3. The Koreans are top notch and the official language of the headquarters is English. The food served in the CG mess is strictly American. If that all seems somewhat unfair to you, it reflects how deeply the Koreans value our commitment. I keep looking for some form of hostility over the situation, but I've yet to see it. The Korean officers will seem somewhat reserved when you first meet them, but once you get to know them you will find they are warm people with a great sense of humor.

"The American officers don't know what to think. They wonder where you came from and why. I am curious to see how General Pace handles that. If you want to make a good impression, you should search out the Korean Deputy Commanding General and introduce yourself to him first, and ask him to introduce you to the others. He is a Major General and his name is Lee Duk Qwan. I will point him out to you. General Pace will not be there at 1830. He always shows up at about 1845 in order to make a grand entrance. He wants everyone there before he arrives. By the way, in Korea the surname come first, so you should address him as General Lee. You will also find out that most Koreans have one of three surnames: Lee, Pak, and Kim. It does get confusing at times. Both the G-3 and G-2 are Colonel Lee."

At 1830, Pete and Rich walked to the CG's mess. Just like the billets, from the outside the building was very undistinguished, but inside it was quite remarkable. It had a beautiful stone fireplace, carpeting on the floor, painted murals on the walls, expensive furniture, and a huge mahogany bar. The tables in the dining room were covered with fine linen. The place settings were of the finest Noritake china, and each place had a silver napkin ring and goblet. The lighting was indirect and subdued. Pete immediately noticed that the people in the room were not divided by nationality. Each group was composed of both Koreans and Americans. Rich told Pete that the gentleman at the far end of the bar was Major General Lee and that, as predicted, General Pace was not yet present. It was time to go for it.

Pete walked over to General Lee and introduced himself. "Good evening, sir. I am told that you are Major General Lee and that you are the Deputy Commanding General of the First Combined Field Army. I am Colonel Goodwin. I have just arrived this afternoon. I am delighted to be here and happy to make your acquaintance."

"Good evening, Colonel," replied Lee in perfect English. Pete was soon to learn that all of the Korean officers spoke near perfect English – this was part of their training. "I have been looking forward to meeting you ever since General Pace told us you were coming. I understand that you have a schedule of meetings with the staff starting tomorrow morning and that we will meet at 0930. So let's save our business until then. Allow me to introduce you around. As you might already know, addressing everyone as Colonel Lee gives you a 50% chance of being right."

Lee was very careful to make all the introductions on the basis of proximity. There was no favoritism according to rank or nationality. It was quite pleasant and without even a hint of business. The protocol was obviously social. At just about the time Pete had completed his rounds, General Pace came through the door. In contrast to the others, he was dressed in in his perfectly tailored battlefield garb and had a strictly non-issue Magnum .44 in his side holster.

Great entrance, thought Pete, wondering how much of this was orchestrated for his benefit.

"Good evening, gentlemen," boomed Pace. "I apologize for being late and out of uniform, but my meeting with the Eighth Army Commander and his staff went much longer than I anticipated. Those staff midgets just don't seem to appreciate the fighting qualities of the ROK forces. If they had been on Bradley's staff in World War II, we would just now be approaching the Rhine."

Pete marveled to himself at how many points Pace had made in his entrance opener. General Pace was clearly no dummy. He anticipated the worst.

Sure enough, at that moment, General Lee took Pete over and introduced him to General Pace. Protocol had been served.

General Pace took his pistol belt off and instructed his aide to ensure that the pistol was unloaded. He then turned to Pete and invited him to go to the bar and have a drink with him.

Pete wondered to himself what the right drink might be. This was apparently part of the test. He hoped the general would order first. No such luck. General Pace asked Pete what he wanted and Pete told him a dry martini on the rocks would do. Wrong answer. Pace announced audibly that he would have a *man's drink* – bourbon neat. Strike one. After the drinks were served Pace turned to Pete and asked, "What makes you think you could make a good Chief of Staff?" The room got very quiet. Everyone was waiting for the answer.

Pete anticipated this question. "Sir," he said calmly, "I have had a variety of jobs in the Army, some of them most difficult. At least, according to my superiors, I have accomplished all of my duties well. I have never before been a Chief of Staff, and certainly not at this level. I am a ranger, paratrooper, and hold the CIB. I have survived a tour in the Pentagon. Based on a previous tour in Korea, I have much admiration for the people, government, and Army of Korea. About the only answer I can give you is that you will have my loyalty, my integrity, and my honest effort. I hope that will be enough."

"Good answer, rattleass, we will find out soon enough. Now, let's eat." The score was now one apiece.

Dinner was an experience. Pace pointed out to Pete that everyone had a designated seat and that Pete's was at the head table. Pace dominated the conversation and never addressed a question or comment to Pete. He spent the entire evening talking about the inadequacies of the Eighth Army staff. After dinner, Pace informed Pete that there was to be the normal staff briefing at 0800 in the morning and that after that, he wanted to see Pete alone in his office. Then, Pace got up and returned to his quarters.

Rich told Pete "You are lucky tonight, sometimes the general likes to party all night and expects the staff to party with him. He has the constitution of an ox. He wipes all of us out and never seems to show any ill effects." Pete was doubly grateful that there was no party tonight, since jet lag was starting to catch up to him.

Pete returned to his hootch and found that his boots were shined, his fatigue uniform freshly pressed, and that all of his patches, nametags, unit insignia, insignia of rank and branch had been sewn on. Amazing. At that point Pete literally collapsed into bed wondering what tomorrow would hold. He was sure that it would be interesting.

Rich thought about inviting Pete for a nightcap but changed his mind. Pete was already asleep.

Chapter Eight

So, Sandy," Pete continued, "That was the first day of my second tour of duty in Korea. Have you had enough? Am I starting to bore you with my memories?"

"On the contrary, General, this is starting to get interesting," replied Sandy, truthfully. "Please go on. It obviously could not have been too bad, since you are sitting there with three stars and the powers that be seem to want you badly in Washington to discuss Korea."

"Well, the next morning Chan awakened me at 0600 and told me that breakfast in the CG mess started at 0630. As opposed to my first tour in Korea the hootch was warm and there was a pot of hot coffee in the living room. I thought I had it made. How was I to know that the following winter during the oil embargo, when the temperature was 10 below zero, we would be without heat? But that is another story. Anyway, after a nice hot shower, with the water having the same peculiar smell of 20 years earlier, I shaved, dressed and made my way to the mess.

"I forgot to mention earlier that the waitresses in the mess were exceptionally good-looking Korean women. Later I found out that many senior American officers had Korean girlfriends, and when it was time for the officers to return home, they tried to find the girls a good job. Which brings to mind another interesting thing about the Korean culture. If a woman becomes a "business girl," as they call it, to support her family, there is no disgrace. In fact, it is never mentioned. When a girl leaves home to join the profession, she changes her name. When she is finished, she changes her name back and it is as if the previous person never existed."

Pete arrived at the mess at exactly 0630 and found the room already half-full. He took his designated seat and found a copy of that morning's *Stars and Stripes* newspaper at his place with his name on it. Another small, but important, benefit. He noticed that everyone had a copy and that they were all reading it. Conversation was practically nil except for pleasantries. Pete was starting to learn that part of the culture of having a successful mess was not to conduct business there. He also realized that people were keeping a distance from him.

At 0645 General Pace arrived, said a general good morning, took his seat, and started to read his *Stars and Stripes*. Breakfast was ordered by filling out a chit. The choices were what you might find in a good restaurant and the meal itself was delicious. Pete decided right then and there that he would have to watch how much he ate and get plenty of exercise. You could look around the room and see that not everyone did so. By 0730 everyone had left. Rich had pointed out where the morning staff briefing would take place and wished Pete lots of luck. Rich would not be there. General Pace kept the attendance to the minimum he thought necessary. When Pete got to the briefing room he spotted name cards at every seat. He was to sit on General Pace's left and the Deputy CG was on Pace's right. The briefing went about as usual. First, the Intelligence officer G-2 told what is going on in the world and in Korea, then the Operations officer G-3 described the significant activities of the day, and finally the Administrative officer G-1, and the Logistics officer G-4 explained their activities. Pace asked a few questions and made a few remarks and that was it. Or so Pete thought.

Suddenly, Pace turned to Pete and said, "Goodwin, I think the morning briefings can be improved upon significantly. Tell me what you will change within a week. Meet me in my office at 0830."

Pete got to the CG's outer office at 0800. He wanted to meet General Pace's personal staff. Pete had learned that in the Army, just as in any large enterprise, it is essential to get along with the boss' immediate family. In this case, the personal staff consisted of two aides, one U.S. and one Korean, a warrant officer Administrative Assistant, a secretary, and the Secretary of the General Staff. This last position was unique to the Army. Its function was to assure that the right paper got to the right person at the right time. Whereas, the job of the Chief of Staff was to assure that the paper or action was right and properly coordinated with all concerned parties. It was obvious to Pete that he and the SGS had to get along. Their jobs were mutually dependent.

Pete spoke with each of these and said basically the same thing, "I will keep you informed, I will never lie to you, and we are not in competition. We each have an important job to do and I don't need any more work. I believe that our task, individually and collectively, is to make General Pace look good and be good." The personal staff was polite and receptive, but being old soldiers they were stubborn and critical. They did, however, appreciate Goodwin's first gesture.

At 0830 the general's secretary instructed Pete to enter. General Pace was seated behind his desk and immediately got up, walked around the desk, and put out his hand. A good sign. Pete wondered what to do next and took the safest course of action. After shaking the general's hand he retreated a step, saluted, and said, "Colonel Goodwin reporting as ordered, sir."

"Let's knock off the bullshit." Pace responded. A very bad sign.

Pace directed Pete to sit down in one of a pair of chairs next to a coffee table and then sat down in the other. He asked Pete if he would like a cup of coffee, and how he'd like it. As if by magic the general's secretary appeared with the coffee matching Pete's request. Pete thought, "I wonder how he did that?"

"Welcome to Korea and the First Combined Field Army," stated Pace, "I suspect that you already know that I fired the previous two Chiefs of Staff. I inherited one of them, and the other was forced upon me. This time I selected. I decided upon you after talking with Colonel Castle and reviewing your file. Probably the thing that impressed me the most was the stand you took on Vietnam. Your record in Vietnam was as good as anyone's, but, later, in your Army War College thesis, you concluded that the war was a lost cause and explained why. At the time, I did not agree with you. You turned out to be right. What I am looking for in a Chief of Staff is an independent thinker, not one tied to the conventional wisdom of the past. Obviously, you will disagree with me at times and that is OK, but only in private. If you can convince me, fine. If not, publicly support me or turn in your suit. Fair enough?"

Pete responded with the best answer possible, "Yes sir."

"OK, let's be a little more specific," said Pace. "This is a good headquarters with a very important mission, even though those midgets in Washington don't seem to understand that. Soon, they will understand why. My job is to make sure that the troops are ready and willing to fight. That is why I spend most of my time out in the field and why I don't waste my time with meaningless paperwork. Don't get me wrong. Some paperwork, such as good war plans and good resource allocations, are essential, but mostly it's garbage. My two previous Chiefs of Staff could not seem to tell the difference.

"There are two things I expect from you. One is quite obvious, the other is not. I want you to assure that the staff actions in the headquarters are done properly and that the accompanying paperwork is right. I want to see only what I need to see. In many cases, that means I trust you to make decisions in my name. If this works out the way I envision, at the beginning you will ask for my guidance before acting, then later on as you learn my mind, you will tell me after the fact what you have done, and eventually you will only selectively inform me of what you have done.

"My second task for you is more to a warrior's liking. I think that the war plans for the defense of Korea are all wrong. I am not going to tell you why I believe that. I want you to become familiar with the war plans, get to know the terrain and the capabilities of our forces and come to your own conclusions. I want to know your opinion of the present defense strategy and how you might change it. I won't tell you why now, but I think we have about six months before significant changes must be made. I hope you will arrive at a similar conclusion. I want your analysis in two months.

"One final point. I selected you, which means I'm I am stuck with you. Therefore, I want you to be a success. That is why I told you to change the morning briefing. It ought to be easy. That will give you early credibility. Your answer to my question as to why you would be a good Chief of Staff was excellent. I had to do it. Questions?" Pete was silent. "I will expect you here at 1700 this afternoon to tell me about the day's staff activities and to sign whatever needs signing. Good luck. Dismissed."

Pete looked at his watch and saw that it was 0900. He had half an hour before his meeting with General Lee, the deputy CG. He turned to the general's secretary. "I know that this sounds silly," he said, "but I wonder if you could tell me where my office is?" After a short, but good, laugh the secretary showed him to a building adjacent to the CG's office. As they were walking, Pete asked two more questions. "Do I have a secretary, and if so, and what is his or her name? I understand I have a deputy. Where is his office and what is his name?" That got a real guffaw.

"Your secretary's name is Sharon. She is American and the wife of an officer in the signal corps. She is here as an unauthorized dependent, but no one seems to mind. Just don't advertise it. Your deputy is colonel Kim Jook Wan. His office is right next to yours. And here you are. I need to go back to my office now."

"Thanks," said Pete.

Pete entered and introduced himself to Sharon and immediately apologized. "I know this is extremely rude but they have me on an impossible schedule this morning. I need to talk to you at length sometime today in order to learn my job. But that will have to wait for a few hours. Please indulge me. And now, where do I find Colonel Kim?"

"Right here, Colonel Goodwin," replied Kim, standing in the adjoining doorway. "I have been waiting for you. Your schedule has been distributed through the headquarters since yesterday. We are scheduled to meet after your meeting with General Lee at about 1030. I have been the acting Chief of Staff for a month. We have no crises that I know of right now. Everything is under control. I will have a briefing prepared for you at that time. Allow me to escort you to General Lee's office. If we leave now we will just get there in time. You'll like General Lee. Except for the fact that he is needed here, anywhere else he would certainly be a three star Corps Commander. Here we are. Good luck. I'll see you in about a hour. *Ciao.* Yes, I speak Italian too. I was an attaché in Rome."

Pete was starting to feel quite humble as he walked into the General's office.

"Good Morning, General, thank you for seeing me," said Pete. "As I told you last night, I am delighted to be here and I hope that I can live up to your expectations. I was last in Korea 20 years ago and am absolutely astonished at the progress that has been made. It's obvious, at least to me, that virtually everything I thought I knew about Korea is now outdated. I have much to learn."

"Tell me what you think you know," responded Lee.

"I think I have been assigned to a superb 12 division Field Army that very few people understand and appreciate. The American people, and most of our own Army, believe the U.S. is carrying most of the burden in the defense of Korea. They also don't believe that there is a viable threat from North Korea. The President is talking about removing U.S. forces. I think this is false. But I talk too much. The real issue is what I *don't* know. I hope you will help me learn."

"Very good," said Lee, "I think we will get along. You are right. Most Americans do not understand Korea. Some think of us as little yellow brothers. The Korean people are a very proud people – we are extremely proud of what we have accomplished over the last twenty years. It is commonly believed that we are just now approaching what economists call the "economic take-off point." I believe that in less than twenty years we will have a viable automobile industry, one of the world's best ship-building industries, and a significant portion of the computer industry, because we are committed, we work hard, and we place an extremely high priority on education. Our kids go to school 240 days a year, compared to American children's 180 days. And it is considered a family disgrace if a child does poorly at school. That is what you and I are here to protect. It is apparent that the DMZ and the North Korean forces are only about 30 miles from Seoul, our capitol and center of commerce. In about twenty years, we will be so strong that North Korea won't dare attack unless they are going for mutual nuclear destruction. They just might be crazy enough to do that. But that is the future. Our problem is now."

"Many Americans come to Korea with the mindset that they know better than we, and attempt to impose their culture upon us. I do not see that in you. The real problem is that the U.S. Government and miliary do not sufficiently appreciate how capable our forces have become. This has been accomplished at great sacrifice. We need to acknowledge this improvement and instill into everyone that we can't be beaten. This requires a change in attitude in the Eighth Army, your Pentagon, and your political leadership. I am asking for you to help us by strengthening our reputation.

"As far as ordinary staff work is concerned, the best I can say is that this staff, which you will find to be very good, has tolerated what previous

American Chiefs of Staff have directed. But in doing so, we have wasted a lot of time that could otherwise be spent preparing for combat. I ask you to cut down on the unnecessary. General Pace is attempting to cut down at the commander level. But it also needs to be done at the staff level. For example, this morning, General Pace instructed you to improve the morning briefing. I agree with him. What we have here is a group of Koreans trying to emulate the U.S. model for briefings. It doesn't work with our culture very well. Talk to the staff, get their opinions. That is enough for today. I, too, have a busy schedule. But, my door is always open. I hope you will take the attitude that you are the Chief of Staff for the entire First Combined Field Army and not just for American interests. Thank you for coming by."

Pete realized that the meeting was over. "Thank you, sir. You have given me much to think about. After I have had a couple of weeks to assimilate and consider what you have said, I hope you will let me come back and make a proper response."

Pete returned to his office, asking people along the way for directions. He detected that people wondered how good a Chief of Staff who can't even find his own office would really be.

Colonel Kim met Pete upon his return to the office. "How did it go?" asked Kim.

"It was totally different from what I expected," Pete admitted, "I have a lot of deep thinking to do. First, I need to empty my mind and get rid of all my preconceived notions. I want the staff to tell me what I need to hear, and not what they think I want to hear. Please relay that message to them. I am very serious. I want the truth, warts and all. There is something very worthwhile to protect and defend in Korea. Therefore, I need to know the real threat, including North Korean capabilities. Then, I need a no-nonsense evaluation of our troops and any ideas, no matter how farfetched, of what we can do to make us better."

Lee appeared quite pleased at Pete's short speech. Over the last year, he become tired of these career-serving, self righteous/egotistical Americans who wanted to tell everyone what to do, make a reputation, and get out fast. These Americans viewed Korea as a place to get their "ticket punched." Most Korean military professionals already knew what the problems were and how to fix them. Unfortunately, nobody listened. Maybe, just maybe, Pace and Goodwin could change that, Kim thought. It would require a complete change in attitude among members of American military and political circles. Nobody liked to be told that the conventional wisdom of the last 20 years was wrong, especially when many had their reputations on the line. The hardest nuts to crack would be the garrison commandos of the U.S. Eighth Army, most of whom had never been north of Seoul. Their jobs depended upon the assumption of a long protracted war.

At that moment, Kim felt better than he had felt in years.

"Colonel Goodwin," said Kim, "Let's go to the command briefing room. I have you set up for two hours of briefings this morning and two more after lunch. That is enough for one day. Tomorrow, if it is all right with you, you will pay informal office calls on the staff. The briefing that you will receive today is the standard command briefing – not exactly what you said you wanted. However, I will convey your desires to the staff tonight and I promise you that in your private one-on-one meetings you will get what you want. Shall we go?"

Pete understood what was going on. It was obvious that the Koreans liked General Pace but had been inhibited in their effort to work effectively with him by the closed minds of the two previous Chiefs of Staff. The Koreans needed to feel Pete out before deciding whether or not to trust him. Opposing higher authority is rarely career-enhancing. Pete felt he had made the right moves so far, but there was a long way to go. The one-on-one meetings tomorrow would be instructive. Pete further realized that the worst possible thing he could do would be to criticize and start issuing orders. Listen politely, he reminded himself, and ask lots of questions. Usually people have a lot they want to tell you, but won't volunteer it. Instead, they will give you a subtle signal, hope you catch it, and ask the right question – that way they are covered. This was a technique Pete had mastered when he was an Inspector General.

Chapter Nine

Kim and Pete entered the briefing room and the SGS called attention. Pete asked everyone to please be at ease introduced himself around the room, even though he had met many of the officers the night before at the mess. This time there was an additional advantage. Everyone wore a sewn-on name tag. Pete had never been good at remembering names unless he could read them at the same time he was hearing them. He noticed that the Korean officer's name tags were in both Korean and English. He decided right then he was going to do the same thing as soon as he could. He also noticed that there were no junior officers present except for those operating the briefing aids. Colonel Kim took charge of the meeting. He announced that the first briefing would be by the G-2 Intelligence Officer.

"Good Morning, Colonel Goodwin. I am Colonel Lee. As you will find out, if you have not already, there are many Colonel Lees in the headquarters. To tell us apart we have adopted a convention. My full Korean name is Lee Jae Joon, so everyone calls me JJ, or JJ Lee. I hope you will find that acceptable. Now for my briefing.

"This map shows Korea and the First Combined Field Army's area of assignment. You will note that we are responsible for roughly the western half of the country. For your information the ROK Third Army has responsibility for the eastern half. The G-3 will expand on that in detail later. For orientation these lines mark the DMZ and the 38th parallel. You will note that in the western part of our sector the DMZ runs along the Imjin Gang, Gang being Hangul for river."

"Hangul?" asked Pete.

"My apologies, sir," responded Lee. "The name of our language is Hangul."

"Sorry," said Pete, "I should have known that. Please continue."

"The DMZ along the Imjin is quite far south of the 38th parallel because that it is the natural defensive line between north and south and that is where the Korean war ended. You will further note, that further to the east, the Imjin bends to the northeast and then north until it peters out in the foothills of the mountains. At this point it crosses the 38th parallel. After that the DMZ is entirely north of the 38th parallel and follows the ridgeline of some very tough mountains, running northeast for a while, and then east. Again, this is where the war ended in 1953 and, in this sector, is the natural defensive line between north and south. I would like to point out the Chorwan valley which is considered to be the primary avenue of approach into the south. It is this valley approach that our current war plans view as the primary threat corridor."

Something in the back of Pete's mind went "tilt," but he kept his mouth shut.

"That is a very brief terrain analysis," continued Lee. "Now a brief discussion of the weather. You will note that Korea is a peninsula and that our latitude is about the same as your Valley Forge. We like to use that analogy because it impresses upon Americans how cold it can get in the winter. Our climate is one of extremes, very hot in the summer, short spring and fall, and very cold in the winter – so cold that the rivers freeze rock solid for about four months."

The "tilt" signal went on again in Pete's mind but he remained silent.

"Now for the enemy. The North Koreans have the fourth largest army in the world, about 900,000 strong. They are well-trained and well-equipped primarily by the Soviet Union. Since the war, the Chinese have really taken a hands-off approach. The North Korean government of Kim Il Sung is an absolute dictatorship and has complete control of the armed forces. Whether it is fear, loyalty, or indoctrination, if Kim says attack, they attack, regardless of the consequences. They have consistently stated that they will destroy South Korea and have rejected all attempts to work out a peaceful solution. In our area, they could put 400,000 troops into the field, supported by armor and air. They are constantly testing our readiness with patrols and amphibious raids on our coast. Most recently, we discovered that they have built two tunnels, each over a mile long and large enough for a man to walk upright under the DMZ. We don't know their purpose, but there is much about the North Koreans that we don't understand. Because of their closed society we have had little success in putting agents into North Korea. Our intelligence comes primarily from satellite observation. We know their capabilities. We do not know their intentions.

"Based upon their present dispositions and combat readiness, they could launch an attack equivalent to two Corps or 100,000 men, without warning, 200,000 men with about 48 hours warning, and the whole 400,000 with a week's preparation. The present dispositions are something of a puzzle. They are really not where they should be if the Chorwan Valley approach is the primary threat corridor."

Again Pete told himself that he must be careful. These clues were almost too easy, as though he were being manipulated. More likely though, others had missed the point. He told himself to play it cool.

"Colonel Goodwin, that completes my briefing. I am looking forward to discussing this with you at much greater length tomorrow," concluded Lee.

Kim then introduced the G-3 Operations officer. There was a murmur of laughter in the room.

"Colonel Goodwin, I am also Colonel Lee," the speaker said. "My full name is Lee Chi Na, so, of course, everyone calls me China Lee, which I have been told is the name of an American striptease dancer. I don't mind. At least everyone remembers my name. And now, once the chuckling stops, I will try to brief you on the operational situation."

Pete was glad the Koreans included him in their little joke.

"The First Combined Field Army consists of twelve divisions, 11 Korean and one U.S. They are organized into three corps of three divisions each and two separate divisions including the 1st Korean Marine Division that is on the left or west flank in the marshes and tributaries on the coast, and the U.S. Second Infantry Division, which is the Field Army reserve since it is the most mobile of our divisions. The Korean divisions are similar in size and structure to a U.S. infantry division. Each corps has a corps artillery and the other normal organic support troops.

"The combat readiness of our forces is what in your army you would call C-1, that is, completely combat ready except for one area. We believe that we do not have sufficient new technology weapons, such as the TOW antitank guided missile and the Redeye antiaircraft missile. We have requested support in these two areas, which request was favorably endorsed by General Pace but is still being considered by Eighth Army. I hope that decision will be forthcoming.

"The Strategic Defense Plan for Korea envisions several things: a North Korean attack along the Chorwan valley approach, a strategic defensive for a period of time, trading space for time, and finally a counteroffensive some months later. You will note from the map that our successive lines of defense are based upon and positioned in accord with the major attack in the Chorwan Valley. We have been studying the new NATO strategy and are beginning to think that a forward defense, as they have implemented, might be more appropriate. This comes about as a result of the increased lethality of modern precision guided munitions. The balance of war has returned to the defense. Of course, a revised strategy would require the tools of war to implement it. The two go together."

Pete spoke up, "Colonel Lee, I was told that I was going to get the standard command briefing. Is that what I am hearing?"

Colonel Kim responded. "No sir, we have been working on this briefing under the direction of General Pace for a month. No one else has heard it except for you. He told us to give it to you and get your reaction. That includes the intelligence briefing as well."

"I'm not going to give you my reaction today," Pete answered. "I have heard and understood every word you say. I need time to think. Please continue."

Colonel Kim was satisfied. He would definitely report this back to General Lee. Colonel Goodwin would not accept assertion, but had an open mind. It will be most interesting to see how Goodwin will act, Kim thought. He guessed that Goodwin would investigate independently and reach his own conclusions. Kim would recommend to General Lee not to push too hard and that Goodwin got the message. But Kim did not know that Goodwin would take what had been said and eventually improve on it considerably.

"Well sir," said Colonel China Lee, "that just about completes my part of the briefing. Do you have any questions?"

"I have many questions, but as you realize, I have been in Korea this time less than 24 hours. I will give you my questions when I think I am ready to ask intelligent ones. But thank you very much for an excellent briefing."

At that point, Colonel Kim asked the other staff members if any one of them had any questions or comments. Pete was getting the impression that dissent and free discussion were unfortunately not encouraged in the headquarters. Pete had studied the works of Deming and based upon his own experience, understood that quite often the best ideas come from below. It was necessary to establish a philosophy and a mechanism for facilitating this, though he did not know how well it would fit into the Korean culture. He would have to be very careful. Maybe the revision of the format for the daily staff briefings might give him an insight.

Kim ended the morning portion of the briefing and instructed everyone to reassemble at 1330.

Pete and Kim walked directly to the CG mess since it was approaching 1230. Pete made some complimentary remarks on the quality of the briefing but refrained from commenting on the substance. Kim did not press him.

Lunch was very good, as Pete had expected. As with breakfast, you filled out a chit at lunch. The choices ranged from a full lunch, to a sandwich, to a salad. There was no alcohol served and the bar was not open. Pete opted for the salad. That was a mistake. Fresh greens approved by the medics were still hard to come by in Korea. This resulted from 2000 years of using human waste to fertilize the soil. Pete mused to himself that this might also explain the odor in the shower. It reminded him that thirty years ago this area was virtually medieval and that twenty years ago it was a devastated war zone. The contrasts were mindboggling. Twenty miles to the south was a thriving modern city with skyscrapers, subways and shopping malls. Twenty miles to the north was a combat zone with bunkers, barbed wire and all the accouterments of war. Right in the middle was Camp Red Cloud and the First Combined Field Army who's mission was to keep the two separate. Pete decided to order a sandwich instead.

At 1330, the briefings started again. This time the briefers were both American, the G-1 for personnel and administration and the G-4 for logistics. Pete listened to the briefers courteously but didn't like what he was hearing. The briefers were speaking about everything but significant facts.

When they had finished, Pete asked, "How does the personnel and logistical situation affect the combat readiness of the Field Army?"

The answers were not very explicit.

Pete then asked, "How do we determine the personnel and logistical status?" The answer relied on national reports.

"Do we have any independent way of ascertaining the status?" he asked, frustrated. Again, the answer was no. "When we determine that personnel or logistics shortfalls are negatively affecting combat readiness," Pete wondered, "what do we do, how do we influence the improvement?"

The answers by both the G-1 and the G-4 were predictable and disheartening. "Sir, these are a national responsibility. We really don't get involved."

Pete broke his own rule of just listening. "Gentlemen, I could not disagree with you more. I see this as your primary responsibility. Please see me within a week as to how we can accurately judge the effect of personnel and logistics on our combat readiness and how we can cause necessary improvements. These are the kind of reports that should be occupying your time. In this command, we should not be concerned with chapel attendance, number of troops who buy savings bonds, and so forth. Those matters are important but are not our mission. When we meet next, bring a list of all reports that are made to higher headquarters with no direct bearing on our mission. It is my intent to either cancel them or hand these tasks to someone else. I know this will displease Eighth Army. Colonel Kim, after discussion with General Lee, I wonder if you might want to follow my advice. We have a typical alliance problem here. We must always get along with our higher national headquarters, and we must also realize that we have a unique perspective."

Kim responded, "Colonel Goodwin, I personally agree with you. I think General Lee will also. Let me get back to you right away."

And with that the briefing came to a close. Pete asked Kim if they might now be able to spend some private time together and returned to Pete's office. Again, Pete had to ask Kim if he would show him the way. Kim laughed aloud. So much for the stoicism of the oriental.

Pete opened the conversation over a cup of coffee. "Colonel Kim, let me express to you what I think our relationship should be. We had a good example of it at the briefings today. We both have two different jobs, one allied and one national. I see you as the Chief of Staff for those matters that are strictly Korean. I am the Chief of Staff for those matters that are strictly American. Together we are the Chief and Deputy Chief of Staff for allied matters. The problem is that these issues will occasionally overlap. That is unavoidable. The way we should approach it is with complete trust. I promise you that I will tell you everything unless I am absolutely prohibited from doing so. I hope you will be able to do the same with me."

Kim responded, "Colonel Goodwin, I fully intend to do just that. In fact those were my instructions from General Lee. It has not been so open in the recent past due to the attitudes of previous Chiefs of Staff."

"Let's return to this discussion after we have both had time to think about it and can discuss specifics rather that generalities." said Pete. "And now, I need to talk with you and the SGS about staff activities for the day. General Pace instructed me to come see him at 1700 and brief him on the day's activities."

Kim answered, "The SGS and I are prepared to do just that. But you will not have to meet with General Pace today. He called in and said that he was invited to have dinner and spend the evening with the ROK III Corps Commander. So, we all get a chance to relax tonight. You will see a very different personality in the CG mess and far fewer people. Some of the Korean officers will take the opportunity to have dinner with their families, some of the Americans with their girlfriends. On that latter point, at some time you are going to have to decide whether or not to intervene. General Pace pretends it does not exist."

The meeting with Colonel Kim and the SGS fortunately did not last long. By luck, and as Pete suspected, by intent, the paperwork flow was relatively benign. Nothing controversial and nothing that couldn't wait until tomorrow. Pete intended for that to change, but not quite yet. He had a lot of ground work to lay first. He decided to go to his hootch and catch a short nap. He was suffering the effects of jet lag. This time he was determined to find his hootch on his own. After a number of wrong turns he eventually found it. People who saw him thought he was making a walkaround inspection tour.

When he got to the hootch, Chan was there pressing clothes. Pete asked Chan if he could do something for him. He wanted Chan to put his nametags in both English and Hangul, knowing that all the officers in the headquarters read English, but in other places many did not.

Chan responded that it would be done by morning. Two days later, Pete noticed almost all the American officers had done the same thing. Point made.

After speaking with Chan, Pete set the alarm for 1800 and hit the sack. He did not fall asleep immediately with the day's events still passing through his mind. He felt pretty good, but realized that he had made one big mistake that everyone was too polite to correct. He had continually used the label South Korea instead of the preferred Republic of Korea. Though it might seem minor to most Americans, the difference was very significant to the Koreans, who also disliked being referred to as South Koreans.

After a long nap, the alarm sounded at 1800 and awakened Pete. At first he was completely disoriented. He almost never took an afternoon nap and usually woke up at the right time without the aid of a clock. It took a couple of minutes for him to realize where he was. He stumbled to the shower and took a cold shower followed by a hot one. He noticed the same smell. After that he dressed and walked to the mess, arriving at exactly 1830. He was the only one there. He understood what Kim had been talking about. This was relaxation time.

Pete walked over to the bartender, introduced himself and asked for a Vodka on the rocks with a twist of lemon. He might as well relax, too.

He struck up a conversation with the bartender. Pete had found, over time, that bartenders like to talk and can be a very good source of information.

"Tell me about yourself," said Pete.

"My name is Pak Smy Li," said the bartender. "Of course, everyone calls me Smiley. I have been the bartender here for almost 10 years. Because of my command of the English language and my length of time spent here, I am the president of the Employee's Association of Camp Red Cloud. We are not a union and have no power to strike, but on occasion, it is right that our views become known. The Association works both ways and is most strict with the employees as well. You will seldom see any thievery here, and when it does occur, our system finds and returns the objects immediately."

"Tell me more." Pete was intrigued.

"I escaped from what is now called North Korea during the war and was immediately drafted into the ROK army. After serving three years, I was discharged. I found work here as a houseboy and eventually worked my way up to bartender. I am not well-educated, but I do read a lot. My wife and I have four children, all of whom are going to the university. My sons want to be businessmen and my daughter wants to be a doctor. This never would have happened to me except for the war and what has happened since. I am a lucky man. Please excuse me, I see that more officers have arrived and are looking for a drink. I wish you the best, sir. There are few secrets at Red Cloud and, so far, we like what we see."

Pete wondered how many other Americans took the trouble to ask Smiley about himself. Pete sensed that there was more to this man than met the eye. He would not be a bit surprised if Smiley owned some of the laundries, restaurants, and tailor shops in Uijongbu. He was to find out later that Smiley was one of the richest men in Uijongbu.

Rich walked in and took a seat by Pete. "I don't know whether you know this or not," he said, "but I'm late because the staff is already starting to react to you. Colonel Lee had us go through all our reports to determine what we do and don't need and what information we need that we don't now have. We have just started and already we are quite surprised by the results. The G-1 and the G-4 are both in a state of shock, but they are good people and know that you are right. They like the idea of being warriors rather that ash and trash collectors."

"I'm sorry that I put you and others through a drill this afternoon," Pete replied. "I did not expect that sort of immediate response. I have found that when response is this quick, people have been wanting to do it and simply needed an excuse or a catalyst to get them started. I am already convinced that this staff is capable of fighting a successful battle. What is in doubt, however, is whether or not we have the forces and the plans. This I hope to find out in short order.

"But enough about business. What is tonight going to be like? Colonel Kim told me that not too many people are going to be here."

"That is exactly right," assured Rich. "On a night like this, we usually forget about the seating arrangements and all sit together. It will be very informal. Let's relax and have another drink. I sometimes think that Pace does this intentionally. He does not enjoy being on center stage all the time."

The evening went by without incident. Most of the officers watched a movie while Rich got a bridge game going. Pete was invited to play but declined on the basis that he hadn't played in years. And, after observing several hands, he was glad. These guys were cutthroats who took the game seriously. Pete decided to restrict his card playing to poker night where he might have a fighting chance. It turned out that he would pay dearly for this assumption.

Chapter Ten

Pete had made all of his private office calls on the staff of the First Combined Field Army and was extremely impressed by the quality. While it was stated in many different ways, the overall theme was consistent: We are better than most people think and we can win this war if it comes to that, we just need to get our act together.

The next afternoon, Pete made his first 1700 office call on General Pace to go over the staff activities and to obtain Pace's necessary signatures. The meeting did not go well. It was preordained not to. Pace had a point to make. Pete had spent the better part of the afternoon getting the papers right. He had driven Sharon, his secretary, almost to distraction. Each paper had a one-page summary sheet on top with a recommendation as to Pace's action. Signature tabs were in their appropriate places as is done in the Pentagon. Pete arrived with his stack of papers and took his seat.

"Proceed," was all Pace said.

Pete took the first paper and handed it to Pace. "Sir, this is our response to a request from Eighth Army about the alert system. It seems that several weeks ago, due to an international incident totally unaffecting Korea, the Pentagon sent out a rocket to all Commanders in Chief to raise their Defense Readiness Condition (DEFCON) by one notch. Eighth Army simply passed the message on. Everyone seemed to have forgotten that because of our location and mission, we were already at DEFCON 4, while the rest of the world was at DEFCON 5. Given the situation, for us to go to DEFCON 3 would have been a big mistake. It would have been unnecessarily provocative and very expensive due to the fact that we would have had to move all of our units into their battle positions and break open the ammunition containers. Once these containers are opened, they must be used. It could have been a disaster but Colonel Lee, the G-3, overruled and requested guidance. What we are saying in the response is to *specify* the DEFCON desired, not simply "increase one level." Common sense."

"Would you stake your career and reputation on this being the right action?" Pace asked.

"Sir, that is the staff recommendation," Pete answered incorrectly. "The decision is yours."

"Well rattleass, that is not the way we are going to do it around here. Let me tell you a little story," said Pace. "Several years ago I was on the staff of the National Security Council at the White House under Dr. Kissinger. I had prepared a paper for him at his request and sent it to his office. Later that day he called me in and asked me if this was my best effort. I told him that maybe I could do a little better. He instructed me to go back and work on it some more. When I took it back the next time, he asked me again if it was my best effort. This time I said, "Yes Sir." Kissinger then said he would read it.

"My point is a simple one. It is one thing to get guidance from the boss on a controversial issue. It is quite another to avoid blame by asking the boss to make decisions that you should be making. I want you to make sure that the papers I have to sign are right and that you and the staff will base your reputations on them. Are the rest of the papers right?"

"Sir, I would like one day to comply with your desires," answered Pete.

That night and the next day Pete went over the staff papers very carefully. He first tried to put himself into Pace's mind. He then called in the primary action officer of each paper and walked himself through every step of the action, asking questions like: What was the issue, what were the facts and assumptions bearing on the issue, what were the options or alternatives, what were the relative advantages and disadvantages of each option, and what was the preferred option. In about half of the papers, the action was right; in the other half, additional work was needed.

That evening, Pete returned to Pace with the revised stack of papers. In addition to the papers, he had attached a one-page summary describing the contents. He informed Pace that the papers were right and that Pace should sign them.

Pace thanked him and told him to leave the papers. "I am going to study them carefully and see if we are in agreement. I will let you know. Dismissed."

Pete understood what was going on. Pace had issued his guidance clearly and was now determining whether Pete was capable of complying. This also had a ricochet effect on the staff. Just as Pete was being scrutinized by Pace, the staff was being scrutinized by Pete. More attention was now being paid to the correctness of staff actions, and Pete was caught clearly in the middle.

The next morning, Pace called in Pete and told him that he had signed the papers. He repeated that this was what he expected. He then asked Pete if he had attained any additional insights.

Pete told Pace that he thought much of the present staff work was inappropriate to the headquarters because of its tactical nature and was wasting valuable time and effort. Both the U.S. Eighth Army and the Korean Support Command were giving the headquarters the administrative paperwork that they should do themselves. Pete also told the general that he was in the process of putting together a list of these useless reports and would get back to him ASAP. Pete thought there was a lot of much needed, combat-readiness, information missing. The rule of thumb should be if the information was needed for assigned mission completion, we should have it; if not, we shouldn't. Pace agreed, telling Pete to keep at it.

The subject of the morning briefing was next. Fortunately, Pete had discussed it with most of the staff and with General Lee, and was prepared.

"Sir," said Pete, "Right now we have the briefings six days a week and they have become very stereotypical – all information and no decisions. I suggest we change the briefing to three times a week and make them more of an information and decision-making format. There are many topics on which a good briefing can legitimately ask for a decision on the spot. Think of the time and effort we could save. I also suggest that we expand the attendance. These staff officers need to see you in action. Many of them have never seen you or spoken to you. They need motivation, just like the troops in the field. I would suggest that we begin with the normal G-2, G-3, G-1, G-4 briefings, followed by topics of command interest that need a decision, but not exhaustive staff work. I would also recommend that the action officer, rather than his boss, give the briefing. Finally, I would like to change the thrust of the G-1 and G-4 briefings to that of combat readiness. General Lee agrees with my recommendation."

"Do it," were the only words from General Pace.

Within the next several weeks, things started to come together. The three morning briefing a week became fun and informative. Sparks flew, good decisions were made, the mission of the Field Army became better appreciated, and Pace had a great stage and captive audience. The audience loved it. It was great theater. Everyone looked forward to the briefings instead of dreading them. Action officers even vied with one another to present the special topics. This competition resulted in higher quality presentations.

Staff work improved, too. It was no longer possible to hide behind the anonymity of the staff process. The guilty party, or the staff hero, was always identified. It was amazing what clear-cut lines of authority and responsibility did to individual motivation. The question "Is this right?" became the staff watchword.

Scrubing the administrative staff actions was more difficult since that took cooperation from higher headquarters. The key question was "Why is this information needed?" Quite often there was no good answer. Sometimes the Field Army just stopped sending the report and waited for a reaction. There never was one. By cutting out the unnecessary reports, it was possible to put the G-1 and the G-4 directly into the combat-readiness business.

What was needed most was assimilation, analysis, conclusion, and recommendation. Eighth Army was not amused when Pace sent a letter to the Eighth Army Commander and a copy to the Korean Chairman of the Joint Chiefs of Staff, stating that the undermanning of the Second U.S. Infantry Division was unacceptable because it placed the mission in jeopardy. Before that time, Eighth Army had taken the position that the status was within acceptable limits, but the numbers, once Pace had a system for getting that information, said otherwise.

The reason that the undermanning was bad was because the United States was then in the process of changing from a draft to an all-volunteer Army. The Korean government, once aware of the situation, had a ready solution. Near the end of the Korean War, U.S. units were at low strength and were augmented with Korean soldiers. It worked well for all involved and the Korean soldiers loved it for the simple reason that U.S. units lived better than Korean units. The program was reinstituted until the U.S. brought the division up to strength, which they eventually did out of embarrassment.

The 1700 evening meetings between Pete and Pace were going very well. Pete had now been exposed to Pace long enough to know his way of thinking and to anticipate his reactions. Pace had learned to trust Pete and had confidence in his judgment. One night, after going through the staff actions, Pace asked Pete if he would like to have a drink and just chat for a while. Pete was delighted.

"Well, rattleass, you have been here for about a month and your performance has been marginally acceptable," Pace praised. "Do you mind if, in private, I call you Pete?" Pete told him he didn't mind and waited for the inevitable next line. "You may call me General or Sir."

"Sir, I would be honored."

"OK, Pete." said Pace, "How far have you gotten on the second task that I gave you, that is, the analysis of the strategic defense plan and our ability to execute?"

Pete responded. "I have been a headquarters commando for the last month and really have not had the opportunity to get out in the field, get to know the commanders and the troops, and physically walk the terrain and defensive positions. I really haven't had the time to study the existing plans all that much, but am now ready to do so. According to your schedule, I still have a month on this issue and I would like to take that month rather than give you an incomplete and halfbaked answer. My major insights, so far, are that the Koreans see the need for change; but we need to change the wherewithal, that is, the plans and the resource allocations, in order to make a *significant difference*. The present plans and resources are, as I see it, *self-fulfilling prophecy*. They assume early North Korean success, a withdrawal

South of Seoul, major reinforcement from the U.S. and finally, several months later, a counter-offensive. If people are told they are expected to retreat – they will."

"OK," said Pace, "Take your time. I think that you are on the right track."

The next morning, Pete went to Colonel Kim and asked two favors of him. "I would like to spend my Saturdays and Sundays learning the terrain of the Field Army, seeing the defensive positions, and talking to unit commanders at all levels. Will you set this up for me? Also, I wonder if you have a military history of Korea going back as far as possible. I am interested in studying historical invasion routes. I have a suspicion that recent history may have taught us erroneous lessons about the Chorwan valley."

Kim responded, intrigued by the second request about the history, "Certainly. If you don't mind, I will instruct officers of the staff to accompany you. You will need an interpreter. It will do some of the Korean officers good. Of course, General Lee will want to know what you are up to."

Pete then called in the G-3, the G-4, and the U.S. Air Liaison Officer. He also asked Colonel Kim to be present since it was essential to mutual trust that General Lee remain constantly informed.

"Gentlemen," said Pete, "I want you to undertake a study for me. We now have the time to do this sort of thing since we have cut down on a lot of unnecessary reports. I have the impression that our present defense plans are based on outdated technology and, possibly, on a misreading of history. Ask yourselves two questions. First, given the location of the DMZ, if you were the North Koreans, where would you attack and how? Second, and based upon your answer to the first question, how could we use the capabilities of present technology to enhance our defense? Do not be resource constrained. Calculate what would be needed to defeat an attack with a forward defense without major penetration, and then to rapidly destroy the North Korean forces. Please keep this effort to a small trusted group. It would be premature for this effort to become common knowledge. This is a matter of some urgency. I want your preliminary *results within a month.* Air, if you need cooperation with U.S. Air Forces, Korea, let me know. I think I know how to get it."

"Colonel Kim," asked Pete, "Is there anything you would like to add?"

"No sir," said Kim. "Other than please keep me informed."

Both Pete and Kim knew that this was the right way to do it. If the effort turned out badly, Lee and Pace could blame it on the lunacy of two staff officers. After all, they were taking on the conventional wisdom of 20 years. They were both keeping General Pace and General Lee informed privately.

On Saturday morning, after breakfast, Colonel China Lee and Pete climbed into a waiting UH-1 helicopter. They had decided that the first step should be to overfly the entire Army area to get a feel for it. They would start on the west coast and fly just south of the DMZ. To comply with the armistice agreements they would fly a mile south of the DMZ at about 5000 feet altitude. Fortunately, it was a nice day with unlimited visibility. They could see about 20 miles on either side of the flight path. Pete was reminded how, even at only about 5000 feet, it was virtually impossible to see military emplacements. Both sides were using effective camouflage discipline. Pete was interested in two things, the location of the units and the difficulty of the terrain. Colonel Lee had to help in the former. He had with him a detailed military installation map and was able to point out where both the North Korean and ROK forces were located. He was also able to give Pete the general direction and location of the North Korean units that were over the visible horizon. The tour over the DMZ reinforced what Pete had already surmised from studying maps. Other than the Imjin Gang the terrain in the western part of the sector was flat and open. In the east it was extremely mountainous. After going the length of the DMZ, and after refueling, Lee & Pete proceeded to do multiple north to south routes along what the military called lines of communication – the routes along which supplies and troops are moved.

Pete noted that each corps had one major route and several minor ones. While the major ridgeline ran approximately east-west, there were several valleys that ran basically north-south. It was in these valleys that the lines of communication were established. Pete took special interest in the Chorwan valley. It was quite wide in places, with occasional choke points that could be more easily defended. The valley was about thirty miles in length and most of it was in ROK hands. When the war ended the DMZ was established at the most northern part of the valley. Pete asked China Lee to show him where the 38th parallel crossed the Chorwan. It was close to the south end of the valley, just before the terrain turned relatively flat without many natural barriers.

The next several weeks were spent in making ground visits to each of the corps and divisions. At each visit the commander insisted on giving Pete the standard dog and pony show, that is, the command briefing. Pete listened with interest and asked the requisite questions to show interest, but never to the extent of exposing his misgivings. In every case the briefings reflected strict compliance with the standard assumptions and direction of the accepted strategic defense plan. Pete then asked to be taken to the forward defense positions, where he could observe for himself the battlefield, preparation of positions and fields of fire, and proper identification of key terrain features. He found that north-south movement of troops was relatively easy. East-west movement was virtually impossible due both to the terrain and the mindset of the commanders. One thing that very much impressed Pete was the fighting spirit of the ROKs. These guys would not cut and run. They deserved plans and resources that matched their fighting spirit. By the end of the month, Pete felt that he had a proper appreciation of the existing situation.

One apparent thing was the disposition of the three ROK corps. Two corps were compressed into less than half of the Army sector in and around the Chorwan valley and the mountains. One corps was stretched very thin, covering more that half of the sector in the west behind the Imjin Gang. The U.S. Second Infantry Division, which was the Army reserve, was centrally located, but the existing road network made it easier to reinforce to the east than to the west.

At month's end, Pete figured that he had gotten about as much out of his personal inspection tour as was possible. It was now time to get back together with his appointed study group.

Pete asked his group for their preliminary findings. They emphasized the preliminary nature of the findings, but the results were consistent with Pete's expectations, essentially what the staff was alluding to on his first day in the headquarters: that the North Koreans should attack in the winter on the Kaesong Munson approach in the west when the Imjin Gang is frozen solid, that the First Combined Field Army was poorly positioned for this direction of attack; and that with a repositioning of the Army and a reasonable amount of modern weapons they could be stopped cold.

The following day Pete and Kim asked for a private meeting with General Pace and General Lee. Pete and Kim gave them the first findings of their investigation. They also gave them the results of a separate Air Battle Analysis that had been performed. Early in the staff study, it had become apparent that the air battle should not be dependent on the ground tactical maneuvering. On the contrary, it was actually hampered by being so dependent if the objective was to first destroy the combat effectiveness of the North Korean air threat. This point of view would be difficult for the military to accept. People had become dependent on the availability of tactical air-ground support. It took a lot of convincing to most people to demonstrate that the use of ground launched, precision-guided munitions that were now becoming available could do the job. Priorities were essential.

Pete told General Pace that the Air Battle Analysis would not have been conducted except for Pace's intervention with the Commander in Chief, U.S. Air Forces in the Pacific. Initially, the Air Force and the Navy were not interested in the effort. But, once forced into it, they became enthusiastic when they realized that the concern was to determine the proper application of air power instead of merely subscribing to old stereotyped thinking. The conclusion was that the North Korean air threat could be rendered combat ineffective in about five days if two U.S. Navy aircraft carriers were available, in eight days if they were not.

After heated conversation and questions, Pace asked, "Where do we go from here?"

"Sir," Pete replied, "our next problem is to convince everyone else. That is not going to be easy. We are challenging 20 years of conventional wisdom from Seoul and Washington. But, I have an idea on that." Pete turned to General Lee. "Sir, I understand that the Korean armed forces have established a computer assisted war gaming agency in Yong Dong Po just outside of Seoul and that it was modeled after the U.S. Strategic and Tactical Analysis Gaming agency in Washington. I wonder if it would be possible to get their help on this?"

Lee thought for a moment and then responded, "I can certainly look into that. What is it you would want them to do?"

"It would be my guess," answered Pete, "that they have fully analyzed the present strategic defense plans already. If so, they probably have the terrain, weather, troop locations and threat parameters digitized into their data base. We should request two separate games.

"The first game would use the present defense plan to include location of friendly units and available resources. The size of the North Korean threat would be as we know it now. The difference would be how the North Koreans attacked. Instead of as we now presume, I believe they would do it in the middle of winter, starting with a feint in the Chorwan valley of sufficient size so as to cause friendly forces to occupy their main battle positions, and then coming with an armor heavy, mobile main attack along the Kaesong Munson Uijongbu axis. If successful, they would separate Seoul from the main body of our forces and take them in the rear. A classic envelopment."

Pete continued, "The second game would use the same North Korean tactics, but in this game we would have repositioned friendly forces, added precision guided modern weapons to the force mix, and implemented the air campaign strategy of our Air Battle Analysis. If we are right, we would stop them cold and destroy their ability to attack for years to come."

Lee asked General Pace if he agreed. Pace nodded.

"All right," said Lee, "I will try, but I am going to need Colonel Kim full-time on this. I very much appreciate you keeping him in on this. This is the way it is supposed to work. Separately, we probably could not have gotten this far. Together, I think we just might pull it off."

After the meeting ended, Pace asked Pete to remain behind.

"Pete, I'm about to tell you something in the strictest of confidence. I could have told you this earlier but, for reasons you will soon understand, I decided not to. As you are probably aware, every day I am visited by two officers of a Special Intelligence agency from Seoul. You may have seen them. They are both armed. One stands outside my door to make sure no one enters. The other sits in my office. They show me what is referred to as the "Black Book." This book is a summary of intelligence in the world gathered by special intelligence sources. Readers of the book are specifically not told what the sources are in order to protect them, although it is certainly possible to speculate because of the subject matter. Obviously the sources include Signals Intelligence, that is, listening in and code breaking, agents, moles, and satellite imagery, and probably others that I can't even imagine.

"Something is starting to develop. There is reason to believe that the North Koreans may, and I emphasize the word may, be thinking about some type of action against the Republic of Korea. They are certainly intensifying training and preparation. We have a feeling something is going to take place in the winter. That is why I gave you the task that I did. I wanted to see if there was some rational explanation possible that was not dependent upon access to this special intelligence. You may have hit on it. But even if the North Koreans are not up to something, your suggestions seem logical and pertinent. I believe that implementing them would have a significant deterrent effect. One other thing from this information. It appears that the Russians are also up to something. However, it is far too early to draw any reliable conclusions. I could, if I desired, make this information available to you on a daily basis. But I am not going to for your protection. I don't want you worrying about inadvertently disclosing this information. You can always say, since it happens to be true, that you reached your conclusions from commonly available information."

Pete had mixed emotions, but realized that Pace was right.

General Lee and Kim had succeeded in getting the cooperation of the ROK War Gaming Agency. The first game was relatively easy to do since it really only involved the repositioning of the North Korean forces. The results were as Pete had predicted and created much consternation at both Korean and U.S. higher headquarters. Many people disagreed with the results and declared the logic flawed, not wanting to believe. In fact, many excursions, with varying parameters, were run. But the results were almost always the same. The Eighth Army commander still was not ready to believe. He expected that the Koreans had an ulterior motive and were cooking the books. So he had the game run in Washington by the Strategic and Tactical Analysis Gaming Agency. Again the results were about the same. Now he was ready to believe!

Suddenly there was intense interest in the outcome of the second game.

People were now looking for a solution to a problem. The hardest part of the second game was in getting the U.S. to release the effectiveness parameters of the new precision guidance munitions so that they could be interjected into the outcome models. It took a decision from Washington to get them and this never would have happened except for the results of the first game. These results caused a turnaround in thinking. It was no longer deemed a mistake to expose the effectiveness of your weapons if it accomplishes the mission of deterring aggression. It was also hard to get some of the ground-oriented commanders to accept the air strategy. That was solved by running the game twice, once with the old air strategy and once with the new. Once these people saw the results they were convinced, albeit begrudgingly. The Eighth Army commander insisted that the second game also be run in Washington. As in the first game, the results were predicted. Everyone finally agreed that it was now time to take the necessary actions. It is one thing to fight a war on paper or on a computer. It is quite another to make it a reality. One of the hardest parts was convincing commanders at all levels to adopt the new strategy. An Army is not like a battleship where, when the captain says "hard rudder aport," everyone turns to the left. Instead, this plan of action must be executed by literally thousands of individual decisions.

The war game process and the acceptance of the results had taken several months to complete, and fall was approaching. It was everyone's intent that the change in the strategy, the movement of the units, the development of each unit's implementation plan, and the acquisition of and training in the precision guided munitions, be accomplished as soon as possible. Still there was much doubt that all of these tasks could be accomplished by the winter freeze. It was now the time for a little cover and deception while the changes were taking place. After all, the name of the game was deterrence and deterrence is a state of mind. What the opponent *believes* is all-important.

Pete suggested to Pace and Lee that it would be most advantageous to run a Field Army-Wide Command Post Exercise all the way down to regimental level. A CPX, as it is usually referred to, involves all the headquarters, but not the troops. In this exercise, a general scenario is written, a special staff playing the part of the opposition is formed, and a controller group whose duty is to control the play and interject events into it is established. This would serve several purposes. The staffs would be trained on the new plan and many unknowns would come to light that could then be addressed. Most important, inevitably, the North Koreans would find out about it and start worrying about the possibility of failure after the element of surprise had been lost.

The CPX took about two months to set up. Many units were going to move, and in fairness to the commanders and staffs they had to be given the opportunity to reconnoiter their areas of responsibility. Virtually every unit had to revise its war plans. Staff and controllers had to be trained in the use of the precision guided munitions, even though they had not yet arrived in quantity. The list was endless, but eventually, it was time. The Army was ready and it was crucial to run the CPX before the rivers froze solid.

The CPX continued as planned, although an oil shortage due to a Middle East crisis, cut down on the heating of office facilities. People just dressed more warmly. One room in every office complex was kept warm so the troops could take an occasional break. One morning, General Pace showed up wearing a black turtleneck sweater under his battle jacket. Within a day, everyone had obtained a black turtleneck sweater. It became the "unofficial" uniform of the headquarters and totally violated U.S. and Korean regulations. Staff officers especially liked to wear their sweaters on visits to Seoul because they believed it set them apart from the rear area types. This was just another manifestation of the change in the attitude of the headquarters. You could see it in their swagger, you could see it in their eyes - "we are different from you," they seemed to say, "we are better than you, we took you all on and won."

The CPX accomplished exactly what was intended, though virtually every mistake in the book was made and nothing went exactly as planned. Importantly enough, gaps and shortfalls were identified. Nothing occurred that couldn't be fixed. Better unit locations were discovered changing original plans. A better estimate of the needed precision guided munitions was made. In some instances the quantities arrived at by normal usage factors developed elsewhere were too few and in other cases too many. That was what a CPX was for – to catch problems before actual combat took lives.

A few weeks after the CPX, Pace called Pete into his office. "I know I told you that I did not want you to be exposed to the "Black Book", but I think you will enjoy this. The North Koreans are aware of our CPX. It appears that their scale of war preparations has diminished considerably."

BOOK 2

THE THREAT

Chapter Eleven

Pete's last three months in Korea went by very rapidly and his role in the headquarters had changed from that of innovation to compliance with innovation. He still ran the morning briefings and still had a 1700 meeting most nights with General Pace, but things had settled down to a routine. The major effort in the headquarters was to monitor the changes that had been brought about. The relocation of the three ROK corps was going well, the precision guided munitions had arrived and training on them was underway, and most of the plans had been revised. The next big challenge was going to be a joint Korean Army Headquarters / Eighth Army CPX. In essence, the intent was to determine how well these two headquarters could support the tactical activities of the Combined Field Army. Pete suggested to General Pace that the real purpose was to train and test the two higher headquarters, and therefore, instead of bothering the corps and divisions, let the Field Army be a response cell representing all of them. This was appropriate since these higher headquarters did not communicate directly with the corps and divisions in any case, they always went through the Field Army. Who cares who is on the end of the line as long as you get the right response? Besides, the corps and divisions had more important things to do.

And then it was time for Pete to leave. General Pace was staying on. The Koreans had convinced him to stay and, as an inducement, had brought the general's family to Korea and built them a beautiful villa just north of Seoul and staffed it completely with servants. The speeches were all from the heart that night and Pete was touched deeply. The final event of the night was a presentation to Pete of a statuette of Ulchi Moon Duk. Ulchi Moon Duk was a legendary hero of Korea who had beaten a Chinese invasion of Korea in the ninth century. Pete mused to himself that in his study of historical invasions of Korea about a year ago, it was the tactics and strategy of good old Ulchi who convinced him to concentrate on the Kaesong Munson approach.

The plane ride back to the United States was very pleasant The Koreans had arranged for Pete to fly first class on Korean Air Lines. This is the way to travel, Pete thought to himself, not knowing then that this was the only time in his life he would get to fly first class on a commercial airliner.

Pete had been assigned to be Deputy Commander of the Southern

European Task Force in Vicenza, Italy. It was great living and the job was not all that demanding. Pete and his family got to see Italy, ski the Tyroi, and learn how to fly gliders. Pete was still a colonel. He had passed the last year of normal eligibility for promotion to Brigadier General. He still had six more years of active Army service and was trying to decide whether or not to take early retirement.

One day, the message came in. Pete had been selected for promotion to Brigadier General and was assigned to the Pentagon. It seemed that General Pace was the president of the selection board that year and Army custom dictates that each president of the Brigadier General selection board is given a personal selection of his own.

*　　*　　*

"Well, Sandy," said Pete, "That was my second tour in Korea. I hope you can see where I got my love for Korea and why some think that I know a little bit about it. Whoa," Pete checks his watch. "I guess that I must have talked long enough, unless I have screwed up the the time change again, we should be arriving in Washington shortly. Just for the Hell of it, I think I'll take Beth up on her offer and watch her land from the cockpit."

The landing, of course, was perfect and Pete complimented Beth, thanking her for a great flight. "Anytime General," Beth told him, "and good luck."

The VC 135 taxied right up to the Special Air Mission gate reserved for VIPs. The door was opened and Pete and Sandy emerged, followed by Airman Newton with their bags. At the bottom of the steps was an Army sedan with three star plates on the front. The driver of the sedan took the bags. They were greeted by an Army Sergeant Major.

"Sir," said the Sergeant Major. "I am Sergeant Major Rinaldi, the senior enlisted aide to General Hampton, the Chief of Staff. He has asked me to meet you and make sure that you are properly taken care of. We have met before."

"My God, Rinaldi. Is that really you? The last time we met was at Yonson in the middle of nowhere on a very dark and cold night." He shook his hand. "This is Sandy, my aide."

Rinaldi shook Sandy's hand and turned back to Pete.

"Yes, sir, General. I remember it well. If you do not recall, you pulled my chain pretty hard twice that night. But over the next few months, I admired what you did with C Battery and, somewhere along the line, decided to make a career of the Army. I have no regrets. I attached my vehicle to a star, General Hampton, and here I am. Usually, the Chief would send a colonel or major to meet a VIP, but I specifically asked if I could do it. I will act as your escort while you are in Washington."

Pete reflected to himself on the establishment of the rank of Sergeant Major back in the early sixties. The higher the rank, the higher the pay, responsibility and dignity. One of the best ideas the Army ever had was implementing Sgt. Major. These guys were good. If most of them had initially gone to OCS at the beginning, they now would be senior officers. Today, Sgt. Majors wouldn't trade their positions for the world. They ran the real part of the Army, as opposed to their staff officers at the Pentagon, and they knew it. Woe be unto a new Second Lieutenant who crosses the Battalion Sergeant Major, thought Pete.

"Sir," said Rinaldi, "Let me take you to the VIP quarters here at Andrews. Normally we would take you to Fort Myer, but as you will learn, it is best if we don't make a big deal over your presence quite yet. We are talking about plausible deniability. I hope that doesn't sound too spooky."

It was only a five minute trip to the VIP quarters. Sandy and Pete were met at the door by an Air Force steward who showed them around and overemphasized the fact that the quarters had two bedrooms. In addition, it had a combination living room-dining room and a kitchen. The steward gave them the phone number where he could be reached immediately and asked if they had any clothes that needed pressing. Finally, he said that he would be in at 0700 to fix them breakfast, and asked what they might want to eat. Rinaldi promised to pick them up at 0900. Then, both Rinaldi and the steward left.

Suddenly, unexpectedly, Pete and Sandy found themselves completely alone for the first time. One could cut the tension with a knife.

"Sandy," said Pete. "I know that we are both tired. If I have the time-change figured out right, it is ten o'clock here in Washington it is four in the morning according to our biological clocks. Please hang in there with me. I have something very important to say and I may not find a better time. I need a drink, may I fix you one?"

Sandy demurred. "If this conversation is going where I think it is," Sandy replied, smiling, "I better keep a level head. But you go ahead."

After getting himself a scotch and soda, and after taking a big swallow, Pete sat down, across the room from Sandy. "Sandy, we have been together now for over a year. You are the best aide that I have ever had. But as you might have suspected, there is more to it than that. I thoroughly enjoy your company and when I am not around you, something is missing from my life. I don't know what is going to happen tomorrow, but either I will retire as scheduled, or I will go to Korea. In either case, I want you to come with me, and I don't mean as just my aide. I have fallen in love with you and I want you to be my wife. I realize there is an age difference, but there is still a little bit of life left in these old bones. If you reject my proposal, I want you to continue to be my aide, but only if you feel comfortable. Either way, I will understand. If we go to Korea and you accept my proposal, we will have to keep it to ourselves for a little while, at least until we get there. I don't expect you to answer now, but please think about it."

"Pete," Sandy said with a satisfying look on her face, "what the hell took you so long? Hasn't it been obvious that I feel the same about you? Of course, I will marry you. But we must keep it to ourselves for a while. I am convinced that you are needed in Korea and we should do nothing to jeopardize that." Sandy went over to Pete and sat beside him. "Please forgive me for being forward, but I know of no reason why we should not start the love aspect of this right now. I am going to take a bath and make the necessary preparations. After I have finished, I want you to shower and shave. Boy, it feels good giving you orders for a change. Once we have both cleaned up, I will have that drink. I guess we'll wait and see what happens next. I do have some ideas."

Sandy's first idea was to lure Pete into her bedroom, since she had, among other things, put on her best perfume, which she carefully brought along. Her other ideas were more basic. She knew how to please a man. Before women were admitted to the Corps of Cadets, everyone thought of West Point as a monastery. But you simply don't put that number of very attractive young men and women together in a close environment without certain predictable results. Especially when West Point selects only the brightest young men and women and then teaches them initiative. There was always a way to get around the strict fraternization rules. The stories about a Woman Regimental Commander of the Corps of Cadets and her male, football player, Executive Officer were the stuff legends are made of.

Needless to say, Pete and Sandy didn't get much sleep that night. Pete had been a widower for four years and Sandy had been divorced for two years. Neither of them had fooled around in the interim. The awakening of old passions was immediate. Pete wasn't all that bad, but Sandy was unbelievable. Finally, Pete was worn out and had to ask for a respite. Whoever said that women were the weaker sex, Pete wondered. And then they slept, clutching each other tightly all night, saying silly things before they fell asleep. This was not the right time to discuss the affairs of the world. They now had more important things to discuss.

At six AM Sandy awoke Pete and told him that he had better go into his own bedroom and mess up the bed to make it appear that he had slept there. She then went into the kitchen and fixed a pot of coffee. Over coffee she gave Pete some advice. "Women are much better actors than men, especially honest men such as yourself. Men usually wear their emotions on their sleeve." Sandy took a sip of coffee, "Now remember that when we are in public together, we must be strictly General and Aide. When you happen to catch my eye, it must be all business. It is not going to be easy. I am sure that during the day we are going to have either reveries about either last night or fantasies about the nights to come. I know that I can handle it since I had lots of practice at West Point. But you will have to work on it." Pete smiled and Sandy checked her watch. "The steward won't arrive for about 30 minutes. Do you think we have time for a quicky?" Pete looked surprised. "I have lots of surprises in store for you, old man. I am going to make you a very happy married man. Since you are known for making good decisions, I am going to prove to you that I was one of your best." Pete was speechless.

As expected, the steward arrived precisely at seven. Pete was at the breakfast table having a cup of coffee and reading the newspaper. Sandy was in the bathroom taking a shower. The steward could not help but notice that Sandy was singing in the shower and that Pete was humming along the same melody.

Sergeant Major Rinaldi picked up Pete and Sandy right on time at 0900. Rinaldi noticed that they both looked refreshed, and Pete had a real spring in his step.

"Good Morning, Sergeant Major. A beautiful day," said Pete as he sat down in the car. "Do you have any idea what is going on? The Chief mentioned Korea and told me that I had a series of appointments today."

"Sir," replied Rinaldi, "You have a 1000 meeting with General Hampton and from what I understand, subsequent meetings with the Secretary of Defense and the President. Times for the last two are still being worked out, but should be sometime today. We didn't know that you would be bringing your aide, but General Hampton has invited her to all of the meetings. He understands that on something like this everyone needs a back-up. We actually have plenty of time. Is there anything that you would like to do or see on the way?"

"Yes, please, Sergeant Major, how about a quick stop at the Vietnam Memorial. It always reminds me of a leader's responsibility to the people and the troops to make good decisions. I'm struck by the irony of the Vietnam War being lousy but having a memorial, and the Korean War being justified and so far having no memorial."

Pete asked Sandy if she had ever seen the Vietnam Memorial? "It is magnificent," he claimed, "As you have probably read or heard, after a lot of controversy, they first added bronze sculptures of men in combat and, more recently, women in combat. I think it adds greatly to the effect."

Sandy replied that she had not seen it since they had added the women-in-combat sculpture. She had read that all the women in the sculpture were actually medical personnel. She wondered to herself what the memorial for the next war would look like now that women were actually given combat roles.

After spending an hour at the Vietnam Memorial, they arrived at General Hampton's office at exactly 1000 and were ushered right in. Pete immediately noticed that the Secretary of Defense was present. Hampton made all the introductions and explained, "Our time schedule has been moved up. We will see the president at 1130. The Secretary and I decided that, in the interest of time, we would have a joint meeting. Mr. Secretary, would you like to begin?"

The Secretary of Defense was an old Washington hand and a real smoothie. He had been practically forced on the previous President due to the inconsistent path of Foreign and Defense policies over the last several years, and the new President kept him on. His first action was to tell Sandy how wonderful it was that women were finally being recognized for their talents, and how she graced what was otherwise a meeting of old fogies. He managed to do this without patronizing. A real talent, thought Pete, and much appreciated. The tone was set.

"Tell me, General," said the Secretary of Defense after the pleasantries, "How current are you on what is going on in Korea?"

"Sir," Pete responded, "I get the daily intelligence briefs from both the DIA and CIA. I also get a SI black book brief every day. Being located in Germany, I know that I do not get all of it, but only what the intelligence community thinks that I need to know. In addition, because of previous assignments in Korea, I believe that I have a good appreciation of the country. I do know that for over 40 years the North Koreans, technically the Democratic People's Republic of Korea, have constantly said that they would destroy the U.S. lackey Republic of Korea. Up to now, we have been able to prevent that from happening, although in some cases it was a near thing. Recent intelligence suggests that the North Koreans are in the process of developing a nuclear weapon, if they don't already have one. It is a sad fact of life that today that if a nation has the technology infrastructure to include nuclear power plants, they can also develop nuclear weapons. The North Koreans certainly have the technology in addition to the will, to make it happen. What is really frightening, unlike the other nations of the world that we suspect have nuclear weapons, they would use them for offensive purposes other than defense as a final measure of desperation. They are not really rational people.

"They see that they are falling behind South Korea in every category, including population, economy, trade, allies, and world acceptance. They just might be willing to make the last throw of the dice. The fact that Kim Il

Sung has died and that his successor, Sung Jae Won seems to be cast from the same mold but is really a total unknown, makes it even more dicey. At least Kim was predictable; Sung is not."

"General," said the Secretary of Defense, "you have told me all I need to hear. Actually, I have a lot more on my mind but one of the reasons I have survived so long in this town is that I have learned not to steal the President's thunder. After the President is finished with you, assuming all goes well, we will have much more to discuss. Why don't we all wander over to the White House now. Captain Parker, of course, you are invited. The President is a sucker for a pretty face. And I mean that with the best of intentions, not like some in our recent past."

Sandy could not believe what a day it had been. She accepted a proposal of marriage, had one of the best nights of lovemaking in her life, and was now going to see the President of the United States. It doesn't get any better than this, she thought, wondering what tomorrow would bring.

They all climbed into the Secretary of Defense's stretch limousine for the ride across the 14th street bridge, to Pennsylvania Avenue, and then to 1600, the White House. They were expected. The gate guard waved them straight through, and they were met by the Chief of Protocol. The Marine sentries opened the doors for them. One of whom winked at Sandy. Without a wait, they went straight into the President's office. Attending the President was the National Security Advisor.

"Come in, Lady and Gentlemen," said the President after the National Security advisor had announced them. "I am delighted to see you. No, I take that back. Do not take this personally, but I wish there was no reason for this meeting. I am under a very rigid time schedule today, so let's skip the pleasantries and get right to it. As you are aware, I am what some would call an accidental President. My predecessor lost his office because the American people and their elected representatives lost confidence in his ability to conduct foreign affairs, so they elected me. At this time, I have some very tough and extremely controversial decisions to make. Because of the nature of these decisions, I expect to be a one term President, which is fine with me.

"The foreign policy of the United States is a mess; Bosnia, Haiti, Somalia, Russia , Japan, Korea, you name it. We have been adrift for several years. We made big threats and then were unwilling to back them up. We seemed to change our minds everyday. Nobody had the slightest idea what we stood for. It is my job to change that, but I need time and help. General Goodwin, that is why I have asked for you to come. Korea, while not topping the list right now, certainly has that potential. I was told many years ago when I was in the military to evaluate enemy capabilities, not their intentions. As far as I am concerned, North Korea has the capability of nuclear weapons and is capable of using them. I have not been able to get very good information and advice from our senior Americans in Seoul, so I am cleaning house. I discussed this with the Republic of Korea President about a week ago. Your name came up. In case you didn't know, the Korean President is Lee Duk Qwan. He told me that you served together in the First Combined Field Army in the mid seventies. I believe that he was the Deputy Commanding General. He specifically asked for you if you were available. He told me that some day I needed to hear the details of years past in Korea and I hope to do so, but not today. What I want from you is quite simple. Namely, what the Hell is going on and what should I do? President Lee has suggested that I make you the Commanding General of the First Combined Field Army. I want you to take command as soon as possible.

"I have one little bit of good news for you. I am recalling the present Ambassador. I am going to replace him with one of the most astute international businessmen in the country and, admittedly, a political advisor and contributor of mine. I trust him implicitly. He tells me you know one another. His name is James Noonan. Perhaps "Noonie" rings a bell? He claims that you owe him a few."

Pete was euphoric over this unexpected news.

"I believe this is what is called a mission type order in the military. Lord knows that trying to run Korea from here hasn't worked. Sort of like trying to turn a screw with a 15,000 mile screwdriver. Any questions? Thank you and good luck. Young lady, thank you for coming also. I understand that you will be accompanying General Goodwin to Korea. Take care of him. The country needs him."

With that, the meeting ended. Pete wondered if there were any secrets in Washington, or maybe it was a lucky guess from a very astute politician. In either case, it was an order that Sandy go with him – one more thing Pete would not have to justify.

Chapter Twelve

At the same time that Pete was meeting with the President, another meeting was taking place in Pyongyang, capitol of the Democratic People's Republic of Korea, commonly known to the rest of the world as North Korea. The meeting was chaired by Sung Tae Won, who had taken over the Presidency of North Korea after the death of Kim Il Sung. Because of the iron hand of Kim Il Sung over the decades and the many bloodbaths that consolidated power, the transition appeared completely safe. No one who valued his life argued with Sung Tae Won. General Yi Bong Su, Supreme Commander of the DPRK armed forces, Dr. Chan So Dung, Chief Scientist of the DPRK, and General Li Joon Duk, Commander of the DPRK Security Services were all in attendance.

Sung Tae Won spoke first, "Kim Il Sung, the Heavenly Leader for life of all Koreans, had been following your activities closely and was very pleased. He kept me informed. I need to determine how much progress has been made since your last meeting and learn your future plans. I think it would be most useful if first we reviewed what has occurred to date. Who will speak?"

Dr. Chan So Dung, the Chief Scientist spoke up. This was in accord with a previous agreement by the three participants other than Sung. They had met earlier and gotten their stories straight. It was dangerous to have a disagreement in front of Sung. He was not a rational person and, if displeased, was known to order summary executions. The only law in the DPRK was the personal law of the President. The fact of the matter was that these three people, dedicated communists all of their lives who owed their positions and power to absolute loyalty to the regime, were starting to have individual misgivings. But not enough to share with the others and certainly not enough to do anything rash. They could not afford to trust one another. Yet.

"Comrade Leader," said Chan, "I will start, since so far, this has been primarily a scientific and technological effort. I have kept in total coordination with General Yi and General Li. They are fully aware of our efforts and fully support them." All in the room understood what Chan was doing. If things go wrong it is better to share the blame. Lock the others in. Chan continued. "As you are aware, we first started developing nuclear power plants for the production of electrical energy over 10 years ago. Our shortage of electrical power and the natural resources to produce it was well known throughout the world. There was no objection since we gave the rationale that this would make us energy independent and, therefore, reduce our potential for aggression towards energy-rich nations. We received much help and did not have to hide our effort. Many nations wanted to sell and we bought. It was another indication of the foolishness of the Capitalist system, and proof that we will eventually beat them in spite of the present deviationism of China from Russia." Chan figured that this gratuitous remark couldn't hurt, and he even got an approving nod from Sung.

"The design for our nuclear power plants came from an international consortium led by France. The technology was well-understood and well-established. Essential to nuclear power is a source of radioactive material. Many nations were willing to sell it to us as long as we signed a statement promising that none of the radioactive material would ever be used in the manufacturing of nuclear weapons. We signed the statement since, as I will explain in just a moment, it is virtually impossible to detect such a diversion.

"The radioactive material of choice for weapons is Plutonium, technically Plutonium 239. All elements are composed of a number of particles called protons, electrons, and neutrons, in varying amounts. A so-called stable element, that is, one that is not radioactive, has a like number of protons and electrons. A radioactive element does not. Since nature is always striving for balance and stability, the radioactive element will constantly attempt to throw off the excess to achieve stability. This is called decay. The number 239 associated with Plutonium is a way of counting the number of protons and neutrons. The larger the number the heavier and more complicated the element. For example, hydrogen which has only one proton has been given the number 1. Plutonium actually was discovered as an artificial element. In 1940, at the University of California, scientists were experimenting with the possibility of making artificial elements. They did this by bombarding what at that time was known as the heaviest element, Uranium, with deuterons, a form of neutron. They produced Plutonium 239. The name Plutonium comes from the planet Pluto. The scientists who named it believed that they had found the fartherest out element on the Periodic Table. They saw very quickly that Plutonium had both a weapons potential and an energy potential.

"The reason that Plutonium had both potentials is that a fission nuclear explosion and the production of nuclear energy are really about the same thing. One is controlled and the other is accelerated and enhanced. I used the word fission. The other word you sometimes hear with a nuclear explosion is fusion or thermonuclear. That is a different but related phenomenon. We do not have a thermonuclear capability and I will discuss it no further, unless you desire. The key word in fission is neutron, one of the parts of the atom, as I mentioned. When a neutron is emitted it produces energy, but it also does something else. It can cause other neutrons to be emitted by literally striking them. This can be controlled. If one neutron release does not cause another release, nothing happens. If one neutron release causes one other to be released, you have a controlled chain reaction. This produces energy in the form of heat which can be used to run electrical turbines. If, however, you can cause one neutron release to cause more than one other, the result is a nuclear explosion, if you take a few additional steps. I will get back to those steps in just a moment.

"The key to all of this is that we produce Plutonium in our nuclear energy system. We can convert it to weapons use because it is not hard to do. That's what all the fuss is about right now. When Uranium is used in a nuclear power plant it decays until it is no longer producing efficient heat but, at the same time, some Plutonium is produced. The Plutonium is contained in the rods that can be withdrawn. These rods can be converted to weapons-grade Plutonium quite easily. The International Atomic Energy Agency wants to inventory our spent rods to see that we don't do so. The fact of the matter is that this is an inexact science and the inventory only makes it a little more difficult, not impossible. Let me give you an example. The United States produced Plutonium at its Hanford facility from 1944 to 1987. During that time they said they produced 66 metric tons, 53 of weapons grade and 13 of reactor grade. They now say that they probably produced about 67.4 tons and can't account for the missing 1.4 tons. This is enough to produce 300 nuclear weapons the size they dropped on Nagasaki. They now say that they did not lose or divert the 1.4 tons, but rather that that is how inexact the calculations are. We can make use of this inexactness to divert enough Plutonium to make between five and ten weapons without being discovered. I believe, Comrade Leader, that this is enough to satisfy your needs."

"Yes, Comrade Doctor," Sung responded, "five to ten weapons will be adequate for our plans. I will be asking General Li and General Yi about that in just a moment. But first, I would like for you to tell me more about the manufacture of the nuclear weapons and how they can be delivered where we want them."

Chan cringed inwardly at this request. He could explain the manufacture of the weapons, no problem. The delivery of weapons, however, was a different matter. Things were not going too well in that area. Perhaps he could divert some of the blame to Li and Yi, but he had to be careful. This was not the time to make enemies.

"Thank you, Comrade Leader," said Chan, "I am always grateful for your appropriate questions and your ability to make the right decisions. It allows poor scientists such as myself to get on with my work in support of the beloved Fatherland. Let me first address the manufacture of the nuclear weapons, since that development directly affects the issue of delivery means. Delivery means must accommodate the size, weight, and sensitivity of the nuclear weapon. This, of course, will be our first nuclear weapon, but not our last. Because of the rightness of our cause and the divine guidance of our leader, Kim Il Sung, and yourself, we will eventually outstrip the decadent west. But because of our Asian heritage and our understanding of Confucius, we must be patient. What we are developing will be what you want for now.

"The development of a nuclear weapon is no longer a physics or science problem. We have had access to Soviet and Chinese information on this for decades. Even if we had not, it is a matter of common knowledge and has been published in the open press. An issue of the American *Popular Mechanics* magazine several years ago rendered all the specifications necessary. The keys to manufacturing weapons include simply engineering, technology and quality control. The weapon must be built to known exacting specifications. This was a problem in the past, but the west, in their decadence, gave us the necessary tools. Modern computer technology with its computer-assisted design software and its computer-assisted manufacturing software has given us everything we need to meet the necessary tolerances. What is more amazing is that we bought all this computer technology on the open market. We did not have to acquire it through intelligence means. Although, I am completely confident the General Li's Security Services would have been able to do so.

"The design is quite straightforward. You must start with a mass of radioactive material. At a certain size and dimension the neutron release, sometimes called the neutron flux, will not be enough to cause other neutrons to release. There may be some interactions with other nuclei, but not enough for anything meaningful to happen. But if you could suddenly compress the radioactive mass into a much smaller configuration, the neutron flux would increase exponentially and you would have a nuclear explosion. That is the trick. This compression must be almost instantaneous and totally symmetrical. If it is too slow, it does not work. If it is not symmetrical, you just blow a hole in the side without a nuclear detonation. Mechanical means are not fast enough for the compression. It must be done with an explosion of high quality powerful explosives. Technically, this is an implosion, since the force is directed inwards rather than outwards. Roughly, what we do is place a sphere of Plutonium 239 inside the device. We surround the sphere with explosive. When this explosive is detonated, the inwardly directed force compresses the Plutonium Sphere. When it gets small enough it achieves what is called critical mass and a nuclear detonation takes place.

The physics are much more complicated than that, but that is the general idea. The real problem is to getting the explosive to all detonate simultaneously and symmetrically. The technology to do this is known and we have it. I am totally confident that our device will work and will produce about 20 Kilotons equivalent of TNT, approximately the same as the weapon at Nagasaki, with a similar design. Since we will not have the opportunity to test the weapon, we decided on the conservative, but sure, approach. With the Plutonium we have already diverted, we will have two usable weapons within two months. With the Plutonium we will divert soon, we will have an additional five weapons within six months.

"That brings me to the delivery means. This is more than scientific effort. It is primarily a military one. I will make the initial remarks and then turn the presentation over to General Yi. As I said, our weapons are similar to the one used at Nagasaki. You will recall that the Americans used a B-29 to deliver one weapon, and even then the airplane was stressed. The weapon was very large and very heavy, as is ours. We simply have no viable airborne delivery means. None of our rockets or missiles can do it. The only aircraft that we have is a heavy, slow, cumbersome commercial transport. Unless it was a sneak attack disguised as a commercial airliner of another country it probably would not make it. I believe that we will have to find another way, this is not my direct area of responsibility. Do you have any further questions for me or should I turn this over now to General YI, the Supreme Commander of the DPRK armed forces?"

Neatly done, General Li thought to himself, as Chan smoothly placed the ball in Yi's court.

"Dear Comrade Leader," said Yi. "I completely agree with Comrade Doctor Chan's technical evaluation of the delivery means. But how do the nuclear weapons and their delivery means fit into the strategic plan for their use? If we got into a nuclear exchange with the United States over Korea right now, we would not win. We have two, perhaps ten, weapons and they have thousands. Our delivery means for a nuclear exchange with the U.S. are inadequate. But if our intent is to achieve a quick tactical advantage, produce terror, and test the resolve of of the United States and their lackeys in South Korea, we do have the capability. We have one advantage that the soft Americans and South Koreans do not have. We have soldiers, sailors, and airmen who are totally dedicated to the Beloved Chairman and would willingly give their lives in a one-way mission. We have several feasible possibilities. We could infiltrate the weapons into South Korea and set them off on the ground. We could send one or two of our old AN-27 transports straight into a city close to the DMZ, such as Munson or Uijongbu. If this option were selected, I would suggest Tong Du Chon Ni, where the U.S.

Second Infantry Division is located. It is only 15 miles from the DMZ. Finally, as you are aware, we have recently purchased 20 old Golf class submarines from Russia, ostensibly for scrap metal. We are in the process now of building at least two reliable submarines from the assorted parts. It is true that we have no way of launching missiles with nuclear warheads from these submarines. But we can drive them right into harbors such as Inchon and Pusan and set the nuclear weapons off. I am confident we can do all of these things. The armed forces stand ready for your command. What we need now is your strategic concept."

"Phew," though Li to himself, "the ball is now in Sung's court."

"Well said, Comrade General," replied Sung. "I am now convinced that we can manufacture and use these weapons as we desire. You are right that it is now time for me to give you our strategic concept so that you can start to make your plans. But first I would like to hear what General Li, our Chief of Security Services, has to say."

Li knew that it was now his turn in the barrel. He had hoped to get through this meeting without having to say much. Li had gotten in the habit of using American slang since he had spent many years of his life as a clandestine agent in South Korea with American forces.

"Comrade Leader," said Li. "My responsibility is to judge the fighting capabilities of the South Korean and American forces. We should not underestimate their capabilities. But as important as their capabilities is their resolve. Even today the South Koreans do not believe they can go it alone. They feel dependent upon the United States. This is the area of greatest weakness. The United States right now is simply not in the mood for a fight anywhere in the world. They seem to have lost their will and are turning inward to address their social problems. They talk big, but always back down when faced with a major confrontation. They now say that they would fight, but only if it is in their national interest. However, lately they keep redefining this national interest to fit the situation. One thing that I have learned about the United States is that from time to time they go through periods such as this and eventually regain their resolve. My estimate is that whatever we are presently contemplating, the time to act is now. We have little to fear from the United States. They will bargain with the devil if it means avoiding a fight. This includes abandoning old allies. They have done this all over the world in places such as Israel, Formosa, and Nicaragua. As stated by General Yi, the Security Services await your orders."

Li was very concerned about the way the meeting was going. He, Chan, and Yi were telling Sung exactly what he wanted to hear instead of what he needed to hear. Li had learned this during his many years as an agent penetrating the U.S. army. You have to tell the boss the truth to get the best results. The difference was that in the U.S. Army this kind of talk was encouraged, while in the DPRK, it could get you shot. Li was to learn later that Yi and Chan had the same thought.

"Thank you, Comrades," said Sung. "I am satisfied with your progress. It is now time, as you mentioned, to go to the next step, which is the development of our strategic plan. I do not need to tell you that the fate of our beloved Fatherland will depend on your efforts. Everything must be done properly and there will be no excuses for failure. I hope this is clear."

Li understood fully that Sung was looking for a place to blame if anything goes wrong and that they were it.

"First," continued Sung, "we must examine the present situation. South Korea is growing stronger and not because of their own efforts or the superiority of their system, but because of the resources being poured into South Korea by the United States and Japan. The United States has for years been trying to isolate us and bring us down. Our traditional allies, China and Russia, have surrendered to the Yankee Dogs. We must act to regain our rightful place, which is literally being pulled from under us unlawfully. We have accomplished miracles due to our independent efforts. We must act now, act alone, and we must not fail.

"Second," he continued, "we only desire to have our rightful place among sovereign nations. We have many specific goals. We must be recognized by all the nations of the world as an independent and sovereign nation. That includes burying once and for all the fiction that the division of the Korean peninsula was only temporary. We must have a seat in the United Nations. We must receive economic aid from the United States, Japan, China, and Russia. We must have Most Favored Nation trade status with the United States. The United States must withdraw all its forces from South Korea and stop subsidizing their economy. South Korea must reduce its armed forces down to a size that cannot be used for aggression and withdraw all forces at least 20 miles south of the DMZ. We have many more goals, but these are the major ones. How do we accomplish them? That brings me to my third point.

"Finally, we must recognize that no amount of pleading, begging, or negotiating can possibly achieve this, even if we were willing to completely stoop beneath our dignity and culture. We should not have to beg for what is rightfully ours. Even if we did, the Americans, who in spite of their indecision and fear, still control the international agenda and would be able to block us. Not because the world respects them or is afraid of them, but because other nations want something from the United States and are more than willing to trade the legitimate rights of the Democratic People's Republic of Korea to get it. The days of strong and courageous leaders are over. Most leaders are a bunch of cowards.

"The way we accomplish this is by force or the threat of force. Here is where we have a big advantage. The threat of force must be credible, that is, your opponents must know your capabilities and believe your willingness to use those capabilities. The West, led by the United States, has much force but is not willing to use it. They are Paper Tigers. We have had our present conventional force for years. The new element is our possession of nuclear weapons. The West speculates that we might have them. At the appropriate time we will tell the world, without apology, that we do. This will change the entire equation. The rest of the world prefers to avoid conventional conflict but, on occasion, will resort to it. The threat of nuclear war will make the world irrational with fear. Once we have announced our possession of the nuclear weapons, we will demand, not beg, for the legitimate rights I just described. If the West gives in, we will have won and our names will go down in history. If the West does not, we will attack. Our attack will include the use of nuclear weapons. We will cease our attack only if the West acquiesces to our demands. I know they will. They do not believe that Korea is worth further nuclear conflict and the chance of it spreading. I'm sure General Li would be able to spread enough propaganda for people to fear possible Chinese and Pakistani involvement.

"That is enough for today. Do any of you have any questions or comments?" Nobody ever responds. "Good. Let us meet again in a month. Besides an update on the weapons development, I would like an outline of the strategic plan to include aspects of military, diplomatic and psychological warfare. Dismissed."

Li glanced at the faces of his compatriots and saw fear, but he said nothing. As opposed to the others in the room, he had spent many years in South Korea and many years with the American armed forces. Sung Tae Won's concept would gain complete approval in the DPRK since it was the truth as they believed it. But Li knew that, although partially true, there were enough false assumptions to make the plan questionable at best. But Li wondered what to do. If he objected, he would disappear and would not be able to accomplish anything. He told himself to think carefully and search for a way. He could not foresee that in about two weeks time, a solution from an unexpected source would present itself.

Chapter Thirteen

After the meeting with the President, the Secretary of Defense's entourage got back into the limousine and returned to the Pentagon. The Secretary invited them all to his private dining room for lunch. The dining room was medium-sized, but beautifully appointed. Usually, certain members of the Secretary's immediate staff, such as the Assistant Secretaries of Defense, were invited to eat there, but not today. This was going to be a private working lunch. The dining room attendants were all active duty Navy personnel who had high security clearances because of what often was discussed there. They had also been vetted for their ability to keep their mouth's shut. The choices on the menu ranged from a full lunch to a salad. No alcohol was served. A few years ago lunch was free and was considered a perk that went with the job. This was not true anymore because of a hypocritical move by Congress several years ago. While the Senators and Representatives still kept their perks, they demanded that Executive Branch members pay for theirs. However, the Secretary of Defense did have an appropriated fund to pay for guests of State.

During lunch, the Secretary got right to the point. "General Goodwin, I think the President was pretty clear. What are you going to do?"

"Sir," Pete replied, "if I had the answer to that right now I would tell you. I don't. I do know that the Republic of Korea's forces are quite good and should be able to defend the country with U.S. help. It has been this way since the mid-seventies. The possibility of the North Korean development of nuclear weapons is a change in the equation. At this juncture, I have not had time to figure how or why they would possibly use them. I do know for sure that we cannot attribute to the North Koreans the same degree of rationale that we normally use in our decision-making process. That is a mistake we often make in our evaluations, assuming that our opponents think the same way we do. I need to learn a lot more both here in Washington in Korea. Actually, I would like to ask the same questions in both places. Quite often perceptions and understandings are quite different the further you get from Washington. My first task will be to ascertain whether we are all singing off of the same sheet of music. With what is going on right now I can almost guarantee that that is not the case. My questions are the obvious ones: what is the best information on the North Korean development of nuclear weapons; how might they intend to use them, what is the status of North Korean conventional forces; what's the best assessment of political stability in North Korea; what is the status of Korean and U.S. forces; what is the present status of war plans and reinforcement plans? And we need an assessment of the attitudes of Japan, China and Russia. I know this is a big order, but I think it's essential."

The Secretary agreed. "I will set up the briefings you asked for right away and we will start this afternoon. I know that everyone will scream to high heaven that there is not enough time to prepare, but that is good. We won't end up getting the homogenized, "everybody agrees" briefing. It will be raw data, which is exactly what I want you to get. I have more confidence in you drawing the conclusions than some of the professional staff officers who do not want to offend anyone. By luck, no, I will take that back. By intent, Ambassador Designate James Noonan will be here in about an hour. The President and I want him to attend the briefings with you. I will attend also. I am looking forward to the questions the two of you ask. I am sure there will be many that I never thought of. This should be fun. There are going to be some mighty unhappy staff officers around here tonight. I know that State is going to be unhappy but the President told me that he would take care of that."

Pete understood the Secretary. He could ask anything he wanted to. No area was off-limits. Of course, the Secretary could disassociate himself from the questions if that was politically desirable and the President could distance himself if it became necessary.

The briefing started at 1400. It took place in the Secretary of Defense's personal briefing room. Pete could not help but notice that there were armed sentries at the door carefully checking identification cards against a list. Some people who insisted that they be allowed in were turned away by the sentries. Pete also noticed that as they were entering, a "sweep" team (checking the room for listening devices) was just leaving. The room would be secure. Pete and Noonie had met about ten minutes before the briefing. It was "old home week" and they exchanged war stories. Pete found out that Noonie had recognized the potential of Korea and had made a fortune there. As they entered they were still in animated conversation with lots of laughter and smiles. This worried many of the staff officers present, since their friendship might affect their individual departments by placing the Washington game of divide and conquer in jeopardy. State and Defense were supposed to be mortal enemies. Many careers depended on this confrontation.

The Secretary of Defense started the briefing. "Gentlemen, I apologize for the short notice. Let me set the stage and establish the ground rules. I have asked for five primary briefers: one to address the possible development of nuclear weapons in North Korea, one to address the political-military situation in North Korea, one to address the political-military situation in South Korea, one to address the political situation in the countries adjacent to Korea, and one to address the U.S. status of forces and plans for Korea. This briefing is at the direction of the President of the United States, although its content is my responsibility. There will be no restrictions on information due to security categories. That is why attendance at this meeting has been limited. I have directed that the briefers be the desk officers in the various agencies involved. We are, of course, interested in your assessments but we must have the raw data too. While this is primarily a Department of Defense meeting, I have invited officers from State, CIA, and NSA to be here. Please feel free to comment if you feel it appropriate. This briefing is being held for Mr. James Noonan, who will be appointed as the Ambassador to South Korea, and General Peter Goodwin, who will be appointed as the Commanding General of the First Combined Field Army. The President has already made these decisions and has communicated with the leadership of Congress. The confirmation of the appointments is assured and not subject to question. Do any of you have any questions? No. Good. I will personally moderate the proceedings."

Pete and Noonie exchanged glances. They had both been around long enough to understand how unique what had just been said was. This was not business as usual. It was clear that the President and the Secretary were serious about this and that bureaucratic obfuscation would not be tolerated. The tension in the room was suddenly palpable.

"Who will discuss the North Korean nuclear weapon development situation?" asked the Secretary.

"I will, sir," answered a middle level staff officer from the office of the Assistant Secretary of Defense for Science and Technology, giving his name. "Let me first describe the design and functioning of a nuclear reactor and the properties of the materials used within one. The first consideration is radioactivity. Radioactivity is the emission of particles and rays from an unstable element. For our purposes these are Uranium 235 and Plutonium 239. Let me tell you about each."

Pete soon realized that the briefer was padding his briefing in order to avoid the uncomfortable questions. He figured that it was about time to set the tone for the meeting and interrupted.

"Excuse me, sir," said Pete. "What you are saying is of extreme interest, but I would like to get to the point of this meeting. I would like to ask a few specific questions. We all know that Plutonium can be produced by the North Korean energy program and is the material of choice for weapons. I

94

have read that the amount produced is not an exact science. Given the efforts of the International Atomic Energy Agency, is it possible for the North Koreans to divert Plutonium to weapon's use and do it without detection?"

"Sir," responded the briefer. "We have no indications of that."

"That was not my question," replied Pete. "I would appreciate it if you would listen to my question. Can the North Koreans divert Plutonium to weapons use without getting caught?"

The briefer got the message. "Yes, sir. It would be difficult, but yes, they could."

"Now for the next question. Have we any indications, positive or negative, that they have done so? I would like both your and the CIA response to this."

Both Defense and CIA responded that there were no such indications, either through technical or intelligence means.

"OK," continued Pete, "we'll let that rest for awhile. My next question is assuming the North Koreans have Plutonium, either through diversion or some other means, are they capable of manufacturing a nuclear weapon? If so ,when, and describe it."

"The answer to your question," said the Defense briefer, "is definitely yes. They have the technology, and when they use it depends on when they made the decision to start. Given our knowledge of their technological base, it would take them about two years. If they started two years ago, they could have it now. As you know, they have had reactors and, therefore, Plutonium for over ten years. The weapon would be crude and similar to the one that we used at Nagasaki. Delivery would be a problem. It would be too large to fit in a missile. What they are doing in this regard is more a matter for intelligence."

"That was going to be my next question," said Pete. "CIA, can you help us on this?"

The representative from CIA responded. "We agree with Defense that they have the capability for building one. We simply have no information on whether they have done so in the past or are doing it now. The building of such a weapon takes very little space and is not detectable from the air using any of our sophisticated technology. In other words, we don't know, one way or the other.

"Mr. Secretary, may I say something else, please? You may recall that several years ago, under the previous administration, we were restricted in our ability to conduct HUMINT, that is, human intelligence, the use of spies and agents. The rationale was that our technical means were sufficient. They are, if you are looking for an aircraft carrier. They are not if you are looking for something like this. I would suggest, in the name of my Director, that you might want to discuss this with the President."

The Secretary gave a noncommittal nod.

Pete continued. "I know we are getting to the far end of speculation, but I have to ask. If they decided to build these weapons, how many would they have now?" Both the Defense and CIA guessed somewhere between two and eight.

"I have one other question in this area. I will ask it now but I don't want an answer until the end of the briefing. I want you to have time to think about it and to answer in the context of the other briefings. If they have somewhere in the vicinity of two to eight weapons and they are hard to deliver, what the hell would they use them for?"

"Mr. Secretary, that's all this briefer has for now."

The Secretary replied. "You are doing just fine. Let's continue with the next briefer, who will be CIA addressing the political-military situation in North Korea."

The briefer from CIA had gotten the message. He was glad that he had not gone first. "Sir, I will not go back in history to discuss the DPRK except where it necessary for understanding the present situation. The political situation in North Korea is absolutely stable. There are no indications whatsoever of unrest or dissidence. Kim Il Sung had complete control until his death. He had arranged for his son, Kim Chong Il, to be his successor, but nobody knows what happened to Kim Chong Il. After he disappeared, Sung Tae Won took over without a ripple. The transition appears to be completely accepted and not challenged. Kim Il Sung had not made the error the Soviet Union made with the Warsaw Pact nations. He fully understood that the communications technology revolution is dangerous to a dictatorship, in that informed people will not be slaves. He had complete control of all information coming into North Korea. Possession of a short wave radio is punishable by death. The people knew only what he wanted them to know. Sung Tae Won, his successor, is a pragmatist and understands the power equation. He will not do anything foolish. Kim's son, Kim Chong Il, would have been another story. He believed his own rhetoric and propaganda and was capable of anything, no matter how far-fetched. Nevertheless, we are entering a very dangerous period in that part of the world.

"On the military side, nothing much has changed for a number of years. North Korea still has the fourth largest Army in the world and the sixth largest Air Force. The Navy is relatively inconsequential, other than the 20 Golf class submarines they recently bought from Russia. Their armed forces are well-equipped, well-trained, and highly motivated. Their biggest problem is that of advancing age. With the demise of the Soviet Union and the orientation change in China, they are not getting new equipment other than what they buy on the open market. That worked for awhile, but now even that is starting to dry up. Israel no longer sells them the tools of war and neither does South Africa. Iraq, which used to be a major supplier, has problems enough of its own. On the surface, this sounds like good news, but may be a partial answer to your question. They can see their military capability slipping away from them over time. They may be up to something before it gets too late. I can talk for hours, but if I have understood you correctly, I think this is the info you want. Do you have any questions, sir?"

"No thank you," said Pete. "That was excellent."

The Secretary of Defense was astonished. He had never gotten that kind of to-the-point briefing from the Agency in his life. "I agree," said the Secretary of Defense. "Excellent briefing. What did you say your name was? Now let us call on State for an evaluation of South Korea."

State mentally revised his briefing as he was walking to the podium. The rules had changed and he did not want to be caught short. Gone were the days of the safe, but meaningless, briefing. Bullshit had gone out of style, at least here.

"Thank you, sir," replied State. "I must start off a with a little bit of history at the risk of your displeasure. South Korea has never been monolithic in its governmental affairs. Since Syngman Rhee became President of South Korea in 1948, it has had a history of coups, counter coups, revolts, and political assassinations. Park Chung Hee took over by force in 1962 after an intense power struggle with Kim Chong Pil, the Chief of the South Korean Central Intelligence Agency. Park stayed in power until he was assassinated in the mid-seventies. Since then, power has been transferred by parliamentary means, but never easily. The point I am trying to make is that politics in South Korea have always been volatile and continue to be so. The people are intensely patriotic. The leader and form of government are always at risk. we would be well advised not to confuse the two.

"I make this point in order to try to understand what is presently going on in South Korea. Privately, behind the scenes, the South Korean leaders are worried and are asking for our help. Publicly, they refuse to acknowledge that there is any problem. They discount the North Korean development of nuclear weapons and, recently, have stated that the 20 old Soviet Golf class submarines recently acquired by the North Koreans are for scrap metal purposes only and represent no threat. They are worried about the reaction of the South Korean people. They understand how hard the South Koreans have worked to achieve progress and wonder if the people would be willing to go to war if it was avoidable. If the North Koreans made a request for concessions on the part of South Korea and backed that request up with the threat of nuclear weapons, they are not confident they know how the people would respond.

"That brings me to military assessment. The fighting capabilities of the Korean armed forces are really not my purview, but from what I have been told, they are excellent and capable of withstanding a North Korean conventional attack. I leave that evaluation to the military. My concern is the political stability of the armed forces. If it appeared that the South Korean government was going to reach some form of accommodation with North Korea detrimental to South Korea, I think they would take over the government. Either way South Korea loses. If the military takes over, I believe that they would lose worldwide support. And that may be a partial answer to your question, General Goodwin. That concludes my briefing. Do you have any questions?"

Pete was about to leap out of his chair when Noonie reached over and touched his arm and whispered, "Down Boy. This is my territory."

"Sir," responded Noonie, "that was a very negative assessment. Is that your opinion or the opinion of the State Department?"

"It is my own," replied State. "To my knowledge the State Department has not made such an assessment."

"Thank you for your honesty. Make sure that I have your name and telephone number. I leave for Korea tomorrow. I have spent much of my life there. I know most of the people in high level government, and I speak their language. I believe they trust me and will confide in me. Let me make my own private assessment and we will get back together. I think we have time, not too much, but enough."

The next briefer was also from State. "Sir," said State, "you wish for my assessment of Korea's neighbors on this issue. They have been remarkably silent. They have taken no positions. Russia is doing so because of their own immense problems elsewhere. They feel it of minimal interest. Russia will probably only get involved if they can perceive some political gain without political cost or risk. China remains totally aloof. At the present, they can see no advantage in supporting North Korea. China is trying to get along better with the United States. They would never go to the extent of supporting the United States. Their remaining neutral on the sidelines is the best we can hope for. Japan is the wild card. The Japanese look upon the Koreans as an inferior race. One thing that is reasonably sure is that they will only do what they perceive to be in their best interest. That is one hard lesson we have learned over the last several years. Do not place your trust in Japan. Friendship and treaties have nothing to do with it. It is all economic bottom line for them. The other aspect of Japan is that, because of history, they will become totally irrational over the issue of nuclear weapons, especially so close to them. If the North Koreans use or threaten to use nuclear weapons, expect no support from Japan. All in all, we can expect no support from

Korea's neighbors. That is a negative outlook, but an honest one. Questions, Sir?"

"None," said the Secretary. "I agree."

"Finally," said the Secretary, closing the discussion, "we will have the Army give us the status of forces and war plans in Korea. As you all know, years ago, Army was appointed the executive agent for the Defense Department for military affairs in Korea. Your turn, Army."

" Yes, Sir," replied the Army Colonel. "I am most lucky to be the last briefer. I have the advantage of listening to the other briefings and understanding the thrust of your interest. I hope I don't blow it. I will summarize. The armed forces of the Republic of Korea, together with our forces in place, and those U.S. Rapid Deployment Forces earmarked for Korea are adequate to repel a North Korean conventional attack on South Korea under any of the standard scenarios which range from a no-warning surprise attack to one of a full build up with the attendant warning and reaction time. This is a result of a change in the defense strategy of Korea 20 years ago, with which General Goodwin is fully familiar. But as I was sitting here listening, a thought crossed my mind that I believe is germane. I ask you to indulge me. When I make a statement such as I just made, it is based on the ability to fight. There is something else. You defeat an opponent when you destroy either his ability to fight or his will to fight. You will recall that in World War II we never destroyed the Germans' will to fight. We ultimately destroyed their ability to fight. In Japan during that war, we did not destroy their ability to fight, but rather their will to fight. That came about with the use of nuclear weapons. In all of our assessments of a possible Korean war, we have always assumed the non-use of nuclear weapons and complete confidence in the South Koreans' will to fight. From what I have heard today, these assumptions may need to be reexamined. It could be a new ball game. Anything else, Sir?"

"Very good," said the Secretary, essentially taking over the meeting. "I think it important that I summarize what has been said. If you disagree with me or have anything to add, do so. As you can see, this is somewhat of an unusual meeting for Washington. Tell us what we need to hear, not what you think we want to hear. Anything you say will be protected as long as it is honest and not self-serving.

"This is my summary," began the Secretary. "First, it is entirely possible that the North Koreans can develop nuclear weapons if they have not done so already. These weapons would be few in number and have limited delivery capabilities. But they would be nuclear with all that that means. Second, North Korea is facing a decision point, which includes a change in leadership to a less predictable one and they see their conventional forces starting to deteriorate. They may see this as a window of opportunity or a last throw of the dice. We have no way of knowing, but it doesn't make any difference if they decide to act. Third, we are confident that our defense strategy of Korea is viable under present circumstances. We are not so sure of this if nuclear weapons enter the equation and this entails both military and political considerations. I will now try to answer General Goodwin's question as to 'what the hell they would use them for?'

"I think at some point they will announce that they have them and ask for some form of international conference to right their grievances. The grievances will be carefully crafted and sound reasonable but, if accepted, would change the balance of power in that part of the world. We would be on the defensive in the court of world opinion. If we do not accede, they will probably attack and use them. If their attack is relatively successful, they would ask for an armistice that consolidates their gains and renews their demands. The world would probably acquiesce rather than risk the spread of nuclear war.

"However, having said that, we must understand that this is just one meeting. My conclusions reflect the world as we here in Washington perceive it. Ambassador Noonan leaves for Korea tomorrow. General Goodwin will leave within the week. They are going to pursue the same questions there. In about two weeks, I am going to reconvene this meeting and give you the latest perceptions from there. Once we have common perceptions, or have clearly identified the differences, we will start making decisions. I want to stress two things. The decisions will be made in Korea. We are in a supporting role. We obviously have the power of veto, but running this sort of effort from Washington has never worked. Second, by direction of the President, I am in charge here in Washington. Bureaucratic rivalries will not be tolerated. Finally, this meeting is to be classified Top Secret UMBRA Eyes Only. Look that up in your security manuals. Dismissed."

"Ambassador Noonan and General Goodwin, will you do me the courtesy of meeting with me in my office for a few minutes, please. Captain Parker, you are, of course, invited too."

They entered the Secretary's office. The Secretary closed the door and flipped on the red light switch, signaling he was not to be disturbed unless it was a matter of national importance or a personal call from the President. He asked Noonie, Pete and Sandy if they would like to have a drink. "I was in the Navy and, as they say, the sun is over the yardarm, that is, it is after five o'clock. I am going to have one. It has been that kind of day. I think we have earned it. I hope you will join me. We all have a designated driver."

That was an offer they couldn't refuse. Pete had a vodka on the rocks, Noonie, a scotch and soda, Sandy, white wine, and the Secretary, a bourbon and branch water. They sat down around a comfortable coffee table and the Secretary opened the conversation. "For this puzzle palace, that was a remarkable meeting. I can't remember such straight talk. I think that the participants understand the gravity of the situation and are tired of the indecision of the last several years. What did you learn?"

Noonie answered first. "I learned that there is more that we don't know than we know. This was an extremely valuable meeting in that we now know the right questions. Hopefully, we can get the answers and decide what to do. I have a question" Noonie glanced at Pete. "Do we have any means to determine whether or not they are actually developing nuclear weapons?"

The Secretary shook his head. "None that I have been able to ascertain, but I will try again. That is one of the problems of an isolated country without allies. We can't even find out from their friends."

"What about you, Pete ?" asked the Secretary.

"I think that the first task of both Ambassador Noonan and myself will be to assess the political reliability and resolve of the Koreans, both military and governmental. I personally do not believe that they will fold, but then I have not been there for 20 years. I think that we have just about exhausted the productiveness of today's meeting. You can't analyze what you don't know."

The Secretary read the signal. He would have liked to have more to tell the President but this was enough for one day. One of the problems of the previous administration was that people had no incentive to tell the truth. Everything was sugar coated, which was fine for a while, but eventually caught up with you.

At that point it was obvious the meeting was over. The Secretary asked Pete when he was going back to Germany. Pete replied that the sooner the better since there was little else that he could accomplish here. He had to go to Korea and there was no reason for delay. The Secretary anticipated this and informed Pete that the same VC 135 that had brought him to Washington would take him back at midnight. Midnight was always the preferred time to leave for Europe, since with the six hour flight and the six hour time difference, you would arrive at noon. You could put in an afternoon's work, go to bed reasonably early, get a good night's sleep, and be ready to go the next day without the effect of jet lag. The key was not to sleep on the flight and not to take an afternoon nap.

The Secretary told Pete that he had a surprise for him. "Pete, one of the privileges of this office is that I run the Military Academies. I know that you have a son at West Point and I have arranged for him to meet you at your quarters at Andrews. The steward there will fix you an excellent meal so that you can visit with your son without interruption. I hope that I have not presumed too much and that that will be all right with you."

Pete told the Secretary that he was very appreciative of his kindness. The Secretary caught a look between Pete and Sandy.

Pete and Noonie said their goodbyes and agreed to meet just as soon as Pete arrived in Korea. At that point, Pete and Sandy got into their sedan and returned to the Andrews VIP quarters. Neither of them said a word. Rinaldi figured that it was because of the crisis in Korea, but was completely wrong.

Fortunately, when Pete and Sandy arrived at their quarters, Pete's son, Stephen, had not yet arrived. Sandy asked Pete what they should do. Pete responded that he had the greatest of confidence in Stephen and the best thing to do was to tell him the truth. Sandy would have liked to have had more time but she agreed.

She raced into the bathroom to get cleaned up and change clothes. She wondered what were the right clothes for a general's aide to wear after spending the previous night screwing a West Point cadet's father. She decided on a fresh captain's uniform, which was definitely what she had been planning to wear (or more accurately, *not* to wear) tonight. Then, she started to see the humor of the situation, began giggling and finally laughed out loud. Pete heard her and determined that if he lived to be a hundred, he would never understand women.

The Air Force steward understood perfectly. He told Pete that he would fix the meal, select and chill the wine, pack their bags for them, and then leave. Rinaldi had already arranged to pick up Stephen and get him back to West Point for morning classes. It seemed that Rinaldi and the steward had spoken during the day and had figured it all out. They make an officer's life easier so that the officers could do their job, which included taking care of their men. This was their job. Besides, Rinaldi liked Pete and he couldn't say that about many officers.

The steward was as good as his word. By seven o'clock, the meal was fixed and was kept warm in the oven while the wine was being chilled. Pete and Sandy were in their best uniforms, which they would wear on the airplane. The bags were packed and ready to go. They had not touched the wine. Knowing what was in store, they had both opted for a stiff drink.

Stephen Goodwin, First Classman, West Point, arrived right on schedule. Rinaldi had seen to that. Pete and Sandy were waiting for him in the living room of the VIP quarters.

"Hi, dad," said Stephen. "I don't know what you are up to this time, but you sure must have a lot of clout. My Tactical Officer told me that he had gotten a call from the West Point Superintendent telling him to get me down here to see you. The Supe said that the original call came from the Secretary of Defense, himself. What's going on?"

As Pete was about to respond, his heart skipped a beat. Every time he saw Stephen, he was aware of how much he looked like his mother.

"Stephen," said Pete. "Up until several days ago, I thought I was about to be put out to pasture. I am the last of my class to be on active Army duty and that is because my promotions always came later than the others. I met with the President of the United States today, who gave me another job. I am to go to Korea and see if I can do something about the mess that seems to be evolving there. This may be one of the shortest assignments in history. They seem to be looking for a miracle worker and right now I am flat out of miracles. But I'm going to give it my best shot.

"We can talk about that later," Pete explained, taking a sip of his drink. "I have something else I want to tell you about. I didn't know you were coming until about two hours ago. The Secretary of Defense thought he was doing me a favor. He was absolutely right, but in a way he never imagined. This gives me a chance to tell you something important face-to-face. I would like to introduce you to Captain Sandy Parker, my Aide. She has been with me now for over a year. The simple fact of the matter is that I have fallen in love with her, asked her to marry me, and she has accepted. I hope that you will approve. I loved your mother for over twenty five years and was never unfaithful to her, but she is dead, and I can't bring her back. Knowing the kind of woman your mother was, I think she would have wanted me to be happy."

Stephen responded immediately. "Dad, I am very happy for you. I know how much you loved my mother. Just so you know, I have been expecting this. Rock Kowslowski told me and Pete about you two several months ago. He said that it was just a matter of time. He also stressed that Sandy was the right person for you, that you two were meant for each other . . . given what has happened to the both of you. Captain Parker, can I call you Sandy?" Stephen asked, smiling. "There is more than enough of my father for both of us. I'm sure we will become best of friends in time."

At that point, Captain Alexandra Parker, U.S. Army and graduate of West Point, came totally unglued. Tears rushed uncontrollably down her cheeks as she rushed over and hugged Stephen. She excused herself telling Pete and Stephen to have a drink while she repaired her "camouflage paint," or what West Pointers call makeup.

"Wow," said Pete, "I don't know if you realize how much I have been worrying about your reaction to this. I am so happy right now I could burst. The President has given me an important assignment, a wonderful lady has agreed to be my wife, and you have approved, I appreciate very much what you told Sandy. That was very important to me. How about a drink? From what I understand from present West Point regulations, although all we old grads believe that the Corps has gone to Hell, you can have a drink as long as you are twenty miles from West Point."

Stephen asked for a beer and Pete noticed that he drank it from the bottle. He had noticed during the last few years that this was considered the macho thing to do in the eyes of young officers. "Tell me, dad," asked Stephen, "what the Hell is going on in Korea? We read the papers, we talk about it, but no one seems to have a good answer."

"You are right on that," Pete answered. "Why don't we wait until Sandy gets back to discuss it. I have given her my thoughts and she has attended the same meetings that I have. I have found that her counsel is always wise and it will give her an opportunity to talk. Ask her questions, draw her out. It will give you a chance to know her better. You will find out that this lady has a first class mind. Even if I didn't love her I will need her help in Korea. So, while we are waiting, tell me about West Point."

"OK," replied Stephen. "As you know, we graduate in several months. Pete Kowslowski and I have both selected Infantry and have signed up for jump school and Ranger school. That means that along with our two months graduation leave, we will finish the Infantry basic officer's course next spring where we will both be assigned to the 82nd Airborne Division. What happens after that is anybody's guess. One thing that we have learned over the last several years is that the future is almost totally unpredictable. After the demise of the Soviet Union and the Warsaw Pact there was a lot of talk around the Academy that there would be no more wars and no more use for us. Boy, were the experts wrong. If anything, we are going to be needed more than ever in this insecure and uncertain world.

"I saw your letter to the Superintendent in the Association of Graduates magazine three months ago where you accused West Point of trying to become more like Harvard Business School and less of a school for warriors. That created a lot of controversy, but most people think you are right. The Association of Graduates has appointed a Blue Ribbon panel at the request of the Supe to study the issues. My guess is that we will come about half way back. I sense a real mood at West Point to get back to the basics of soldiering."

Sandy emerged from the bedroom. She had taken off her Army jacket and tie, loosened the top buttons of her blouse, and had let her long red hair down. The effect was spectacular. Pete and Stephen simultaneously said "wow."

"OK, guys," said Sandy, giving the orders. "Why don't you two take a seat at the dining room table and one of you open the wine. The dinner is already fixed and if we leave it in the oven much longer it will dry out. I will serve."

"Yes, Ma'am," replied Stephen without even a hint of sarcasm, thinking to himself that this, indeed, was one special lady.

Once the meal was served, everyone starting talking at once. There was so much to say and discuss that many times they stopped, laughed and said "You first," "No, You first." Stephen took over. "Look, guys, we have two very important things to talk about, Korea and you two. Why don't we take the most important one first. Sandy, please tell me about yourself. I want to know you." That got Stephen a nice glance from Pete.

"Thank you, Stephen," said Sandy. "That's only fair. I believe that I already know you quite well the way your father and Rock constantly talk about you and Rock's son Pete. I am the daughter of a Midwest lawyer who served in the early part of the Vietnam war as an enlisted man. He developed a real admiration for West Pointers. I had no brothers and when the opportunity came along, he encouraged me to go the Point. I never regretted it. I graduated number 11 in my class and won my Army "A" in both cross country and track. Upon graduation, I went Field Artillery since they would not allow women to go Infantry or Armor. I married a West Pointer. It all seemed so perfect for a while. But eventually his career and mine started getting in the way of each other. Although the Army will assign married couples together if it is at all possible, sooner or later, one partner will have to take less than a career-enhancing job in order for them to stay together. Neither of us were willing to sacrifice and we divorced the best of friends. We had no children. My former husband continues to do well and just made the accelerated list for promotion to major.

"A little over a year ago, I was assigned to the Artillery section of your father's headquarters. A month or so later the word came down that Pete was looking for a new aide, having fired his old one, and I applied for the job. Pete has never told me why he selected me. My friends tell me it was because of my legs. One day I'll get Pete to tell me the truth."

Pete remained very quiet. If the truth be known, he had selected Sandy for a combination of reasons. One was that she appeared competent, another was that there was a real push going on in the Army to further women's opportunity, and the last was that Pete had noticed, as had everyone else in the headquarters that Captain Alexandra Parker had great legs, as well as her other observable component parts. He had made the right decision, at least partially for the wrong reason.

The conversation then turned to the reason why Pete had been called to Washington. Pete told of the day's events and the problems that the new President was facing. A lot of the conversation centered around the drift of U.S. foreign policy in the last few years. Stephen observed that there was much dissatisfaction among both the faculty and and the Corps of Cadets at

West Point, but being good soldiers and in strict accordance with the Constitution, the people at West Point were keeping their opinions private. The attitude was similar to what Pete and Sandy had heard from the President.

Sandy interjected that she was a witness to history. She had seen a President of the United States and the Secretary of Defense admit that the present structure and might of the country simply did not know what to do and asked Pete and his friend, Ambassador Noonan, to see if they could figure it out.

Stephen asked Pete who Noonan was. Pete told him the early Korea stories when Noonie was the battalion scrounge. That got a lot of laughs. The Korean war seemed like the dark ages to present day West Point cadets. It was beyond Stephen's comprehension that the U.S. Army would ever have a food shortage. Pete smiled and told Stephen to remember that remark on about the fourth day out on the long patrol at Ranger School. They intentionally lose the rations in order to see who can gut it out. It is quite amazing what happens to normally rational human beings when they have gone without food for over three days. That is where you find out who the warriors really are.

The three of them engaged in the best kind of dinner conversation, one rambling from topic to topic without any apparent thread. Sometimes they would discuss West Point, sometimes Korea, and sometimes, love. The time flew by quickly and Rinaldi knocked on the door indicating it was time to leave. They were all disappointed because they were enjoying each other's company and wanted to talk some more. Rinaldi had a surprise. Pete's VC 135 was going to take Stephen to Stewart Air National Guard Base just outside of West Point and then continue on to Europe. It lengthened the trip by a half hour and gave them more time together. Pete was very happy. Stephen was turning into a great young man and he and Sandy were getting along magnificently. Korea seemed to pale into insignificance in the overall scheme of things.

Chapter Fourteen

The VC 135 lifted off from Stewart Air National Guard Base. The trip up from Andrews had been uneventful and Pete and Sandy had another hour to talk with Stephen. Stephen said goodbye after a lot of hugs and kisses and promised to keep in touch.

The plane climbed out to cruising altitude and Airman Newton came to the passenger compartment and asked if there was anything they wanted. Pete and Sandy both asked for a good drink. Newton returned in just a moment with the drinks and an ashtray. Before making himself scarce, he told them that Captain Powell welcomed them aboard and invited them to come up to the flight deck. Sandy was busting to tell someone her news and asked Pete if she could tell Beth Powell. Pete said sure, but please ask Beth to keep it to herself for a while. Sandy laughed at that and informed Pete that if the women at West Point had not been able to keep their mouths shut, they and a like number of male cadets would have never graduated.

Sandy went forward to say hi. Beth suggested to her copilot that he might want to take a break and invited Sandy to take the right seat.

"Greetings again, Sandy," said Beth. "Why is it that I get the feeling that you want to tell me something? You have the glow of a woman in love. Am I right?"

"Right on, Beth," replied Sandy. "I never could keep a secret from you. If I tell you something, will you keep it in the strictest confidence?" Beth nodded in the affirmative. "These last 26 hours have been the most unbelievable in my life. Last night General Goodwin, Pete, told me he was in love with me and asked me to marry him. And I accepted! The rest of the night was not all that bad either. Today, no, I guess it is actually yesterday now, I met the President of the United States and the Secretary of Defense when they gave Pete a new mission and command. We are going to Korea, where Pete has been asked to try and straighten out the mess over there. Earlier this evening I met Pete's, son who is a West Point cadet, and the reason for our stop at Stewart, who accepted me into the family. Now, that is what I call a day."

"Wow," responded Beth. "That is some news. I am very happy for you. I thought that when I went into the Air Force, I was going to have the adventurous life. I don't think anything can top what has happened to you. When are you getting married and the other stuff?"

"I don't know," said Sandy. "Pete has to close out of the 11th Corps in Frankfurt and get to Korea as soon as possible. We really want to keep this quiet until we get there, and even then we will have to determine exactly the right time. Oh, I see what you are driving at. No, Pete didn't ask me to marry him just to get me in the sack. On the contrary, that was my initiative. Pete is a gentleman and under his rules we probably wouldn't have bedded down until after we were married. While I'm on that, I understand that this bird has a pretty comfortable bed. Any chance that we could use it with your and your crew's discretion?"

That got a real laugh out of Beth. "Sandy," she said, "the passenger compartment is yours. Nothing that happens there is any of the crew's business. Welcome to the five mile high club. You won't be the first. What you have told me about your general's mission also explains something else. We were scheduled to return to Europe at about noon yesterday after the mandatory crew rest. At noon we were told to remain at Andrews and take you back. That worked out very well since this plane was almost due for its 100 hours maintenance check, so we did that yesterday afternoon. You can tell your general that not only am I a good pilot but, as far as we know, this plane won't fall out of the sky during the trip. Now why don't you go back and make your General happy. You have more important things to do than talk to me."

Sandy returned to the passenger compartment where Pete was waiting for her. Pete told Sandy that he was sorry about what happened to her previous marriage and asked if she would be willing to discuss, not her personal experience, but the difficulties of women graduates of West Point.

"Sandy," said Pete, "I was in the Pentagon in the mid seventies when the Congress was debating whether or not to allow women to attend West Point. I was put on a task force to convince them not to do so. We were unsuccessful, as you know. After that, I was put on another task force to make the transition go as well as possible. At that point we were not going to sandbag the effort. The properly constituted government of the United States had spoken and, we, as soldiers, were obligated to make it work. My concern then, and it continues today, is that while women at West Point can be outstanding cadets, whether they will be around for the long run. West Point is not in the business of training Lieutenants. It is in the business of training future leaders of the Army and the country. It doesn't matter what kind of cadet you are if you do not stick around long enough to realize your potential. I know that that is spoken like a true male chauvinist pig, but I think it is a legitimate concern."

"Pete," replied Sandy, "you probably can't imagine how many times I have been involved in precisely that debate. At West Point it seemed so easy. We all believed that we would have no trouble combining a marriage and a family with a career, or in some cases, who needed a marriage? It is obviously not easy at all. We are just now approaching the fifteen year mark of women graduates so it is too early to tell. But the evidence thus far is not too good. My personal experience attests to that. There is something important that happens that most people don't understand. I don't want to inflate your ego too much, but the simple fact is that West Pointers spoil women for other men. That leaves us with an impossible choice. Do I marry someone who doesn't measure up to my requirements or do I marry a West Pointer with the inevitable career conflicts? And there is obviously the other problem. When is the right time to start a family? From what I have seen, there is no right time. It always entails a compromise. There are very few success stories, but they do occur. One of my classmates married a doctor who was fed up with big city hospitals and the pressures of a medical partnership. He also loved to travel. He was delighted to be appointed as an Army contract surgeon and, as such, he had his own status and credibility. But situations like that are few and far between. And, of course, there are very few women West Pointers who marry a very successful Lieutenant General, at least not while they are Captains. When you think that through, the probability is that a woman will not stay for a full career and possibly make General. The bottom line is that I am happy that I went to West Point and that is good enough for me. And since we are on that subject, this is as good a time as ever to bring up a very important matter." Pete lifted his eyebrows in curiosity. Sandy looked down and then turned to Pete with a smile, "I want a child."

Sandy had dreaded making that statement but it was better to do it now than later. If Pete did not want a child, Sandy was unsure what her decision would be. Either way it would be bad. She hoped she would not have to make a choice.

Pete reflected on that for a minute. Impinging on his thoughts were just how lonely he had been for the last several years. He knew that he couldn't have it both ways. If he said no, he might lose Sandy, or, even worse, eventually make her embittered. Finally he spoke, "Sandy, if you want a child, then so do I. I have never had a daughter and I have always regretted it. Let's just hope that it is not too late for me. I promise you I will give it my best effort. Last night you were the forward one. Now it is my turn. I see no reason why we shouldn't get started right now. They tell me that this bird has a sofa that turns into a pretty good bed."

"Well," thought Sandy to herself, "I certainly don't have to make the preparations that I made last night. I'm glad Beth told me what she did about the passenger compartment. First I need to tell Airman Newton that we do not wish to be disturbed."

The flight turned out to be the most pleasant one Sandy had ever experienced. It went by very quickly and in order to not upset their biological clocks, they did not sleep, at least not in the literal sense.

About an hour before arrival, Pete went up to the pilot's compartment and thanked Beth for a great flight. Beth responded that the U.S. Air Force had always been dedicated to the support of the Army and that no mission was too difficult. She accompanied this statement with a wink. The copilot was completely puzzled as to what was going on.

The VC 135 landed at Frankfurt International right on time at 1200. Rock Kowslowski was waiting to pick them up. He was grinning from ear to ear. It seemed that Stephen had told Pete Kowslowski about Pete and Sandy and that young Pete had called his father. So much for secrets. But, Pete didn't really care. His life was going to improve no matter what happened. For whatever odd reason, he suddenly wondered what being at 35,000 feet might do to one's sperm count. He didn't have any complaints and heard none 'from Sandy. He thought of the old joke, "Thank you for flying United."

Rock took the luggage and asked Pete if he wanted to go to his quarters or straight to the 11th Corps Headquarters. Pete thought for a minute and decided on Headquarters, adding that he had a very refreshing trip. I'll bet, thought Rock to himself. As they stepped into the car, Rock looked at Sandy and Pete in the rearview and said, "the Chief of Staff, Colonel Tanaka, is waiting for you. He asked me to tell you that everything is going just fine with the deactivation and the only decisions that you need to make are connected with your own ceremony."

This was one thing that the Secretary of Defense and Pate had not discussed. What was he going to tell everyone? He decided that he had better get on the phone as soon as he got to Headquarters to get some guidance. He did just that and was told that all wheels had been greased and he could now tell people that he was going to Korea to become the Commanding General of the First Combined Field Army, but not why. It would best for the time being to treat this as just another assignment, nothing special.

That afternoon Pete and Sandy thought it best if they did not spend the evening and night together. No sense complicating what was already a delicate situation.

The next morning was the inactivation ceremony of the United States Army 11th Corps (Dreadnought). The ceremony had been in the planning process for months and was one of those occasions that everyone hoped went smoothly. Present were the Chancellor of the Federal Republic of Germany, now called simply Germany, the Supreme Allied Commander of

Allied Powers Europe who was a U.S. Army four star general, The Lord Mayor of Frankfurt, and the Commander in Chief of the U.S. Army in Europe, including many more. The place was packed. Arrayed on the parade ground were bands from both Germany and the U.S. Army, and company-sized detachments representing each of the Brigades of the 11th Corps plus one from each of the nations of NATO. All in all, over 10,000 personnel were present. The flag detachment was breathtaking, National colors of each of the nations, Brigade colors of every Brigade, and over 300 guidons from every unit of the 11th Corps.

One of the aspects of a ceremony such as this was the firing of a cannon salute. Pete was the honoree, and the number of rounds to be fired for a Lieutenant General was 19. Four stars and above get 21. This was always a traumatic experience. It was very easy to screw up a cannon salute and everybody knew it when it happened. Pete noticed that not only he, but every other senior officer, was counting the number of rounds on his fingers. His mind took him back to Fort Hood and his battalion command there. Two other battalion commanders had been fired for messing up the salute battery. He had been given the mission. At about the same time, he had had assigned to him a Lieutenant that had been fired from another battalion. Pete had always had the attitude that you could find a job for anyone if you tried hard enough. After talking to the Lieutenant, Pete decided to give him the salute battery function. The kid was a natural. For the next year and a half, all cannon salutes in the Division and the Corps were done by his salute battery and were flawless.

The speeches were excellent and heartfelt, but as the outgoing commander, Pete was to give the main address.

After the obligatory welcome to the visiting dignitaries, Pete made his remarks. "Soldiers of the 11th Corps, this is one of the saddest days of my life, but it is also one of the happiest. It is sad in that one of the proudest outfits in the U.S. Army is going to be deactivated here in Germany. 11th Corps Headquarters will be removed from the active list. Fortunately, the Divisions and separate Brigades will remain intact but will be reassigned to other Corps in the United States. As a Corps however, we will cease to exist. I am fully confident that you will give your loyalty to your new commanders just as you have given it to me. More importantly, we can confidently say to the world, what a soldier should say, 'Mission accomplished, Sir.'

"Reflect upon what we and our predecessors have accomplished. The 11th Corps was established in Germany at the beginning of the cold war along with the VII Corps to our south. Our mission was simple, deter aggression by the Soviet Union and the Warsaw Pact, and should deterrence fail, defeat them in battle. I don't mean to imply that we did this alone. It was a combined effort of all of the countries of NATO. It is now forty years later. Did the Soviet Union attack? Of course not, but why not? It is my opinion that they would have attacked at any time they believed at any time they had achieved what is considered adequate 'correlation of forces,' that is, they thought they could beat us. This never happened. They kept trying to achieve such a force until it finally broke them. They ruined their own economy as well as those of their allies and literally fell apart. Please think about that. We won without having to fight and without incurring casualties.

"If that had been all of it, I, and I believe you, would have been left with a certain feeling of incompleteness. We knew we were good but we thought we would never have a chance to prove it. Well, we did have such a chance. We were selected, as was the 18th Airborne Corps, to be the major U.S. forces in the Persian Gulf War against Saddam Hussein and Iraq. What we did there will be studied for years in the history books as the way to fight a modern war. We were the armor heavy left hook of the enveloping move-ment around Saddam's forces. We destroyed 42 of his Divisions with less than 500 casualties of our own. We proved how good we were.

"And now, it is time to go home. We have worked and fought ourselves out of a job here. Your country needs you elsewhere, but let there be no doubt, this world is just as dangerous as it has always been, the new danger is just of a different type and is in a different place. Just look at the over 80 battle streamers on the Corps colors. They cover many wars and many years. The last streamers are yours.

"So now, let me leave you with something I hope you will carry with you the rest of your lives. 'Mission accomplished, Sir.' Pass in review."

After the troops had marched off there was a reception in the Officer's Club. Everyone meant well and all the right words were said, but Pete couldn't wait for it to be over. He was in no mood to party. Deactivation was not unlike going to a funeral of a very good friend who lived a wonderful life.

Following the reception, Pete asked Colonel Reuben Tanaka, his Chief of Staff, and Sandy to meet with him in his office. He told Reuben that he was to stay here in Frankfurt until all the administrative and logistical aspects of the deactivation were completed. Then he would bring Tanaka to Korea if he still wanted to come. Pete summarized the events and meetings that took place in Washington. Pete also told Tanaka that he wanted him to arrange for Rock Kowslowski to join him.

Reuben responded, "General, I am going to show you how quickly this deactivation can be done. I figure that it will take me about a month. I'll see you in the Land of the Morning Calm."

The next day Pete and Sandy left for the United States in CINCUSAFE's VC 135. Beth was once again the pilot and informed Pete that the CINC asked her to tell Pete that he would like to have his airplane and pilot back as soon as Pete was finished with them.

About an hour after the plane took off, Airman Newton told Pete that he was to come to the pilot's compartment to take a phone call from the Secretary of Defense. The Secretary told Pete that he needed to delay his trip to Korea for several days. It seemed that in fairness to the outgoing commander of the First Combined Field Army, the Koreans and the Army command wanted to bestow appropriate honors. The question to Pete was where he would like to spend three or four days. The Secretary felt that since time would not be productive in Washington perhaps a short vacation would be in order. Although he did not tell Pete, the Secretary had already asked Beth if Captain Parker was accompanying him.

Pete thought for a moment and responded that he would love to have a few days in San Francisco and that the VC 135 could be diverted to Travis Air Force Base just outside the city. Pete also asked if protocol could arrange for a rental car and lodging at the Sheraton Fisherman's Wharf. The Secretary answered that it would be done, have a good time, and that he would be in touch.

Beth listened to the conversation and was already programming her inertial navigation system. After doing the calculations, she changed her flight plans and arranged for refueling at Pease Air Force Base in New Hampshire. She also asked Pete if he would tell Sandy to come up when she got the chance. She then did something that confused the copilot. After asking the copilot to take the controls, she got up, kissed Pete, and told him that he was a very lucky man and to take good care of Sandy. Pete smiled.

Pete walked back to the passenger compartment with a broad grin on his face. Sandy immediately noticed that something was up. When Pete had been called forward, she had anticipated bad news. This did not seem to be the case.

"Sandy," Pete said, "you are not going to believe this. The Secretary of Defense wants us to delay our arrival in Korea for several days because of protocol problems there. There is no reason to go back to Europe nor is there any reason to go to Washington. So, we have three or four days to ourselves anywhere we want . . . within reason of course. I had to make a quick decision so I decided upon San Francisco which has always been one of my favorite towns. I hope that that is all right with you. We will fly into Travis Air Force Base, rent a car, and stay at the Sheraton Fisherman's Wharf. I don't know how you are fixed for clothes and I know I need some, but one thing about San Francisco is that they have great places to shop. I personally like Nordstroms at Union Square the best. There are so many wonderful things to see and do there. But I'm yammering like an adolescent. What do you think?"

"Sounds great," Sandy replied. "I have never been to San Francisco, but everything I've heard about it sounds wonderful. Really, it doesn't matter where we go, as long as I'm with you. How long will we be there?"

Pete responded that he didn't know, but that it should be at least three days. The Secretary would call. At that point Sandy suggested that since the trip was going to be longer than expected, maybe it would be a good idea if they got some sleep. As they turned the sofa into a bed, they giggled like teenagers.

The plane arrived at Travis Air Force Base at just a little after noon. Pete and Sandy went forward to say their goodbyes to Beth who told them that she was taking off immediately before Pete had a chance to commandeer the airplane again. A staff car met them and took them and their bags to the rental car agency. The Captain, who had been designated by the base commander to meet them, asked if there was anything he could do for them. His feelings were slightly hurt when they responded that they really wanted to be left alone.

The trip to Fisherman's Wharf took about an hour and a half driving through some very beautiful country. Sandy was amazed at how much the temperature dropped when they crossed into Marin County. Pete explained that they were now under the influence of the cold water of San Francisco bay rather than the warm desert around Travis. He repeated the Mark Twain statement that the coldest winter he had ever spent was a summer in San Francisco. Pete explained that San Francisco has a reputation for being cold and foggy, and sometimes it is, but usually it is cool and sunny – about as perfect a climate as is possible. It just makes you feel good. And then they approached the Golden Gate Bridge. Sandy was awestruck. The bridge itself glowed in the sun but the top of the main supports were in light wisps of fog. To the far left and down was the beautiful small town of Tiburon. Scanning clockwise was Angel Island, then in the distance Oakland, the Bay Bridge, and then San Francisco itself. The blue waters of the bay surrounded San Francisco and behind the city were steep hills rising into the fog. Further to the right were the green expanses of the Presidio and then the Pacific Ocean. On totally clear days you could see the Farallon Islands, but today they were obscured by fog. Pete explained that because of a combination of wind and sea, the fog was usually like that. San Francisco was almost always in the sunshine and the fog stayed overhead or out to sea. Pete also pointed out Fisherman's Wharf from the bridge. One of the features of the topography was that San Francisco looked as if all the roof tops were white, even though this was not really the case. It is truly a shining city by the sea, or Baghdad by the Bay, as columnist Herb Caen called it.

"Is San Francisco as beautiful close up as it is from this distance?"

Sandy asked.

"Unfortunately, no," replied Pete. "Some parts are even more beautiful, such as Golden Gate Park. Others have succumbed to the ills of modern society. It used to be the case that San Francisco was considered naughty but nice. Now, many parts are dangerous, crime-ridden, drug-ridden, and full of homeless. Man has, in many ways, ruined what was one of civilization's most wonderful products. But despite that, it is still my favorite city in the United States. The difference is that now you have to know what to do and where to go. I used to love staying at the St. Francis Hotel at Union Square right downtown. I consider it too dangerous now. That is why we should stay at Fisherman's Wharf. It's safe and clean all the time and we can go to the other areas of our choosing in the daytime. Some of the best things to see and do are outside the city and I have in mind a schedule for us, but I'm not going to tell you what it is. I want each experience to be a surprise."

"I love surprises," Sandy said.

They rolled up to the front entrance of the Sheraton where the attendant took their car and the bell hop took their luggage. As Pete was about to register, the concierge came over and asked him if he were Mr. Goodwin. Pete said yes and the concierge said, "Sir, I don't know who you are but I got a call from corporation headquarters that you and the lady are to be treated extra special. Follow me please. I'll take care of all the administration for you later. Did you have a good trip? I understand it was a long one." He then ushered Pete and Sandy into a corner suite that had a panoramic view of the whole bay. "I hope this will be satisfactory. I'll leave you now, but please let me know what arrangements I may make for you. I am here to serve you and have been told that I'm pretty good at it by such people as our Secretary of Defense, who is a major stockholder in the corporation."

Pete attempted to tip the concierge but was rebuffed. After the concierge left, Sandy wanted nothing more than to take a nice hot bath. While she was in the bath, Pete fixed himself a drink, took his shoes off, and gazed at the bay, thinking that he might wake up any moment and find that this was all a dream. But dream or not, he intended to enjoy it to the fullest. For the next several days, Pete would do his best not to think about Korea, although he knew it would be impossible. He thought that he had figured out what the Secretary of Defense was up to; he was giving Pete the opportunity to prepare for what awaited him in Korea. So, if this was a dream, the next few months were going to be a nightmare. Pete speculated that the fate of millions of people rested upon the accuracy of his assessments and the nature of his decisions. At one end, this was a compliment to his abilities, but on the other, it was an act of some desperation. Never before had he had such a clear cut opportunity to be either a hero or a bum. An old Teddy

Roosevelt speech labeled "The Man in the Arena" came to mind.

"It is not the critic who counts," stated Teddy Roosevelt, "not the one who points out how the strong man stumbled or how the doer of deeds might have done them better. The credit belongs to the man who is actually in the arena, whose face is marred with sweat and dust and blood; who strives valiantly; who errs and comes up short again and again; who knows the great enthusiasms, the great devotions, and spends himself in a worthy cause; who, if he wins, knows the triumph of high achievement; and who, if he fails, at least fails while daring greatly, so that his place shall never be with those cold and timid souls who know neither victory nor defeat."

Pete was amazed with himself that he could still quote the speech verbatim after all these years. He had always kept the speech in his note card file. Sometimes he used it in speeches, and sometimes he just read it to himself when things were not going all that well. These were words to live by and always made him feel better when he had difficult decisions to make. But enough of that, Pete thought to himself. Although not yet sanctified by marriage, he was a bridegroom and was going to enjoy it.

Sandy came out of the bath. She was a vision to behold. Obviously, she was not in the mood to explore the streets of San Francisco quite yet. It then occurred to Pete that he was easy.

At about four in the afternoon, Pete and Sandy decided to come up for air and explore their surroundings. That night, they had decided to stick close to Fisherman's Wharf. Pete called the concierge and asked if there was a clothing store near by where they could buy some casual California clothes. He also asked the concierge to make a dinner reservation at a nearby restaurant that was quiet, informal, and intimate rather than a tourist trap. The concierge directed them to a clothing store and assured them he'd take care of the reservation.

They walked two blocks to the place recommended by the concierge. It was called California Dreamers, Ltd. It was exactly what they were looking for. The manager was waiting for them at the door. The concierge had called and the manager was most appreciative of the business that was directed his way.

With the advice of the manager, Pete and Sandy bought similar outfits appropriate to the weather and the northern California lifestyle: light sweaters, chino cavalry twill pants, comfortable walking shoes, and reversible windbreaker jackets. They laughed at themselves for looking like the cover models of *Yuppies Monthly*. They changed into their new clothes and the store manager offered to deliver their old clothes back to the hotel. But Sandy had a better idea. She preferred the store manager donate the old clothes to the homeless shelter. She considered this an important symbolic break and Pete agreed.

They were now ready to see the delights of San Francisco. Pete took Sandy first to Ghirardelli Square, which adjoins Fisherman's Wharf. He explained that many years ago the entire area around Fisherman's Wharf was raunchy and in decline. What is now called Ghirardelli Square was an old abandoned chocolate factory. A group of businessmen had a vision and invested large amounts of money to turn the old building into a series of shops and restaurants. Their idea worked and now Ghirardelli Square is prosperous and one of the most popular tourist attractions in San Francisco. This move, Pete explained, caused imitators such as the Cannery Next Store, which was once an abandoned cannery factory.

"I first visited Ghirardelli Square about two years after it opened," Pete said. "On the second floor was a theater that continuously showed 'The Fantastics.' Next door was a restaurant called The Seawitch. The waiters at the Seawitch were the cast of the theater. They would break into song and invite the customers to join in. It was a fun place. Now those two areas are expensive shops for tourists. All over the place were small mom and pop eateries where you could get delicious food for cheap. Now the big chains have forced them out. Some call it 'progress.' But, as I said earlier about San Francisco, even though I regret the change, it is still more fun than anywhere else."

One of the best things about the area was the street performers. This had not changed. San Francisco took a very relaxed view of these performers. As long as no one complained, they could put on their acts and collect donations from the audience. Pete's favorite was a guy who called himself the "living TV show." He had taken a large cardboard clothing wardrobe, cut a hole in it approximating a TV screen, stood inside and pretended he was a TV program. He was actually quite good.

After wandering around for a couple of hours they went back to the hotel and found out where their dinner reservation was. The concierge told them and, in response to a question, also said they were properly dressed. The place was ideal. It was off the beaten tourist path on a side street without a view, but it was exactly what they were looking for, quiet and intimate.

Over dinner, Pete told Sandy some of the things he had learned about San Francisco over the years. "This is a strange place. I hear you can drink yourself to death and nobody minds. You can be openly gay, catch AIDS, and die and that is accepted. You can go out and jump to your death off of the Golden Gate Bridge and become a statistic since the newspapers keep a running tally. But, smoke a cigarette in a public place and you'll be run out of town. Don't ask me to explain it. It is part of the fascination of this unusual town. I love it."

After dinner, Pete asked Sandy if she was or up to another adventure that would take about two hours. Sandy responded that she felt fine and hoped that the evening would never end. Pete took Sandy to the park near the square, which was the terminus of the Powell and Hyde cable car line. He explained that if you want to ride the cable car, a weekday evening is the best time to do it. Any other time it is just too crowded by the tourists. They bought their tokens at the vending machine and Pete pointed out that the change was in Susan B. Anthony dollars, about the only place left in the country that actually used them, typical of San Francisco. When it was their turn they helped rotate the car around on the turntable, as was expected of the passengers and climbed aboard.

Pete told Sandy that up until a few years ago women were not allowed to stand on the outside steps, they had to sit inside. It was a major issue in local politics to change that rule. Standing outside was dangerous but was part of the fun. The conductor clanged his bell and they were off. After climbing a very steep hill and turning left toward downtown San Francisco, Pete mentioned that this hill seemed even steeper on the return trip. As they went down Powell Street, Pete pointed out all the great hotels such as the Mark Hopkins, the Fairmont, and the St. Francis. He also showed Sandy Union Square and pointed out the drug deals going on. When they got to the end they stayed on board for their return trip, which irritated the large number of people waiting to get on. About halfway back they made the right turn that would take them down the hill to Fisherman's Wharf. As predicted, the view was breathtaking, as was the steepness of the hill. Sandy clutched Pete and asked if this was really safe. Pete answered, "Not totally, but was worth it."

When they got to the end Sandy admitted that she had had enough for one day. Two hours of standing on the outside steps of the cable car in the cool night air together with the tension of the ride had gotten to her. Besides, she was looking forward to using what energy she had left for more constructive purposes.

For the first time in a long time, they slept in late the next morning and had their breakfast delivered to the suite. Pete told Sandy that there was no rush but in order to do the things he had in mind, they needed to leave at about 11 o'clock. While Sandy was in the bath, Pete asked for his car to be brought around and for the concierge to make a reservation for him. This time Pete knew exactly what the reservation should be. He hoped it was still as nice as he remembered.

Sandy and Pete crossed back over the Golden Gate Bridge and stopped in the artist town of Sausalito. Pete pointed out that the mayor of Sausalito for many years was San Francisco's most prominent madam. As they toured the small art galleries, Sandy fell in love with a beautiful painting of San

Francisco and Pete bought it for her, knowing full well that this painting, while an original, probably had many copies. So what, Pete thought, it would be the only copy in their house, wherever that house might be, and would one day make an important memento.

They then headed north again until Pete spotted the sign he had been looking for. It led to a relatively narrow Marin County road. By this time Sandy was starting to get curious and asked Pete exactly where they were going. Pete responded that over the years he had brought many people to this place and that none of them were enthusiastic when he told them beforehand. But once they had seen it, they were enthralled. So, he decided to keep it a secret.

They passed a sign welcoming them to the John Muir Woods National Park. Sandy was skeptical, but kept her mouth shut. They parked the car, and started walking down a path. The path had been well conceived, since nothing was visible until you turned a corner, and there, as big as life, was a magnificent redwood forest in all its glory. Pete had been through this forest enough times to know to remain silent. Words were insufficient. The beauty of the place was overwhelming. Ancient redwoods, technically giant sequoias over 300 feet high and 2000 years old, were in profusion. A walking path had been cleared along a running stream and Sandy and Pete walked along it for hours saying very little. Sandy was in awe and Pete felt a sense of spiritual well-being.

As they were leaving the Park, Sandy told Pete that this was the most beautiful place she had ever been. Pete smiled calmly and informed her that pollution was slowly killing off the redwoods elsewhere. But here, because of the proximity of the sea and the prevailing winds, it was not yet a problem although he assured her that man will probably find a way to fix that.

As they left, Sandy asked Pete if the rest of the day could top this. Pete replied that he certainly hoped it would but she would have to wait and see. On their way back to San Francisco, Pete turned off and drove to the town of Tiburon. Pete explained that Tiburon was Spanish for shark and was one of his favorite towns.

They pulled into town and parked the car. "Four years ago my wife died," Pete explained, "and my son entered West Point. I was assigned to the Pentagon and had been a two star general for almost five years. I was coming up for mandatory retirement and didn't have the slightest idea what to do or where to go. I took a month's leave to try to make a decision. I first went to San Francisco and was not satisfied. One day, after driving around, I stumbled upon Tiburon, and I rented a small apartment there by the week. At the end of two weeks I decided that this was where I wanted to stay. I found a townhouse, which I will show you in a moment, and was about ready to sign a contract when I got a phone call. I had been selected to receive three stars and command the 11th Corps. The Army gave me a "take it or leave it" choice and needed an answer immediately. Of course I said yes and the rest is history. And, just think, if I had not taken the job I would have never met you. Maybe someday we will want to return."

Sandy just smiled.

They walked the main street of Tiburon, which was only about two blocks long. They passed several boat docks and restaurants until they came to a beautiful set of townhouses called Tiburon Point. "These townhouses are well built," Pete said, "and have a magnificent view of the bay and San Francisco as you can see. They were featured in *Architectural Digest* for their style. Unfortunately, they sit right on the San Andreas fault, though that does not stop anyone. I guess the attitude is that if you are going to die, this is the best place to do it. I agree, in a way. Now, I think it is time to have dinner. I'm starving, how about you?"

Pete took Sandy to a restaurant on the waterfront called, "The Dock." He had checked with the concierge that morning to ascertain if the restaurant was serving a certain meal. They entered just as the place was opening. This was intentional, so as to avoid the crowds, get a seat by the window, and watch the sunset as it reflected off San Francisco. Pete asked Sandy if she would allow him to order the meal. He asked for a bottle of cold Joseph Phelps Johannisberg Reisling '72, sourdough bread with unsalted butter, a lettuce wedge salad with the house bleu cheese dressing, and seafood ciappino – a form of bouillabaisse native to the bay area, consisting of abalone, shrimp, crab and other seafood stewed in a tomato garlic base and served in a bowl. It is very messy, and the restaurant recommended bibs. The meal was as excellent as Pete had hoped and Sandy dug in. The lady could really put it away when she was hungry. There was not much conversation due to the food, the view, and the fact that Pete and Sandy no longer felt a need to make polite conversation. Many of their thoughts passed unspoken and at times simple eye contact was enough.

After dinner they did not linger. It had been a long, terrific day and they wanted to get back to their suite and be alone. They were starting to understand that neither of them much cared for large, loud parties and bars. That was good.

During the next two days, they did everything. They went to Golden Gate Park where Pete played a trick on Sandy. He asked Sandy if she liked the wonders of nature in the park, to which she responded positively. Pete then informed her that everything in the park was man-made. After the San Francisco earthquake every tree was cut down for new construction. The place was a barren pile of sand. A Scotsman by the name of John McLaren built the park on his own without using public funds. Pete got a kick in the shins for that one. They went to the Cliff House near the park where they saw the seals and drank Ramos Gin Fizzes, drove the coast highway down to Monterey and Carmel along the Big Sur country, and saw Stanford University and Palo Alto. It was wonderful. But inevitably the call came and it was time to go to Korea the next day. Transportation was arranged.

Chapter Fifteen

The Korean Air Lines 747 SP had been in the air for almost eleven hours and was approaching Kimpo Airport.

During the flight Pete had lots of time to reflect on the last ten days. Once an old bachelor who was about to be put out to pasture, Pete was now in love with a beautiful and talented woman who loved him back and had been given the most important assignment of his life. His emotions were mixed. On the one hand, he looked forward to the challenge. On the other, he wondered if he was up to it. Time would tell, he thought, repeating the words of Teddy Roosevelt in his head.

In Korea, Pete and Sandy were met by the Ambassador of the United States to Korea, the Honorable James Noonan. This got them very special treatment at the airport. They climbed into the Ambassador's limousine and headed for his residence. On the way to the residence, Noonie told Pete that they had much to discuss, but there was nothing that had to be decided until tomorrow and it was better to wait until then. Several people from both the Korean government and the U.S. military had requested an immediate audience with Pete but Noonie had refused. He did not want to repeat his own mistake of trying to do too much too soon. That was how bad decisions were made. He did have one piece of good information for Pete. The President, using his power and influence, had "frocked" Pete to be a four star General and Sandy to be a Major, the rationale for Sandy's promotion being that the aide of a four star General is usually at least a Major. Frocking meant that you wore the uniform but didn't get the additional pay until the formal process took place. It was a matter of prestige. With the people that Pete was going to deal with, the additional star would help. It would put them on an equal par. This was important in Asian culture.

Pete and Sandy were shown to separate bedrooms, which were adjoined by a connecting door that could be opened if both sides turned the latch. They were told to get cleaned up and take a nap if they wanted one, and that dinner would be casual at about 8 PM with cocktails at 7:30. Because of the circumstances Pete and Sandy took their naps in separate bedrooms.

After a refreshing nap, Pete and Sandy went downstairs to the drawing room at 7:30 and were met by Noonie and his wife, Jo Ann, whom Pete had never met before. By tacit agreement the conversation did not deal with the primary business at hand but was limited to pleasantries and getting acquainted. Jo Ann, being a diplomat's wife, immediately perceived that Sandy was a bit insecure about being there. She was also intuitive enough to understand that the relationship between Pete and Sandy was more than just business. She took it upon herself to make Sandy feel at home. Pete and Noonie noticed that the women had gone over to the corner of the room and were having a very private conversation that included peals of laughter. Pete and Noonie could only guess as to what they were talking about, and when Pete momentarily caught Jo Ann's eye he gave her a nod of gratitude.

Dinner was taken in the private family quarters. The food and wine had been placed on a buffet table so that no servants were present. They served themselves. The conversation at dinner was limited to getting to know one another. Jo Ann made sure that Sandy got to talk about herself first. At a certain point she looked over at Pete and with a gesture silently asked for his approval. Pete nodded yes and then Sandy told Noonie and Jo Ann about themselves. Jo Ann reached over and kissed Sandy and Noonie shook their hands. This was especially meaningful to both Pete and Sandy since in this environment Sandy was going to need a lady friend very much. Noonie talked about his experiences since he and Pete were together in Korea.

"After I left the Army, I tried several jobs and found that I was not very good at working for other people. I tried my hand at many things, barely managing to scrape along. I felt that I was at a dead-end. One day, I read an article on Korea that seemed to indicate future opportunities. I decided to take a flyer and took a look at it. In the end, I sold out and came here. It wasn't easy at first, but being here during the war helped a little. My first venture was starting a monosodium glutamate factory just outside Uijongbu. MSG was just getting popular in the United States and I caught the curve at just the right time. Let me give you a number that astonishes most people. In 1970, the Korean Gross National Product measured in U.S. dollars was $8.1 billion. In 1992, it was $294.5 billion. In the same time period, the per capita income went from $252 to $6749. Part of the present problem is that the South Koreans have made great economic progress while the North Koreans have not. I went along for the ride and contributed to part of it. I do have a certain degree of credibility in this country, as, I have found in the last week, so do you. Lots of people remember what you did in the the mid seventies. I guess that is why the President sent us. But we can get more into that later."

Jo Ann and Sandy never said a word, but by the looks they exchanged it was clear that these two guys didn't keep secrets from them but had to keep up the necessary appearances. They would find out later by way of pillow talk.

After dinner, Noonie invited Pete into his den for an after dinner drink and conversation. Jo Ann knew the drill. She told Sandy that she had been here less than a week and was still trying to find her way around the mansion, finding delightful surprises everywhere. Sandy was the first person she wanted to show them to and together they could explore. She also wanted to have a girl to girl talk with Sandy. She was worried about what might be about to happen and needed a trusted lady friend herself. The diplomat's wives she had met so far were shallow and artificial. The U.S. Army senior officer's wives seemed to resent her.

Pete and Noonie sat down in two comfortable chairs after fixing themselves drinks. Pete mentioned that this drink tasted almost as good as the beer Noonie gave him the night they first met. Noonie mentioned that he was glad Pete had knocked before bursting in that first night. His .45 was loaded and a round was in the chamber.

Noonie confessed to Pete his worries. As far as he could tell, the Koreans were far more fearful than they were letting on publicly. How much they were willing to resist and how hard they would fight seemed to be dependent on their confidence in the United States. Right now, they didn't have much confidence. They read the U.S. newspapers and news magazines and, like everyone else, were confused as to the U.S. understanding of the situation and what actions the U.S. might take. They were fully familiar with the technique of leaking trial balloons to the press to determine public reaction. Much had been written in the U.S. press lately that was totally contradictory. In fact Noonie was getting cables from the State department asking him for his opinions on these various media stories. The emphasis right now all seemed to hinge on the military assessment. Clever people were arguing that policy making should be based on possible military outcomes, as opposed to based on the national interest. One well-publicized Pentagon analysis stated that if the North Koreans invaded, they would control Korea in four weeks regardless of U.S. actions.

"I think we only have about a month," Noonie told Pete, "before that we have to have a solid no-shit military appraisal and we are depending on you for it."

"I think the article you are referring to is the one that appeared in *Time* magazine," Pete said. "I couldn't help but notice that in the front of the magazine there was a short blurb on how good the author of the article was. If that is the best *Time* can do they might want to stick to *People* magazine. The first thing that caught my eye was the map of Korea beside the article. It was wrong and misleading in every detail, whether because of intentional disinformation or sloppy journalism. They had the Munson valley and Chorwan valley threat corridors in the wrong places, plus the Korean and U.S. forces in the wrong locations. I don't know if the North Korean forces locations were right or not but the text was inconsistent with the map. The text stated that most of the North Korean forces were located next to the DMZ but the map showed otherwise. Virtually everyone quoted in the article said Seoul would be destroyed. Based on what my experience, I don't believe it.

"The analysis reflected the typical amateur bean count approach. They count their goodies and then count ours and whoever has the most is declared the winner. If that were true, France would have beaten Germany in World War II, we would have won handily in Vietnam, Lee would have never won a battle, and Saddam would have won in the Persian Gulf. As a matter of historical interest, over half the battles in history have been won by the side that was numerically inferior in troops and equipment. Alexander the Great beat Darius at the battle of Arbela with 35,000 troops to Darius' 1,000,000. You win wars with superior tactics, superior equipment, superior logistics, superior training, and superior motivation, all of which I believe we and the South Koreans are better at than the North Koreans. The bean counters haven't ever figured out how to put these factors properly into their computer models.

"My job is to give you my assessment of the fighting capabilities of the South Koreans and my best professional judgment as to the outcomes of the various feasible scenarios. I know one thing that would be most useful. Please ask the Pentagon and State to put a lid on all this speculation. Ask them to stick to the nuclear issue and to get commitments from allies. One thing for sure, you won't get a commitment from anybody if you have already forecast defeat. I know the President is new and has inherited a lot of amateurs, but if he is not careful he will have a self-fulfilling prophecy on his hands. Now please tell me about the civilian side of the equation, although I know that it is hard to separate the military from the civilian, especially in Korea."

"Pete," said Noonie, "I will answer that in just a moment. But first I need to tell you something. You are the first military officer that I have talked to who has made any sense whatsoever. I have been constantly bombarded with computer program results that seemed to fly in the face of all logic. When people would tell me that the North Koreans have 10,000 artillery pieces and rocket launchers to our 5,000, I would ask how good they were and where they were located. I could never get a direct answer. I asked, assuming that most of their tanks are located north of Pyongyang, wouldn't we know if they moved? But I wander. The reason that you were chosen is that you have a reputation for giving honest and correct appraisals. The President knows that your career almost came to an end when you questioned the Vietnam war. The fact that you seem to disagree with the doom and gloom crowd makes me feel much better already. I know that you wouldn't be saying this if you didn't believe it. But if you change your mind, please let me be the first to know.

"Now for the answer to your question that I alluded to earlier. If the government of the Republic of South Korea decides to fight, they will. The history of South Korea is replete with military losses – but losses that they have always overcome. Even at the height of military disaster, they have always had one of the highest birthrates in the world. That does not happen in a nation that accepts defeat. My judgment is that the Koreans are proud of what they have accomplished in nation building and would hate to lose the fruits of their efforts. But they are willing to accept devastation rather than surrender. The point is that they do not believe that great devastation need occur if they get the support of the United States. As they see it, the choice is not surrender, but rather the price of fighting for their existence. They will fight alone if need be, believing that they would win, but at a terrible price. It would almost be easier for the United States if the Koreans decided to reach an accommodation with the north. There might be some room for maneuver, but never if it placed the viability of the Republic of Korea in future jeopardy. I think that is one of the things that the North Koreans are up to right now. They hope the United States, Japan, and China might be willing to do a "Munich" to avoid a conflict, especially a nuclear one. That has political appeal but would be the worst possible thing, even worse than fighting a war in the immediate future. The next phase, maybe five years from now, would be disastrous. There are times when you must make a stand and this is one of those times. The issue is not, to my way of thinking, whether we make a stand or not, but rather making the right stand. Which brings me back full circle. We must have a good assessment of all the possible military outcomes to decide the most intelligent course of action. I know this was more than you asked for, but I wanted to share my thoughts with someone I trust. Are we in agreement?"

Pete now understood why the President had selected Noonie for this job. Noonie was no striped pants cookie pusher or political hack. He was a diplomat in the finest sense of the word. How funny. Pete thought. Who would have ever thought that two lieutenants sharing a hootch in the cold of Korea many years ago would be having this conversation?

"We are in total agreement," Pete responded. "I am about ready to fall asleep after the last couple of days. I will be ready to go to work tomorrow. Do I go up to the Field Army or do I first do a round of meetings here in Seoul?"

Noonie instructed Pete to attend military meetings in Seoul tomorrow and then go to his headquarters in Uijongbu and asked him not to make any direct decisions yet, but rather attain information. Noonie and Pete would meet again in about a week and decide where to go from there.

Pete reflected for a moment. There was no question that Noonie was the President's man and was in charge. That is how it should be, unless the diplomat tries to be the military commander. Pete did not believe that would happen. He fully expected Noonie to accept his military judgment as long as he was able to explain his reasoning. Everyone needs someone to critically question him, which is exactly what he intended doing with Noonie's judgments. Pete was confident that they could pull this off, the only question was the cost. The price of appeasement was the highest of all and neither Pete nor Noonie would have any part of that, regardless of the consequences. Pete went back to his room where he noticed that Sandy had opened the latch to the connecting door on her side.

Pete and Sandy were awakened by a discreet knock on the door at 7 AM. Pete raced through the adjoining door and answered from his own room. The Korean maid smiled at Pete and informed him that breakfast would be served at 7:30. The maid then went to Sandy's door and made the same announcement, however unnecessary. At 7:30, both Sandy and Pete entered the dining room, dressed in their best, freshly pressed, Army Green dress uniforms. Pete's real leather shoes sparkled with a very professional spit shine, since he had never been able to bring himself to wear the recently fashionable, uncomfortable patent leather shoes. In some ways he considered it cheating to have shined shoes without work. Noonie and Jo Ann were in the dining room waiting for them.

"Fix yourself some coffee and have a seat," said Ambassador Noonan. "One of the perks of this job is that I have the cables and press summaries delivered to the residence early in the morning so that I can read them at leisure. You might as well know that I share them with Jo Ann because I value her advice. I really had to battle the spooks over that, but they relented when the President suggested that she have a Top Secret clearance. Read this one. Some senators are suggesting a preemptive strike on North Korea as a way out of this mess. I will talk to the President later today and pass along your suggestion that Washington cool it for a while. The President has a real political problem here since the situation has gone too far. Knowing that you and I need time, he also knows he must show decisiveness. I think we must give him something to say publicly that will buy us and him some time. Any ideas?"

Many ideas were debated around the table and it was actually Jo Ann's idea that they finally agreed upon. She believed it best to send an eyes-only message to the President requesting authorization allowing Pete and Noonie to address a joint statement from Korea. This would give the President distance and the opportunity to say he and his advisors were studying the statement.

The statement would say that Pete and Noonie were the most qualified to address the issue. As they saw it there were two separate but related issues at stake. The first was the possible North Korean acquisition of nuclear weapons. The second was the possibility of a conventional attack in the near future on South Korea. It was their professional opinion that if the North Koreans launched such an attack, the South Koreans, with the planned response from the United States, would be sufficient to defeat the attack. Yes, there would be casualties, but not anywhere near some extreme estimates coming from Washington.

Noonie said that he would go to his office and get this request out right away. He hoped to have a response from the President by evening, so Pete and Sandy should plan on staying one more night in Seoul before heading to the Field Army headquarters at Uijongbu. Noonie also told Pete that he had only one appointment all day, though it was liable to last that long since it was with the Republic of Korea Chairman of the Joint Chiefs of Staff. His name was General Lee Chi Na. Pete said that he knew Lee Chi Na and that they had worked closely together two decades ago on a matter of equal importance.

Noonie put on his Ambassador's hat to make sure he was not misunderstood. "Pete, today is the day for getting information. The most important thing for you is to see if you can find out the South Korean military's plans. Of course, their objective is to find out the U.S. plans. Explain that you have just arrived and need time and that it is most important to hear their ideas. One thing you might do is ask them their opinions on the *Time* magazine article – they've read it. If they play ignorant take this copy with you and show them. Make no commitment, explaining that we will make the right commitment once you and I fully understand the situation. Stress that we will not abandon them in any case, but that we need to decide exactly what to do. This is a tough assignment, but has to be."

A Korean Army staff car picked up Pete and Sandy in front of the Ambassador's residence precisely at 0900. They were met by a Korean Colonel who spoke perfect English and informed them that he was General Lee's senior aide. Pete and Sandy wore the insignia of their new rank. Sandy's major's insignia was easy, but Pete's four stars had been hastily fabricated by a Korean jeweler during the night. At breakfast, Noonie had presented them in the name of the President.

The ride to the ROK military headquarters took about a half hour. Pete was familiar enough with Seoul to know that they had taken the most impressive, rather than most direct, route. He also noticed that they were being followed by several cars with rather serious-looking passengers. Pete and Sandy rode in a Mercedes and from his days in Germany Pete knew the sides and windows were bulletproof. In front of the headquarters, an honor guard was waiting for them. Pete told Sandy, loud enough for the aide to hear, to enjoy this because nobody does it better that the Koreans. Flags, national anthems, 21 gun salute, trooping of the line, inspection of the troops. In Pete's eyes, it was perfect. Pete noticed that the entire honor guard was six feet tall or more. He remembered reading somewhere that in the last two generations, after centuries of a meager subsistence diet, the average height of the South Korean had increased by six inches due improved nutrition. Indeed, the Koreans were a beautiful race of people.

After the ceremony, General Lee invited Pete and Sandy to his impressive office. It had more computer equipment than the President's oval office, but perhaps only for show. General Lee offered his visitors a choice of coffee or Gin Seng tea, the latter being the traditional Korean drink for power and fertility.

Chi Na Lee opened the conversation in perfect English. "Well, Pete, what has it been, twenty years? It looks as if the world has treated us kindly. I thank you very much for coming back to Korea, and especially for bringing your aide. As you must be aware, when we heard you were coming, we did as much research on you as possible. I am most impressed. Major Parker, I hope we get a chance to talk about women at West Point. We designed our Korean Military Academy after West Point but we have not yet admitted women. We are considering doing so and I would very much like your advice. But that will have to wait. I have scheduled a series of briefings for you, remembering how you improved the morning briefings at Uijongbu years ago." General Lee looked at his watch. "I see that it is about time. Shall we go? Pete, Major Parker, please follow me."

This was a defining moment. Fortunately for Pete, the difficult decision as to what to do if Sandy were not invited would not have to be faced. When they got to the briefing room, General Lee and Pete sat alone at the center table, with officers in descending order of rank at the back with the rest of the aides and Sandy behind them.

General Lee Chi Na started the briefing and introduced Pete. Pete was grateful to know that the briefing would be in English. Years ago there was a certain amount of resentment among Koreans that meetings such as this were always conducted in English, but in the last several years they recognized that English was the language of business worldwide and that most military forces in the world accepted English as the language of combined force activities. The Koreans are not stupid, Pete thought. General Lee was of the opinion that his command of English, which he mastered when he was the G-3 of the First Combined Field Army, probably contributed greatly to his present position. He introduced the first speaker as the Assistant Chief of Staff for Intelligence, a fancy term for G-2.

As the briefing started, Pete experienced an intense feeling of déja vu. He had heard all of this twenty years ago at Uijongbu when the briefings were altered to the satisfaction of General Pace, the Commanding General. And besides the obvious weather and terrain, the enemy forces were surprisingly the same as he remembered – location, size, equipment, everything. For a moment, it was as if the world stood still. When the briefer finished Pete asked an important question.

"General, as I am sure you know, I was the Chief of Staff of the First Combined Field Army some twenty years ago. Back then we put together the best intelligence briefing possible so that we could properly estimate the situation. I was struck by how similar your briefing was to the one of twenty years ago. Perhaps it would be useful if you could tell me how the situation has changed since then."

The officer was prepared for the question. "Sir, the numerical count of North Korean forces has not changed and their locations have changed very little. Although they have modernized their equipment by one generation, it is still inferior to ours. The comparisons between the capabilities of theirs and ours are properly the purview of the Assistant Chief of Staff for Operations who is next to speak. They have continued to dig in and fortify their positions but this effort is mostly lost if they leave the positions to attack. In the last ten years they have increased their artillery and air defense weapons by about a third. It is interesting to note, too, that the bulk of their armor is still in the vicinity of Pyongyang and has been there for years. Over the past several years, we have observed a general decrease in training activities, which probably means that they are having replacement spare-parts problems and fuel problems. One thing that we have not observed is any relative decrease in training activities. This is important since a large decrease might indicate a stand down in preparation for a major effort. As a general answer to your question, for a combination of reasons, some positive, some negative, the North Koreans are only marginally better for offensive operations than they were twenty years ago. But, they are considerably better for defensive operations, including most importantly, air defense. One other point: they are very dependent on centralized command and control. This is their greatest vulnerability. I hope I answered your question, sir."

"Yes. Thank you very much," said Pete, knowing better than to ask if everyone agreed. If there was disagreement Chi Na Lee would say so later in private.

The next speaker was the Assistant Chief of Staff for Operations, ACOS

OPS in Armyspeak. It was his task to relay the status of friendly forces and war plans, and to make the relative force comparisons between North Koreans and their allies. He commenced by saying. "Sir, just as the ACOS INTEL, much of what I am going to tell you has not changed that much over the last twenty years. As a matter of fact, more change took place in the year that you were here in the mid-seventies than has occurred since. That is because we thought we finally got it right then and have had no reason to change. The First Combined Field Army still has twelve divisions, eleven ROK and one U.S. and as you know, they are positioned as shown on the map, defending the Munson and Chorwan valley approaches. The real difference has been that with U.S. help, although I stress that we have been paying for it ourselves since our economy strengthened, we have been continuously upgrading our equipment. Our real problem is not quality but quantity. We can defend ourselves quite well for about a month, but without resupply, we will run short, especially in precision-guided munitions. We are very dependent upon the air reinforcements that are called for in our joint U.S. ROK war plans. The bottom line is that we believe we can do very well if the North Koreans attack as long as the planned U.S. support comes through as scheduled. However, one thing puzzles us; we and the U.S. have been wargaming what might happen for over twenty years. Each time a significant change in structure or armament has occurred, we have rerun the game. The results have been consistent: relatively heavy, but acceptable, damage to civilian populations due to artillery fire; a rapid winning of the air campaign, although North Korea will have some initial success; limiting their penetrations to north of Uijongbu; and then a counteroffensive limited only by our own objectives. The only difference in the previous situation and the present one is the possible North Korean acquisition of nuclear weapons – yet this does not change the tactical balance. Obviously, it has the potential to significantly change things in the future, but we are concerned with now. After all these years of agreement on tactical outcomes, we are now reading in the U.S. press predictions of almost total destruction and defeat. We wonder what is going on? Were we wrong in the past or is some political factor at work here?"

Silence filled the room. Pete recognized a beautifully laid out trap and was grateful for the advance briefing he had gotten from Noonie. He knew that his future credibility depended upon his response. He asked General Lee for permission to leave his seat and address the audience.

"Gentlemen, as you know, the United States has a new President and administration. This came about because of the previous administration's handling of foreign affairs. Ambassador Noonan has been here for a week. I arrived yesterday. Neither of us have participated in the analyses and estimates that have been produced in the United States. I think you know that both the Ambassador and I have extensive service in Korea. The President briefed both of us personally and his instructions were to find out what is going on, make our own independent evaluation, and report back to him personally with our recommendations. I hope you will give us a little time, though it shouldn't take more than a month. I will tell you one thing. I will not be a party to appeasement or the abandonment of the Republic of Korea. I would rather turn in my suit first."

General Lee nodded his approval, which was not lost on the rest of the audience, and asked Pete if there was anything further that he wanted to know. Pete responded that he would like to have in writing the ROK comments on the reinforcement and logistical support plans and wanted to know the ROK estimates of the shortfalls. He also wanted to know those aspects of existing plans that were critical to the defense – that is, those promises that had to be kept. Lee agreed and told Pete that he would have everything within a week. And with that the meeting came to a close. Much more needed to be discussed, but those were mostly details that would be better addressed at a later date.

General Lee, Pete, and Sandy returned to Lee's office. Lee noted that it was about time for lunch and invited them. With a smile, he guaranteed that it would not be *kimchi*, a traditional Korean dish made out of fermented (some say rotten) cabbage, heavily spiced with garlic and unknown substances. To Pete, this was good news. After a meal of *kimchi*, for over a week everyone around you knows. Pete had once heard someone say that after *kimchi* your breath could knock a buzzard off of a manure wagon, or honey wagon as the Koreans called it.

Instead, the meal was *bulgogi* – marinated thin strips of beef cooked over a charcoal brazier, accompanied by Korean rice, which the Koreans claim is superior to any other rice in the world, including Japanese rice. General Lee asked Pete and Sandy if they would try some Korean white wine. Lee told them that the wine industry was just now getting started, thanks to the help of Californians with their Napa Valley expertise. Although the wine was not all that good, Pete said it was better than many expensive wines that he had tried in fancy restaurants. He also warned Lee that if the wine industry in Korea progressed the same way that other industries had, California better look out. Sandy then told Lee the California joke that the way to make a small fortune in the wine industry was to start with a large fortune.

Near the end of the meal, General Lee brought up a very sensitive topic. He mentioned that the United States still had the U.S. Eighth Army headquarters in Korea and that the Commanding General of Eighth Army was also the Commander in Chief of United States Forces in Korea and Commander in Chief of United Nations Forces in Korea. This latter title was a carryover from the Korean war of the 1950s and was a real convenience in international diplomacy. This concerned Lee for two reasons. The first was that ambiguous chains of command were always detrimental to military operations; and second was that technically the ROK armed forces were under the operational control of the Commander in Chief of United Nations Forces.

Pete responded that everyone agreed that the primary battle would be fought in the zone of the First Combined Field Army, of which he had been appointed the commander. It was the intent of the President of the United States that Eighth Army recognize its supporting role, not its tactical one. He hoped that the ROK armed forces headquarters had the same understanding. Lee agreed wholeheartedly. He answered Pete that he would do his best to help him in this difficult arrangement and really didn't see any problems since the bulk of the allied armed forces in Korea were Korean. As he saw it, the task was to get Pete the needed tools of war and to hold him responsible for the conduct of the actual conflict. Pete did not mention that the President, at Pete's request in anticipation of this issue, had given the Eighth Army commander some very specific orders: to support Pete; stay out of his hair; or come home.

After lunch, General Lee took Pete and Sandy on a tour of his underground headquarters, which was a well-kept secret that had been built during the construction of Seoul's subway system. The headquarters was self-contained and designed to withstand everything but a direct nuclear hit. The communications were redundant, with external antennas hidden all over town and the adjacent mountains. Lee felt that he could conduct his part of the war successfully from here and had no plans to move out. They would fight and win, or die. This reminded Pete that in the seventies, the South Koreans built an underground Command Post at Camp Red Cloud in Uijongbu. With the present North Korean artillery threat, Pete knew he had better quickly find out how good it was.

The meeting with General Lee was ended at three in the afternoon. Pete asked if General Lee would mind having the car take him to Eighth Army Headquarters. Pete felt that the sooner he made peace with the Commanding General, the better. The trip took only a few minutes since the two headquarters were located quite close together. On the trip over, Pete used the car's cellular phone to ask if the CG would see him. The response was a cold, but polite, yes. Pete entered the office, asking Sandy to please wait outside since this was liable to get ugly.

Pete saluted. "Sir, I am sorry that I could not see you earlier. My President made it quite clear that he wanted me to start with the Ambassador and the Chairman of the ROK Joint Chiefs because of the politics of the situation. I appreciate very much you seeing me on such short notice. I was told that I would spend the whole day with General Lee, but we finished early, so I took the chance."

General Armstrong, CINC U.S. Forces Korea, CINC UN Forces Korea, and CG of Eighth Army asked Pete to sit down, wondering for a moment, what to say. He was scheduled for mandatory retirement in two months. In addition, it was common knowledge that he had prostate cancer. Therefore, whatever was going to happen and whatever had to be done he would not be around to see to conclusion. Up until now, Korea had always been the least desirable and least prestigious of the Army's four star positions. It was in many ways a political convenience rather than an actual command. The UN part of his title was a historical accident that resulted from the Russians having missed a meeting. Besides, the only troops he had were Koreans and Americans, hardly a United Nations force. Ninety-five percent of the forces were Korean, but the Koreans wanted a U.S. boss to strengthen the commitment. Armstrong had virtually no U.S. Navy forces permanently assigned to him, but could draw from other commands in times of crises. The same was true of U.S. Air Forces Korea. He had a total of 35,000 U.S. troops from all services, most of them in the Second U.S. Infantry Division, which was under Pete's command already. On the Korean side, Armstrong was technically in command of 700,000 troops. No, this was not the time to be in a blue funk about fate, thought Armstrong. Pete made the first gesture, now it was up to him to help make it work.

"Pete," said General Armstrong, "I believe that is what they call you – so I hope you don't mind my doing so – welcome to Korea again. Thank you for coming by. I am aware of the protocol delicacy of your position. Who is your primary boss in this odd situation? If you find out please let me know. I never have figured it out. I have heard a lot about you and I think you are the right man for a very difficult job. I intend to support you fully. One of the neat things about having cancer and retiring in two months with four stars is that I can do just about anything I want. How about joining me for a drink? I am sure that we could both use one, especially you." Pete nodded and asked for a vodka on the rocks. "How did you and Chi Na Lee get along? I understand that you know one another from years back."

General Armstrong finished fixing the drinks and took his seat, not behind his desk, but in a chair facing Pete. This was one of those subtle signs that people with power sometimes use. Sitting behind the desk tends to say 'I am superior to you and I don't want to get too close.' Sitting away from the desk is a gesture of friendliness.

Pete was most appreciative of the kind reception and took an immediate liking to Armstrong. He decided to confide in him. He informed him of the President's assurance that he was prepared to take decisive action, but wanted a fresh appraisal of the situation. Pete summarized the briefing with the Secretary of Defense and repeated the apparent frustration of the middle level officers in Washington over the inaction and inconsistent action of the last several months. Pete then talked about his meeting with Lee Chi Na and the ROK Joint Staff earlier that day. At this point he was not ready to draw any conclusions, and when he did it would be with the President after obtaining agreement from Noonie.

General Armstrong was especially interested in the list of shortfalls and critical planning items that General Lee was going to furnish to Pete. Armstrong admitted that for whatever reason he had never managed to hit it off with Lee Chi Na and never had won his confidence. "What has been going on for weeks," Armstrong told Pete, "is an international game of responsibility avoidance. The Koreans have been saying 'we will fight if you guarantee your support.' Washington had been saying, 'we will guarantee our support only if we know you will fight and the losses won't be too high.' The Koreans have been saying publicly that there is no problem. Washington has been saying that it will be a disaster. What nobody seems to be doing is separating the issues. Yes, the North Korean acquisition of nuclear weapons will be a big problem and the more they have the bigger the problem will get. We must stop them by whatever means is necessary. But they don't have them yet. What we need to do now is concentrate on the fighting of the potential conventional war. For whatever reasons, Washington has been pressuring me to paint a negative picture. I can only speculate why, but that sure would support appeasement if that is what they have in mind."

General Armstrong then asked Pete to forgive him but he had another appointment. Pete told him that he was going up to Red Cloud the next day to get the feeling from there. He asked Armstrong's permission to come back and talk with him once he had a better grasp of the situation. He also asked him if it was possible to get transportation back to the Ambassador's residence. Armstrong assured him he could but the reminder that Pete was staying there elicited another question. Armstrong asked if Ambassador Noonan was really the President's man. "Absolutely," answered Pete, who went on to explain his personal relationship with the Ambassador and his confidence that the President's confidence was well placed. It came as a shock to Pete that Noonie had not yet gotten around to meeting with Armstrong. No wonder Armstrong is somewhat bitter, thought Pete, making a mental note to raise the point with Noonie that night.

Dinner that night at the Ambassador's Residence was again a private affair involving only Noonie, Pete, Jo Ann and Sandy. As the night before, there were no servants present. This was to be a working dinner. Noonie asked Pete how his day had gone and Pete summarized his meeting with Lee and his staff and his private meeting with General Armstrong. Of special interest was Pete's response to the question asked by the Korean ACOS OPS. Noonie thought that Pete had hit exactly the right balance. Sandy interjected that, from the back of the room, she perceived a very positive reaction from the staff officers and commanders assembled. Pete asked if Noonie had received an answer to the cable that had been sent this morning as a result of last night's conversation. Noonie responded in the negative but reminded everyone of the time difference. While it was 8:00 PM in Korea it was 8:00 AM in Washington. Washington had acknowledged receipt of the message and had assured that it would receive the President's immediate attention.

Noonie asked Pete his thoughts on the day.

"I have been here only one day," Pete answered, "so that anything I say is preliminary, but I detect a consensus that is quite different from Washington's. Everyone is concerned with the North Korean development of the nuclear weapon without seeing it as an immediate threat. They make a clear delineation between importance and urgency. I am convinced that the South Koreans will fight if attacked, regardless of what the United States does. I am also reasonably convinced that the North Korean attack will not be successful if the U.S. does what it is committed to do under present war plans. But I want to defer temporarily on that last point. Everyone agrees, as do I, that the war, if it comes, will be fought primarily in the First Combined Field Army's zone. I need a couple of weeks to see all the commanders and troops, walk the terrain, inspect the prepared positions, and, most importantly, assess the fighting spirit. I would be surprised if I change my mind, but I feel it necessary that I see it all first hand."

"The nuclear issue is another matter. There is very little that we can do from here about that except show total resolve in support of the sanctions that are being considered, unless Washington wants to consider a preemptive strike. Right know I don't think that is a good idea and I hope you ask the President to involve us in any discussions to that effect. You know, if you fold the two matters back together, that is, the nuclear problem and the North Korean attack problem, into one issue, the best thing that could happen is for the North Koreans to attack, for the attack to be unsuccessful, and for our counteroffensive to destroy forever their ability to develop nuclear weapons. I know this alternative sounds radical, but realistically, what other choice do we have for doing so if sanctions don't work?"

The dinner partners gasped as Pete seemed to advocate war. But Pete stood firm and said. "Suppose it was five years from now and the North Koreans had developed many nuclear weapons and sold some to Khadafi and Saddam. That would be a very bad situation. We would be facing nothing less than nuclear terrorism."

After that, the dinner conversation became somewhat subdued. Nobody had much to say. Without intending to, Pete had identified the critical flaw in the situation. They could win the battle, that is, deter a North Korean attack from happening now, and lose the war by not preventing North Korea from developing an arsenal of nuclear weapons. It was a Pyhrric choice. The only good news was that near the end of the dinner, Ambassador Noonan had received a cable authorizing him to make the recommended statement in his and Pete's name. The President mentioned in his response that almost everyone in the administration, except the Secretary of Defense, had advised against it. The President did give himself an out. He told Noonie that the statement had to be made extemporaneously in response to a planted question at a news conference. The statement would start off with a *mea culpa* that this was Noonan's and Goodwin's opinion and was not necessarily that of anyone in Washington. It would be most interesting to see the reaction, thought Pete.

After mentioning to Noonie that it would be appropriate for him to pay a call on General Armstrong, Pete and Sandy excused themselves and went to bed. Jet lag was catching up with them. After they left, Jo Ann and Noonie remained for an after dinner drink. Jo Ann remarked that she really liked Pete and Sandy and now understood why Noonie talked about Pete all the time. She gave her opinion that if any two people could solve this mess, it would be her husband and Pete. She then told Noonie that Pete and Sandy had reminded her of something that had recently escaped her attention, so why don't they go to bed early for a change. The world could wait.

At 0900 the staff car from the First Combined Field Army showed up in front of the Ambassador's residence to pick up Pete and Sandy. It was accompanied by two machine gun jeeps. In the staff car was the Deputy Commanding General of the Field Army, Major General Kim Jook Wan, who had been Pete's Deputy Chief of Staff years ago. The bags were ready and Noonie and Jo Ann accompanied them to the door. The Ambassador shook their hands and kissed Sandy. Jo Ann kissed both Pete and Sandy. This show of affection was not lost on General Kim, nor was it lost on the North Korean Security Service agent across the street whose job it was to keep surveillance on the Ambassador's residence.

General Kim saluted Pete, "Welcome back to Korea, General, it has been a long time and I still remember our last duty together. Most of us who were once associated with you and General Pace have prospered. We owe you our gratitude for then and look forward to the future. May I congratulate you on your fourth star. It is long overdue. And now, will you please introduce me to your aide."

Pete made the introductions, not knowing that the maid for their room was an agent for the South Korean CIA. General Kim was already aware of their relationship and considered it very positive. No real man would put his loved one in harm's way. This was a vote of confidence in the ability of the First Combined Field Army to defend Korea. They would make good on their nickname, "The Shield of Seoul."

BOOK 3

THE PLAN

Chapter Sixteen

The staff car pulled out into the traffic. Pete noticed that the normally chaotic traffic was somewhat quiet. He observed the Korean traffic police taking special measures to assure their prompt passage. Leave it to the Koreans, thought Pete, nobody is better at attention to detail than they when they want to make an impression. Pete remembered that during the last time he was in Korea, a North Korean delegation, under United Nation's auspices, was to come to South Korea for talks. Their route would be from Panmunjon to Seoul and they would arrive in two months. During that two months the South Koreans built a four-lane superhighway called Route 1 over thirty miles in length connecting the two cities. Every military compound along the route was fronted with a large fence that could not be seen over or through. On each fence was a sign identifying it as something else, such as an orphanage or hospital. Unfortunately the talks were unproductive.

They headed north out of Seoul on Route 33 – a four-lane divided superhighway in the center of the country. Pete recalled that on his first tour in Korea, Route 33 was a dirt road, and on his second it was a two-lane asphalt road. He was told that it petered out north of Uijongbu since there was no desire to give the enemy a good road network. General Kim pointed out something else. Every so often, running perpendicular to the highway, were fortified tank barriers as far as you could see. Where these barriers intersected the highway, the highway narrowed to two lanes, and directly over the two lanes appeared large structures. Kim explained that these structures were masses of reinforced concrete that could be dropped on the highway by explosive charges, thus completing the tank barrier.

Pete pointed out the large mountain right in the middle of the valley between Seoul and Uijongbu that dominated the terrain for miles around. This mountain was one of the most heavily fought over during the war because of its tactical importance and had changed hands over 10 times. It was now something of a vacation spot and people loved to come climb it. Pete had done so once himself with a group of Korean officers on a Saturday mandatory physical training test. Kim mentioned that at a certain stage in the alert system the mountain top would be occupied by South Korean Artillery observers.

140

They were approaching the outskirts of Uijongbu where it was apparent that the population and building density were less. Kim told them that this was intentional due to the proximity to the DMZ and artillery weapons. Kim also stated that, contrary to what you read in the paper, Seoul is not in standard artillery range. It is not really in the FROG missile range – a missile that the North Koreans have in quantity. It is, however, in SCUD missile range, the missile that Saddam used in the Persian Gulf war. Kim also mentioned that the staff had prepared a complete briefing on the subject of artillery and missile vulnerability and would include it in the General's incoming briefing schedule.

Kim then broached a delicate subject. "Sir," he said to Pete, "your aide, Major Parker, will be the only woman assigned to the staff. We want to make sure that she will be billeted properly and in accordance with your desires. All officers, Lieutenant Colonel and below, are presently billeted two to a hootch, which would not be appropriate in this case. We have taken the liberty of building a new hootch, separate from but adjoining your hootch, for the Major. It will have its own bath. I hope that this will be satisfactory."

"When did you start building?" Pete had to ask. "When did you know that my aide was a woman?"

Kim smiled, "Yesterday. I think you know that when we want to do something fast, we can. We are not as restricted as your Army in the various regulations pertaining to construction projects. The billet is ready for occupancy, although we still have some minor things to do, such as painting but at least Major Parker can choose her own colors. Do you recall the expansion of our par three golf course when you were here before? The previous Commanding General was a golf nut and wanted to expand it to a full size nine hole course and gave you the job. You found out quickly that U.S. Army regulations precluded you from doing so. You came to me. I went to the Deputy Commanding General, General Lee Duk Qwan, who is now the President, with the problem. He authorized the work which included acquisition of land, movement of the perimeter fence, and building the course. We finished it in two months, including growing the grass."

"Neatly done," thought Pete to himself. "Kim has reminded me how efficient the Koreans are but also that they don't forget a thing and will remind you of old debts when appropriate."

The staff car pulled up to the front gate of Camp Red Cloud, named after an American of Indian descent, who had won the Congressional Medal of Honor during the Korean war. The road to the parade ground was lined with Korean and American soldiers carrying the guidons of all the company-sized units in the Field Army. On the parade ground was an honor guard ready for his arrival. As was expected, the ceremony was flawless. Pete was asked to give a speech and gave essentially the same speech he gave at the meeting at ROK Army headquarters the previous day. Everyone then went to their billets to get cleaned up and change clothes. It was time to get into battledress. When they got to their billets, Pete noticed that Sandy's hootch was indeed adjacent to his and had a connecting door.

Kim informed Pete that lunch would be at 1200 and that no further activities were scheduled for the morning. He did ask where Pete wanted Major Parker to sit in the CG mess. Pete responded that she should sit with the rest of the aides and majors. Anywhere else would be inappropriate, at least for now. Pete had really not thought things through about how to handle his and Sandy's relationship at Red Cloud. Things had moved too fast. But then an idea struck him. He would have to discuss it with Sandy.

Pete was met at the door by his houseboy, who turned out to be Mr. Chan – the same who had been his houseboy twenty years ago when he was Chief of Staff here.

"Good morning, General," said Chan. "I am delighted to be able to serve you once again. Welcome back to Korea. When we heard that you were coming there was great joy since we all remember what you did here before. I will be your houseboy. Major Parker will have a housegirl who happens to be my daughter. I have trained her well and I assure you that she will be most satisfactory. Please let me know if she is not. In Korean families we can correct these sort of things quite quickly. I congratulate you on your recent promotion to four star general. I assumed that the battledress you brought with you does not have four stars or the First Field Army shoulder patch. I have taken the liberty of having a battlejacket made up for you with the proper insignia so that you can wear it immediately. While you are gone today I will do the same with the rest of your clothes. Before you ask, we have done the same thing for Major Parker. My daughter is with her now. I am very proud of my daughter. She is presently a pre-med student but given the present circumstances, I felt her place was here. As a good Korean daughter she, of course, accepted my decision. While you are changing your clothes please let me have your combat boots. Americans have never shined them properly. I would be ashamed if my general was not the best dressed officer in the headquarters."

Pete was surprised and pleased at this turn of events.

Pete knocked on Sandy's door and asked if she was "decent." Sandy told him to come in and then introduced him to My Li, her housegirl. Pete asked if everything was OK and if she needed anything. Sandy said no and My Li just giggled, covering her mouth with her hand as most Korean women customarily do. Laughing is all right as long as you cover your mouth. It is actually an endearing gesture. It was obvious he was intruding, so Pete returned to his hootch. He was very grateful for Chan's arranging for Sandy to have an intelligent Korean woman to talk to and ask questions.

At 1200, Pete and Sandy walked over to the mess. Pete told Sandy that, at least for now, she should do her aide act and she was not to be a part of a reception line. Pete suggested she find the other aides and introduce herself, blend into the background and give the officers of the headquarters time to accept her on her own terms. Sandy understood and had no problems with Pete's guidance, although she did say that Pete would pay for this later that night.

General Kim met them at the door and, sure enough, the officers of the headquarters were lined up by rank to meet him. The first officer in line was a U.S. Brigadier General who was the Chief of Staff. He did not appear happy.

General Kim introduced Pete down the line. The Chief of Staff told Pete that he needed to speak to him as soon as possible, suggested 1700, and Pete agreed. The remaining introductions were perfunctory. Pete observed that he did not know any of the officers other than General Kim and that the size and composition of the headquarters were the same as he remembered them. The G3 and the G2 were Koreans, the G1 and the G4 were Americans and all were Colonels. The new twist was that there was an Army artillery officer who was a Korean Brigadier General. Pete would need to know more about that. After the reception they sat down to lunch. Pete knew enough to set the tone. The officers sat at a number of round tables, eight to a table. Pete's was the head table with himself, the three other generals, and the G staff. Pete told them a little about himself and pointed out his old seat of twenty years ago, then asked each of them in turn to tell him something about themselves.

Pete noticed that the waitresses were still some of the loveliest Korean women he had seen. He concluded that the old practice of senior American officers who left Korea was still being done. One waitress showed extreme interest in Sandy. Most Korean women had never seen a woman army officer before, much less a beautiful one, and could not take their eyes off of her red hair. As was usually the custom of the mess, no business was transacted during lunch, and Pete intended to keep it that way. Everyone needs a time and place to relax.

After lunch, General Kim suggested that they go to the briefing room and get started. He noticed that Sandy was surrounded by the other American and Korean aides. Whether this was friendliness, or something else, remained to be seen.

Although Pete noticed immediately the same old briefing room, the briefing aids were now state-of-the-art computer systems with computer-assisted graphics. He wondered what would happen in the time of a complete loss of power. He decided he would have the power turned off in a couple of weeks to see if it is possible to become too dependent on computers. After all, in a real combat situation, the loss of power is common. He recalled that once, years ago during a training test of his artillery battalion at Fort Hood, the evaluator pulled the plug on his Field Artillery firing data computer. Fortunately, he had trained his Fire Direction Center in the use of the old manual firing tables and graphs and passed while some other battalions did not.

The briefing started as usual with the G-2, who gave them the assessment of the weather, the terrain, and the enemy. It was quite similar to the briefing that Pete had received the previous day in Seoul. The numbers, locations, and combat readiness evaluations were the same. The key was that while the enemy had the capability to attack, in spite of all the rhetoric, no overt signs of them preparing to do so had been observed. Their capabilities were known, but not their intentions.

The briefing by the G3 followed. As before, it was quite similar to that of ROK headquarters. The G3 gave the status of friendly forces, their locations, and their plans. He concluded that, given the nature of the threat and the nature of friendly forces, the First Combined Field Army could successfully limit the depth of the North Korean penetration to north of Uijongbu and, if the U.S. support came in as promised, within a month be ready to go over to a counteroffensive. He then mentioned the shortfalls that worried them. The first was strategic and tactical warning. You could not keep your troops in a state of full readiness for extended periods of time. They lose their edge, and the equipment starts to deteriorate. Pete asked what the predicted warning time was and what the most desirable time was for completion. The G3 responded that they hoped for 12 hours, but 24 would be welcomed.

Pete had an idea, but kept it to himself because it would require a commitment not presently in U.S. support plans. He had used this plan in the Persian Gulf War to great success and was surprised that it had not received much publicity. The G3 also mentioned that the defense was contingent upon the release from U.S. supply dumps of most of the precision guided munitions. They were in the country but not in the hands of actual field commanders. Pete knew that this was a question for General Armstrong and would ask it as soon as he could. The G3 then concluded his part of the brief.

The Army Artillery Officer commenced his briefing by stating the unusual nature of the assignment. He had been assigned for less than a week, in response to analyses appearing in the U.S. media about the North Korean artillery and missile threat. ROK headquarters wanted to know the true situation. The Korean Brigadier General seemed upset, not out of nervousness, but of anger. The professionalism of the artillery had been questioned and he took it personally, as did Pete, who was a "Red Leg" himself (slang term for artillerymen the world over).

"Sir," said the general, "to start with, I completely disagree with the analyses that are being published in your media. The only thing that they have right is that the North Koreans have 10,000 artillery pieces and missile launchers and we have 5,000. What is more important is the condition of the weapons, the accuracy of the weapons, the amount of available ammunition, the lethality of the ammunition, and, most importantly, command and control and target acquisition capability. In each of these areas our artillery is superior to theirs. I am very upset that your media gives the impression that the North Koreans have zeroed in on and can destroy Seoul. That is simply not true. In their present locations, no North Korean artillery can reach Seoul, though their 170 millimeter gun, which they have very few of, might just reach the outskirts. The same is true of their FROG ground-to-ground missile acquired from the Soviets. In all candor this is an old, worn out piece of junk that presents more danger to the firing crew than anyone else. Their SCUDs are another matter, although the North Koreans have fewer than the Iraqis had, and we now have the Patriot system for defending against them thanks to the U.S. In sum, the North Koreans present only a moderate threat to Seoul from their present locations, and if they should attack their artillery will be needed for the land battle, not civilian terrorism. One last thing. We need more counterbattery radar. With it we can locate their positions after they fire once or twice. I hope you can assist us in this. I promise you one thing. Our artillery will not abandon their guns. They will fight and, if necessary, die by their guns."

Next in order was the G1, who explained that the forces of the Field Army were at 100% strength and in some cases, such as infantry units, which take the highest casualties, above that. He also mentioned that the Republic of Korea had gone to wartime alert and all reserves had been called to active duty, which meant all able bodied men below the age of 50. Most of the reserves were in combat support roles away from the zone of the Field Army, thus releasing younger men for front line service. All in all, the personnel situation was excellent.

The G4 was last. His brief, for the most part, was also upbeat. They had all the needed logistics of war, with some exceptions. Fuel oil and gasoline were good. Ammunition was good, with the exception of precision guided munitions mentioned by the G3. And Korea had plenty of food. He caveated his brief with the notation that he was talking about the initial parts of a war. In about thirty days, they would become dependent upon the supply lines from the U.S. contained in agreed upon operations plans and wanted confidence that this would occur. Without confidence, they would ration war items from the beginning, which would put the outcome in doubt. Fortunately, the items that were most critical could be flown in since they were relatively low tonnage.

Pete got the message that the South Koreans would fight and were confident that they would prevail without huge devastation to their country as long as the United States did what they had agreed to do. He detected a feeling that he had experienced in the 11th Corps prior to the Persian Gulf War. These folks had been preparing for war for over 40 years and wanted to show off. They were actually spoiling for a fight. Great.

When the briefing was over. Pete thought it appropriate to make some concluding remarks. He repeated himself from the morning honor ceremony. "I will have no part of appeasement or the abandonment of the Republic of Korea. I have heard you clearly and will get to work on your suggestions immediately because I agree with you. But remember, I have only been here less than six hours. Please give me a little time. Chief, I want to start visiting the units in the field tomorrow. Please leave the U.S. Second Infantry Division until last. I would appreciate a schedule by this evening. This was a great briefing. Any questions?" Nobody had questions, so Pete dismissed everyone.

Pete and Sandy returned to his office. The Chief of Staff was waiting for him. "Sir," said the Chief, "there is nothing in the day's paperwork that is urgent enough for your attention. I can handle it if you would like."

Pete took the chance and said, "OK Chief, that is fine with me. Please let me know about those things you think I need to see. Are we ready to meet now as you requested, or do you need a little more time?"

The Chief said he needed about fifteen minutes to get rid of the daily minutia and then would be right in.

A few minutes later, Brigadier General Thomas Alexander, U.S. Army, Chief of Staff of the First Combined Field Army, knocked on Pete's door and was told to go right in by Sandy who remained outside. Pete had told her that this was to be a very private conversation. Pete was sitting behind his desk and directed General Alexander to take a seat in front of the desk. Pete wanted to know what was bothering Alexander before getting friendly.

General Alexander took his seat and thanked Pete for seeing him on such short notice.

"What's on your mind?" asked Pete.

"Sir," said Alexander, "I think you should know the whole story about what has been going on around here. The implication in the media is that the previous commander and I were a couple of stumblebums and a significant part of the problem. Several months ago, word came out that the North

Koreans may have developed nuclear weapons. We received a very complete analysis from American intelligence sources on this development. The thought, even then, was that it was a probability. We received, at the time, very specific orders from Washington to make no comments on the issue, positive or negative. We were then asked for our estimate of what would happen if the North Koreans attacked. Our response was essentially what you heard today during your incoming briefing – mostly positive. We were then told that we would make no public pronouncements and refer any inquiries to Washington. In essence, Washington, for whatever their reasons, did not want the world to know our position.

"Your predecessor was a good man who had never been in Korea before this tour of duty. I don't believe that he ever completely understood the Koreans or was fully accepted by them. His timing was also very bad. His tour in Korea was about to end, but in anticipation of what might happen, he had requested an extension to see it through. This happened at the same time there was a change of administration in Washington. The new President seemed to want to show that things were going to be different and the most public way of doing this was to relieve personnel on the spot.

"But that is history," said Alexander. "My point is that you are not changing the position of this Field Army now but rather will be able to tell the truth. That is good and I want you to know that you have my full support. But one thing really bothers me. Why would the previous administration want to paint the picture that the North Koreans would be very successful if they attacked? That makes no sense to me at all."

This same question had been bothering Pete and he was just now starting to figure it out. "General, what I am about to give you is my personal opinion. I have discussed it with no one else. No one. Would it not be the case that a doom and gloom assessment could be used as rationale for either a preemptive attack or a surrender of sorts? I believe that one of our jobs is to assure that no such rationale exists for either the hawks or the doves. I would appreciate your thoughts on that."

General Alexander asked if he could have some time to think that one over. It was a more Machiavellian idea than he was used to.

"I know that soldiers are not trained to think that way," Pete told him. "That reminds me of an old aphorism that was attributed to Clausewitz. 'The soldier who fears the enemy's general staff is a coward. The soldier who fears his own general staff is a wise old warrior.' Let's talk about our relationship. I expect you to run the headquarters and bring only those administrative matters to me that I must see. Twenty years ago I was sitting in your seat and one of the country's best generals was sitting in this one. The first night I brought him a stack of staff actions, he looked me in the eye and asked me if they were accurate. When I said they were, he signed them without reading them. That makes the Chief's work a lot harder. I won't go quite that far, but I will place my trust in you until you prove I shouldn't. And now, I have some work to do. I hope to see you at dinner tonight."

"Of course," said General Alexander, realizing that he was going to have to change his plans. He had scheduled a nice private dinner with his Korean girlfriend and she would not be happy. Korean women, when unhappy, have a habit of taking their boyfriend's belongings out into the street and burning them, much to the amusement of all the neighbors.

As soon as Alexander had left, Pete put in for a secure voice phone call to Ambassador Noonan. It took a couple of minutes to set up since the codes had to be entered and authenticated. Years ago, a secure phone call was possible but very hard to understand. You sounded as if you were in a cave by a waterfall. Now it was pretty close to being normal.

"Noonan here, is that you, Pete?"

"Roger that, Noonie. I have had a pretty good day and have some thoughts I would like to share with you. Certain things are starting to get clearer. Although I haven't made my field inspections yet, I find a remarkable consensus everywhere I go. We can beat a North Korean attack as long as U.S. support is forthcoming. The interesting part is that this is not a new assessment. This assessment was being suppressed by the previous administration in Washington. The previous administration was characterized by indecision and the former President was being advised by two separate groups: the hawks, who were advocating preemptive strikes on North Korea; and the doves, who were advocating concessions and, basically, surrender. What they had in common was that a negative prediction of the outcome of a North Korean attack were supported by both of their positions. The message that you sent the President the night before last was the right one. Have you been able to make that statement yet?"

Noonie replied that he was scheduled for a press conference at 9:00 AM tomorrow. He also stated that he had received a personal, private message from the President thanking him, and Pete, for the suggestion. Among other things, it had helped the President identify those disloyal carryovers in the administration.

"Noonie," Pete continued, "there are several items of essential equipment that don't appear in our present plans. One is counterbattery radar. This device picks up an artillery round as soon as it is fired, calculates where it came from, then directs friendly artillery fire on the firing gun even before the round hits the target. It is very advanced technology, but requires a lot of training and coordination. Another is the Air Force AWACS system, which is an airborne command and control system. It is the key to fighting and winning an air battle. Still another is called JSTARS, which stands for Joint Surveillance and Target Attack Radar System. The Army developed this system just in time for the Persian Gulf War. It is a converted Boeing 707 outfitted with computers, downlooking radar and infrared sensors. It has a "real" time down link to the command centers on the ground and takes a picture of what is going on. One JSTAR flying south of the DMZ could see approximately 100 miles into North Korea. It would greatly enhance warning in that as soon as the North Koreans started the engines on their tanks we would know it. I don't have the precise numbers that we would need right now, but agreement in principle would speed up the process. You can tell whomever you speak to that I consider all this technology essential and the need immediate."

Noonie said that he would get right to work on it and that he would bring General Armstrong into the loop. At Pete's suggestion, Noonie had called upon General Armstrong and felt that they now had another ally.

After his phone call to Noonie, Pete went to the door of his office and told everyone that he was through for the day unless anyone had anything so important that it could not wait. Of course, there was nothing that fell in that category. These were smart people who recognized an order when they heard it. After the others had left, Sandy showed Pete something she had found. Directly behind Sandy's desk was a picture that, when removed, revealed a peephole into Pete's office. Pete now understood how the coffee appeared magically some twenty years ago. Sandy also showed him some buttons concealed under the overhang of Pete's desk. The red button meant "Please interrupt me and stop this appointment. Use any excuse," and the green button meant "I do not want to be disturbed unless it is really important." The yellow button meant "catch my secret hand signal."

Pete told Sandy that dinner in the CG mess was at 1900 hours and cocktails were at 1830. It would be better if they did not go together. Pete said that he would go at 1830 and that Sandy should arrive about ten minutes later. Pete wanted to observe the effect of Sandy's entrance. Pete also told her that the dress would be casual and asked what she was planning to wear. Sandy told him it was none of his business. While they were in San Francisco, Sandy had secretly gone back to California Dreamers, Ltd. and bought the perfect outfit. He would see it for the first time along with everyone else. And then she told Pete that she had to go to her hootch and do girl things. If she needed any help My Li could take care of it. Pete feigned annoyance but Sandy saw through it in a flash and gave him a quick kiss.

Pete had time to take a nice hot shower and as he did, noticed the same smell of 40 and 20 years ago. Ironically, he found that comforting. After the shower, Pete noticed that Chan had laid out his choice of the appropriate dress for the evening meal. It was the outfit that he had bought in San Francisco. Pete mused that in a day or two Chan would suggest a visit by the Uijongbu tailor who would probably be a relative of Smiley, the old bartender. Pete wondered what had happened to Smiley and decided to ask Chan.

Pete arrived at the mess on time and went to the bar to order a vodka on the rocks. He was met by an Army Warrant Officer. On occasion the Army does something smart. Commissioned club officers never worked out since they felt that club duty was detrimental to their career. So the Army established a Warrant Officer club career program, to which enlisted mess stewards could apply. For them it was upward social and career mobility. The only problem was keeping them in the Army. The civilian food service industry recognized their value and offered them more money than the Army ever could. The Army Warrant Officer informed Pete that they didn't use cash in the club. All expenses would be recorded and an end of the month bill would be presented. You didn't have to sign anything, it was done for you. The gratuity was included. Several officers sidled up to Pete and made brief polite conversation but, according to the rules, business was not to be discussed unless initiated by Pete, and tonight he had no intention of doing so.

When Sandy walked in, the room temporarily quieted down. She was wearing a brushed denim shirt and skirt that tastefully showed off her great figure and legs. She had taken down her long red hair to its full length and was wearing just the right amount of makeup. Pete enjoyed watching several of the junior officers in the mess rush over buy her a drink. Only a few of the more observant senior officers in the room saw the wink passed between Pete and Sandy.

Dinner that night was subdued as everyone tried to figure out Pete. What discussion topics did he like what topics displeased him? Pete decided to break the ice and spent most of the time describing his first tour of duty in Korea. He made a point of talking about Ambassador Noonan. Knowing that Pete was the personal friend of the U.S. ambassador was always worth a few credibility points.

As he was talking, Pete noticed that the aide's table, which was usually considered Siberia and a place to be avoided, had suddenly gained a new popularity. Officers were vying to be seated there. The club officer had seated himself there for a change.

Chapter Seventeen

At the same time the officers of the First Combined Field Army sat down to dinner at the CG's mess in Uijongbu, Major General Li Joon Duk, Chief of the Democratic Peoples Republic of Korea's Security Services, was alone at his desk in Pyongyang, capital of the DPRK. Li was worried. He had followed the events of the last several months, and especially the last several weeks, and saw potential disaster in the offing. Sung Tae Won, the new President of North Korea, was becoming more and more irrational. It had been his personal decision to withdraw from the treaty that had been signed years earlier with the United Nations International Atomic Energy Agency, even though Dr. Chan So Dung, the DPRK Chief Scientist, had told him it was unnecessary. Chan had told Sung that the Plutonium had been hidden so well that the inspectors would not find it. The development of nuclear weapons could continue as the North Koreans appeared to cooperate. But Sung had ruled otherwise. He took great pleasure in rubbing the noses of the United Nations and United States in the situation. He was convinced that they would do nothing meaningful about it and that the sanctions would have little effect because of the hypocrisy of Japan and China. According to Sung, the plans of the Great Leader, Kim Il Sung, were going perfectly. In a very short time, the United States would be humbled, the running dogs of the puppet government of South Korea would be neutralized, and the DPRK would be recognized as a power to be reckoned with on the international stage. Sung was prepared to continue development of nuclear weapons and use them in conjunction with an attack on South Korea if the world did not meet his demands.

Li was sure that the world, led by the United States would not meet North Korean demands. He was also sure that, if war came, it would result in the defeat and destruction of North Korea in spite of what the U.S. media was saying. That part of the situation puzzled Li. Why would the U.S. media claim that North Korea would prevail when it simply wasn't true? Li needed better intelligence on that question and decided to task his agents in the United States and South Korea to see what they could find out.

Li also reflected on some recent conversations he had with Chan, the Chief Scientist, and General Yi Bong Su, the Commander of the DPRK

Armed Forces. He never met with these two people at the same time, but rather met with them one on one. This way he kept plausible deniability if he were accused by one or the other. He suspected that Chan and Yi were also meeting one on one. Li could tell that they also were worried, but no one was yet ready to openly share their feelings, much less discuss what to do. Chan had made the first overture in a very clever way by stating how wonderful it was to have a leader like Sung Tae Won who could see the future more clearly than an ordinary person, such as himself. Li interpreted this remark as an ironic way of saying he disagreed with Sung. That took courage.

At a recent meeting with Sung, Li, Chan, and Yi had made a suggestion to the effect that there might be a better, less risky, way that would meet all of the Great Leader's objectives. The suggestion was to wait a few years until a number of nuclear weapons are stocked up, and furnish some of them to Libya and Iraq, or possibly Iran, depending on who offered the better deal. In the interim, North Korea would cooperate and pledge not to attack South Korea, perhaps recognize South Korea and allow such things as family visits. The rationale that, in a few years, the North Korean position would be secure and virtually unassailable. The only risk was that the United States might get worldwide agreement to create meaningful sanctions or possibly launch a preemptive strike on the DPRK's nuclear facilities. But this would be virtually impossible if North Korea appeared cooperative.

Sung became very angry and dismissed the suggestion out of hand. Using the ultimate argument in North Korea, he said, "That is not in accordance with the wishes of the Great Leader, who's never wrong. This is the best time."

Li, Chan, and Yi figured out independently that Sung's position of leadership was not as secure as everyone believed and that in order to obtain it he may have made certain promises of loyalty at Kim Il Sung's death bed. Another thought crossed Li's mind. If North Korea waits a few years, the overall situation will get even worse and North Korea will still be destroyed. The only difference will be the damage to the rest of the world. Maybe someone like Sung found satisfaction in world destruction. Li did not. He was not that much of a zealot. Maybe, just maybe, all things considered, getting it over with now instead of later might be better.

Li decided to abandon this train of thought and get on with the day's ordinary but necessary business. The most enjoyable part of his business was reading the intelligence reports from the world. Even with the collapse of the Soviet Union and the Warsaw Pact Li still had reliable sources the world over. As was his custom he demanded the raw reports. He intentionally did not allow for others to summarize the data for him. This took more of his time but he considered it time well spent. Quite often the best intelligence is what you get from reading between the lines. The lack of intelligence when there should be some in a certain area is often a very good indicator that something is going on and is being concealed. Li enjoyed the game.

One of the items that caught his attention came from an agent in Seoul, of which Li had many. It announced the arrival of General Peter Goodwin, who was to take over command of the First Combined Field Army. This confirmed an earlier report that he had received from one of his agents in Germany. The agent's code name was Nimbus, but Li knew that her real name was Brigitte and that she worked in the U.S. Army headquarters in Frankfurt. Her information on the Persian Gulf War had been very valuable since it convinced North Korea to not openly support Saddam Hussein. You don't support a loser. Li knew General Goodwin very well although Goodwin did not know this. Maybe Li could turn this to his advantage. He would have to think about it.

That night, General Li could not sleep. There were so many things on his mind. He had been a dedicated supporter of the DPRK all of his life and had risked his life many times. When he thought about it, the fact that he was still alive was good luck. What's more, he had raised a great family and had gotten them out of harm's way in the present situation. That would not be true if this insanity continued much longer. He had to do something but he didn't know what. And then a wild thought struck him. When it first occurred he immediately rejected it, but as he tried to think things through, it kept returning. He knew better than to put any of his thoughts on paper. That would probably mean instant death for him, although maybe not his family since they were in Australia. Li was very proud that he had been able to arrange that and had convinced his superiors that it was a good cover and deception plan. After many years as a deep cover agent in South Korea Li had been called back to North Korea. During his years in South Korea, as part of his cover, Li had raised a family and amassed a considerable fortune. It was quite easy to do. In the early days of South Korea, venture capital was hard to come by. Whenever Li needed some for his various enterprises, it was always forthcoming from North Korea. He was always very careful to assure that the North Koreans made a profit. Of course he kept some for himself. When the time came, Li convinced his superiors that part of the cover plan should be his emigration to Australia. This was easily arranged. Li continued to correspond with his old associates in South Korea by the simple device of having his mail delivered to Australia and then forwarded to him in the diplomatic pouch. He answered by the reverse route.

The more Li thought about it the more feasible the plan appeared. It just might work and would save what Li had strived for all his life, which was now different from what Sung was advocating. Li did not agree that the destruction of South Korea, while a laudable goal, was worth the destruction of North Korea. The price was much too high.

If his plan was to work, it would require the support of Chan, the Chief Scientist, Yi, the Commander of DPRK forces, and of Peter Goodwin, Commander of the First Combined Field Army. It was as high risk as possible, but Li simply could not think of a better alternative no matter how hard he tried. He would first have to approach Chan and Yi, and he recognized the danger in doing that. It probably wouldn't work, but he had to try. He concluded that the personal risk was higher if he did nothing. Therefore, he would do it.

The next morning Li invited Chan and Yi in for a meeting. He did it in his office totally in the open except for the subject matter. They spent several hours discussing the implementation status of Sung's instructions to them. The needed a reason for the meeting and it was certain that the agenda and minutes of the meeting would be scrutinized. Then near the end of the regular meeting, Li outlined his plan to them. After a brief hesitation, Chan agreed. Shortly thereafter, so did Yi. They both recognized that they had placed their fates in one another's hands. This was not altruism. It was a cold evaluation that it was the least risky path. Doing nothing assured dire personal fates, since when Sung's plan failed, as it surely would, they would be the scapegoats with the predictable consequences. Li's plan had a chance. Sung's was doomed to failure. The choice was really not all that difficult.

Two mornings later Li received his normal media summary from the night before. This was a standard practice throughout most governments. In the U.S. Pentagon they called it the 'Xerox News'. People got up early in the morning and clipped from the world news sources the articles they believed the decision makers would need to see. In North Korea there was one difference: most lower level personnel got a censored version. Only a select few got what was really being said and written. Li was one of the latter, especially since it was his department that published the document.

The lead article was from the *Washington Post* quoting Ambassador Noonan's press conference of the day before. It stated that Noonan and the newly arrived commander of the First Combined Field Army, General Peter Goodwin, agreed that the South Korean Armed Forces, together with the planned U.S. support, could successfully defend South Korea with only moderate casualties and temporary loss of ground – and in a short period of time should be able to go over to a counteroffensive if the political leaders in both countries so directed. In response to the question why this was a different analysis than had been coming out of Washington, Noonan coolly replied that this was the first analysis that had come from people who were in a position to really examine the situation. Any difference would have to be explained in Washington. He and Goodwin stood by their statement.

Li made a point of instructing his administrative assistant that he wanted to see any response the Washington media made to the statement immediately. Something very significant was happening here. They appeared to be calling Sung's bluff. This did not displease Li at all. It fit in very nicely with the outline plan he had discussed with Chan and Yi. He knew that Sung would soon ask for his opinion. His answer would be that the U.S. is getting desperate and had lost its senses. He would congratulate Sung on being right and do his best to further his megalomania. Li decided that he had to find a way to meet with General Goodwin, regardless of the risks. Fortunately he still had a large number of agents in South Korea, including a few at Camp Red Cloud in Uijongbu. For the first time in weeks, Li felt that there may be a way out of this mess. Little did he know that Pete Goodwin was thinking exactly the same thing at the same time.

Chapter Eighteen

The week since his arrival in Uijongbu had gone by rapidly for Pete. As scheduled, he had visited every unit of the Field Army and talked to the commanders and men. He had gone to virtually every outpost and front line location. With very few exceptions, he had agreed with the tactical deployments and the defensive positions. More importantly, he had judged the fighting spirit of the troops and commanders. They were ready, motivated, confident, and spoiling for a fight. On the other hand, certain negatives were universally expressed. One was that, although they had sufficient supplies to sustain an effective defense they lacked assurance that necessary resupply would be forthcoming. Another was that so much had been said about the North Korean artillery capability, that while the troops felt they could survive, they were worried about that families and the civilian population might not. Still another was that they simply did not know when the North Koreans would attack. Commanders knew that you can sustain a top level of readiness for only so long. It was the old cry wolf tactic. If you keep raising your enemy's concerns up to a high pitch and then back off, sooner or later the reaction becomes less enthusiastic. The U.S. had found this out the hard way at Pearl Harbor, as did the French in World War II.

Pete was addressing these issues. He had received the shortfalls list from General Lee Chi Na, the ROK Chairman, according to previous agreement. The list was remarkably similar to his own list, as well it should have been. He had arranged a meeting with Ambassador Noonan and General Armstrong, the CINC, to discuss the list. Together they had sent a message to the President and the Secretary of Defense requesting the needed equipment and commitment. This did not come as a surprise to the President, since Noonie kept the President informed by secure voice telephone calls almost every night. The commitment had been made and the equipment began to arrive. Pete knew that timing was critical. It would take several weeks to integrate the new equipment into the force and to train all personnel on its use. One of the reasons for the time criticality was that they were getting into deep winter and the Imjin Gang was starting to freeze over solid. As Pete had determined many years earlier, this was the most probable time for a North Korean attack.

The first items to arrive were the AWACS and JSTARS aircraft. This was because they were capable of flying the Pacific with refueling. It had been decided to base them at Kadena Air Base in Okinawa. The flying time across the Sea of Japan was less than an hour and it was possible to secure the planes against possible local guerrilla attack. The Japanese were not happy about this but agreed when they were told that these were not actual weapons but rather command and control means. This was sophistry, of course, but it gave the Japanese a political crutch. The counterbattery radars also began to arrive. The U.S. Army and Air Force sent ground detachments with the planes to make the necessary interfaces with the Korean and American troops. To start with, the U.S. detachments would operate the equipment, then turn it over when the local ground forces were properly trained. Pete was really looking forward to this.

These technologies were truly "force multipliers" – a term that had recently come in vogue. A force multiplier allows much more effective use of available means. The key to all three of these technologies is that you know where the enemy is and what he is doing and have a more rapid and accurate command and control method for directing your own forces. For example, in the old days, counterbattery fire was very time consuming and not very accurate. With the new technology, when the enemy fires an artillery round at you, he can expect accurate and deadly return fire on his positions while his round is still in the air. This is most discouraging. For years, artillerymen had felt that they were relatively invulnerable unless they were physically overrun on the ground. With the new technology, this was no longer true. They were now prime targets.

Pete knew that he had no one on the staff of his command who had the expertise to oversee the integration of these new technologies into the force. He had requested that the Pentagon send over an officer who had this expertise and who spoke Hangul, with the rank of at least Colonel. Wonder of all wonders, such an officer existed and was on the way.

By mutual agreement the coordination of the air battle, and therefore the use of the AWACS, would be directed at United States Forces in Korea headquarters located in Seoul, the field operating agency being located at Osan Air Base just South of Seoul. This was proper and in accordance with agreed doctrine. On the other hand, the land battle would be run by the First Combined Field Army at Uijongbu, and therefore the JSTARS and counterbattery radars would be coordinated and directed from there.

The infighting and the backbiting from Washington had abated. One of the advantages of the modern world was that almost everyone watched CNN news. Pete had noticed that the 'talking heads' who advocated preemptive strikes or surrender were suddenly nowhere to be seen. World opinion seemed to be shifting, although the predictable accusations of U.S. warmongering were being made by those who did not like the United States. Saddam and Khadafi were the most outspoken. Pete considered this a compliment.

Amidst these development a quite different but equally important matter was also on Pete's mind. One evening after dinner he broached the subject to Sandy. He suggested that he ask the Field Army Chaplain to come see him the following day at 5:00 PM after he had returned from his daily round of field inspections. Sandy agreed enthusiastically.

The following afternoon, shortly after Pete had returned to his office, in walked Chaplain, Lieutenant Colonel, U.S. Army, Francis Xavier Murphy. Pete offered Chaplain Murphy a seat and asked him if he would like a drink.

Father Murphy replied. "General, I would very much like to share a drink with you. That is one of the advantages of being a Priest in the Holy Roman Catholic Church, as opposed to being a Baptist. We see nothing wrong with drinking alcohol as long as it is done in moderation. Would you happen to have a wee bit of scotch? That is one of the many things that I admire about the Presbyterians who invented Scotch. Except for a small problem with Henry VIII, we Catholics and the Presbyterians would still be one church."

Pete answered. "How about a little Glenfiddich? That is my favorite scotch and I will join you. How would you like it?"

Murphy replied that he would like it neat, the way the Scots drink it. A Scot had once told him that unless you can cut it with the cool water of a highland spring, that was the only way. Pete took his with ice and water.

After they had relaxed and made small talk for awhile, Pete got to the point. "Padre, I would like for you to perform a marriage. It will not be a Catholic marriage, but rather a Protestant one. Can you do that?" Pete used the term Padre since he had never been able to say Father to someone younger than himself.

Murphy chuckled and responded. "General, that is one of the things I like about being an Army chaplain. Other than giving the Catholic sacraments to non-Catholics, I can do just about anything. We have very liberal dispensations from the Mother Church. I am famous for my Bar Mitzvahs. Who do you want me to marry?"

"Me and my aide, Major Alexandra Parker," replied Pete. That was the first and only time that Pete would see Murphy at a loss for words. "Until we get this set up, can you keep it a secret?"

Murphy regained his composure, and after taking a gulp of his scotch responded. "Sir, I am a Jesuit. Secrecy is our business when we are not saving souls. As you are aware, in order to perform a marriage between two Americans in Korea, I need the written permission of the embassy in Seoul.

This normally takes several weeks."

Pete had already spoken to Noonie, who had agreed to make sure the paperwork would be accomplished by noon the next day. Noonie had also agreed to be the best man and Jo Ann agreed to be the matron of honor.

Pete assured Murphy that the paperwork would be in his hands by noon the next day and that he be ready to perform the ceremony in the CG mess at 5:00 PM. He did not want to have the ceremony performed in the local Army Chapel because the audience would be mostly Koreans, some of whom felt uncomfortable in a Christian Church.

Murphy said. "No sweat. But I do have one obligation. I need to talk to the two of you privately to assure myself that this is according to God's purpose. I hope you understand."

Pete completely understood and called in Sandy, who had been waiting anxiously in the next room. Murphy talked to them for about an hour and assured himself that they were indeed in love and that there were no legal or moral reasons why they should not be married. The fact that Sandy had been divorced was not a problem, since Murphy would not perform a Catholic ceremony but rather an ecumenical one.

Murphy finished by asking Pete and Sandy if they would join him in a short prayer. Neither Pete nor Sandy were ardent church goers but this just seemed right. Murphy's words were exactly right. Murphy then asked what he should wear and Pete asked him if he would object to battledress. Murphy thought for a moment and said that that would be appropriate and save him the question of wearing traditional Catholic vestments.

After dinner that night Pete asked General Alexander if he would have all of the officers of the headquarters assembled in the CG mess at 5:00 PM tomorrow. He had something very important to say. Alexander asked him what it was and Pete told him he would have to wait. Pete knew that you normally shared your secrets with your Chief of Staff, but in this case Alexander would have to trust him. When he found out what it was he would completely understand. That night after dinner Pete and Sandy talked for a long while and assured themselves that this was right. Pete said that he was going to wear battledress and asked Sandy what she was going to wear. Sandy had already thought about this and had made arrangements. She told Pete that it was wrong for the bridegroom to know this sort of thing in advance but that he would be proud of her. Pete knew he would.

The next day Pete went through the motions of his job, but the officers of the headquarters could not help but notice that the General was somewhat distracted. They were further puzzled when the Ambassador from the United States to South Korea arrived unexpectedly with his wife at 4:00 PM. They figured that it had something to do with the scheduled meeting and wondered what it was all about.

At precisely 5:00 PM Pete addressed the gathered officers and introduced Chaplain Murphy. Murphy gave a short homily on marriage and asked Pete to please come forward. Pete was joined by Ambassador Noonan. This got a real reaction from the assemblage, but nothing compared to what happened next. Murphy then asked Alexandra Parker to please come forward. Sandy emerged from the adjoining game room where she had been waiting. She was accompanied by Jo Ann, her matron of honor, and My Li, her attendant. She was dressed in a beautiful multicolored Han Bok, the traditional dress of celebration and marriage in Korea. It was not white since that is the color of mourning in Korea. She was beautiful and Pete noticed that even the most battle hardened of the group were misty-eyed. As he gazed around the room he could see a certain look of chagrin on the faces of some of the junior officers. He also noticed that in the back of the room stood all the waitresses of the mess dressed in their own Han Boks. This could only mean that someone had told them about the marriage ceremony, but that was OK considering the circumstances. It was probably Chan or My Li. They were crying their eyes out both because of happiness and also of their own situations. Murphy performed a short but appropriate and very beautiful ceremony. Pete then asked if he could address the audience.

"Ladies and Gentlemen," said Pete. "Thank you for honoring me and my new wife, Sandy, by being here for our marriage. I am a very happy man. I think that I have found the perfect wife. You might be aware that under U.S. Army regulations I could send my wife back to the United States. I am not going to do so, for two reasons. The first is simply that I need her. She is the best aide that I have ever had. The second is that I see no danger for her. I know how good you are and I know how good the troops under our command are and I have complete confidence that we will accomplish out mission and quickly defeat and repel the North Koreans if they are dumb enough to attack. I don't know that I can give you a better gesture of my confidence than keeping my wife at my side. I expect that some of you will see some awkwardness in the situation. I do not. Think about the relationship of any general's aide to the general. When the aide tells you something, you assume that it comes from the general. When you tell the aide something you assume the aide will tell it to the general. Nothing has changed. We have agreed that my wife will continue to sit at the aide's table at meals. She will continue to do the same duties as she is doing now. If I become displeased with her performance, that is my problem, not yours.

"Now it is time for a little celebration. I invite all of you to join us for champagne, and I mean every one in the room, including those of you in the back. This is a special occasion. Ambassador Noonan and his wife have done us the honor of joining us. Please introduce yourselves to them. As some of you may know, the Ambassador and I shared a tent in the middle of the Korean winter not far from here many years ago. Let me warn you, he speaks fluent Hangul. And now let's party."

Pete's speech was almost instantly repeated around the entire Field Army. Soon every one knew that the Commanding General had enough confidence in them to keep his wife on the battlefield. It made them feel confident and proud. Li's agent in the headquarters had Li informed by the next morning.

After the party, Ambassador Noonan and his wife returned to Seoul. Before leaving, Noonie passed along the congratulations of both the President and the Secretary of Defense, whom he had kept informed. That got a real pleasant response out of Sandy, but made Pete wonder if it were possible to have any secrets in Korea. Sandy and Pete then returned to their hootch. Fortunately Pete's bedroom was big enough for both of them. They decided not to go to the CG mess for dinner, but rather to have their meal served to the hootch. They were within earshot of the CG mess and, from the sound, there was one Hell of a party going on. Thank goodness the next day would be Saturday. That would make it easier on everybody, which was why it had been planned that way. Right after dinner, Pete and Sandy went to bed, but sleep did not come easily. There was so much to say and some of it actually made sense.

The next morning Pete and Sandy walked to the CG mess together. They no longer had to keep up their pretense, although Pete wondered if they had fooled anyone in the first place. Since it was Saturday they were dressed in casual civilian clothes. The custom around the headquarters was that, so far as possible, Saturdays and Sundays were to be days of relaxation. All offices were to be manned but not necessarily at full strength. Also, it was 9:00 AM. Breakfast was served later on the weekends.

Pete and Sandy entered the mess and took seats together at one of the available tables. This was another of the customs. On weekends the CG's main table in the mess was closed and people sat together as they arrived. The informality contributed to the cohesion of the headquarters. This time there was some initial awkwardness. What do you say to a four star general and his aide, who happens to be his wife, on the morning after their wedding? 'Did you get a good night's sleep?' just didn't seem appropriate.

Pete broke the ice by breaking another custom. Instead of talking business, he asked those at the table what they were planning to do that day. Most answered that they were going to combine work with pleasure. Some would play a short round of golf on the Red Cloud nine hole course, some had a tennis game planned, and some were going to take a terrain walk. This

latter activity was ideal for the situation. The walk was good exercise and
you could study and become familiar with the ground you might be fighting
over in a short time. Pete asked where they were going and was told up the
Munson valley to the Imjin Gang for a picnic lunch. Pete was disappointed
that Koreans only were going and said so loud enough for everyone to hear –
which was easy to do, since everyone in the mess was clandestinely listening
to him anyway. This had the desired effect and pretty soon a couple of
American officers came up and asked if they could join. Then Sandy said
she would like to go too. Pete was hoisted on his own petard. He couldn't
say no, so decided to make the best of it and warned the other officers that at
West Point Sandy had been an All-American track and cross country star and
he hoped they would be able to keep up with her.

He did not go on the terrain walk since he had walked that ground many
times in the past and knew it like the back of his hand. Besides, U.S. Army
Colonel Suwang Han, technically Han Su Wang the way the Koreans write
it, was scheduled to arrive from the United States in a couple of hours.

Pete had received Colonel Suwang Han's bio, called in Armyspeak, his
ORB (Officer's Record Brief) the day before. Colonel Han was a naturalized
American citizen of Korean heritage who was a specialist in tactical
Command and Control systems. He seemed to have all the right tickets:
Army War College, Vietnam, Brigade command, specialty ratings in
Research and Development, Systems Analysis, and Force Development. Pete
also noted that Han had started as an enlisted man with a high school educa-
tion, had gone to OCS, and along the way had gotten a master's degree in
electronics. He had done it the hard way, which was always a very good
sign.

Pete was pleased with this evidence that the American dream was still
alive and well. Anyone willing to work instead of claiming that government
owed them a free ride, could still make it. The performance of the Koreans,
the Vietnamese, and others from Asia proved it. This was especially true in
education. Pete had always been a member of the PTA in all of his postings.
He had come to the conclusion that access to a good education was still
there. Somehow or other certain Americans had come to the conclusion that
lack of a good education was the fault of schools and the teachers. The fault
lay with parents who failed to properly discipline their children. This was
not the case with Orientals. They understood the value of education. They
were astonished when they arrived in the United States to find that the
opportunity for a first-rate education was available to their children. Only the
rich and privileged had that access in their home countries. Pete remembered
an incident at Stanford University a few years earlier. He had been scheduled
to attend a computer seminar there because the Army was entering the

computer age and wanted some of the senior officers to get a basic course. He was having lunch with a group of Stanford professors and the topic of conversation was what to do about the next year's entering class. It seemed that the results of the entrance examinations had just been published, and based on criteria that had been in existence for years, over half of the new entering class would be Asian-Americans. The argument, which was not resolved while Pete was there, was whether or not to change the system. Pete did not know how the argument came out, and he was smart enough to keep silent and not express an opinion.

Pete walked to his office, where the daily message board and the Special Intelligence Black Book were waiting for him. His Secretary of the General Staff and Administrative Sergeant Major were grateful that this was Saturday. Usually Pete saw these documents at 6:00 AM, which meant they had to get up at 4:00.

Pete looked at the message board and asked the SGS if there was anything in there of importance. The SGS replied that he had tabbed the message giving the status of the equipment Pete had requested. The equipment was not arriving as fast as had been promised, and there were the usual bureaucratic excuses. Pete called Noonie on the secure line and asked if Noonie had seen the message. Noonie said yes and that he had already fired off a rocket to Washington after discussing the matter with General Armstrong. Noonie then asked Pete if he had read the Black Book yet. Pete said no and Noonie told him to read it carefully. They would get back together later, since they couldn't discuss the subject matter even over the secure phone.

Pete could not ask the SGS about the Black Book since only he was authorized to see it. As a matter of fact, the two officers who accompanied it were armed and authorized to shoot rather than let it fall into the hands of anyone not on their list. Pete asked them to enter. One did and gave Pete the book. He remained, carefully watching. He was not allowed to let the book out of his view. The other officer remained outside guarding the door. This was heavy stuff.

Pete thumbed through the book and found the item that Noonie was referring to. It was a CIA report on North Korea. As was the practice, it in no way, explicitly or implicitly, identified the source. It was also fully caveated that this was unverified information, not processed intelligence. It was given a rating of 'E-5' which was the lowest level of authentication. The 'E' meant that the source was unknown. The '5' meant that there was no way of verifying the information by other means. The essence of the message was that there appeared to be an emerging North Korean faction not in complete accord with Sung Tae Won. There were some in North Korea who were concerned about the way things were going and who were starting to be worried over the consequences. The item did not give any kind of evaluation as to how widespread this dissatisfaction might be or its future implications. The fact that there might be discord in the DPRK was significant enough all by itself.

Another item in the book about North Korea referred to public statements from Sung that he might be willing to keep the International Atomic Energy Agency Inspectors if the nations of the world, especially the United States, would be willing, in turn, to make certain unspecified accommodations. The item warned that several explanations were possible. Maybe Sung had come to his senses, which the CIA doubted. Maybe North Korea had hidden sufficient Plutonium already and could allow the inspectors to continue without any damage to its nuclear program. Or maybe the other shoe was about to drop. The North Koreans might be about to make very significant demands requiring the surrender by the South Koreans.

Pete gave the book back to the officer and thanked him. Pete did not attempt to discuss the contents with the officer, since the officer was prohibited from doing so.

Pete reflected on what he just read and then reminded himself that his job was different from Noonie's. His job was to be able to fight and win the ground war if it came. These other items were important and related, but not directly his concern. He hould not think about them since they did not impinge on his mission. In a few days he would find out just how wrong he was.

After the Special Intelligence officers had left, the SGS knocked on the door and said that Colonel Han had arrived and asked if Pete wanted to see him. Pete went to the door of his office and introduced himself. He asked Han when he had last slept and eaten. Han told him that because of the time change he wasn't exactly sure, but it had been a while. Pete suggested that the SGS take Han over to the mess and get him something to eat and then get him settled. After a short nap and a shower they would meet at 4:00 PM. That would be soon enough. However, this wasn't totally altruistic on Pete's part. It was the first time he had been separated from Sandy in several weeks and she was somewhat in danger. He really would not be able to concentrate upon what was sure to be very technical material until she was safely back. On an intellectual level Pete knew that this was how it would have to be, but he was not sure he was ready to handle it emotionally. He did not want to lose Sandy and there was more than one way that could happen.

Sandy returned at 3:00 PM. She was cold, dirty, exhausted, and very happy. She told Pete that this had been one of the best experiences of her life. Initially the ROK officers tried to walk her into the ground. They were testing her. After awhile they told her that General Goodwin had warned them of her prowess in track and cross-country and that they had wanted to find out for themselves. The good news was that she was able to keep up. The bad news was that some of the other Americans could not. Her personal escort during the terrain walk was General Kim, Pete's deputy. He pointed out to her a tactical analysis of the terrain, where the key defensive positions were, where the killing grounds would be, where the counterattacks would be launched from, where the best observation posts would be, and where the North Korean most probable avenue of attack would be. When they got to the Imjin Gang, she saw how the river was starting to freeze over and how it would be a clear shot to Uijongbu if not properly defended. She had studied all this sort of thing at West Point and at Fort Sill, but had never actually witnessed it. She felt that she had been accepted by the Koreans more than she had ever been accepted by the American Army.

She also said something else that Pete was already beginning to suspect. The Koreans had arranged to have lunch upon arrival at the Imjin. Because it was somewhat cold they served a dish that the Koreans believe protect against the cold. They told her that it was called kimchi. She did not feel it was appropriate to refuse. And now she had an unsatiable desire to brush her teeth and use some mouthwash. Pete agreed.

Sandy asked to be excused. She wanted nothing more than to get cleaned up and take a nap. She was really exhausted, but in a good way.

Pete was very proud of her and most happy that she had returned safely. How he would handle the kimchi residual would have to wait until that night. He was looking forward to supper to see how the Koreans reacted to the day. He was sure it would be extremely positive.

Soon Colonel Han returned. He looked much better. Pete asked him in and offered him a drink. He found that Han shared his fondness for vodka on the rocks. It was actually a little early for Pete, but his concern for Sandy and her safe return seemed to make it all right. For Han, it didn't make a bit of difference. Just like everyone else who flies over from the U.S., his biological clock was completely screwed up. His body thought it was four in the morning.

After the pleasantries, Pete showed Han the message regarding the arrival of the equipment.

"This is not that much of a problem," said Han. "On the one hand, it is slower than I would like, but on the other I think we initially underestimated the train-up time. The JSTARS is actually quite easy. The interface is with senior headquarters only. Except for the technicians who turn it on or off, all the staff officers do is read the results and make their requests. The counter-battery radars are a much different matter. Enough people and equipment came with me to start. Would it be possible to have artillery firing into an impact area by tomorrow? The first thing I need to do is calibrate the equipment and make sure it is working properly. It is rugged equipment, but malfunctions occur. By Monday I hope to be able to give a demonstration to senior officers, and once I have their confidence I will train the Artillery battalions in the corps. In the U.S. Army there has always been an argument as to whether this is an intelligence system or a tactical system. This thing belongs with the Artillery Battalions, not in the Division G-2 sections. I might need your help on that."

Pete called the Army Artillery Officer, who agreed to meet immediately with Colonel Han and get the arrangements started.

Dinner that night at the mess was very relaxed and friendly. Sandy was surrounded by Korean officers who had obviously began to accept her as an equal. They were also fascinated by a woman who was beautiful, smart, and could walk them into the ground. Korean society, for all its advancements, had not yet achieved anything like that. Pete introduced Colonel Han to all the officers. He started every conversation in English and then at the appropriate time made a smooth transition into Hangul. They loved it. Early on Sandy asked Pete if they could go. She was tired and wanted to brush her teeth again. As they left, all the officers in the mess said good night. Some of the American officers felt a touch of loneliness since they were in Korea without their wives. The Koreans, on the other hand, were beaming. Among other things, kimchi is supposed to make you a better lover. It is supposed to have a high quantity of vitamin E.

The next morning, Colonel Han told Pete that he had made all the necessary arrangements with the Army Artillery Officer and was going to set up his counterbattery system and try it out. He asked Pete if he would like to see it in operation, but to wait until about 2:00 PM so that he had time to work the bugs out. Pete agreed. They drove to the site. Han was waiting and explained what was about to happen.

"What I am about to show you is relatively simple in concept but quite difficult in execution. It would not be possible except for recent advances in computer technology to include the rather esoteric field of Artificial Intelligence. We have been able to do most of this for years but until recently it took hours, sometimes days, of computations, which made it virtually useless on the battlefield.

"An artillery round, when fired, theoretically follows a parabolic trajectory. Rene Descartes, a Frenchman of the 18th Century, figured out all the equations of parabolas in a field of mathematics called analytical geometry, which was the necessary forerunner to calculus. He showed how, if you knew three points of a parabola, you can calculate the equation of the parabola. Unfortunately, the artillery round follows what is called a perturbated parabola – that is, the parabola is warped by various physical influences.

These include the density of the air, the direction and speed of the wind, the temperature, the rotation of the earth, and others. Fortunately we can program all of these into the computer. Some are constants, others are variables.

"Next we need to know the precise location of the Radar. Years ago this took field survey, which was also very time consuming. We now have a gadget called NAVSTAR GPS. The United States has ringed the earth with a series of satellites with well-known predictable orbits. The NAVSTAR sends a signal to three or more of the satellites and, based upon the time it takes to get a return signal can immediately calculate the exact location of the sending system, including its altitude. Again, the theory behind this has been well-known for years and the geometry is taught in high school. It took satellite and computer technology to do it. One of the beauties of the system is that it is so easy to use. A soldier pushes a button asking 'where am I?' and the NAVSTAR tells him.

"What we want to know, of course, is the location of the artillery piece firing the round. This takes us back to the geometry I explained earlier. We have developed Radar sensitive enough to pick up an artillery round in the air. The Radar tells the computer where the round is, including its altitude at an instant in time. In essence, it gives the three dimensional coordinates of the location. Milliseconds later it repeats the process and continues to do so until it gets a good track. This usually takes less than a second. With these several locations plotted and the local wind and density parameters entered, using the computational software the computer can tell you in near-real time where the round will land and where it came from. One of the difficulties that the technology had to overcome was tracking the same round when multiple rounds are in the air. This is where Artificial Intelligence applications come in. The AI determines which round is the one being tracked and tells the Radar to forget the others until the solution for it has been calculated.

"Now we are going to try it out and see if it works. We have made a few test firings and everything seems to be working perfectly. Your Artillery officer has placed six guns or howitzers of various calibers at locations unknown to me. He has also selected various impact points throughout the range. Firing all his rounds at the same target makes it too easy. He knows where they are and has surveyed coordinates for each of them. We will start off simple. One round will be fired and we will tell you where the firing position is located, where the round will land, and, as a bonus, the type of weapon that fired it. This last bit of information was made possible by using a lot of captured weapons and ammunition and running enough test firings to allow the AI module to make a "best guess." Nothing in warfare is absolutely certain."

When an artillery round is fired in your vicinity you can usually hear three sounds. First you hear a distant thump of the round being fired. As it passes overhead, if it is above the speed of sound you hear a crack, and if it is below the speed of sound you hear a shushing whistle. Finally, you hear the sound of detonation when it strikes the target. As a matter of fact, one thing good commanders teach green troops is 'thump crack' procedures. If you hear both thump and crack, they are probably firing at you. If you hear only the thump they probably are not. "General, if you would please, fire 1."

They heard the thump of the first round being fired. The Radar slewed around automatically and pointed up. A green light came on and a set of coordinates appeared in the display. Han pushed a button and a piece of paper he called 'hard copy' came out of the machine. On it were listed the coordinates and altitude of the firing position, the target and the probable type of weapon. Han explained that in order to make it accurate one more thing had been programmed into the computer. The landing point of a round depends on the altitude of both the firing point and the target. For years, the U.S. Defense Mapping Agency had been preparing digitized maps of potential trouble spots throughout the world – that is, maps that have been reduced to computer language. Fortunately, Korea was one of them. This information had been programmed into the software before the Radars had been sent to Korea. The software procedure first assumes that both the target and the firing point are at the same altitude as the Radar. It then compares the calculated points with the map and if the altitude is different it makes a correction. It repeats the process until there is no difference. This is called successive approximation and takes only milliseconds.

The Artillery officer compared the hard copy with his notebook and nodded. The test was repeated five more times with the same results. They then started all over again, firing simultaneous multiple rounds. Watching the radar was fascinating. You could physically see it complete one solution and then automatically slew to another round and solve the next one. Everyone was impressed. Colonel Han asked the Artillery officer if it were possible to have the Corps Artillery commanders as well as the Division Artillery commanders and their operations officers there the next day for a repeat demonstration. The agreement was immediate.

"How soon can we have these operational throughout the corps?" Pete asked.

Han replied. "According to the schedule of arrival that you showed me yesterday, all the equipment and personnel will be here by the end of the week. That amounts to about sixty complete sets to totally outfit all the artillery battalions of the corps. Fortunately each of my team chiefs accompanying the Radar is capable of doing what I did today. We will need priority on available range time and training ammunition. So all in all, I would say two weeks, tops, with the priority units somewhat sooner. Why don't I work that out with your Artillery officer. This is a job for 'Red Legs.'"

Pete noted that Han was not only a good technician, but a great politician also. The Artillery officer had a broad smile on his face. He would show those rear area commandos in Seoul a thing or two. They would see just how good artillerymen can be in defending South Korea and keeping artillery fire away from Seoul. He asked Pete if he could bring the Corps artillery commanders to dinner that night and have them meet Colonel Han. He was in a hurry to get started.

Pete and Sandy stayed late at the mess that night. The last couple of days had been very good. Colonel Han and the artillery generals had been in animated conversation all evening and looked as if they might go on forever. Sandy suggested to Pete that they join the bridge game that was about to start and Pete reluctantly agreed. Sandy was a whiz but Pete was completely out of practice. They got slaughtered. Sandy realized that they were badly in need of practice if they were going to play against this gang of cutthroats. As the game was about to break up, an American officer came over and mentioned that they might want to see something on the CNN News TV program. It showed a former President of the United States meeting with Sung Tae Won. If you believed it you would think the crisis was over. The American officer muttered out loud, "I wonder who is bullshitting whom." "Sorry, Ma'am," he said to Sandy. Sandy said, "No problem. I was thinking the same thing."

Pete went back to his office and called Noonie on the secure phone and asked if he had seen the program. Noonie replied that he had and had talked with the President. The President was furious. This had gone far beyond the intended scope. He then told Noonie that he and Pete were on the right track and to hang in there.

That evening as they were preparing for bed Sandy asked Pete if he could still smell and taste the kimchi. She was not happy when Pete said yes, and what's more it would be with her for several more days. She then asked Pete if it would be better if she slept in her own bed that night. Her feelings were hurt. Pete said, "No way."

By the middle of the next week, Pete was satisfied that the implementation of the counterbattery radars was going well. He had finished all of his initial field visits and was satisfied with the deployment of his army. It was now time to turn attention to the JSTARS. The first aircraft had arrived at Kadena in Okinawa. It was intended that there be a total of four so that continuous surveillance could be maintained. Colonel Han was supervising the installation of the ground read-out equipment in the underground command bunker. Additional ground equipments were being installed in Eighth Army and ROK headquarters, but they were informational backups. His was to be the primary operational one. Han said that tomorrow they would make the first trial runs with the actual aircraft, but that first he had something most interesting to show Pete and the rest of the officers. He had some tapes that had been made during the Persian Gulf War which demonstrated the capabilities of the JSTARS system. He offered to play them. Pete called the staff together and told Han to do it.

Chapter Nineteen

Colonel Han called the officers to order and began his explanation. "Gentlemen, as you have been told, JSTARS stands for Joint Surveillance and Target Attack Radar System. The U.S. Army copied the basic idea from the U.S. Air Force, although the purpose is somewhat different. The Air Force AWACS is a modified Boeing 707 chock full of Radar and other surveillance equipment together with lots of computers and communications gear. The JSTARS is the same. The difference is that the AWACS keeps track of both friendly and enemy aircraft and actually directs the air battle. The JSTARS tracks the enemy and gives the information to a ground system, such as the one you see in front of you, and the land battle is controlled from here, not the aircraft.

"Let me describe briefly what is on board the JSTARS. It has a combination of television cameras, some of which are low light level, Radars of differing purposes, and infrared sensors. These are all connected together by a series of computers. Here is how it all functions. We first establish what we call a base datum – that is, we will fly the JSTARS aircraft up and down the DMZ 24 hours a day for as long as we have time, collecting data. Over time we will produce a very accurate picture of where the enemy is and his routines. This is for the base datum. For example, you know that in order to keep tanks operational you must start the engines once a day to keep the seals moist and the batteries charged. By using the infrared sensors we will be able to track such events. We will also be able to track their daily supply runs and so forth. In other words, we will establish a base activities datum against which deviations can be immediately identified. We will establish these datum for day and night and in all types of inclement weather.

"We also have the capability to zoom in on a particular area or take a wide panoramic view. If and when things start moving we can put several days of activities into something like a movie so we can see the evolution of the action. We can do this at whatever speed we wish. One caution: We can not become too dependent on JSTARS. We must keep all your other intelligence gathering means functioning. Prior to hostilities, JSTARS will function well. When the war breaks out, it must dive for the ground and has no chance of survival until we regain air superiority. That should take two or three days. During those two or three days JSTARS information will be sparse. If a need is extremely urgent, we can send up a JSTARS with aerial escorts but the decision to do that will have to be made on a case by case evaluation.

"Before I show you the Persian Gulf War tapes, please remember that because of the rather unique circumstances of the war, JSTARS was able to operate with relative invulnerability any time it wished. This will not be true in the opening stages of our war. Because of the foolishness of Saddam, the U.S. was able to run a 34 day air campaign before the ground war commenced. We also had six months for our force build-up. The point I'm trying to make is that you should view the tapes to understand the technical capabilities of JSTARS, not to predict battle outcomes."

Colonel Han proceeded to run the tape, stopping every once in a while to give an explanation. He showed what the first day's tape looked like and then compared it with the tape of two weeks later. He emphasized that there had been very little movement or change in the Iraqi forces but that it takes time to build up the composite picture. He made a special point that what they were seeing on the computer screen in front of them were not the actual sensor images being received by the JSTARS. After being received, these images were processed by the computer into standard military symbols. In other words, the image of a tank appeared as a certain type of image blossom. The blossom would be compared with a blossom data bank in the computer and the computer would determine what it was and display the appropriate symbol. Han also explained the Artificial Intelligence module in the Computer. If certain image patterns started to appear, the AI module would indicate that something important was happening and allow the operator the option to look more closely or change his surveillance priorities.

One of the Korean officers had a very good question. "Colonel Han," he asked, "we have known for years that the North Koreans are very good at digging in. Almost everything is underground. How can the JSTARS observe them?"

Han responded, "Even equipment that is underground must be fired up occasionally. If it is not it ceases to be reliable. That is why we have to establish the datum. We might not catch them the first couple of times. But even underground there must be a way to vent the heat and fumes. We ran many trials at Fort Huachuca using enemy equipment in various bunker and soil conditions. These results were then programmed into the software memory. A tank is a tank is a tank. It just produces different sensor images given different conditions. The computer can tell the difference and make the proper identification."

Han then showed them the difference in application once a war get's hot and mobile. Prior to the start of a war the JSTARS is primarily used for static intelligence. After the war has started it is primarily used for battle management and more for massed formation movements than individual targets. The software had been built that way. Han again told them that the datum runs would begin tomorrow and should be considered at the beginning as raw unsubstantiated information. He requested that his initial results be compared with already existing intelligence to see how closely they agree. If there was major disagreement there needed to be some serious thinking. Pete told the group that he wanted to be immediately informed if there was such a disagreement.

Pete then got up to address the group. He said, "Gentlemen, I want to pick up on something very important that was said by Colonel Han and that is the danger of overgeneralizing from the results of the Persian Gulf War. I am afraid that the United States and possibly other nations have come to the conclusion that U.S. technology has made the fighting of war easy and predictable. I noticed that the U.S. Army Field Manual, FM 100-5, Operations, has been rewritten since the Persian Gulf War and depends heavily on the results of that war. To me this could lead to fatal error and I don't intend allowing that to happen here. The circumstances surrounding the Persian Gulf War were almost obscene in the advantages to the U.S. and allied forces. Saddam started the war betting that no one would react, and in so doing gave the world the rationale for justifiable war. The fact that his possession of Kuwait would give him a stranglehold on the world's supply of oil added to the rationale. I think that many of you were here in the winter of '74 when the Arabs cut off the oil. Korea's oil came from Kuwait. It got mighty cold that winter. Saddam then placed his forces in the worst possible place. He had some 42 divisions blocked on three sides by the border with Iran, the Sea, and Kuwait City. Any military man could see what an envelopment around the west flank would do. Please don't get me wrong on this. The U.S. and allied forces were superbly trained, equipped and led and they deserve all the credit in the world, but it was a once in a lifetime set of circumstances that I don't expect to see repeated, certainly not by the North Koreans. I will go so far as to say that the force we sent to the Persian Gulf would not have done much better in Vietnam than the force we did send. Similarly, I think the force that we sent to Vietnam would have done about as well in the Persian Gulf as the force we did send. I am still confident that we will prevail here, but it won't be the walkover that it was in the Persian Gulf."

This put a real pall on the audience, which is exactly what Pete intended. Being overconfident is just as bad as lacking confidence. The balance is important.

At dinner that night General Kim Jook Wan, the Deputy Commanding General, asked a question. "For the last several days during the briefings on the counterbattery Radar and the JSTARS we have heard the term Artificial Intelligence mentioned. I wonder if anyone can tell me exactly what it means."

Colonel Han was about to answer when he got a signal from Pete that he wanted to answer the question. "I first got involved in this several years ago when I was in the Pentagon. I was very dubious at first. The subject had been oversold and many unfulfilled promises had been made. The proponents tried to convince people that Artificial Intelligence could replicate the functions of the human mind. I became involved with a corporation in Palo Alto, California that made no such claims. They were proposing what they called Artificial Intelligence Expert Systems Decision Aids. What they were saying is that certain people can be classified as experts in their fields and that by capturing how these experts made their decisions, their expertise could be made available to those who were not so expert. They were not proposing a machine that made decisions, but rather a machine that offered advice based upon what a true expert might do in a given situation. I thought that this idea had merit and funded it.

"The first thing I found out was that AI, as they called it, was based upon a form of mathematics called symbolic logic. They informed me that many advances in the world have been made by exploiting mathematics that had been originally developed in a theoretical way without any anticipation of practical use. For example, you heard a few days ago about Rene Descartes and analytical geometry in the development of artillery fire. It is also the case that analytical geometry was necessary to the development of space orbital mechanics. If you want to orbit the earth you achieve the equation of a circle or an ellipse. If you want to escape earth's gravity, you achieve the equation of a parabola or a hyperbola.

"Another form of mathematics which had no original purpose other than intellectual satisfaction was the binary number system, that is, the number system base two with only zero and one. When John Von Neumann was starting to think about computers which really are only a series of on-off switches, he knew that the math had already been worked out.

"Now back to symbolic logic. This mathematics discipline is based upon a simple precept: If A is true then B is true. This can be either a fact or a rule. For example. if I am a Virginian, then I am an American. As you develop the discipline the logic becomes more complicated. If A Is true then B is true. If B is true then C is true. Therefore if A is true then C is true. And so on. Normal computer programs require exact algorithms that must have a complete data set before a solution can be reached. But real life is not that way.

Most decisions are reached through inexact and incomplete information. Experts do it through a combination of rules and facts and, as I mentioned, the mathematics of this has already been established. So you interrogate an expert and capture his expertise and put it into the computer.

"This is not as simple as it sounds. We are only now realizing how complicated the human mind really is. Say that you want to drive a car from point A to point B. The people who are developing AI figure that the driver has stored in his mind about 6,000 rules and facts and applies them to his driving at a rate of about 300 a minute. Capturing those 6,000 rules and making a machine that can apply them at 300 times a minute has only become possible with fifth generation computers. The AI in the JSTARS is quite rudimentary. The rules are simply these. If the image looks like this, then the object is probably this. Or, alternately, if there are a certain number of events of this kind, then it is probable that this is going on. Have I confused you enough?"

There was no discussion although Pete did get an approving nod from Colonel Han, who made a mental note not to underestimate Pete in the future.

The next couple of weeks went by rapidly. All the counterbattery Radars and their crews had arrived and training was just about complete. The Koreans were ready to take over most of the operations. However, the U.S. crews felt a degree of ownership in the Radars and volunteered to remain. The Koreans acquiesced immediately since U.S. commitment was very important to them. The JSTARS datum base was pretty much complete and differed only in small detail from that developed by other intelligence systems over the years. There did not appear to be any significant troop movements, nor were there any discernible changes in North Korean activity patterns. This increased Pete's confidence in the warning time he might have and he brought down the readiness level a notch. This would allow time for training, maintenance of equipment, and rest. The trick is to be at the maximum level of readiness at exactly the right time. Being too early or too late are both bad. Pete spent many agonizing hours trying to think of things he had overlooked. This was the hard part. When you are first in a situation such as this there is so much to do that you don't have time to worry. But now, you want to make sure that you have considered everything.

This brought him back to an old dangerous thought that he had had before. The North Koreans had become reasonable and were starting to make what on the surface appeared to be reasonable requests. They said that they did not want to develop nuclear weapons and pledged not to do so although they had not agreed to any meaningful way of being checked. In return they were asking that the armed forces of South Korea be reduced to

100,000 men and be withdrawn from the DMZ. They had also asked for large amounts of economic aid. The problem was that this was receiving much support from some countries of the world and from some of the liberal fringes of the United States. On the other hand, another group was advocating a preemptive strike against North Korea. This is where the Persian Gulf War mentality worked against common sense. Many Americans felt that war was now pretty easy to win and would have few casualties. Pete knew different.

But Pete also knew that were the world to accede to the North Korean demands they might well regret it when five years later North Korea had nuclear weapons, had sold a few to terrorist nations, and had weakened South Korea. Another scenario crossed his mind. If the South Koreans saw the situation going against them, they might initiate a war on their own. Who knows how that would come out. No matter how Pete thought about it he kept coming back to the same conclusion he had that night with Noonie, Jo Ann and Sandy. It would be better to get it over with now than five years from now. Dangerous thinking. He knew that he could not and would not ever propose this to Noonie, the Secretary of Defense or the President. That was not his job. However, little did Pete know that that decision was going to be made for him.

That night as Pete was getting ready for bed he noticed a note on the pillow of his bed. It was in a sealed envelope and addressed personally to him. It was hand printed in perfect calligraphy. The contents were unbelievable. It claimed to be from the Chief of the North Korean Security Services and that he and Pete knew one another. It stated that he was worried about the present situation and the fate of both North and South Korea. He thought that he and Pete could avoid a disaster by working together. He stated that he was putting his life in Pete's hands and at present was within one mile of Pete's headquarters. He asked for a one-on-one meeting with the provision that Pete tell no one except his wife and aide. He gave the details of how the meeting could be held without anyone ever finding out, in case they could not agree. Pete had to admit that the plan for meeting was ingenious and demonstrated a very precise knowledge of how Camp Red Cloud operated.

Pete called Sandy over and asked her to read the note. She was astonished and asked Pete if he was going to do it. Pete told her that he had to. Very few times in life is a person afforded the opportunity of doing something as important as this. He knew that it might be a trap and that his life might be in danger, but his instincts told him no. Part of the arrangements for the meeting showed that the writer did indeed know Pete very well. Pete told Sandy that she was to tell no one. The note said that Pete would be back in his hootch safely by 0500. If he was not, Sandy was to go to Seoul and show the note to Noonie and let him decide what to do. Pete knew that Noonie would be upset no matter how it came out, but that there was no alternative. Sandy knew better than to argue and told him how much she loved him and that she would not sleep a wink that night.

In Korea, north of Seoul, there is a curfew for all vehicles and personnel from 2400 until 0400. It is strictly enforced. It is a "shoot first and ask questions later" type of situation. Because of this, many of the necessary functions of life are planned around the curfew. One of these is the nightly pickup of garbage at Camp Red Cloud. The garbage trucks finish by 2300. They then go to the municipal garbage dump outside Uijongbu where the garbage is sorted carefully throughout the night. Americans throw out much that is of value and this is a very lucrative commercial activity. What many did not realize was that this is also a very lucrative intelligence gathering function, since Americans are somewhat careless in what they throw away. Li, many years ago, had recognized this and taken over the garbage franchise. He made money and got good information.

The result was that the routes and timing of the garbage trucks were known and accepted. Only their absence would cause anyone to think about them. At 2330 Pete was standing in the shadows outside his hootch next to one of the Dempsey Dumpsters. He felt foolish but recognized the simple brilliance of the plan. The driver of the truck looked out the window and said to Pete. "I am told that you are a rattleass." Pete responded. "That is true and I am told that you are a midget." Brilliant. The best code exchanges are those that are simple, show a knowledge of the situation, and couldn't possibly be accidental.

Pete got in the front cab of the truck and lay down on the floor. The truck was waved right through the front gate of Red Cloud without being asked to stop. After all, this happened every night, and who wants to inspect a load of garbage? The ride to the dump took about 20 minutes and Pete knew enough not to try to involve the driver in conversation. When they got to the dump the driver pointed out what appeared to be an old abandoned army bus and nodded. Pete got out. While he could see no one he was sure that they were there. The door opened and Major General Li Joon Duk, Major General, North Korean Security Services, better known to Pete as Smiley, the bartender, greeted him.

Chapter Twenty

"Please come in, General Goodwin," said Li. "I thank you very much for taking the risk of coming. I owe you an explanation. But first, I would like to offer you some refreshments. I have coffee, Gin Seng tea, and one of your favorites, vodka on the rocks. I know that that is one of your favorites because many years ago I was the bartender at the CG Mess at Camp Red Cloud. What would you prefer?"

Pete responded that the situation was so unusual that a vodka on the rocks would taste very good. He asked Li if there were no concern that he had been followed or had some form of location sensing device on him. Li smiled and said that he had enough agents in the surrounding area to know that Pete had not been followed. Also, he had technology in the garbage truck to assure that Pete did not have any type of electronic device on him.

"General Goodwin," said Li, "let me start by telling you about myself. You asked me this question twenty years ago and I told you the truth except for one very important detail. Near the end of the Korean war I was selected by the North Korean Security Services to penetrate South Korea and become a deep cover agent. I was drafted into the South Korean Army and served with some distinction. After the war I was discharged and became a house-boy at Camp Red Cloud. Eventually, I became the bartender. The story I told you before about my family is true. I have a wife and several children, all of whom are successful. Shortly after you left Korea in 1974, I was recalled to North Korea. I will explain the reason for that in just a moment. To explain my sudden departure, some of my contacts in the South Korean government arranged for me and my family to emigrate to Australia. My family is still there but I am obviously not, although officially I still reside there. After being recalled to North Korea, I worked my way up and now am Chief of the Security Services of the DPRK.

"Now, why should you believe anything that I say? Allow me to establish my credibility. I know how successful you were in command of the 11th Corps and especially in the Persian Gulf War. I know this because I have had an agent in the 11th Corps headquarters for years. You know her as Brigitte, your secretary. She was not difficult to subvert. She was a lonely spinster who was easily seduced by a handsome and well-trained East German agent. I know that this sounds contradictory but she was loyal to the 11th Corps.

She would never pass along any information that she felt would hurt the Corps. Mostly she told us how good you were. Her intelligence contributed to the Soviets throwing in the towel and ending the cold war. They concluded that they could not win. She told me how well the U.S. forces would do in the Persian Gulf and that is one of the reasons North Korea took a hands off approach to that conflict, unlike Hussein of Jordan and Khadafi of Libya. She also provided my first indication that you were coming to take over command of the First Combined field army. I hope you will keep this in mind when you decide what, if anything, to do about Brigitte.

"But there is a more important story to tell concerning the reason that I got recalled to North Korea. In 1973 you were assigned to be the Chief of Staff of the First Combined Field Army under General Pace, the Commanding General. You undertook to examine the strategic assumptions of the defense of South Korea. We followed your work very closely because there was something else going on of which I don't believe you were aware. Of course, you know that Kim Il Sung invaded South Korea in June of 1950. He almost won. Then later, after the invasion at Inchon and the advance to the Yalu river by MacArthur, he almost lost. He would have except for the intervention of the Chinese. He swore that he would attack again and that the next time he would win. This almost happened in 1974. Very few people know the story. It may never be known, although with the collapse of the Soviet Union it may be found some day in the archives.

"In 1973 your American Army was virtually combat ineffective, as was the political will of the American people. This was the result of your experience in the Vietnam War. You had drawn down your forces everywhere to support the war and as it was being lost you had riots in your streets. Your Army in Europe and in Korea were a hollow shell. You were at your lowest ebb during the entire cold war following World War II. As you know, in those days the Soviet Union was our closest ally. China had a different agenda and had virtually abandoned us. The Soviets have always wanted to conquer the remainder of Europe and were prepared to do so if they ever achieved what they called sufficient "correlation of forces." By this they meant that they would attack if they ever perceived a high probability of winning. In early 1973 they came to us with a plan. We were to make a surprise attack on South Korea along the Kaesong Munson approach during the coldest part of the winter and defeat the bulk of the South Korean forces. It was assumed that the Americans would react and bring to Korea the remainder of their strategic reserve. We anticipated a standoff.

"Then, when the Americans were completely involved in Korea, the Soviet Union and the Warsaw Pact would attack during the spring across the northern European plain and take all of western Europe. The plan appeared foolproof, with little risk. U.S. strategy at that time was called the 'one and a half war' strategy. That is, you had the forces to fight one major war and one minor war simultaneously. I think you know that, at best, you only had the forces to fight one war at a time. We agreed to use the Soviet plan. Then something happened. We started to get inklings of the changes to the defense of South Korea that were being initiated by you and General Pace. We concentrated our intelligence effort on these changes. By February of 1974, we decided that our attack would be unsuccessful and that the United States would not have to commit their strategic reserve. Unless someone helped us, which seemed totally unlikely, the result would be the destruction of North Korea. We opted out and told the Soviet Union that the opportunity had been lost. In my opinion that was the beginning of the end of the cold war. They had lost their last and best chance. The total strategic equation had changed, although some, like Kim Il Sung, could not accept it.

"The reason that I was recalled was twofold. First, in order to gather the necessary intelligence about the status of your defense and the effect it might have on our attack, I had to take many risks that I ordinarily would not have taken. I was coming under suspicion. The second reason was that Kim Il Sung was appreciative of my efforts and wanted to reward me by bringing me back to the worker's paradise of North Korea. Let me say that I viewed the move with mixed emotions. I have been a dedicated communist all my life and a loyal subject of the Democratic People's Republic of Korea. But for some reason, perhaps because of my life in South Korea and my contact with Americans, my loyalty is to my country and not to the leader. I know what Sung Tae Won intends doing and I am convinced that it will fail and result in the destruction of North Korea and South Korea, and possibly other areas of the world. I must do something to prevent it.

"Let me tell you about our intentions. First, we are developing nuclear weapons. There is no ambiguity there. We will have two operational within a month, although we have problems with delivering them. At the appropriate time we will announce our possession and offer to dispose of them only if the world would accede to our modest and reasonable requests. The essence of the requests will basically neutralize the defensive capabilities of South Korea. However, we will not actually dispose of the nuclear weapons. We will hide them and continue to produce them. We already have agreements and arrangements with several nations that you label as terrorist to purchase them. In fact, they are giving us credit now against future delivery so your much talked about sanctions won't work. The plan is to several years from now attack South Korea. Here is where I differ completely with Sung Tae Won. He believes that faced with such a situation the rest of the world will acquiesce rather than fight. I don't. I believe that the United States would fight and would use nuclear weapons if necessary. My country would be destroyed.

"I have allies in North Korea who are willing to work with me. We know that we are placing our lives in jeopardy but we have a plan. We don't actually need your cooperation to carry it out but it would be much better if we could find a way to work together. Here is the plan."

Pete listened intently for over three hours. He asked many questions and played the role of devil's advocate. He looked for a fatal flaw in the plan. It was obvious that the plan was full of risks, but Pete came to the conclusion that there was even more risk in doing nothing. Pete made no commitments nor did Li expect him to. Li was actually rebelling against his government, while Pete would need the approval of his. As the discussion went on Pete found himself making suggestions on how the plan could be improved. The suggestion involving nuclear weapons intrigued Li although he said he would have to discuss it with his confederates. Pete asked who his confederates were. Li responded that if they had another meeting and Pete had by then received permission to proceed, he would tell him. Pete told Li that he had to discuss the plan with three and only three people: Ambassador Noonan, the Secretary of Defense, and the President of the United States. Li agreed, and in a show of great insight authorized Pete to discuss it also with the beautiful Major Parker.

It was approaching 0400 and Li told Pete that it was important that the garbage truck return on schedule while it was still dark. Pete agreed. Li displayed a sense of humor by calling the truck "Garbage Six." Li was using the convention of the United States Army that the commander's vehicle always had the number six. They shook hands and Pete asked how he could get in touch with Li after he had talked to the necessary people. Li replied. "Simple. Go to the bartender of the CG mess and ask "What ever happened to that old rattleass, Smiley the bartender?" The bartender will say that he will try to find out. When the bartender tells you that Smiley is living in Australia, we will meet that night. The time and method of transportation will be the same, but the location of the meeting will be different. That, of course, is for my protection."

The trip back to Red Cloud was uneventful, although Pete noticed that the driver gave each of the gate guards a small bundle of old clothes found in the garbage. This was expected and part of the routine. The truck stopped outside of Pete's hootch and Pete went inside. Sandy was asleep in a chair and Pete noticed that she had gone back to smoking again. Pete went over and kissed her. She jumped up and almost knocked him down in her enthusiasm to hug him. Pete teased her by saying that maybe he should go off on these secret missions more often, as he was beginning not to feel properly appreciated. For a second, Sandy thought he was serious, but then started crying and laughing simultaneously.

"Pete," said Sandy, "can you tell me what happened?"

"Sandy, you are not going to believe this. I know that I can not possibly get back to sleep, so why don't we fix a pot of coffee and I will tell you the whole thing."

For the next two hours Pete recounted his entire conversation with Li including the fact that Li volunteered letting Pete tell Sandy. Pete asked Sandy what he had on his calendar for the day. She replied that there was nothing that couldn't be canceled. Pete knew that the very first thing he had to do was discuss this development with Noonie. It was not going to be fun. Noonie was likely to go ballistic at first, but would probably come around soon. After all, Pete had given away nothing, made no commitments, and gained some very good intelligence.

Right after breakfast Pete called Noonie on the secure voice phone and requested an immediate meeting. He told Noonie that it was extremely urgent and of critical importance. Noonie asked what it was all about and Pete told him that he did not want to discuss it over the phone and Noonie to please trust him. They agreed to meet in an hour. It occurred to Pete that there was at least one advantage in the front lines being so close to Seoul.

The ride to Seoul took about 45 minutes. On the way Pete realized that he had been so intent on the combat posture of the First Combined Field Army over the last several weeks that this was the first time that he had been south of Uijongbu since his arrival in South Korea. He was curious to observe how the people were reacting to the possible danger and to his having decided to drive rather than take his helicopter. He noticed apparent total normalcy. The people were going about their business, and if there were additional military forces around he did not see them. He could see no sign of panic whatsoever.

Pete's Army sedan arrived at Ambassador Noonan's residence precisely at 0900. Pete and Noonie had agreed that it would be better to meet there than at the embassy. He told the driver to pull around back and wait for him and be available since he did not know how long the meeting would last. Pete entered through the front door, where he was saluted by the Marine Corps guards. His entrance was noticed and recorded by the North Korean Security Service agent whose job it was to observe all comings and goings.

Pete was greeted by Noonie, who suggested that they go upstairs to his private office. Noonie told Pete that because of the apparent seriousness of the meeting he had just had the office 'swept' for electronic listening devices. It was clean. After getting a cup of coffee, they took their seats.

"OK, Pete," said Noonie. "what the hell is this all about?" Pete immediately noticed that Noonie had put on his ambassador's hat.

"You are not going to believe this," replied Pete. "Something very strange has happened, and if this had turned out badly you would have me on the next plane out of here or have me shot. Let me show you something first." Pete handed Ambassador Noonan the note that he had gotten from Li. Noonie read it and then read it again.

"Holy shit!" exclaimed Noonie. "You are not going to do this, are you?"

Pete responded that he already had. He figured that if he had asked Noonie, it may have taken weeks to get an answer and the answer might have been no. This way if it worked out well there was no harm done, and if it did not work out well the only loser would have been Pete. Noonie and the President would have deniability and a real good diplomatic debating point.

"Jesus," said Noonie. "Do you realize what might have happened?"

Pete responded that he was very aware of the risks, but the fact of the matter was that he was safe, and he asked Noonie to please defer judgment until he had heard what was discussed. Noonie began to calm down and accept the situation. After all, no harm had been done and maybe something positive would even result from Pete's action. Noonie had learned over the years to trust Pete's instincts.

Pete then spent a couple of hours describing the meeting. He started by explaining the transportation arrangements in the garbage truck, which got a smile from Noonie, who took some satisfaction in visualizing a U.S. Army four star general lying on the floor of the cab of a garbage truck. He had to admit that the concept had been brilliant. Pete then told Noonie about Major General Li Joon Duk and his history as the former bartender of the Red Cloud CG mess. Pete opined that from the conversation he concluded that there were still North Korean agents in the compound, which wasn't all that bad when one considered that what they had to report was the excellent combat readiness of the First Combined Field Army. He then told Noonie what Li had to say about the close call in 1974 and the possible start of World War III. Noonie, who had been a CIA agent for years with a businessman's cover, did not comment, although he knew that what Li had said was true.

Pete then described to Noonie the plan that Li and his confederates had hatched up. He explained the rationale behind it and argued that they would probably do it with or without U.S. participation. He reiterated Li's point on which he fully agreed that if something were not done now the consequences for the future would indeed be dire. Pete said that he thought it was in the best interests of the United States and South Korea to participate in some way. Noonie temporized and said that this kind of decision was way beyond his and Pete's level of authority. This would have to be brought to the attention of the President of the United States. Noonie told Pete that he would contact the President right away and try to arrange a meeting. This was too important and too sensitive to do over phone or cable means. Either way the President would decide that there could never be a record of what had transpired.

At that point, Noonie decided to change gears. He asked Pete to give him his evaluation of the combat readiness of the First Combined Field army. Pete responded. "If the North Koreans are dumb enough to attack, we will beat their ass. If you want all of the details, I can give them to you." Pete was now establishing the fact that diplomats should only go so far in interfering with military matters. Noonie got the signal and agreed. "Great," said Noonie. "We have worked together very well so far. If there is anything else you need and are having trouble getting it let me know."

Pete asked Noonie when he might be expected to hear from the President. Noonie said that he could not predict but that he would emphasize to the President that it was extremely urgent. The President owed him a couple and it would probably be soon. In a couple of days Pete would be astonished to learn how soon. With that it was time for Pete to return to his headquarters in Uijongbu. He returned to his car and left. The length of time of his meeting was carefully recorded by Li's agent. He was disappointed that the listening device he had placed in the Ambassador's office at Li's direction had been discovered and removed. He was also disappointed to learn that the glass in the ambassador's office had been changed and that it was no longer possible to hear conversations through the window using parabolic antennae. Security was much better that it had been in the past when, under the previous ambassador, the place had been a sieve.

Chapter Twenty One

Things had become relatively routine at Camp Red Cloud. One could feel an attitude of quiet confidence. The JSTAR flights were going well and the intelligence picture and enemy routines were well established. The training on the counterbattery Radars was complete. The troops were ready. To assess their readiness Pete ordered a series of Command Post Exercises for senior commanders and staffs. CPX's, as they were called, were designed to furnish commanders and their staffs with different situations to see how they would react. The controllers, who also played the part of the North Koreans, were accomplished sadists, which was a requirement for the job. They enjoyed embarrassing the friendly forces. After each war game iteration there was a critique demonstrating what went right and what went wrong. The main point was to train the commanders and staffs without exhausting the troops. Another point was to see the reaction to the unexpected. After all, the enemy doesn't always do what you expect him to. The commanders and their staffs performed well, giving Pete even greater confidence.

The only negative news was that Brigadier General Alexander, his Chief of Staff, had turned out to be an alcoholic and was heavily involved indiscreetly with several Korean women. Pete sent him back to the states. Pete was furious with his staff, who had known about this and had not told him. He found it out for himself. This did give him the opportunity to bring over as Chief of Staff, Reuben Tanaka from the 11th Corps. This could have created a problem, since the Koreans really don't like the Japanese. But Pete made the point that Tanaka was an American and had never lived in Japan, and what's more, had a Jewish mother. This was hard for the Koreans to appreciate, because like almost every nation other than the United States, racial purity is important to them. This was one of the reasons that he had previously brought over Colonel Han. He was able to point out that in the U.S. Army the only thing that counts is performance. Fortunately, within a few days the Koreans came to believe in the abilities of Reuben. During the CPX's Reuben Tanaka usually played the part of the Field Army commanding general and did so well. Reuben had brought with him, in response to Pete's request, Rock Kowslowski, his long time driver. Things were going so well that Pete was almost getting bored looking for something meaningful to do. That was about to change.

Pete got a call that night from Noonie to be at Osan Air Base at 0900 in the morning. He was to wear civilian clothes and was to bring no one with him. He and Noonie were going to meet the President of the United States in Hawaii. The President had decided to come half way since he did not want Pete and Noonie away from Korea for any longer than necessary. He did not want to go to Korea, which would possibly escalate the situation, and he did not want to get bogged down in the protocol that accompanies a visit to a foreign country. As far as the public was concerned, the President was taking a very well earned vacation and would be staying at the U.S. Army Hale Koa Hotel at Fort DeRussy on Waikiki Beach. Pete and Noonie would sneak in through the back door, hopefully unobserved.

Pete's helicopter landed at the far end of Osan Air Base away from the passenger area as directed by the control tower. Waiting for him was Ambassador Noonan. On the runway was an Air Force VC 135 just like the one that he and Sandy had used a month earlier between Frankfurt and Washington. Pete wondered if it were possible that Beth would be the pilot. No such luck. This bird flew out of Hickham Field, Hawaii. There was so much traffic at Osan, including KC 135 tankers that looked to the naked eye like a VC 135, that they were completely unnoticed, which was the intent. They were whisked aboard and cleared for immediate takeoff. The pilot later told them that they must be special, since with the crowded conditions at Osan tactical aircraft had priority and trash haulers, using the pejorative Air Force term for any airplane that is not tactical, sometimes waited over an hour for clearance. The pilot did not know who they were, since they were in civilian clothes and using assumed names, but he figured that "Mr. Jones" and "Mr. Smith" were probably not their real names.

This time the pilot did not invite them up to the flight deck. His instructions were quite specific. Fly them, be polite, but don't ask too many questions. If they want to talk, that is their business. The steward however did ask them if they cared for anything and they both asked for coffee. The steward then disappeared, indicating a button they could push if they needed anything.

Pete chuckled out loud when they leveled off at cruising altitude and told Noonie that the last time he flew in a VC 135 he had joined a very exclusive club called the five mile high club. He then explained to Noonie exactly what that entailed. Noonie remarked that he might have to mention that to Jo Ann the next time the opportunity arose.

The flight to Hawaii was uneventful. Pete and Noonie spent most of the time discussing and rehearsing what they were going to say to the President. There were two approaches. One was the usual bureaucratic one that presents the decision maker with the options but refrains from making a recommendation. This is called the "no responsibility" option. The other is to go through the options and then make a strong recommendation. Neither Pete nor Noonie were the kind of people who would not put it on the line. That is why the President had chosen them. Basically, they had decided that Li's plan was the best option and would recommend it. They had come to the conclusion that to do nothing was the worst option and would lead to ultimate disaster.

Much of their time was spent just staring out the window and thinking. It is not often when the possible fate of your country rests on whether or not you did your job right.

The VC 135 landed at Hickham during the night when observation was limited. Pete and Noonie were picked up by an unmarked sedan immediately. The driver and the other passenger identified themselves as members of the Secret Service and the President's personal bodyguards. They asked for identification and compared it very carefully with a list in their hands. They asked Pete and Noonie to place their right index fingers into a hole in a small box, which was a new gadget that instantaneously compared fingerprints against a preprogrammed data base. Once satisfied, they became most polite and invited Pete and Noonie to accompany them to the Hale Koa, a drive which would take about half an hour.

Noonie asked Pete what he knew anything about the Hale Koa. Pete responded. "This is one of those oddities that occasionally happens. It could never happen today. The Army and the Air Force have something called AAFES, which stands for the Army and Air Force Exchange Service. It runs the Post Exchanges and other troop welfare activities. It makes a small profit which, by law, must be plowed back into troop welfare. At the height of the Vietnam war AAFES was rolling in dough. They had more money than they knew how to spend. Someone suggested that they build a hotel at Waikiki so that soldiers on R&R from Vietnam could have a place to stay without having to pay high rates. Congress approved. After the Vietnam war ended there was an argument over what to do with it. The decision was to retain it and lots of Congressmen now use it. The average GI can not now afford it since it is required by law to be self sustaining and must charge necessary fees. Most of its present clientele are retired officers on vacation."

The two Secret Service agents had listened carefully since they were curious too. They liked the idea of staying on the top floor of a military hotel on a military base. It made their job much easier and they hoped that maybe they could enjoy a swim at Waikiki beach. The sedan pulled up to the rear entrance and Pete and Noonie were directed to the freight elevator and then to their rooms. The agents told them that they had a half hour to get cleaned up before the Secretary of Defense would talk to them.

Half an hour later Pete and Noonie were escorted to the suite of the Secretary of Defense. He invited them in and asked if they would care for a drink. He told them that he was going to have one, so they accepted the offer.

The Secretary established the ground rules early on. He started off by addressing them as Ambassador Noonan and General Goodwin, not Pete and Noonie. This was going to be all business.

"Let me make something clear from the very outset. No matter what happens, the President does not know that you are here. I was invited to accompany the President on his vacation and I took it on my own to invite you here to tell me what is going on in Korea. It may be the case that after we have talked the President will have time to greet you informally as a matter of courtesy. Is that understood? Now tell me what I need to hear."

Pete and Noonie understood perfectly. They had to first sell the Secretary and, succeeding that, sell the President. If they did not succeed the President still had plausible deniability. Pete had learned to hate that term but understood that it was necessary in a very complex world. He had used it himself in the past.

"OK," said the Secretary, "what is so important that you could not tell it to me over secure communications and so important that it requires the presence of the President? This had better be good. Before you ask. This entire floor has been swept. We are secure."

Noonie said that Pete should be the primary speaker. He agreed with what Pete was about to say and would comment as necessary.

"Mr. Secretary," said Pete, "you will recall the instructions that you gave me when you sent me over here. I was to give you and the President an honest and factual estimate of the situation and suggest what I believe to be the best course of action for the United States. I am prepared to do so tonight, although some things have happened that neither I nor anyone else could possibly have anticipated.

"First of all, I am totally convinced that for now and the immediate future, if the North Koreans attack we can beat them back north of Seoul and be ready to go over to the counteroffensive if so ordered. Our limit of advance should be Pyongyang and the various nuclear facilities in its vicinity. That is about the limit of our logistical capability unless additional forces are sent. In this counteroffensive we can destroy the combat potential of the North Korean armed forces. This includes the air battle, which I believe will be virtually over in three days. With your sending over of the counterbattery Radars, some rounds will unavoidably land on Seoul and its environs, but that will not come near to influencing the outcome of the war.

"This brings me to my main point. I am confident that if the North

Koreans attack in the near term we will prevail and, if ordered, also solve the nuclear dilemma that is worrying everyone. There is a larger issue. This is where I hesitate to get involved, but I think it is necessary."

"Go ahead, General," said the Secretary. "That is what I pay you for."

"OK, sir, here is how I see it. If the North Koreans attack now, we will beat them and solve a very difficult problem. There will be casualties, but they will not be too high and certainly not as high as the prophets of doom and gloom in the media have been suggesting. But what if they don't attack now and instead continue to develop their nuclear weapons, while at the same time extracting concessions from the United States and South Korea affecting the defense? If that happens, think about the decisions that will have to be made several years from now. It will not be a pretty sight. I have been worried about this for some time and have shared my concerns with Ambassador Noonan. Until recently I did not have an answer. Then something happened the other night that is hard to believe but just might provide the answer. I have tried to shoot the idea down because it seems so implausible, but I have come to the conclusion that it is worth trying. I hope you will agree that this is a decision for the President. I have searched my mind and I can not recall any historical precedent."

Pete then showed the Secretary the note that he had received from Li. The Secretary's reaction was the same as Noonie's, including the same expletive. "Holy Shit."

"Next, you are going to tell me that you had the meeting," said the Secretary.

"Yes, sir. I took a chance. I figured that if I asked permission, the opportunity would be lost. Also, if something bad happened you could blame it on me and get a new commander without any harm being done. I got lucky, or at least I think I did. As a result of that meeting I now understand the situation much more clearly and I think I see the best solution to the problem.

"First, there are several certainties. North Korea has developed a nuclear weapon and is in the process of producing many more. The inspections by the IAEA will not uncover this activity. The technology for the inspections is not available and the North Koreans are much too clever at concealing things. They will use these weapons if necessary and they will sell them to terrorist nations to gain hard currency. Kim Il Sung was dedicated to establishing North Korean hegemony over the entire Korean peninsula. Sung Tae Won has continued this pursuit. How he will do it is still being played out and is dependent on world reaction. At some point he will announce that he has nuclear weapons and may actually detonate one to prove it and to frighten the world. He hopes that the world will respond to his demands and surrender South Korea rather than risk a nuclear war. If the world does not surrender, he is prepared to back up his demands with force and attack South Korea. The argument in North Korea now is when. Common sense would tell them that waiting a few years would be their best course of action, but fortunately, they don't have much common sense. That is the basis for Li's plan.

"General Li believes that he and his confederates can convince Sung that if the world does not accede to his demands, the best time to attack is now. Li and his confederates are willing to make sure that we have total knowledge of the attack and that the attack will be halfhearted. Their military will do everything wrong and make lots of tactical mistakes. We will defeat them and go over to the offensive. At the same time Li and his associates will start a rebellion, take over the country, and sue for peace. Obviously there are many details to work out but that is the essence of it. One other thing. Li tells me that whether or not we cooperate, they will attack soon, as they see as that is their best option. Li has come to the conclusion that waiting and attacking later will result in nuclear war and the total destruction of North Korea and South Korea. He will not allow that to happen. There is one more very important element to the plan and that is the use of nuclear weapons. In order for Li's plan to work and to be accepted by Sung, they must use nuclear weapons and believe that they worked. This is important. However, if the North Koreans were to really use a nuclear weapon on Seoul there would be millions of casualties. Here is what Li and I have tentatively figured out. If we do it this way the North Koreans will think the nuclear attack was successful, but there would be few if any casualties." Pete then explained this part of the plan in detail to the Secretary, who admitted that it was ingenious. Pete then said, "It is time to put it on the line. I support Li's plan and recommend it."

Noonie stated that he did too.

"Gentlemen, I am a go-between in this. The President has already gone to sleep and I want to think on it. I am meeting with him at breakfast tomorrow. After that I will tell you if the President wishes to see you. You are right in one thing. I do not recall a historical precedent in cooperating with your enemy's plan to attack you. No matter what happens, this can never be known."

The next morning Pete and Noonie were told that the President would see them at 2:00 PM. The President had a morning golf game with the Governor of Hawaii and saw no reason to cancel it. This gave them a chance to take a swim in the waters of the Pacific off Waikiki. Pete noticed that the water there was starting to get polluted. Isn't it amazing how man can screw up the best efforts of mother nature? Nevertheless, the swim was most welcome and put them in a good mood. The fact that the President would see them was also a very good sign. On the other hand, maybe he was going to fire them. Time would tell. They wondered what the proper dress would be for the meeting. In accordance with their instructions, neither of them had brought formal wear. They decided that sport shirt and slacks would be about right.

Right on time they were ushered in. The President rose to greet them and welcomed them as Pete and Noonie. He offered them a drink. This was a good sign.

The President started right off and said. "OK, gentlemen, let's see if I have got this right.

"The North Koreans presently have at least one operable nuclear weapon and will soon have more regardless of what the United Nation's IAEA does.

"North Korea will use these nuclear weapons if and when they believe it is in their best interest.

"If the North Koreans attack now we will beat them.

"If we accede to the North Korean demands, we will avoid war now but be in an impossible situation in several years.

"If we fight several years from now it is liable to go nuclear, with great destruction to both North and South Korea and possibly other areas.

"Certain North Koreans recognize this and are willing to get it over with now no matter what we do.

"You have made contact with high ranking North Koreans and believe that the best thing to do is have the war now.

"The outcome will be favorable to us and we will be able to reunify Korea under a democratic form of government.

"North Korea will use a nuclear weapon if they attack now, but the damage to South Korea and U.S. forces will be minimal.

"Is that about it?"

As Pete and Noonie were about to respond they got a slight nod from the Secretary of Defense. The meaning was simple. They did not have to sell the President. That had already been accomplished. What was now occurring was politics. The answer was quite obvious and they gave it. "Yes, Sir."

The President spoke again. "As I see it, what you have told the Secretary of Defense is quite straightforward. In no way are you participating with the North Koreans in some form of accommodation. Rather, you are simply giving us an additional form of intelligence. You have obtained a new way of determining what the enemy is up to and you are devising the best form of defense given the new information. Would that be a fair way of summarizing it?" Pete and Noonie nodded. "OK. Now I have to go. I have another important appointment. Actually, I have been invited to take a catamaran ride around Diamond Head and I am not about to miss it. I am sure that you can work out all of the necessary details with the Secretary of Defense. He will be your sole point of contact in this affair. Please excuse me." And with that, the President left.

The Secretary asked Pete and Noonie if they would join him in his suite in a few minutes. They did and, after they had gotten comfortable, the Secretary asked them for their impressions of the meeting with the President. Noonie spoke first.

"We thank you for convincing the President. That took courage. We have both been around long enough to understand that the President must take a hands-off position in situations such as this. He has taken the ultimate risk. He has told us to go ahead. I promise you that we are right and that we will not let you and the President down. Ours is the easier job. We buck the hard decisions up to you. We have our answer, or have I misinterpreted the signals?"

"No," said the Secretary. "You have understood him correctly. You do have the go ahead. But please keep me informed. I will have for you, before you leave, an old form of secure communications to be used on a limited basis. They are called 'One Time Diana Pads.' They are unbreakable, although very expensive. We only use them in extreme situations and this is one of them.

"I thank you for your perceptiveness in understanding the President's position. Unlike his predecessor, he is willing to make the tough decisions but also understands the calculus of power politics. I am, what you call, his "cut out," that is, the means of keeping him one step from the nitty gritty. In order for the plan to work, the United States must take certain positions. We must continue to insist that the United Nation's International Atomic Energy Agency have full access to all of North Korea's nuclear activities. Although they believe that they can conceal their activity, this inserts an element of uncertainty into the equation. We must continue the threat of sanctions, not too stridently, but always in the background. Most importantly, we will resist any form of accommodation or compromise over the defense status of South Korea. We must make it clear that they will not achieve their objectives by threat. We must convince them that if they want to achieve their goals, they must fight. Do you agree?"

Pete and Noonie concurred. They realized that the meeting between the President and the Secretary had not been superficial and that what was said had been carefully thought out.

"Time is very important. Also, I don't want the fact that you are here to become known. Your plane leaves in two hours. Have a good flight; maybe next time you can enjoy the pleasures of Hawaii. And now you must excuse me, I have a tennis match that I don't want to miss." Pete and Noonie got the message. They had better be right.

On the flight back to Korea, Pete and Noonie were very subdued. The decisions had been made. The President and the Secretary of Defense had expressed their confidence in Pete and Noonie and authorized them to pursue the plan. They were good enough politicians to have distanced themselves from dumb mistakes, but they would still have to take responsibility for the overall consequences. The die was cast. The next move was up to Pete. He would have to meet with Li and work out the details. Anyone can have a brilliant idea. The devil is in the details.

Pete and Noonie arrived back in Korea less than 36 hours after they had departed. Noonie's car met him at the Air Base, as did Pete's helicopter. They agreed to talk in a couple of days, after Pete had spoken to Li. There was not much else to say. Pete got back to his headquarters just before supper. Sandy was waiting for him and had a thousand questions. Pete said that the visit with the President had gone well and that he felt more confident than he had in the last month. He told Sandy that they had to go to the mess early so that he could make certain arrangements. Sandy understood and knew that her job was to make sure that Pete was left alone at the bar with the bartender. She was good at that.

Pete went over to the bartender and said. "I wonder, what ever happened to that old rattleass, Smiley the bartender?"

The bartender replied that he had never met Smiley but had heard of him and that he would try to find out. He said he thought it might take a couple of days, but he was absolutely sure that he would be able to get the information. Pete then rejoined the others for dinner.

Chapter Twenty Two

The next two days seemed eternity. Each time Pete approached the bartender he got a slight negative nod. Then on the third day the bartender told him that he had talked to some people in Uijongbu and found out that Smiley had made a lot of money and emigrated with his family to Australia. Some people corresponded with Smiley frequently, and if Pete wanted to get him a message it could be done that night. Pete said he was just curious and wanted to offer Smiley his best. Message sent and received. Tonight was the night.

As before, Pete was waiting outside his hootch for 'garbage six,' which arrived right on time. The rattleass-midget passwords were exchanged. Pete noticed that this was a different driver and wondered just how many agents Li had at Camp Red Cloud. The trip was uneventful and the truck let Pete out at a small farmhouse close to the garbage dump. Li met him at the door and congratulated him on his meeting with the President and the Secretary of Defense at the Hale Koa. Li was making the point that he had many agents all over the world, including the United States, and especially in Hawaii, which has a large Korean population.

Pete decided that two could play that game and asked Li, if he knew so much, how the conversation had gone. Li smiled and responded that it was easy to have dishwashers and maids who could make observations of comings and goings. It was quite another thing to penetrate close security. Li said that most good and reliable intelligence comes from lots of little apparently innocuous bits of information, not from the type of coups that you read about in novels.

They settled down and got to business. It was Pete's turn first. "As you know, I did meet with the President and the Secretary of Defense three days ago. I was accompanied by Ambassador Noonan and I suspect you already know that also. I don't know if you agree with me or not, but I told the President that we will be able to defeat your attack even if you and I do not reach an agreement. It is obvious that you have agents in the First Combined Field Army headquarters and probably in many other places. If your agents are any good, I think you will have reached the same conclusion. That is why I trust you. There is no other explanation for wanting to attack now. You can't win. I think you owe me your answer to that."

Li replied. "General Goodwin, I and my confederates had already reached that conclusion before we agreed to this plan. If we thought we would win or that the world would buckle under to our demands, we would not be having this meeting. We are not doing this to make South Korea stronger or to make the United States look good. We are doing it as the only chance to avoid the destruction of North Korea. That, and only that, is our motivation. This is pure practical politics without any altruism whatsoever. In my business I have found it smart to not trust anyone unless they are acting primarily in their own best interest. Zealots scare me."

Pete pondered what Li had just said. He was exactly right. What they were considering was what was in the best interest of North Korea and the United States, individually and collectively. In a way they were playing God with the interests of South Korea, but fortunately, their plan was also in the best interest of South Korea. This was unusual. Throughout history, when two countries had made an agreement such as this, it has usually been to the detriment of a third party. This was an important point in the negotiations. They now trusted one another, not because they particularly liked one another, but because they had a mutuality of interests.

Pete said. "General Li, as I see it, you now have the hardest job, which is to convince your leaders to adopt a course of action that, as we agree, is not in their best interest. I think it is time for you to tell me how you are going to do that and who your confederates are. I think it is fair for me to ask you to convince me that you can pull it off."

Li smiled at that and temporized by offering to refill their glasses. He then took his seat and responded. "As you Americans like to say, that is the 64 thousand dollar question. I will give you the names of my confederates in just a moment, but I must first tell you what we want out of this. Their cooperation is dependent upon getting reasonable terms. Actually it goes further than that. Getting the people of North Korea to accept this requires that they maintain some amount of dignity. While I believe that the majority of our people now believe that communism is a false god and that Kim Il Sung was a false prophet, they are still a proud people. You must not ask for unconditional surrender. Rather, at the appropriate time we will ask for an armistice. We will agree to dismantle all of our nuclear weapons, pledge to never again produce them, and allow whatever inspections the world wants. We will agree to a plebecite to select our form of government to include some form of mutually agreed confederation with South Korea, if that is what the people want. We will agree to place our armed forces under the command of the United Nations if the South Koreans do the same. As you know, the South Koreans would not be giving up anything since they are already under the

UN. We will open up our borders to trade, communications and free passage. We will renounce furnishing arms to the world and cancel development of the Nodong missile. We will, however, ask for economic aid to rebuild our country and to avoid what has happened in Russia and the former East Germany.

"I know I have not answered your question directly, but in order to get the support of the necessary people to pull this off I have to be able to offer them something reasonable. One other thing you will not have to worry about is what to do with Sung Tae Won. We will take care of that.

"Now, how are we going to do it? During past conversations with Sung Tae Won, he has insisted on an early war and we have tried to talk him out of it. We will now tell him that he was right all along. This is the right time to introduce my confederates, since they will be needed to convince Sung. The two primary ones are General Yi Bong Su, Commander of the DPRK Armed Forces, and Dr. Chan So Dung, Chief Scientist of the DPRK and is responsible for our nuclear and missile programs. I will tell Sung that the U.S. and South Korean forces are not up to the task. Yi will tell Sung that the North Korean forces are ready to win, and Chan will tell Sung that our nuclear weapons are ready and will prevail. In other words, we will reinforce Sung in what he already erroneously believes."

Pete responded that the set of conditions that Li had requested was way beyond what he had the authority to agree to. He would have to discuss them with ambassador Noonan and then the President. He did say that, for whatever it was worth, he would recommend agreement to them.

They then discussed Pete's variation in the plan for the North Korean use of the nuclear weapon. Li told Pete that both Chan and Yi had thought it was a good idea and supported it. Like everything else about this plan, it had difficulties but seemed the best available option. Pete then asked Li if it was time to discuss exactly how and when the attack would take place. Pete wanted to be able to position his forces in the best possible place. Li stunned him by saying that the assumptions upon which War Plan Red Three had been based would be the right ones. That is how they would do it. Pete started to ask Li how he knew about Red Three but decided not to. This was the set of assumptions that Pete and General Pace had put together years ago when they revised the defense plans of South Korea.

It was time for Pete to go back to Red Cloud. It was apparent that they would have to have another meeting after Pete had communicated with the President. Pete would simply ask the bartender if he had heard from Smiley and repeat the process. As before, the garbage truck made it back to Red Cloud without incident, and this time Sandy was asleep in their bed. Much to their mutual delight, she awakened when Pete crawled in between the sheets.

Pete went down to Seoul the next day to tell Noonie what had transpired. Noonie was stoic about Li's terms. They were exactly the terms the U.S. would request if they were bargaining. He told Pete that approval would take a few days but probably would be no problem. He then showed Pete how to use the One Time Diana Pad. The simple concept was brilliant and no one without the other half of the pad could read the message. The Secretary of Defense had the other half. That was the good news. The bad news was that the sender and the receiver each had to spend an hour of their time encoding and decoding the message. In this case it was time well spent.

Pete returned to Uijongbu and asked Reuben how the CPX's were going. The answer was very positive. Pete asked if they had run Red Three recently. Reuben replied that it was the base case and had been run several times. Pete decided not to interfere further. He did not want to give anything away, and besides, maybe Li was playing him for a fool. Still, he knew they had better be prepared for anything. The nuclear incident would be the proof of Li's intentions.

Pete got a call from Noonie the next morning advising him to watch television at 0900 Korean time, which was late in the evening in Washington. The President was going to make an announcement on Korea from the White House. He preferred doing it this way, since he then did not have to subject himself to asinine questions from self-serving reporters who were transfixed with their own brilliance and importance. He would leave the questioning session to the Secretary of Defense.

The setting was the Oval Office of the White House. The President was sitting behind his desk – a desk which had been brought to the Oval Office by President Kennedy, who had found it in the basement. It had originally been a gift from Queen Victoria of England and was made from the wood of a fighting ship.

"Good evening my fellow Americans. Tonight I want to talk to you about a topic of grave national importance. I know that you are aware of what has been going on in Korea. There has been much said on this by the media, by other nations, and by members of both political parties in the United States. Much of what has been said has been contradictory and confusing. Many people wonder what the real situation is and where the government of the United States stands. I intend to tell you what I believe you are entitled to know. I wish that everything I have to say was good news. It is not. But I have enough confidence in the people of the United States to know that, given the truth, they will make the right decisions.

"Much has been said in speculation about whether the North Koreans have diverted Plutonium from their nuclear power plant at Yongbyon and developed a nuclear weapon. I am now convinced that they have developed at least one and are in the process of developing more. I am further convinced that the United Nation's inspection team from the International Atomic Energy Agency will not be able to detect the diversion of the Plutonium. We would be misleading you if we told otherwise.

"Recently, the North Koreans said that they would allow inspectors if the world would accede to their demands. Please think about that. First, as I said before, the inspections would not be able to prove anything. Second, the North Koreans are trying to trade something that they should not have and which they promised they would never do. This is blackmail and the United States will not be a party to it. The United States will never allow the independence of the Republic of Korea to be compromised. We will agree to nothing that places them in jeopardy. We hope to have the backing of the other nations of the world on this but, if necessary, we will stand alone.

"You have heard from many self-appointed experts that the North Koreans can defeat the South Koreans and Americans if they attack. This is utter hogwash. No one wants war, but if they are dumb enough to start one, I assure you that we will finish it. Now, if the North Koreans wish to avoid a war that will result in the destruction of their country, they can do so. First, they must admit and then renounce their nuclear weapon program. They must then allow meaningful inspections of all their facilities instead of the charade that is presently going on. Next, they must open their borders to commerce, communications, and freedom of passage. And finally, they must agree to a United Nation's supervised plebecite on their form of government.

"I know that these are tough conditions, but they are the conditions that the rest of the world lives under today. And, what if they don't accept these conditions? I am prepared to implement sanctions far beyond anything that has been discussed so far.

"I know that this has been a very dire presentation. It would be easy to just ignore the problem for now and acquiesce to the North Korean demands. But think about the future. What would happen some years from now when the North Koreans have many nuclear weapons and delivery means of over 600 miles? What would happen if they sell nuclear weapons to terrorists and terrorist nations? We must act and we must act now. History would never forgive us if we did not. Thank you, good night, and God bless the United States of America."

Pete had been watching the President's address with General Kim, his deputy. Kim was flabbergasted. He told Pete that he thought this meant war. Pete, in turn, felt very guilty that he had not been able to keep Kim informed as to what was going on between him and Li, and hoped to be able to correct that in the near future. However, Pete also realized that this would be a good time to set the stage.

"General Kim," said Pete, "think about what my President just said. He has committed the United Sates to the defense of South Korea. Let's examine the possibilities. First, we could do nothing now and just let things ride. As the President said, think about the future. Second, we could acquiesce to the North Korean demands and the future would get even worse. Third, the North Koreans might accept the President's conditions and we would hopefully solve the problem without war. This might happen with or without sanctions. Finally, the North Koreans might resort to war now. I am convinced, as I hope you are, that we will prevail and solve the problem that way. No matter how you analyze it, the President has done the right thing. We must now wait to see what the North Koreans do. Our job is simple. If they attack we will clean their clocks. I am reminded of a wild statement made by General Pace many years ago. If the North Koreans attack there will be so much of their blood in the rice paddies that the protein content will rise and produce bumper crops for years to come."

General Kim had no response and asked to be excused. Pete knew that Kim was going to his office to report the conversation to his bosses in Seoul. That was what Pete intended.

Later that afternoon the talking heads from all of the news networks were out in force. Universally, they were saying that the President had lost his mind. This made Pete feel good since that was an indication that he was right.

Chapter Twenty Three

The meeting in Pyongyang, capitol of the Democratic People's Republic of Korea, came to order. It had been hastily called by Sung Tae Won, President of the Democratic People's Republic of Korea. The attendees were Commander of the DPRK armed forces, General Yi Bong Su; Chief Scientist of the DPRK Dr. Chan So Dung; and Chief of the North Korean Security Services, Major General Li Joon Duk. Sung was agitated.

"Comrades, I have called this meeting because of recent speech by the President of the United States. I assume that you also heard the speech. Up to now, I have been very pleased with all of your performances and I expect to continue to be so if you have the right vision. The United States President has played right into our hands. We can now do what Kim Il Sung always intended. We also have the justification that the United States of America has threatened our nationhood and sovereignty and, as any free nation, we have a right to protect ourselves. He thought he could intimidate us into surrender. He is totally wrong. Instead, he has given us the opportunity that we have long awaited for. I am ready to take action, but first I want each of you to give me your evaluation. General Li, you first."

Li thought that this was almost too easy. Sung had already made up his mind and was only looking for support. "Honorable Comrade Leader," said Li, "I thank you for this opportunity. As you are aware, up to now I have advised caution. But thanks to your leadership, I have renewed my intelligence efforts and learned that you were right all along. I hope you will forgive me for my past caution. I have concentrated my intelligence efforts on South Korea and have actually made two personal visits to verify what my agents have told me. I have learned that, for all their rhetoric, the United States forces and the South Koreans are not ready to fight. They are scared. They know what we did to them many years ago. We almost won then, and would have won except for the massive infusion of U.S. troops. My agents in the United States tell me that there is no mood for war and there are sufficient votes in the majority party in the U.S. Congress to preclude anything but symbolic action. The readiness of the DPRK forces will be stated by Comrade General Yi, but it is my view that the imperialists will crumble rapidly, especially when overcome with the terror induced by our nuclear weapon." Sung nodded without expression and asked General Yi to speak.

"Comrade Leader," responded Yi, "our forces are ready. We have over a million men under arms, compared to the lackey's 600,000. We have twice their tanks, artillery, and combat aircraft. We have been devising our plan of attack for years, have war-gamed it extensively, and have continuously trained on it. It is interesting that one of the perceived South Korean strengths is actually a great weakness. As you can see from this map, they have established three fortified lines called Alpha, Bravo, and Charlie. They will occupy these lines when they feel threatened. They are guilty of what I call 'Maginot' thinking – I refer to what the French did at the beginning of World War II. When they occupy these lines they will make themselves completely vulnerable to a flanking attack across the Imjin Gang when it is frozen over. In order to draw them into this position, we will start with a secondary attack down the Chorwan valley. They will overreact under the impress of history. Sir, I am confident. We have the forces, the plans, and with your leadership we can not fail."

Sung again gave an expressionless nod of approval.

It was now Chan's turn. "Comrade Leader. We have one nuclear weapon ready for use. At best, we could have another in about a month, but for our purposes one will be sufficient. It is also the case that the imperialists do not know exactly how many we have. Our weapon is too heavy to be placed in an aircraft or a missile, but again, because of our purpose, that is only a minor inconvenience. I have discussed this with Comrades Li and Yi and we have devised a plan that I believe you will like. But before I tell you the plan let me explain what we will accomplish. First, the weapon will be detonated immediately preceding the supporting attack down the Chorwan valley. This will cause confusion and panic and further conceal the location of the main attack. However, we must not detonate the weapon near the front lines because the resulting rubble and radioactivity would be a barrier to our attacking forces. Rather, it should be detonated in a location that hampers the South Koreans and Americans from bringing their reinforcements forward. Finally, the location of detonation must be somewhere that we can transport the weapon to, which brings us back to the method of delivery. Now here is our plan. It accomplishes all of the objectives that I just stated."

Sung listened carefully to the plan, then approved it. He congratulated the men on their ingenuity, not knowing that it was actually the American, General Goodwin, who had suggested it.

Chan had one more thing to say. "Comrade Leader. It is apparent that the plan requires a one-way mission. The people that detonate the weapon must be physically present to do it. There is also a chance that they will be discovered before they reach the intended location. If so, they can still detonate the weapon and not let it fall into enemy hands. This will accomplish most of our objectives. Of course, the soldiers accompanying the weapon must be completely knowledgeable of its workings and totally dedicated to our cause. I request the personal honor of being one of these soldiers. It would be the culmination of my life's work. I hope you will approve."

Sung reached over and embraced Chan, granting him the permission he requested. Chan did not know that Sung was going to order him to do this very thing had he not volunteered.

Sung then asked when they would be ready to carry out the plan. Yi said that two weeks time would allow sufficient preparation and that an attack on early Sunday morning would be best, since many Korean officers were away from their units on the weekends. Li verified that this practice still continued in spite of the present crisis and said it was just another indication that the South Koreans would be unprepared. Also, in two weeks, the Imjin Gang would be frozen solid. Yet another factor was the tides. High tide, which would occur early that Sunday morning, was necessary for the employment of the nuclear weapon. Thus, the date and time of the offensive were set.

Later that afternoon, at one of Li's safe houses, Li and Yi discussed how, without arousing suspicion, they would ensure that the North Korean attack failed. In the end, they decided not to interfere with the initial attack plan that had been approved by Sung and practiced for years. They would have to depend on General Goodwin's prediction that he could stop the attack. If the initial attack failed, or at least did not achieve the expected results, then there would naturally have to be deviations from the plan. This was an area in which the North Koreans were not skilled. They had not been trained to use initiative on the battlefield. They needed to be centrally controlled and did not question orders from higher headquarters. This fact would allow Li to influence the action. He could furnish North Korean headquarters with fictitious and misleading intelligence. The intelligence he provided had to be credible, yet it had to be misleading so that reinforcements and resupply would arrive late or be misdirected.

At the appropriate time a false report of an impending amphibious assault on the port of Namp'o, just to the southwest of Pyongyang, would be spread. At a minimum this would draw off forces from the front lines and perhaps cause a panic reminiscent of the Inchon invasion 40 years earlier. At the same time, a report of the U.S. 82nd Airborne Division about to be dropped on Pyongyang would be made. Again, this would create panic but, more importantly, it would give Yi the rationale to send the 815th Mechanized Corps to Pyongyang, ostensibly to defend it. However, the Commander of the Corps, along with selected staff, was now one of the conspirators. The troops, being North Korean, would do what they were told.

There was one more subtle factor in the plan. By timing the nuclear event for midnight, the U.S. and South Korean air forces would thereby gain a real advantage. While the North had more planes than the South, the South's planes were far more capable of night and limited visibility action, especially with the support of the AWACS. In those critical six hours much of North Korea's air power could be destroyed. Then the command and control centers would be vulnerable, creating a situation where the ground troops, who were dependent on instructions from higher headquarters, would be unable to communicate. At this point Li and Yi would be at greatest personal risk. Even if Sung did not suspect what was going on he would probably still issue a command to have them shot for failure. To prevent this, Li and Yi intended to be with the 815th Mechanized Corps at that time to participate in the takeover of the government. Chan would already be out of harm's way if the plan for the nuclear detonation succeeded.

Li now had to leave to begin making arrangements for his next meeting with General Goodwin. This meeting would probably have to be the last one, for this sort of thing can only be done so many times before people start to become suspicious. Besides, he was running out of clandestine ways of getting in and out of South Korea, which reminded him that he would have to tell General Goodwin where the various tunnels under the DMZ were. There weren't 30, as stated in the U.S. press, but there were eight.

The arrangements for Pete's and Li's last meeting were the same as before, which led Sandy to ask Pete if he was in training for a post retirement job as an assistant driver on a garbage truck. Pete replied with an old joke that the pay and the hours were good and you could have all you wanted to eat. Sandy grimaced at the poor joke, but they both knew that the tension was getting to everyone and that certain excesses had to be tolerated.

Upon Pete's arrival at the predetermined secret location, Li congratulated him on the speech made by the President of the United States several days earlier. It hit exactly the right tone and was the final straw that convinced Sung Tae Won that the time had come to attack. He had taken it as a personal affront.

Li then told Pete of the meeting with Sung and informed him that the decision to attack had actually been made by Sung before the meeting. It would have taken a major disaster to change Sung's mind. The irony of the situation was that, with the coordination between Pete and Li, the major disaster had already occurred without Sung knowing it. Li then informed Pete of the date and time of the attack. Pete already knew where it would come and in what strength.

Li stressed two points. First, the entire operation hinged on the North Koreans believing that the nuclear weapon had been successful, since that was to be the first in a series of sequential events. This meant that the route to the target point must not be impeded, but also that it must not be obvious. Next, Chan would assure that the weapon could not be detonated. Then it was Pete's job to take possession of the weapon without the North Koreans in Pyongyang knowing about it, while leading them to believe that it had been detonated. They went over the plans several times and made a few minor adjustments until they both were satisfied.

Li next made the important point that the reaction of the South Koreans and the Americans could not be premature or it would give away the entire plan. It was for this reason that the nuclear event would be staged first. An obvious response after a nuclear attack on your territory is to bring your forces to full alert. The real key was the immediate air offensive on North Korean forces just after the weapon had been detonated. The first priority targets would be airfields and communications centers. There was no way to prevent the enemy from getting off one air strike, but the intent was that there would be no place for them to return to afterward. This one strike, however, meant that there would be damage to some friendly locations. Li told Pete that the first priority of the North Korean Air Force would include support of their ground attack. Friendly units would have to take their lumps, but contrary to the movies, well disciplined troops properly dug in are relatively invulnerable to conventional air attacks and the North Koreans did not have precision guided munitions.

A subtlety of Pete's and Li's plan was that the South Korean reaction to occupy the defensive positions along lines Alpha and Bravo in the vicinity of the Chorwan valley would actually go more slowly than called for in the War Plans. This would position them much better for blunting the North Korean main attack.

Pete and Li talked for four hours, reviewing every detail of the plan many times, trying to anticipate the many things that could go wrong. They had both been around long enough to know that in combat nothing ever goes entirely as planned. The cover and deception plan involving the amphibious landing and the 82nd Airborne assault on Pyongyang was one part of the overall plan that they reviewed. Both ships and aircraft would be involved, making credible feints, which was another reason for making a successful early air campaign. While engaged in this review, Pete suddenly realized that he would have to bring the Air Force commander in earlier than he had originally planned. It is physically impossible to get a valid Air Tasking Order – as the air war planning document was called – in less than six hours. He would need the approval of the Secretary of Defense to do this.

Finally both were satisfied and the meeting came to an end. Pete and Li stood, shook hands, and wished each other good luck. Both men struggled to find something more to say but no words came. Li then saluted Pete, and Pete returned the salute. Between professional soldiers a sincere salute is often far better than words.

Chapter Twenty Four

During the following few days Pete decided that it was time to bring other people into the plan. This was going to be tricky both in terms of timing and deciding who would be informed. He discussed it at great length with Noonie, who made a few suggestions which he accepted. Noonie then sent a "Diana" message to the Secretary of Defense asking for his and the President's approval. Approval was granted and was accompanied by a personal note from the President to the participants, saying that he was convinced that the information was authentic and stressing the utter necessity of secrecy. In a separate note to Noonie and Pete he told them that there was no reason to tell the other participants the source of the information or that any agreements had been made or coordination arranged. They did not need to know this to do their assigned jobs. Finally, the President told them that he would take responsibility for informing the President of South Korea. Pete knew that he was going to have a hard time explaining the nuclear event, but he would just allude to good intelligence and sources that he could not divulge.

The meeting took place in the conference room of General Armstrong, who was the Commander in Chief of United Nations Forces, Korea in addition to Commander in Chief of United States Forces, Korea. At Ambassador Noonan's request the room had been swept for electronic bugging devices and no aides, secretaries, or other support personnel were present. Attending were Ambassador Noonan, General Armstrong, General Goodwin, General Lee Chi Na, Chairman of the ROK JCS, and the commanders of the United Nations Air Forces and Naval Forces, Korea who were an American Major General and Rear Admiral, respectively.

Ambassador Noonan led. He started by saying that he had already briefed the President of the Republic of Korea, Lee Duk Qwan, and that the President of the United States had also spoken to him. Lee had agreed with what was about to be said and had authorized them to proceed. Noonan admonished them that what they were about to hear was for their ears only. They could not tell anyone else. This information was to assist them in their decisions. Their subordinates did not need to know the reason behind those decisions. For example, the Commander of United Nations Air Forces, Korea had already put together several air campaign packages for the employment of friendly air based upon different assumptions. The information they were about to receive concerned these different packages and the circumstances under which each would be employed.

Ambassador Noonan thought some preliminary remarks were in order to establish credibility.

"Gentlemen," he said, "I think I should start by telling you a little bit about myself. I can be described as an old Korea hand. I first came to South Korea in the early 50's at the end of the Korean War. One of the accidents of life – although you will see later that it wasn't a complete accident – was that I shared a hootch with General Goodwin during those difficult days. After the war I returned to the United States and got out of the Army. Several years later I returned to South Korea because I could see business opportunities. Along the way I made a lot of money, made a lot of friends, and learned to speak Hangul. In the early 60's, at the request of the present President of the United States, I became a parttime operative for the American CIA. Over the years I supported the President financially and politically when he was running for Senator and Governor. When he unexpectedly became the President, he asked me to be his Ambassador to South Korea in order to help him determine the right thing for the United States to do here. This brings us to the purpose of this meeting.

"Let us discuss the present situation. Included within my remarks will be references to extraordinary intelligence that until today was known only to myself, General Goodwin, the President of the United States, and our Secretary of Defense. I implore you to keep this information to yourself. It was a difficult call to decide how much to tell you. We must tell you enough to allow you to do your jobs properly. However, I hope you will understand, at least for now, why I can not tell you the source of this information. Let me assure you that both the President and the Secretary believe that the information is accurate and are willing to stake their futures and the future of the United States on it.

"First, there is no doubt that the North Koreans have an active nuclear weapons program. They have one operational weapon now and in several years will have more than ten. In spite of all the rhetoric that you have heard, United Nations' inspections will not, I repeat, not stop this development from taking place. The North Koreans intend to use these weapons in several ways. They will use them as blackmail if they think they can get away with it, they will use them actively in combat if it seems appropriate to them to do so, and will sell them to terrorist nations. This latter point shows why the oft spoken sanctions won't work. The terrorist nations are now giving North Korea credit against future delivery.

"What are the options? One is that we can do nothing now, which would give the North Koreans time to develop the weapons. I ask you to think about the world several years from now if that should happen. We could try to impose sanctions to cause the North Koreans to cease the development of these weapons. However, I conclude, as does the President, that this will not work. I hope you do also. Something has been suggested along the lines of a preemptive strike on the North Korean nuclear facilities. The people that have suggested this are not military. They remember the Israeli attacks on the Dimona nuclear facility in the Middle East years ago. But this situation is entirely different. In the Dimona case there was one undefended above-ground target. Here there are multiple facilities, underground, which are heavily defended. Even precision guided munitions would have little effect on them. Besides, it would be seen as an act of war.

"It would seem that we have run out of options. We are damned if we do and damned if we don't. But there is one other option. What if the North Koreans attack and the attack is unsuccessful? At that point we would have the freedom of action to solve the problem. I suggest that you think about the President's speech the other night in this context. He was telling the North Koreans that many of their perceived options were no longer realistic and that their assumptions concerning the reaction of the world to their threats were inaccurate. I will now turn the presentation over to General Goodwin."

"Thank you, Sir," said Pete. "The North Koreans are going to attack starting at midnight on the 23rd of this month. I mean midnight dividing the 23rd and the 24th." Pete made this point because 'midnight' was ambiguous in this context and could refer to one of two days. Incredible as it seems, this had actually happened in Vietnam during the Tet offensive. Reasonably good intelligence was available that the North Vietnamese and Viet Cong were going to attack at midnight. In several instances, to their detriment, commanders picked the wrong day. "In the Eastern part of South Korea in the areas of the ROK I, II, III, and VIII Corps, the attacks will be secondary. The first ground attack will be down the Chorwan valley. This will not be the main attack but will be intended to draw our forces into their main battle positions. The main attack will be along the Kaesong Munson approach across the Imjin Gang which is already frozen hard solid. The initial objective will be Uijongbu and then on to Ch'unch'on. If they accomplish this they would be able to envelop most of lines Alpha, Bravo, and Charlie.

"My First Combined Field Army has the ROK IV, VI, and VII Corps as well as the U.S. Second Infantry Division. The North Korean main attack will be in my sector. I am confident that with these forces, recent reinforcements from the United States to include JSTARS and counterbattery radars, and this forewarning that we will be able to defeat the attack and go over to a counteroffensive in less that a week if that is necessary.

"I initially told you that the attack would begin at midnight. Let me explain that because it is critical and gives us a real advantage. The initial hostile action of North Korea will be at midnight. Their ground and air offensive will begin at first light on the 24th. We will have about six hours to conduct the air campaign, spoiling attacks, and counterbattery artillery fire. The midnight event I'm about to describe has been calculated by the North Koreans to spread panic, confusion and indecision and if we did not have this intelligence probably would have done so. Our advantage is that the instant they start the war we will react and hit them faster than they hit us.

"Now I will explain the midnight event. I use midnight since that is when the North Koreans intend doing it. War being war, they may be off a bit. The point I'm trying to make is that we start our war as soon as this event happens. We will establish proper communications to let you know. You may have to start a little earlier than midnight or perhaps a little later. Be ready."

At that point, Pete described the North Korean nuclear attack and how it was going to be combated. This elicited a lot of discussion and everyone in the room tried to shoot down the plan. Ultimately, after thinking it through, they came to the same conclusions that Pete and Li had. The Commander of United Nations Naval Forces, Korea understood clearly what he had to do, but told Pete that in order to do it he must tell several select people. General Armstrong agreed and asked the Commander to come back to him with a plan of action by the next day – one that included who would be told so that it could be reviewed and approved. Ambassador Noonan concurred.

Ambassador Noonan again mentioned the necessity for keeping this information Close Hold and said that since the ground forces and the air forces had several rehearsed war plans and campaign packages it was not necessary for them to know. On the other hand, the naval forces were being asked to do something quite out of the ordinary. He asked that he be advised by General Armstrong as to the naval plan. He further asked the Commander if he would do the first draft by hand, himself, without involving anyone else. The Commander said that he would. The mood was somber as the meeting came to an end.

The next morning Ambassador Noonan and General Armstrong met with the Commander of UN Naval Forces, Korea, who was also the Commander of U.S. Naval Forces, Korea. (This was a carryover from the Korean War when the United Nations had declared the Korean conflict, which had never technically been declared a war, to be a United Nations responsibility. Over the years the arrangements had remained in force to the mutual satisfaction of the UN, the U.S., and the South Koreans.)

The Commander stressed that he understood the criticality of the

209

situation and said that he had devised a plan which he thought would meet the requirements. First, he figured that he would not have to tell anyone in his tactical operations center – in Navyspeak called Flag Plot – what was happening. He would physically remain in the Flag Plot during the critical hours and personally make the necessary decisions. He would put his command on 'Guns Tight,' which meant that no one could do anything without his express authority. He was sure that some of his officers would think that he had lost his mind, but he could handle that. One part of the job would require a SEAL team of about 50 men under the command of a Navy Lieutenant. Fortunately, Navy Seals, being Special Operations personnel, were used to clandestine operations and the necessity for being put into a controlled secure area prior to an operation where communications with the outside world would be prohibited. The Commander stated that in order for the SEALs to do their job they had to be fully briefed and be allowed to rehearse and practice with their unique equipment. They would be in total quarantine the entire time. These were a special kind of people who could be depended upon. This way nothing had to be reduced to writing and no orders to other than the SEALs were required. After a minimum of discussion, the Ambassador and the General approved the plan. Noonie returned to his office and wrote one more 'Diana' message to the President and the Secretary informing them that the operation was under way.

BOOK 4

THE FIGHT

Chapter Twenty Five

Captain Shim, commander of the DPRK submarine Choson Victory, had been called to Pyongyang for a meeting with Sung, General Yi Bong Su, and Dr. Chan So Dung. He had never met any of these people before and wondered what was so important. He anticipated that the meeting had something to do with the fact that his submarine had been ordered to proceed under the cover of darkness to the port of Namp'o on the west coast of North Korea just southwest of Pyongyang. The Choson Victory was named after the Choson Kingdom, which had total control of the entire peninsula in the 15th century.

The Choson Victory was the newest and quietest submarine in the North Korean navy, having been obtained clandestinely at the breakup of the Soviet Union. They had actually bought it from a mutinous Soviet Admiral who had realized that the new Russian government had lost track of its military inventory. Everybody was selling everything, although as far as the Russian admiral knew, he was the only one who had sold a submarine. The reason that the North Koreans wanted it was that it was quiet and could probably escape detection from U.S. and South Korean anti-submarine forces, unlike the 20 Golf-type submarines that they had purchased officially. In fact, the official purchase of the 20 Golfs was actually a cover for this purchase.

Shim was ushered into Sung's office. Sung rose and greeted Shim and told him that he had been personally selected for the most important job in the history of the DPRK. His name would be at the forefront of history and would be remembered forever by every schoolchild. He was a very lucky man. Shim was apprehensive and remained quiet. He realized that something not necessarily good was about to happen. Sung asked General Yi to explain the mission. After the explanation Sung asked Shim if he was prepared to undertake it. Shim thought for a moment and said. "Comrade Leader, I am honored that you have selected me for this historic task. I will do it and I will do it successfully." This was a lie on Shim's part. He realized that the probability of surviving this mission was practically nil. On the other hand, if he refused it, he was certain that both he and his family would be immediately executed.

"Very well," said Sung, "I will now turn you over to General Yi and Dr.

Chan. To show you how much confidence we have in you and the success of the mission, Dr. Chan will be accompanying you. Also, his scientific and technical knowledge will be needed. Effective immediately you are now a Rear Admiral. As such, your family will be moved into more appropriate quarters and furnished with a car and driver. They will receive Admiral's food rations. Good Luck."

Shim returned to Namp'o and his submarine. He was accompanied by Dr. Chan, who needed to take some measurements. Because of the size of the nuclear weapon it could not be put into the submarine through any of the available hatches. A hole had to be cut in the deck. However, they were not simply going to cut a hole, lower the weapon into the submarine, and then weld the hole shut. For the benefit of the crew, after cutting the hole, they were going to install a hydraulic lift and watertight doors. As far as the crew was concerned, the mission was to deliver the nuclear weapon to a group of infiltrators, who would carry it away and detonate it elsewhere. This was a refinement in the plan that had been suggested by the new Admiral Shim. While the crew was dedicated and could be trusted in normal situations, knowing the real mission might be too much for them. There was no reason for the crew to know.

After Chan had taken the measurements, he went to the dockyard commander and issued instructions. The dockyard commander had already received a phone call from the office of Sung about cooperating with Chan and not asking any questions. He was to keep his work force to the minimum needed and select trustworthy personnel. The commander had no way of knowing that after he had completed his work he was to be taken into custody for security purposes. After meeting with the dockyard commander, Chan returned to Yongbyon to begin arranging for the nuclear weapon to be taken to Namp'o. The timing was critical. It could not arrive too early or too late and this was dependent on the progress of the conversion of the submarine. The overall plan allowed two extra days for unexpected difficulties.

Admiral Shim returned to his office to do his calculations and planning. He had originally thought about calling his family and explaining his absence. However, he noticed that he was being closely followed and figured that his phone was probably tapped. He had been instructed to do all the calculations himself and to bring no one from the crew into the planning of the mission. Each individual was to know only what was necessary for him to do his particular job. The first thing that Shim had to do was to select a crew. Usually his submarine had a crew of 120, since they had to have several shifts for round the clock operations over an extended time. Actually, only about forty people were necessary to run the submarine. In this case they would need fewer, since some jobs, like loading and firing torpedoes, would not be done. Shim settled on thirty of his best men. They would be quarantined on the sub. The remainder of the crew would be quarantined on Namp'o base.

Shim also had to do a series of weight and balance calculations based upon the difference of this load from the normal one. A submarine must be delicately balanced: too buoyant and it comes to the surface; too heavy and it sinks to the bottom; if the bow is heavier than the stern, it will go up on end. This balance is achieved by letting in or blowing out sea water from different compartments in the outer hull. This can be done as it occurs but it is far better to be able to anticipate it. The transitions are more smooth and more safe than the unexpected. Fortunately, Chan had been able to give Shim all the information he would need. The calculations were simple, but they had to be right.

The final set of calculations was associated with navigation. He had to arrive at a deserted pier just south of Inchon at midnight of the 23rd -24th of the month. He had to make his passage at high tide. After the Bay of Fundy, the area around Inchon had the second highest tides in the world. There was a 32 foot difference between high tide and low tide. This was the difference between having sufficient depth for navigation and running aground. Depth was also needed in order to escape detection. Because of the relative shallowness of the Yellow Sea, this was not easy. The route could not be the most direct one. He would have to go straight west when leaving Namp'o, then south, and finally, somewhat northeast back to Inchon. It was possible but difficult. The navigation was not all that tough, but the possibility of detection worried him. Chan had told him not to worry, although Shim had no idea why Chan was qualified to make such a statement. Shim did not know that he was intentionally being given a free ride. Shim went over his calculations several times until he was convinced he had them right. Factored into the calculations was the fact that Shim wanted to run as quietly as possible, which also meant relatively slowly. He determined that he had to leave Namp'o at 0100 on the 21st. Once having decided this he changed his crew requirements to 50. He would have to run two shifts after all because the trip was going to be longer than he first thought.

The dockyard work went smoothly. By the 19th, it had been completed. Shim had requested that he be allowed to make two trial runs. The first was to be made before the loading of the nuclear weapon in order to test the watertightness of the new doors. They were watertight. That evening the nuclear weapon arrived from Yongbyon and was loaded during the hours of darkness so that it could not be observed by U.S. satellites or other observation means. Once loaded, Shim took the sub out again to verify the accuracy of his weight and balance calculations. Again they were correct. Admiral

Shim was ready to go and informed the office of General Yi. During the evening of the the 20th, Sung Tae Won visited the submarine and inspected it himself, although he really did not know what to look for. He made the appropriate speeches and told the entire crew that they had been promoted one grade and that their families were being provided extra rations for their heroic deed.

At 0100 on the 21st the Choson Victory started out to sea on its epic voyage. The world would never be the same, although what was about to happen was far different from what Sung Tae Won anticipated.

The U.S. Navy Rear Admiral, who was also the Commander of United Nations Naval Forces, Korea was informed through Li and Pete that the clock had started. The first phase was underway. The Choson Victory was at sea. The Admiral was at his Flag Plot and would remain there for the next several days. He reckoned the probability of detection of the Choson Victory at about 50%. Having thought about this over the last several days, he went to Ambassador Noonan with a cover and deception plan that could be used if the sub were detected, so as to avoid having to attack it. It was quite ingenious and the Ambassador approved it.

At the 0800 watch briefing on the 22nd, the Admiral gave some very specific orders. "I want what I'm about to say to be written verbatim into the Watchbook," (referring to the book of instructions that are carried over from watch to watch). They remain in force until the Admiral changes them. "I want to maintain normal, repeat, normal, surveillance activities over the next few days. I do not want any loose cannons out there running off and doing their own thing. I am ordering 'Guns Tight,' and if there is any doubt among you, that means no one can fire and change the rules of engagement without my express authority. If a contact is picked up I want no action of any kind to include changes in surveillance patterns. If a contact is picked up I wish to be informed immediately no matter the time. If that sounds mysterious to you, the reason is that there are certain things going on that I am not presently permitted to share with you. When the time comes you can be assured that I will tell you what I can. Are there any questions? Make sure that everyone in the Flag Plot gets these orders and that every command down to the last ship and aircraft acknowledges them. And, in this case, I mean a positive acknowledgement. If you do not get a response from someone keep trying until you do. I wish to be informed of anyone who does not acknowledge these orders."

The orders were received stoically by the officers and men of the Flag Plot. They were unusual to say the least. This Admiral had a well-earned reputation for being a fighter and one who encourages initiative in his subordinates. There was something quite unique and important going on. But they had learned to trust this old salt, and if he said so, that was good enough for them.

The Admiral was very unhappy over what he had just had to do. This was not his style. The next two days were probably going to be the most difficult of his life. At the end of Phase I of the operation, if everything went according to plan, he had been authorized by the Ambassador to tell his command what was going on. If things didn't go right, because of his location, he would be dead anyway, as would those in his headquarters.

At about 4:00 PM on the 23rd the Admiral was awakened. He was taking a nap, fully dressed, on a cot in his office. His mouth was vile, since he had drunk far too much Navy coffee over the last two days.

"Admiral," said the Watch Officer, "there is something showing up on our shore radar that I think you ought to see. I apologize for waking you, but you instructed us to do so."

The Admiral hurried to the plotting board, where the yeoman pointed out what appeared to be a submarine contact.

"Sir," said the yeoman, "I can't be sure, but this looks like it might be a hostile submarine. I know that it is not one of ours. Under normal rules of engagement, I would have sent in additional surveillance measures, but you have ordered us not to do so."

The room became very quiet. Everyone was curious as to what the Admiral would do and say. The Admiral was thankful for having the Ambassador's approval for what he was about to say.

"Gentlemen, I congratulate you on picking up the target and for following instructions. I can now tell you some of what is going on. That is an enemy sub. I have known about it for three days through intelligence sources not normally available to this office. That is the Choson Victory, and it left Namp'o at 0100 on the 21st. It contains some high ranking members of the North Korean government who are defecting. It was scheduled to make a normal deployment at that time. So far, we have no indications that the North Koreans know that it is deviating from its planned mission. We don't want to help them in that. The sub is scheduled to make landfall just south of Inchon at about midnight tonight, where it will be met by the South Korean government, who will take possession of it and give the defectors political asylum. Our job is to make sure that it gets through unimpeded. You will not tell this to the fleet at sea. Just keep them away. If any other activity shows up please inform me. Also, keep tracking the sub by inactive surveillance rather than active surveillance. I would like to know if it keeps to its intended track, which I will indicate for you on the map now. Any questions? None? Good, I think I will go get a couple more hours of sleep."

The Admiral knew that he would not sleep and every instinct in his body was to remain in Flag Plot and direct the action. But he had to play the role. "God," he thought to himself, "it sure would be nice to get back to a normal sea command instead of all this spook stuff."

The Choson Victory was on course and on time. Once submerged off Namp'o it had never surfaced, much to the discomfort of Dr. Chan. Like many people, he found a submarine claustrophobic. Shim recognized the symptoms and gave him one of the tranquilizers that are carried aboard all submarines of all nations, although they don't like to talk about it. This reaction can happen to even the most experienced of submariners. The next day Chan was better and apologized for his weakness. Shim explained that it was a frequent occurrence and most people get over it. Chan asked how the voyage was going.

"Dr. Chan," replied Shim, "we are right on time. We are running submerged, but every so often I have to rise to periscope depth to take a position location reading. That is when we are most vulnerable to detection. When I rose to periscope depth about two hours ago our radar detector on the periscope indicated that we may have been detected by a shore based J band radar. By the lack of activity since then I think they missed us. The South Korean's plan of action, once they have a possible detection, is to send out aircraft and helicopters with all sorts of detection devices. This did not happen. We have about six hours to go and this is when you told me you would give me my orders on the nuclear device. I assume it is time."

"Very well, Comrade Admiral," said Chan. "It is time. Can you accompany me to the forward compartment where the weapon is located?"

Shim issued the proper instructions to the Executive Officer and they both went forward.

The weapon was lashed to the floor so that it would not move in case of a violent maneuver. The sailors that had lashed it down had taken special care. They were scared to death. Chan explained to Shim that the weapon would not go off due to any sudden movement. The lashing down was to assure that it would function as designed. It did not look like a weapon, since it was not built with any special aerodynamic purpose in mind. It was not designed to be put in a missile or to be dropped from an airplane. It was just a big heavy box about five feet by five feet by eight feet with lots of instrument dials and a control panel on the top. It looked both ordinary and menacing. Chan showed Shim how the control panel and the dials were used to check to see if the weapon would function as designed. He then handed Shim a key on a chain to put around his neck. He then showed him a second one that he would keep.

"You can see, Comrade Admiral, two key holes on opposite sides of the box. They are far enough apart so that one person can not insert and turn both keys simultaneously. It requires two people. You have one and I have one. At the appropriate time we will turn them together and the weapon will detonate. Our plan is to detonate it when we reach the pier. If, however, at any time from now on you feel that we may be captured or sunk, we must set off the weapon regardless. We will still accomplish the intended effect. In essence we have already achieved our mission. Let me explain.

"The power of this weapon is approximately the size of the one that the Americans dropped on Nagasaki Japan in World War II, which is 20 Kilotons. That means that it has the explosive equivalent of twenty thousand tons of TNT. For comparative purposes one of your torpedoes has about 400 pounds of TNT. But there is more to it than that. When a nuclear weapon goes off it produces three primary effects, which are blast, heat, and radioactivity. Each of these has a different destructive power and, as important, reacts uniquely with the surrounding environment. An air burst – that is, one whose fireball does not touch the ground – produces very little radioactivity but lots of heat and blast. A ground burst, on the other hand, has less heat and blast, but much more radioactivity and fallout. A water burst has even less heat and blast but far more radioactive fallout due to the interaction between the initial radioactivity and the surrounding water. Our weapon was never intended to destroy all of Inchon. Its purpose is to cause panic and confusion and due to the radioactive fallout to preclude reinforcements from going north through the vicinity of Inchon. If we set this weapon off right now, the blast and fireball will be seen in Inchon and Seoul but there will be no immediate damage there. But the radioactive fallout will be huge. This is because the wind is blowing to the northeast. The so called mushroom cloud would rise above us to over 50,000 feet. This cloud would be composed of very radioactive water vapor, which would be carried into South Korea. Our mission would still be accomplished, although somewhat differently than if it is detonated near Inchon. The difference is really between near term and long term damage. The psychological effect, and therefore the panic, would be the same."

There was one other aspect of the nuclear phenomenon that Chan did not tell Shim, since it was the basis for the plan that Li and Pete had worked out.

It was approaching midnight. The Choson Victory was about a half mile offshore and was running at periscope depth. If the charts and the tide calculations were right, they would run aground right next to the pier. Running a ship of war aground was considered the worst of sins for a naval commander. In this instance, it was part of the mission. At 200 yards offshore Shim brought the sub further to the surface, so that the conning tower was above the waterline, and opened the hatch. He had taken the unusual step of putting his executive officer in charge of the landing. He knew that he had to be in the vicinity of the weapon if they were discovered. He had no way of knowing that they had been under constant surveillance for the last three miles. Presently the submarine ground to a halt right next to the pier. Shim anticipated that all Hell was going to break loose, since they had actually just invaded enemy soil. But all was quiet. The lookouts on the conning tower could see nothing of the infiltration party that they had been told was going to meet them. Shim told them to remain alert because they would be there soon. Shim then went forward to Dr. Chan's location to meet his destiny.

Chan took out his key and indicated for Shim to do the same. No words were said. It just didn't seem appropriate. They both inserted their keys and two green lights appeared on the control panel. Chan nodded and held up three fingers for a count down. On the count of three they both turned their keys. Nothing happened. During his final checkout of the weapon, Chan had simply reversed the polarity of the wires leading from the keys to the electrical explosive generator. Instead of getting two 'Go' signals, the generator had gotten two 'No Go' signals.

Shim, who had been prepared for death, was shaken. He asked Chan what had gone wrong. Chan checked the instrument panel and said that probably some moisture had gotten into the mechanism during the voyage. Fortunately, he could fix it, although it would take about a half hour. He suggested to Shim that he might send his crew out to establish a fighting perimeter in case they were discovered. This would buy them the time needed. Also, the crew would be told to make contact with the nonexistent infiltration party. Shim agreed.

Every word that had passed between Chan and Shim had been heard by the joint U.S. Korean SEAL team. They were in their assigned positions. Some were in the water next to the sub, where they had attached listening devices to the hull. The officer in charge pushed a button on his hand-held command and control device that gave a silent order to the SEALs. Step 1 of Phase 1 was complete and now it was time for Step 2. As the crew of the Choson Victory got off the sub and started to form a perimeter, they were taken out by the SEALs' silenced weapons. At the same time an assault team hit the submarine. It was now no time for silent action. The more noise and confusion the better for trained troops used to fighting in the darkness.

The SEAL team advanced to the front of the sub, throwing concussion grenades ahead of them to stun and incapacitate anyone left on board. In addition they were wearing night vision devices and had trained on an exact mock-up for a week. Just before they reached the forward compartment where the nuclear device was located, Admiral Shim realized what was going on and that his mission was a failure. In accordance with the private instructions that he had received personally from Sung he took out his pistol and fired two shots into the head of Dr. Chan. After verifying that Chan was dead he put the pistol into his own mouth with the muzzle directed upward toward the brain and pulled the trigger.

The SEAL team reached the forward compartment a moment later. With hardly a glance at the bodies, the nuclear weapons expert among them checked the weapon. He gave his team leader the thumbs up signal. The leader went on deck and spoke into his radio. "Green Six, this is Blue Six. Phase one of Triton is completed." There was much clean up work to do and much to tell but that could wait.

The Commander of the United Nations Naval Forces, Korea heard the transmission. He gathered his people together and told them what had happened and what was about to happen in 10 minutes.

Chapter Twenty Six

Captain, U.S. Army, Martin Edwards (Commander of D Battery, 1st Battalion, 78th Artillery, Second U.S. Army Infantry Division) was both angry and confused. He had received orders that simply did not make any sense. His Battery was the composite Battery of the Battalion and, as such, he had four M-110 howitzers. The M-110 was a self-propelled 203 millimeter howitzer with a range of over 24,000 meters. It was the most accurate artillery piece in the U.S. Army. Its mission was to deliver general support artillery fire to the entire division. His Battery was good and he knew it. It was also an integral part of the Division's war plans. Over the last several weeks, as things were heating up, he had trained extensively. He had complete target lists of all the potential North Korean avenues of attack. He was ready. And now he was to be detached on a special mission, away from his Division, which needed him.

It was 0800 on the 22nd. He had been told to assemble two M-110 howitzers and their crews with the supplementary equipment to be able to fire nuclear weapons. He was told that no conventional ammunition would be required. That was OK, but the fact remained that he had no nuclear ammunition. It had been removed from Korea years ago. The M-110 is nuclear capable. It can fire nuclear rounds. Nuclear ammunition for the M-110 is called "Dial a Yield," which means simply that by turning a switch the nuclear yield can be 3, 6, or 11 Kilotons. He'd had to scramble all night to gather together the necessary nuclear equipment, since it had not figured into the Division's war plans for years. He did not know where he was going, but two "Dragon Wagons" had arrived during the night to transport the howitzers. That meant they were going some distance. There was also a company of some very tough looking Korean Special Forces. Edwards had been told that before he departed he would be inspected to ensure that he had all the equipment he would need for the mission. He had also been told to have the personnel records available to assure that the troops were trained and qualified to fire nuclear weapons. He had done so and thought he was ready. He figured that this was not for real, but just another type of surprise inspection to keep everyone on his toes. He was about to be proved very wrong.

Right after 0800 Colonel Reuben Tanaka, Chief of Staff of the First

Combined Field Army, arrived to make the inspection. He had been chosen for this job for two reasons. First, he had the complete confidence of General Goodwin to oversee what was a very critical mission essential to the plan that Goodwin and Li had devised. The other reason was that several years ago, Tanaka had been chief of the U.S. Army, Europe's TPI team. TPI is shorthand for Technical Proficiency Inspection. The howitzers of the United States Army of caliber 155 millimeter or larger are nuclear capable. This means that they can fire nuclear weapons and that this ammunition has been developed. It is essential that the troops who might fire these weapons be trained and reliable. The TPI has many parts, one of which is called the "Human Reliability Program." Each soldier involved must undergo a background check and a psychological evaluation. People who handle weapons of mass destruction obviously can't be nut cases. Every member of the team must be "Prefix Five" trained. "Prefix Five" is a speciality designation indicating that one is nuclear qualified. It requires constant training and testing. The unit collectively must be able to demonstrate its ability to fire the weapons safely and accurately. Finally, all the equipment must be present and in perfect working order. The U.S. Army considers this so serious that a unit failing the TPI is declared "Not Combat Ready" and the commander is usually fired.

Reuben was concerned. He knew that since the end of the cold war, the nuclear ammunition had been returned to the United States and the emphasis on the TPI had been decreased. He had one day to determine if D Battery was ready and, if not, to make it ready. Hovering in the background were the Battalion Commander and the Division Artillery Commander. They had been told to be there and to give whatever support was required. Tanaka first inspected the Human Reliability records. He found that two of the personnel had evaluations that were out of date. After questioning the individuals, he gave them a waiver and allowed them to continue. There is an important morale point here. It is best to keep a team together unless there was a clear indication to the contrary. The next items Reuben inspected were the various assembly tools which were required to assemble the nuclear weapon. They were in quite good shape, although one of the special wrenches had a burr on the face of the grip surface. He disqualified the wrench and asked the Battalion Commander to bring another. Then he examined the firing tables and computer data. The purpose of this was to ascertain whether the Battery could fire the weapon at the intended target accurately. They were then run through a couple of target calculations to see if they could actually compute the firing data correctly. They passed. Other checks included the maintenance of the howitzers and vehicles. The standards for maintenance for nuclear operations are higher than for normal operations. Necessary repairs were made on the spot.

The U.S. Army has something called "Equipment Serviceability Criteria" or ESC. The three categories are ESC Green, ESC Yellow, and ESC Red. Red means the equipment is not serviceable and can't be used. Yellow means that there are many deficiencies but that the item may be used in emergency situations. For example, a Jeep can be ESC Yellow if it is missing the windshield, the passenger seat, the spare tire, and one headlight. Green means no deficiencies. For nuclear weapons operations all items of equipment must be ESC Green.

The final check included the ability of the Battery to conduct a safe and reliable road march. Included within this was the method of convoy, road guards, buffer vehicles, vehicle interval, and many more items. The first practice was quite ragged since the convoy consisted of units that had never worked together. After an hour, the kinks were worked out and the convoy was ready to roll. Reuben wanted to get to the firing site with plenty of time to practice and rehearse. The timing of the road march was a compromise. It is more dangerous to move at night due to possible accidents, but you can be observed better by possible enemy agents during the day. Because it would be easier to maintain security where they were than at the firing site, Reuben decided to wait until nightfall. He instructed the Division Artillery Commander that all personnel were to be sequestered.

The road march went without incident and the Battery arrived at a point about 15 miles southwest of Inchon around midnight of the 22nd-23rd. The area had been prepared for them. There were tents to sleep in and a field kitchen. The area was isolated and no civilians could be seen. It was very well guarded. Reuben had flown down in a helicopter. He had carefully monitored the progress of the convoy from the air, and when necessary, had caused the roads in front of them to be cleared. He was now waiting for Captain Edwards. When he arrived, he asked Edwards to accompany him to a tent that was surrounded by barbed wire and guarded by even more troops. In order to enter they had to show identification which was checked carefully against a list. Inside were three metal boxes, each about three feet by three feet by seven feet. They had certain recognizable markings on the top and sides.

"Are those what I think they are?" asked Edwards. Reuben responded in the affirmative saying that they had been flown in from the United States during the day.

Edwards then said that he had never before seen a real 203 millimeter nuclear round. His past experience had been only with training simulators. Reuben told him not to worry. Preparations for firing the simulators and the real nuclear round were identical, They were designed that way. The only difference was what the various components were composed of and the colors of the boxes. Reuben told him that one of the boxes contained a training simulator and the other two contained real nuclear rounds. In the morning Edwards' assembly crew would practice on the simulator until Reuben was convinced that they were competent.

"Now, why don't you and your troops get something to eat and get some rest. For once in your life you do not have to worry about external security. That has been taken care of for you. The first thing in the morning I want both of your howitzers inspected again to ensure that they are in good firing order. Things can come loose during a road march. At about noon tomorrow, I will tell you what you are going to be firing at so that you can compute the firing data several times to make sure that it is right. Any questions? Great. I will see you in the morning. Oh, one other thing. It may make you feel better to know that if we all do our jobs right, not one single human being, enemy or friendly, will be harmed by this weapon."

That made Edwards feel much better.

The next morning all the checks were made. The assembly crew had been practicing. The first time through the routine was quite rough. They were out of practice. But pretty soon they had it right. Then Reuben told them to do it again and started interjecting simulated problems to see the crew's reaction. At last he was satisfied. And besides, he did not want the crew to get stale and overtired. He told them to get some rest.

Reuben then met with the Fire Direction Center and the Battery Commander. He had obtained for them good maps of the area and arranged for frequent meteorological messages. To properly calculate the direction of fire and the effects of the weapon, you have to know such things as the direction and velocity of the wind, the temperature, and the density of the surrounding air.

Tanaka gave the firing instructions. "While we have two howitzers and two nuclear rounds, we will be firing only one. The others are backups. The probability of both malfunctioning is less than 1 in 10,000,000. The purpose of the weapon is not, repeat, not, to cause any damage but rather to create the illusion of doing so. I can not at this time tell you why this is your mission. I assure you that it is important. Think about it. You will be the first, and hopefully the only, Artillerymen, to fire a nuclear weapon in combat and you don't have to hurt anyone. I think that that is a pretty neat mission.

"I have made some preliminary calculations. I want you to verify and refine them. I want a location and height of burst that will make a big noise and lots of flash but will cause no blast, thermal, or radioactivity damage – and that includes fallout and ground induced radiation. Also, the time on target will be at about midnight tonight. I can not give you the exact time, since that is dependent upon another event. However, I want the time on target to be exactly 10 minutes after I tell you to fire. Please make the necessary calculations, to include weapon assembly time, to do so. I would like to see your calculations when you have them."

The nuclear fallout phenomenon is generally not understood. A nuclear detonation produces three types of damage energy: blast, thermal heat, and radiation. The radius of damage of radiation is less than that of the thermal heat, which in turn is less than that of the blast. If the radius of damage of each of the three energies intersects the ground or water fallout occurs. The radiation intersects with the ground and makes it radioactive. The blast throws billions of radioactive particles into the air. The thermal heat causes a violent updraft that carries these particles thousands of feet into the air. They are then carried along by the wind until they cool and fall back to earth. The fallout pattern, called the footprint, can be hundreds of miles away from the initial detonation. If none of the blast, thermal heat, or radioactive effects intersect with the ground, then there is no meaningful fallout.

This gave the FDC the task of making two types of calculations. The first was to calculate the firing data to get the round to the intended point at the intended time. The second was to make all the damage calculations. The real key was to put the round over the right point on the ground and at the right height of burst. Most people do not realize that the damage from a nuclear weapon is primarily caused by its interactions with the ground and the surrounding air. For example, a nuclear weapon designed for very high antiballistic missile defense that detonates exoatmospherically produces almost no blast, since blast is caused by the interaction with the molecules in the air. There are very few molecules at high altitudes. The damage to an incoming missile is caused by the radioactive energy that is absorbed by the incoming missile until it melts and spalls. Fortunately, the manuals have sufficient data and computational algorithms to make the calculations. It was actually a nice challenge for them. To do something that they had trained for all their lives, but not to hurt anyone.

By 2300 all was ready. The calculations had been checked and rechecked. It had been decided to have the firing point just slightly out to sea and south of the island of Wolmi Do. The height of burst would be 11,500 feet. The time of flight would be 37 seconds from the time the round left the howitzer. The nuclear round had three fuses: two were mechanical clocks and one was barometric. It is a principle of nuclear artillery that as much redundancy as possible is built in. Since the time of assembly was longer than ten minutes, it was decided to finish the assembly and check out by 2300. The estimate of the completion of Phase One was only that – an estimate. They had to be ready.

The round had not been loaded in the chamber, since if something happened and the round was not to be fired it would be quite dangerous. An artillery round must be rammed with some force into the chamber of the howitzer in order to seat the lands and grooves, that is, to seal the round in the chamber so that the powder propellant will be totally effective. If a round is not properly seated it will fall considerably short. The only way to get a round out of the chamber other than firing it is to push very hard on the nose of the round from the muzzle end of the howitzer with something called a rammer staff. It is not something you want to do under normal circumstances, much less with a nuclear round. The round was right next to the howitzer and could be loaded in less than a minute. The howitzer would then have to be aimed at the proper elevation and deflection. This could not be done until the round was in the chamber because of the clearance of the open chamber and breechblock to the rest of the howitzer. The entire process would take less than two minutes.

At just three minutes after midnight Tanaka received a call over his radio that Phase one of Triton was completed. He responded. "This is Green six. Acknowledge that Phase One of Triton is complete. Phase two will occur 10 minutes from now. Out."

The Admiral in the Flag Plot now told his people what was about to happen and instructed them to get away from all windows, look away from the location of the blast, and cover their eyes. He also told them that effective immediately they had "guns free." The war was about to start.

At the firing point the round and fuse setting were checked one more time. The round was rammed home, the propellant bags were loaded and counted carefully for the right charge, and the breechblock was closed. The howitzer was turned to the calculated deflection, or direction of fire, and the muzzle was elevated to the right number of degrees above horizontal. These settings were checked by two other people and found to be accurate. Then the Section Chief announced that Section 1 was ready to fire. The response from the FDC was "Stand By," which is common artillery practice, since other words might be misunderstood. At 0014 the command to fire was given, the howitzer was fired, and the round was on its way. All personnel were again instructed to get on the ground, look away from the target point, and cover their eyes. They were not to look for two minutes or, as they were told, they would be blind for life.

At 0014:37 on the 24th of the month, the world changed forever. A nuclear explosion approximating eleven kilotons of TNT went off at 11,500 feet above Wolmi Do Island in the Republic of Korea. The flash could be seen immediately for 150 miles. The sound would take a little longer since sound travels around 650 miles per hour, depending on the atmospheric conditions. The point was that the world would know almost instantaneously, due to CNN, that a nuclear weapon had been detonated in South Korea. Tanaka did not have to announce over the radio that Phase Two was complete.

Many things started to happen simultaneously.

In Pyongyang, Li informed Sung that the mission of the Choson Victory had been accomplished successfully. The nuclear explosion had occurred right on time and in the right place. It would take several days to get an accurate damage assessment, but the lights of Inchon were out and fires could be seen in the vicinity. This was actually true. As part of the cover and deception plan, a Division of the ROK Capitol Corps had immediately gone into Inchon to maintain order. They turned off the city power plant and lit fires in some of the military compounds in the city. Sung now ordered the ground and air invasion of South Korea to begin as planned.

At Osan Air Base, the Commander of United Nations Air Forces, Korea ordered the immediate implementation of his air campaign plan. Since he had been given sufficient warning, the AWACS were already airborne and the first attack aircraft would be crossing the border in about seven minutes. Based upon his reports from the AWACS, he hoped to experience an airman's dream. He would get in the first blow and catch the enemy on the ground.

Pete called his Corps and Division commanders and informed them that the war had started and authorized them to take offensive actions. He told them that a nuclear attack had taken place in the vicinity of Inchon, but that the damage was minimal. He had been assured by intelligence that the enemy did not possess any more nuclear weapons. He expected a North Korean attack to commence at first light, preceded by an intense artillery barrage. He instructed them to implement Operations Plan Red Three.

Tanaka called in Edwards and told him to get back to his battalion as quick as he could. He had a war to fight. He would be escorted by half of the security force and have road clearance. The other half of the security force would remain to clean up and eliminate all traces of what had happened. They would also return the remaining nuclear weapon to Osan Air Base for immediate departure from Korea. He invited Edwards to come see him in a couple of weeks, when he would give him the full story. Edwards had earned it. By morning, the area was as if it had never been occupied and Reuben was back at Red Cloud.

An hour later the President of the United States appeared on international television. He announced that North Korea had infiltrated a submarine into the vicinity of Inchon and that a nuclear explosion had taken place. Damage assessment was not complete, but apparently the North Koreans had miscalculated, since from what they knew to date damage was minimal. He further stated that after consultation with the President of South Korea, he considered this a hostile act of aggression, and under the War Powers Act he was authorizing commencement of defensive and offensive action. The first action would be an air assault on the air bases of North Korea, which was already underway. He ended by saying that he had complete confidence in the fighting qualities of U.S. and South Korean forces, and was sure that they would be victorious, although the cost would not be cheap.

Years later historians would pontificate on how lucky it was that the North Koreans were dumb enough to attack as they did.

Chapter Twenty Seven

The UN Air Commander could now only sit back and wait. He had ordered the start of the air campaign and his planning was complete and his forces well trained. He had been around long enough to know that it was now time to leave everything up to the pilots. Abrupt, unexpected changes would only add to the confusion of battle. Besides, his pilots and crews were far better qualified than he to make the necessary instantaneous decisions.

He had a high level of confidence because he had many advantages. He knew that the North Koreans had about 750 combat aircraft, most of them were one generation of technology older than his. His munitions, both air to air and air to ground, were far superior to the North Koreans. And he had over 1,000 combat aircraft when the reinforcements he had recently received and the Navy aircraft carriers were counted. He also knew that the maintenance of the North Korean Air Force had suffered in recent years due to the embargo of repair parts from Russia and China. At best, only about 80% of the North Korean planes were flyable.

He also had those most important advantages of the Principles of War: surprise and initiative. The North Koreans did not expect him to strike first, so they would not be entirely ready. Also due to the AWACS his command and control was vastly superior to that of the North Koreans. He had another advantage that no U.S. Air Component Commander had ever had – not even in the Persian Gulf War. Through General Goodwin's intercession with the Secretary of Defense, he had been granted operational control of all air assets, Air Force, Navy, Army, and Marine Corps. The Navy and the Marine Corps had screamed bloody murder because this was not in accordance with their doctrine. Past practice was for the Navy and Marine Corps to fight their own air war and to turn over only extra air assets to the Air Component Commander. The Secretary of Defense – using the powers granted to him under the Goldwater Defense Reorganization Act of 1986, had directed the arrangement. The Commander in Chief of U.S. Forces Pacific, who was a Navy full Admiral, said that he could not accept the arrangement, whereupon the Secretary of Defense told him to accept it or retire immediately. He then accepted it.

"All in all," thought the Air Commander to himself, "if I don't win this one with all the advantages I have, they ought to shoot me at sunrise." As it turned out he did not have to be shot.

The first planes in were the F-117 stealth bombers. This technological marvel had been part of the reason that the Soviet Union finally called it quits. For decades the Soviet Union had poured over 3% of their Gross National Product into Air Defense. With the development of the F-117 and the follow on B-2 bomber, all this money had been virtually wasted. There is no way to see them, and hence, no way to shoot them down except through sheer luck. The F-117 is the strangest looking airplane ever built. It is built of a new composite material that does not reflect most radar and infrared detection signals. It has also been built with a configuration of odd angles and physical arrangements that deflect whatever signals are received away from the radar set. Actually the F-117 is not flyable in the normal sense. Because of the angles and configurations, the plane is unstable and can not be controlled by even the best pilots using standard equipment and flying skills. It has a built in computer system to make many of the necessary precise and instantaneous adjustments. The pilot flies the plane in the normal way and is not even aware that the computer is helping him. Due to the computer technology, the F-117 has one of the best survivability rates of any airplane. Those that have been lost were lost almost without exception because of computer malfunction. Standard practice is that if the flight control computer goes, get out. Early on in the development of the airplane there were several Air Force hotshots who believed that they could fly anything. All but one ejected safely. The other rode it in. It was not until the Air Force developed a flight simulator and challenged the pilots to try to fly the plane without computer assistance that they were made true believers.

Preceding the F-117s to the targets were the cruise missiles. The cruise missile has an interesting history. In the Gerald Ford Presidency of the U.S. the administration was anticipating serious arms reduction talks with the Soviet Union over the next several years. It was decided that a prudent move would be to have a few "bargaining chips," that is, items that they could bargain away without too much pain. Since no one could agree that any of the existing weapons systems or developments could be bargained away, there came the suggestion to start some half serious developments and use them. One of these was the cruise missile. The other was what would eventually become to be known as "Star Wars," a ballistic missile defense system. In fact, the cruise missile turned out to be an excellent offensive system.

The principle of the cruise missile is simple and the technology employed is actually quite low tech. It is simply a war head strapped on a relatively slow missile that flies like an airplane. The uniqueness is the guidance system. It has a map in a computer system that guides it to the target. It takes continuous radar pictures of the area beneath the flight path, compares this data with the commanded path and corrects any deviations. The key is to have an accurate map, which the Defense Mapping Agency has been able to do with the advent of satellite photography. Another advantage is that it is unmanned and can fly much lower than an airplane. The radar is called "terrain following radar."

Once the technology had been proven, all the doubters wanted a piece of the action. Prior to this, both the Navy and the Air Force fought against it since it could result in taking pilots out of cockpits, which was the ultimate sin as far as they were concerned. The Navy has two types of cruise missile: one launched from submarines and the other from surface vessels. The Air Force has one, launched from the B-52 aircraft. All versions are essentially the same except for the launching platform.

The missiles being used in this attack were both Air Force and Navy versions. The Aegis class cruiser Bunker Hill was 100 miles off the east coast of Korea just north of the 38th parallel. At 0020 on the 24th it launched 72 Tomahawks, the Navy name for the missile. They were launched in pairs at 18 targets, four missiles at each. Each pair included one large penetrating point – destruction war head designed to burrow into the target and detonate. The other missile contained over 400 bomblets designed to carpet bomb the above ground parts of the target. The reason that two pairs were launched at each target was that these were high priority targets and a high probability of destruction was desired. The targets were the command and control nodes for the North Korean Air Force and Air Defense. The negative thing about the cruise missile is that there is no pilot to report back a damage assessment.

At the same time the Navy was firing its Tomahawks, a flight of U.S. Air Force B-52s from Guam was launching its Air Launched Cruise Missiles. The Air Force had never selected a fancy name for these and simply called them ALCMs. They also launched 72 missiles at the same type of targets with the same rationale. The fact that each service launched 72 missiles was more a political move than a military one. Either service could have launched 144. The reason for the 36 targets was that that was all they knew about. They were sure that there would be more as the situation developed.

Also preceding the F-117s was ground artillery fire on all known Air Defense sites within range. This was done by the U.S. Army Multiple Rocket Launcher System that has warheads similar to the cruise missile but with a range of about 30 miles instead of the 3,000 miles of the cruise missile.

The Air Commander had three squadrons of 18 F-117s each. Two of these squadrons were sent directly in just after the cruise missiles had landed. Timing was critical: too early and they might be hit by the missiles, too late and the North Koreans might have a chance to react. Each squadron had been divided into flights of six aircraft. The first two aircraft in each flight were equipped with the Shrike Anti-Radar Missile. Even if the attack on the Air Defense command and control systems was successful, the North Koreans were known to have many Air Defense weapons capable of independent action that would have to be contended with. Some had their own self-contained radar. These included the SA-8 short range antiaircraft missile, the SA-6 medium range antiaircraft missile, the SA-11 high range antiaircraft missile, and the ZSU 24 and 30 antiaircraft guns, the latter of which had its own radar. Any of these were fully capable of shooting down airplanes. Since the F-117s were relatively invisible to the radars, they were accompanied by some 'Wild Weasel' F-4s. They have one of the hardest jobs in the Air Force. They are designed to alert the enemy and cause him to take action, then get the hell out of the way. They are intentional targets. As soon as a North Korean radar would light up to direct fire at a Wild Weasel, the F-117 would take the radar out with the Shrike, which followed the radar beam back to its source. At least that was the theory. It worked most of the time, but not always. During the first ten minutes of combat two Wild Weasels and one F-117 were lost to North Korean fire. The compensation was that they had cleared the way for the others.

The other four F-117s in each flight were to take out the airfields and the aircraft on them. They knew that many of the North Korean aircraft would be in underground bunkers, where they would be relatively unassailable, but it would be enough for one mission to get those in the open and make the runways unusable.

To accomplish this two different types of munitions were used. The first was the Rockeye Cluster Bomb, sometimes called the BLU. It was a canister that floated hundreds of bomblets down on parachutes. Two clusters on one bombing run could cover an entire airfield. Any airplane within 10 feet of a bomblet impact would be destroyed. The other munition was a French developed Etourd runway penetrator. Again, a series of Etourds were dropped from a canister. Upon impact each would blast a hole three feet deep and six feet wide. While this kind of damage could be repaired, the runways would be inoperable for a critical period of time.

The third squadron of F-117s was being held in reserve, orbiting just south of the DMZ. It was anticipated that unknown airfields and air defense sites would become active as the air battle progressed. If they did not, the F-117s would be sent in to make a second strike on the known targets. But, about a half hour after the first strike, the AWACS starting receiving radar reports of activity from new areas. For the most part they were air defense radars. The airfields had suddenly gone very quiet. The AWACS vectored the F-117s and their accompanying F-4s to the new targets. This time, however, it was not so easy. The element of surprise had now been lost and the mission had not been rehearsed. Consequently, although the attack was successful, the casualties in this squadron were close to 25percent. The AWACS reported that there was no observable enemy air or air defense activity. This didn't mean that they were not there, but rather that they had taken the prudent course of action to be silent for now.

Although the Air Commander knew that the enemy still had plenty of assets, it was now time to send in the next series of sorties. A principle of the air campaign was continuous action. One must never give the enemy a chance to regain his balance. The next wave consisted of FB-111s using the Pave Way system. Pave Way is a laser system. One FB-111 from each flight is equipped with high technology detection devices, including low light level TV, infrared, and several forms of radar. When it detects a target, it designates the target with a laser beam. The following FB-111s were equipped with smart bombs – that is, the bombs have guidance systems built in to them, that follow the laser designator to the target – in this case, command and control nodes, airfields, and air defenses.

The principle was simple in concept, but difficult in execution. If you can destroy the enemy's ability to interfere with your air operations, the remaining targets can be taken out with little risk. Most ground commanders do not appreciate this. They insist on air support to the ground forces. Pete knew that the best air support to ground forces was the destruction of enemy air, and he had supported the concept of the air campaign. The Air Commander was grateful and intended to make sure that General Goodwin would be proved right. The Air Force and its forerunner, the U.S. Army Air Corps, had fought the air doctrine war with the other services for 80 years. Maybe this time they would finally get it right. He knew that the Persian Gulf War had proved nothing. A unique set of circumstances had allowed them to fight the air war and then the ground war sequentially. That was easy and nobody complained. The hard part is when you have to fight them simultaneously, which is almost always the case.

The principle of taking out the air defense and enemy counterair first was well known. In the mid 70's Syria was a Soviet Union client state. The Syrians had avowed the destruction of Israel, and the Soviets were more than willing to help, since in those days the competition for the hearts and minds of the Arabs was at its peak. The Soviets furnished to the Syrians the most extensive set of air defense weapons the world had ever seen. They wanted the Syrians to win, and even more importantly, they wanted to test out the efficacy of the air defensive systems that they had developed at great expense. With the missile batteries, the radars, and the interconnecting communications in place, they had declared Syria invulnerable to an Israeli air attack. The Israelis proved them wrong in one day. The tactics and weaponry they used were similar to what was now being used in North Korea. In one 24 hour period they had destroyed the entire Syrian air defense system and taken out the entire Syrian Air Force without the loss of a single Israeli plane. Needless to say, that air battle was studied intensively by all the nations of the world. Intelligence reported that a Soviet Air Defense Marshal was shot after the debacle.

It was now about 0400 and time to send in the next attack. This attack would be composed of U.S. and ROK Air Force F-16s and Navy A-6s. These were excellent aircraft, but not as night capable as the F-117s and the FB-111s. They would be accompanied by Wild Weasels, as had the original sorties. The Navy did not call their aircraft used for this purpose Wild Weasels. They did not have a nickname. The Navy used a variation of the A-6 called the EA-6B Prowler. It had the same purpose and was almost as capable as the Air Force F-4s. The F-4s were actually a Navy development that the Air Force had recognized as a great airplane and decided to use. Remaining over the target area were the FB-111s that had the Pave Way laser designation system. The Defense Department had insisted that both the Air Force and the Navy use the GBU-15 laser Guided Bomb, which was compatible with the Pave Way laser designator. Because the F-16 and the A-6 were quite visible to enemy radars, as opposed to the F-117 and to a lesser extent the FB-111, it was anticipated that the North Korean air defenses would become active again. This was a necessary calculated risk.

During the intervening three hours the Air Commander's Tactical Operations Center, using information from both the AWACS and the JSTARS, had been able to upgrade their target grid. They had some new targets and the indications were that some of the previously attacked targets were still partially functional. This data was passed to the AWACS and to the Navy E-2Cs, which had the same function as the AWACS. The E-2C is very good at this and was purchased by the Israelis as adequate for their purposes. It was more a matter of distance than capability in the two systems. The priority of attack was Pop Up, that is, unexpected and previously unknown radars and air defense systems first, targets identified during the course of the previous action second, and reattack of old targets third. This was broad guidance only. The pilots flying the missions would have to make the real choices. Their lives were at stake.

Flying overhead were a bunch of very pissed off F-14, F-15, and F-18 pilots. The F-14 and F-18 belong to the Navy. The F-15 belongs to the Air Force. Their mission was Combat Air Patrol, that is, to intercept and shoot down any enemy aircraft that left the ground. None had. All of these aircraft had been loaded with Sparrow, Sidewinder and Phoenix air-to-air missiles.

While each was capable of delivering the same kind of ordinance as the attacking aircraft, they had not been so loaded. There is no feeling worse for a pilot than to have to return to base with unexpended ordinance. It is also quite dangerous, but at a million bucks a copy, you don't just jettison them or shoot them at nothing. Each pilot had the same thought, formulated in different ways: "What idiot thought up this plan?" The Air Commander had the same thought. On the next sorties he would do cross loading so that the planes could do air-to-air or air-to-ground, depending on the situation. This would decrease the ability to conduct air-to-air combat, but it seemed to be a prudent risk. This decision almost proved fatal, but turned out to be positive in the end.

The special meeting was called in Pyongyang by Sung Tae Won. Present were General Yi Bong Su, Commander of the DPRK armed forces, and the commanders of the DPRK Air Force and Air Defense Force. The North Koreans used the old Soviet model that made Air Defense a separate branch of service. It was 5:00 AM.

"Comrade Generals," said Sung. "Please tell me what has occurred. I thought you told me that the Americans and the South Koreans could not possibly attack us this early."

Yi spoke first. "Comrade Leader, our entire operations plan was based upon your guidance. Thus far we have accomplished everything that you asked us to. It is true that the lackeys have attacked earlier than we anticipated, but that is not the important thing. What is important is whether or not they have hurt us. They have dropped lots of bombs and made a lot of noise, but the fact of the matter is that we still maintain our combat capability. The commanders of the Air Force and Air Defense will brief you in just a minute as to the specifics."

What Yi did not tell Sung was that the two commanders were concerned over their failures and were trying to avoid summary execution. They had become willing co-conspirators with Yi and Li. It was their best chance for survival.

Yi went on. "The enemy has offered us a great opportunity. He must pause in his air attack in about two or three hours. His pilots are tired. He must rearm his aircraft and they will be extremely vulnerable on the ground. If we time it right we can catch them and destroy them once and for all. This significant defeat for them together with our start of the ground offensive will probably result in the U.S. Congress suing for peace. I already have it on good authority from Comrade Li that the U.S. Congress is considering impeaching the President. They believe that his speech of last week started the war. That, together with our upcoming victories should get the war stopped in our favor. All in all, except for the Americans attacking first, I see everything going in our favor. I am as confident for success as I was when we decided upon this plan. Allow me to introduce our Air Defense Commander." Yi wanted to make this transition quickly before Sung had too long to think about it.

"Thank you, Comrade Leader," said the Air Defense Commander. "We have been hit very hard by the Air Forces of the United States and South Korea. They have taken out about 50% of our command and control systems, 60% of our long range radars, and about 30% of the missile batteries. However, we have many advantages. Due to your foresight all our systems are redundant. We have always had more than we would actually need. During the night the primary form of attack was from their stealth bomber. As you know, no one has yet been able to devise a way of seeing them by radar. But now it is approaching daylight. I am confident that we can do our task. As we speak, an attack from other than stealth bombers is taking place. We do not yet have a report of the outcome of that attack, but my preliminary reports are that we are inflicting heavy casualties on them. They had the advantages of surprise and night at the beginning, but they no longer have them. They will not be able to do again what they did this night if we take the proper action today."

Sung nodded and asked the Air Force Commander for his view.

"I completely agree with the Comrade General. We have suffered casualties, but nothing that we can not accommodate and nothing that we had not planned for. It is true that they have hit our airfields several times. But what have they actually accomplished? They have knocked down a few buildings, cut out radio communications between bases and my headquarters, destroyed a few of our older aircraft that were out in the open, and made a few holes in the runways. As far as communications go, we have backups and they have already been restored. We already have our labor battalions working and the runways will be back in service in three hours. Almost all of our first line aircraft are safe. Years ago, learning from NATO, we built hardened aircraft shelters. These will protect the airplanes from everything except a direct hit. There have been very few of those. The same goes for our fuel supplies. What I'm saying is that our offensive air is ready. I must also say that we will not win an air war of attrition. Although we will win almost every air battle, eventually they will prevail through sheer weight of numbers. I agree with the Comrade General that the political support for the war in the United States is fragile. All this tells me that we must initiate a maximum strike at U.S. and South Korean air bases this morning. Their planes will be down for rearming, maintenance, and crew rest. They will be at their most vulnerable. Also, daylight will make the odds more even. We can see as well as they can during the day. I recommend a maximum effort air attack at 0900 today. I have already worked out the plans here if you approve and want to see them. To show you my confidence in this attack, I request permission to lead it."

Yi and the Air Defense Commander agreed. Sung also agreed, hardly looking at the plans. He knew that he would not understand them and did not want to share the blame if it did not go well. He denied the Air Commander the permission to lead the attack saying that he was needed in his headquarters. Besides, though he didn't say so, if it didn't go well he wanted him available for punishment.

The three Generals had intentionally underestimated the casualties and overestimated the probability of success of the air attack. Interestingly, they actually agreed with the conclusion. They knew they would not win an air war of attrition. Their best chance was the all-out attack now. It might even work.

Chapter Twenty Eight

Pete had been at his underground command post since 2200 on the 23rd. He had been checking his communications and listening to his special single side band radio that was netted with Green Six and Blue Six, together with selected others. The command post was not actually underground, in that it had been built by burrowing into a mountain. It was higher than his normal headquarters but had enough overhead cover to protect against any known North Korean conventional artillery and air. It had been dug into the south side of a north facing mountain. That was the good news. The bad news was that the command post was small. He had ordered all nonessential personnel to a new set of underground shelters, just built, south of Uijongbu. After their first real argument, it was agreed that Sandy would remain at Pete's side. This was about as clear cut an example of mixed emotions as Pete could ever imagine. Sandy had mixed emotions also. She was not about to tell Pete, but she thought that she might be pregnant. After making her calculations, Sandy had decided that, boy or girl, the initials would have to be V.C. commemorating the unique place that conception had taken place.

One of Pete's previous worries was the vulnerability to artillery fire of the civilian population north of Seoul. He had complete confidence in the counterbattery radars and the return fire procedures that had been developed and practiced. But the fact remained that the first volleys and many leakers would still get through. He had discussed this with his Korean Deputy, General Kim Jook Wan. Kim had told him that much had been done. The ROK Army engineers had issued to each village chief the specifications for adequate individual family shelters. The village chiefs had issued orders for each family to build their shelters themselves. Koreans being Koreans, it was done at no cost to the government. The Mayor of Uijongbu had invited Pete to see the one that the mayor and his three sons had built themselves. Amazing country.

Pete realized that the nuclear event that was to take place around midnight might have a debilitating effect on the First Combined Field Army. He needed a way to instill confidence in the troops and keep up their fighting spirit. At about 2330 he composed a handwritten note, put it into a sealed envelope, gave it to General Kim and asked him to keep it on his person until he told him to open it which would be sometimes after midnight. Kim was curious, but did not speak. He speculated that the note might be some kind of admission of surrender or death wish. He would be proved very wrong.

At 15 minutes after midnight a terrifically bright flash was seen in the sky. Soon thereafter Pete got the message over his single side band radio that Operation Triton had been successfully accomplished. The orders to his command had been prepared ahead of time and were immediately transmitted. The orders said that the war had started, all units were authorized offensive and defensive action, the North Korean ground attack would commence around first light, preceded by an intense artillery preparation, that the U.S. and ROK Air Forces air attack on North Korea had already started, and contained the directive to implement Operations Order Red Three. An Operations Plan becomes an Operations Order when implemented. None of this came as a surprise to his subordinate commanders, who had been briefed earlier in the day. Pete knew that everyone would be concerned about the nuclear attack, which was why he had written the note. He asked Kim to open the envelope, read it, and then share it with the staff and commanders.

The note said. "I know that you and your troops saw the large flash in the sky just after midnight and wonder what it was. Soon you will be receiving information that it was a North Korean nuclear attack. I have known about this for over a week. Some very brave and smart soldiers and sailors undertook a plan approved by the highest levels of both the U.S. and ROK governments. Although a weapon was allowed to detonate, there was no damage whatsoever and no people were killed. The North Koreans do not know this and believe their nuclear attack was a success. It was not. It was a total failure. I can assure you that the North Koreans have no more nuclear weapons. We do not have to worry about that. Now let's do our part and fight and win the ground battle. Please know that this note was written 30 minutes minutes prior to the detonation and placed in a sealed envelope in the possession of General Kim, my deputy, to convince you that I am not just making this up. Good luck."

Lieutenant General Pak Wan Ki, Commander of the III ROK Corps, had waited for this day all of his life. Pak had been a fifteen year old soldier with the III ROK Corps in 1951. During a battle near the town of Nodong, south of the 38th parallel in the eastern part of the country, the III Corps had been hit by an attack from an entire Chinese Communist Field Army. The III Corps broke and ran and was deactivated from the roles of the ROK Army. Pak himself did not run, but was wounded several times, was cut off from friendly forces for twenty days, and eventually made his way back to friendly lines. He brought with him excellent information about the Chinese forces, which helped in the UN counteroffensive. He was allowed to join another

Corps and fought heroically until the end of the war. During the intervening years, he had stayed in the Army, gotten a commission, and had risen to the rank of Major General. He had a personal friend in the Prime Minister and lobbied hard for the reactivation of the III ROK Corps. He called it a debt of honor. The Corps had been reactivated and Pak was put in command. He had been the Corps commander for almost four years, far longer than the normal tour. He had been offered another job and a fourth star. He had refused, since this was his life's work. It also irritated him highly that the North Korean advanced missile under development was called the Nodong. This was a personal insult. He had requested that the III ROK Corps be given responsibility for the defense of the Chorwan valley, considered at that time the most dangerous North Korean avenue of approach into South Korea. He had imbued the Corps with its history and had coined the Corps motto. "Stand and Fight. Win or Die."

Pak knew that he had certain advantages that most military commanders do not have. Through the JSTARS he knew almost precisely where the enemy was and its strength. He knew through the Field Army Commander the time of the attack and the method of attack. He knew what he must do.

Pak had learned every inch of the terrain in the III Corps area during his four years in command. He had required that his subordinate commanders also did the same. They had wargamed and practiced the various scenarios innumerable times. General Goodwin had authorized both defensive and offensive actions within the confines of Operations Plan Red Three. This meant that Pak could mount a spoiling attack and he was not restricted to stay south of the DMZ. This is exactly what he intended to do. He knew that the enemy would attack at first light, which was about 6:45 at this latitude and time of year. He also estimated that, in accordance with North Korean doctrine, the artillery preparation would begin at around 5:45. His spoiling attack would commence at 0400. Under usual circumstances he would never have been able to do this this quickly, but he had been handed a set of circumstances that only came around once in the lifetime of a soldier. He would not let the opportunity pass him by.

A spoiling attack is one of the most difficult tasks in the tactics of war. In essence, it occurs when you know that the enemy is getting ready to attack you and you hit him first while he is going through the many steps preparing for his attack. It is during this time that he is at his most vulnerable. He is not in a defensive configuration, but in an offensive one, and the two are entirely different. In defensive configuration, units are located in depth. In offensive configuration, everything is jammed up to the front. In the several hours before an attack food is being served, letters are being written, weapons are being disassembled for cleaning and checks, staff meetings are being held, vehicles are being refueled, and artillery howitzers are being moved forward and are unable to fire while they are on the road.

Timing is essential, as are the objectives of the attack, which by definition are limited. Hit the enemy, inflict maximum casualties, disrupt his scheme of maneuver and timetable, and get out without becoming completely engaged. A principle of a spoiling attack is that when it is over the attacking force returns to its original position, but it returns fighting, contesting every inch of the way without getting bogged down. Only well trained units can do this sort of thing. Pak had exactly that. The first Regiment of his 23rd Infantry Division was his pride and joy. It was one of the few Regiments that had fought in combat in Vietnam. The commander was the first South Korean to graduate from West Point in a program started some 25 years earlier. He was the only foreign cadet ever to earn an 'Army A' in football. He was an excellent place kicker. He won the Army/Navy game with a field goal in the last seconds of the game and would forever be an Army hero. The commander was also Pak's son. In the ROK Army, nepotism is considered a positive thing. A father would never let his son down and a son would never let his father down. That is not done in Korea.

At 0400 the attack jumped off. There was no artillery or air preparation, since the enemy had to be caught off guard and by surprise. Young Pak was in the lead M-60 A2 tank, which was superior to anything the North Koreans had, other than the Soviet built T-80. He was going right down the middle of the road. Subtlety is not part of a spoiling attack. His initial objective was the staging area of a battalion of T-72 tanks. If he caught them right the tanks would be unmanned and in administrative rather that tactical formation. They would not be massed in accordance with armor doctrine. They would be spread out for protection from air strikes.

Pak's infantry regiment had been reinforced by the 23rd Division's tank battalion. The tank battalion consisted of 54 M-60 A2 tanks. South Korean Army doctrine was based upon U.S. Army doctrine. Tanks never operated alone. They were always integrated into what was called a "combined arms team." Tanks and infantry working together have a synergistic effect, building upon the individual advantages of each. The lead battalion of Pak's regiment was what is called "armor heavy," that is, it had two tank companies and one infantry company. The other two battalions were infantry heavy, having two infantry companies and one tank company. In many ways, what Pak was doing was similar to a cavalry charge, a swift violent frontal attack to the center of the enemy's formation. One advantage that Pak had was that the North Koreans had not secured the high ground on either side of the valley north of the DMZ. They had not considered it necessary since they were the ones who would be making the attack. Pak's attack was in what is called a wedge formation. His lead armor-heavy battalion was in the center and his two infantry heavy battalions were on either flank, slightly to the rear but close enough to keep contact. One of the advantages here was that the valley was just wide enough to accommodate a regiment. Normal doctrine in all armies is to keep a reserve, but not in a spoiling attack.

By 0430, Pak was two miles north of the DMZ. He had swept aside some of the front line North Korean formations and left his two following battalions to take care of them. His primary objective was the tank assembly park. Here he got an unpleasant surprise. Instead of finding a battalion, he came upon a regiment of North Korean tanks from the North Korean V Corps. They had been brought up during the night and had not been observed by JSTARS. In the half hour since the attack started, they had gotten organized. The fighting was brutal. Pak's battalion lost over half of its M-60s, but succeeded in taking out over 150 enemy T-72 tanks – most of the regiment. It was now time to get out. They headed south through the defensive lines established by the two infantry battalions, which would fight a delaying action back to the South Korean lines. As they delayed, they left behind TOW tank killer teams. These were three man teams with a TOW launcher and five TOW missiles mounted on a jeep. They would hide behind rocks and other cover and shoot and scoot. The TOW has a range of over 2,000 meters, more than the North Korean T-72s. The tactic was to wait until the North Koreans got within range, fire, and then withdraw to the next selected position. Each engagement delayed the enemy by 30 minutes, since they would stop, analyze the situation, reform, and start a new attack. The bulk of the regiment returned safely as did ten of the thirty TOW teams. Unfortunately, Colonel Pak did not. He had been killed by a round from a T-72 in the first ten minutes. The regiment brought his body back. General Pak was grieved, but he was a professional soldier. He knew that the spoiling attack had destroyed a North Korean division and delayed the attack down the Chorwan valley by at least a day. He would grieve another day. He had a war to fight and the best he could do for his son was to win it so that his son's death would not be in vain. His entire Corps agreed with him.

During the same time there were several spoiling attacks underway throughout the entire South Korean front. The only exception was in the sectors of the II and VIII ROK Corps on the eastern side of the peninsula. From every indication, the North Koreans did not seem to be preparing for an offensive there. The mission of these two Corps was to defend, if necessary, but to be prepared to launch an attack, on order, towards Wonsan on the North Korean east coast, which was about 70 miles away. This would depend on the reaction of the North Korean 9th Mechanized Corps, which was still located in the vicinity of Wonsan and the North Korean 820th

Armored Corps located southeast of Pyongyang. So far they had not shown much movement. This kind of decision would be made in from two to five days.

From his conversations with Li, from his JSTARS intelligence, and from his own tactical experience, Pete believed that the First Combined Field Army would be hit by four North Korean Corps: the II and IV Infantry Corps, the 815th Mechanized Corps normally garrisoned at Sariwon south of Pyongyang, and the 820th Armored Corps. All indications were that the lead attack would be by the two infantry corps followed by the armored and mechanized corps exploiting the anticipated breakthrough. However, the spoiling attacks had interrupted this sequence. Consequently, the North Koreans would be faced with having to make a change of plans. Pete was preparing for two contingencies. The first was that the North Koreans would attack, as scheduled, that morning. The second was that the North Koreans would delay a day and bring up the other two corps. Either way, Pete felt confident. If they attacked now he would have an opportunity to defeat them in detail, that is, defeat the first attack and then defeat the second. If they waited a day, that would give the air offensive one more day to destroy the North Korean air and air defense forces and be able to divert resources to direct support of the ground forces. As usually happens in war – the unexpected happened. The North Koreans did neither. Instead, they brought up the 820th Armored Corps and attacked at noon.

At 0700 that morning, in the headquarters of the DPRK Armed Forces, there was utter chaos. Reports during the night and early morning were coming in and things were not going as planned. The first reports pertained to the air attacks on DPRK air defense and air bases. They indicated that centralized command and control had been significantly degraded. While much of the air defense and air forces were still intact, the ability to coordinate them had been lost. Units would have to operate on their own until communications could be restored. It was apparent that the enemy was concentrating on this and was continuing the attack right up to the present. Also, the long range radars were almost all gone. While many individual air defense batteries still had their local radars for actual fire control, warning time was non existent. An air defense missile without the radar to guide it is useless. The action was not without its successes however. During the morning attacks by the U.S. and South Korean F-16s, over forty had been shot down, but they still kept coming. One more day and the air defense would be virtually out of business. Something had to be done. They would lose the war of attrition.

On the other hand, the status of the combat aircraft was still quite good. The shelter and revetments program was working. So far the combat airplanes had not been significantly hit. But it was just a matter of time before they would be. Once the air defenses had been taken out, the U.S. and South Koreans would start taking out the shelters one by one using smart laser guided bombs. Anyone who watched the Persian Gulf War on CNN knew this. The North Korean people didn't because of the controlled media, but the leaders did. That is why they had decided to launch a maximum air effort at about 0900. They would go after the U.S. and South Korean Air Forces with priority to command and control and bases. One special group of pilots had been given the mission to ram AWACS and JSTARS.

The ground attack had also been discussed. The enemy's spoiling attacks had been successful, ruining the timetable. They had also lowered the forces available for the attack. Of special concern was the fact that somehow the South Koreans had determined the location of the eight tunnels under the DMZ and had detonated explosive charges just as the troops were supposed to emerge in the rear. Eight regiments were trapped and presumedly lost. In response, it was decided to have an economy of force tactic all along the front and weight the main attack along the Kaesong Munson approach with four corps, three in the initial assault and one as the breakthrough element. The earliest that they could set this up was noon that day and it was so ordered.

One other concern in General Yi's headquarters was the lack of success of the artillery fire. It had not been affected by the air attack of the U.S. and Korean forces and did not seem to have been a target. As a matter of fact, none of the North Korean ground forces had been targets of the initial air assault. This was contrary to all of their expectations. The artillery was at 100% at the start of the attack. For years they had calculated the schedules of fires, as artillerymen call the plan for artillery fire. They had determined exactly how much ammunition to fire at each target. The targets were both tactical and civilian. The short and medium range guns were aimed at the tactical targets in the vicinity of the DMZ. The longer range guns were aimed at the civilian targets. The DPRK artillery had over 8,500 guns and 2,400 multiple rocket launchers. One principle of artillery in all nations is that artillery is not held in reserve. All artillery weapons are brought to the front. This is because that artillery is usually not damaged in combat, since it is located away from the front. That doctrine was about to change. The technology of warfare had changed the rules again. Artillery now was just as vulnerable as everything else. The North Korean artillery was primarily Soviet designed 130 mm and 152 mm guns. These were excellent weapons. They were very accurate, very mobile, had a good range, and were easy to maintain. All in all, they were considered equal to, if not superior to, the U.S. weapons. The key, however, was not only the quality of the weapons, but the quality of the entire artillery system, including expressly the target acquisition system. You have got to know where the targets are and calculate accurate firing data.

The North Koreans had made several blunders in their artillery plan, one of which they had had no way of predicting. If one is subjected to unexpected artillery fire, there are usually severe casualties due to being caught in the open. This did not happen. The South Korean civilians had been warned in time. This is also a problem for troop units. It is always a problem to decide to go underground or not. If you are underground and are attacked on the ground, you usually lose. Similarly, if you are exposed and get hit by unexpected artillery fire, you suffer high casualties. Knowing when the artillery barrage would occur and when the ground attack would start was a huge advantage. The North Koreans also did not initially target U.S. and South Korean artillery units. Their priority of fire was on infantry and tank units. This was a fatal mistake. As soon as the North Korean artillery rounds were in the air the counterbattery radars had picked up the location of the guns. Counterbattery fire was immediate. About 25% of the North Korean guns were taken out within the first 30 minutes. Within the first two hours 50% had been taken out. After that there was a discernible reticence on the part of the North Korean artillery to fire. In Yi's headquarters this was blamed on spies and traitors. In order for this to happen the positions must have been compromised.

All of this led Yi and his staff to conclude that the outcome depended on one massive stroke. It was decided that an all out air attack at 0900 followed by an all out ground attack starting at noon, was their best chance. They were right. It almost worked. The outcome was much closer than Yi had anticipated. He almost won when he intended to lose.

Chapter Twenty Nine

It was 0830 on the morning of the 24th. The AWACS had been on station for 30 minutes at 35,000 feet orbiting south of Seoul having relieved the previous plane. Having received a complete data dump from both the ground controller and the other plane, its computer records were up to date. The crew had been following the action for the last several hours and was ready. All equipment and communications had checked out and were in good operating order. The men had been briefed that they would be in a period of relative lull. The next attacks by the U.S. and Korean Air and Naval forces would start at about 1100.

Airman Burnes was monitoring his radar screen. There were a few planes flying, but not many. All had been positively identified as friendly reconnaissance planes which were taking photographs and other images for post strike analysis. All of a sudden Burnes staring receiving blips from several points heading south. The blips started multiplying. Pretty soon it was obvious that a major North Korean air attack was underway. He started to alert his senior controller, who told him that he had already seen it. The UN Air Commander had been notified and ordered them to remain on station as long as possible. The count kept growing. What started as 50 planes increased to 200, and then over 500. Burnes said. "That's the whole frigging Gook Air Force," using the slang most Americans use for enemy orientals. "I wonder where our guys are." The Senior Controller had already informed ground that he was going to have to get out of there in less than 10 minutes unless help arrived. The AWACS was escorted by a flight of four F-15s, but they would be of little help. The UN Air Commander had already issued the "Scramble Red" call. That call meant for every fighter plane to get airborne immediately, regardless of fuel and weaponry, and fight individually. They would try to coordinate as the battle evolved. All other planes were also to get airborne and head south out of harm's way.

Coordinating the air battle soon became much more difficult. While everyone's attention was to the north, a pair of MiG-29 DPRK fighters came streaking in from the southeast unobserved. Their flight path was outside the known combat radius of the MiG-29. No one had accounted for the probability of an intentional one way flight. If you are not coming back anyway who needs the extra fuel? Their mission was unambiguous. They were to ram the AWACS. The pilot of the AWACS spotted them at the last second and went into a dive. He avoided the first MiG-29, which passed above him. He never saw the second one, which rammed him right in the tail. The explosion could be seen but not heard. A bunch of junk fell to earth, none of which remotely resembled an airplane. There were no chutes. The first Mig-29 still had about five minutes of fuel left, which was not enough to get home. He put his plane into a dive and headed for the Air Control Tower at Osan Air Base. By sheer luck, he took out most of the communications and the UN Air Commander. This was an extreme irony. The commander had 258 combat missions in Vietnam, and although his planes had been hit several times, he had always returned safely without a scratch, and here he was killed by a totally random act. UN Air was now blind and leaderless. The outcome would now depend on individual initiative and, as it turned out, the U.S. Navy. Superior training was about to pay off. This training was the result of intensive air combat training at the Navy Top Gun school at Miramar Naval Base in California and the Air Force Red Flag school at Nellis Air Base in Nevada. The pilots had trained under all possible scenarios, including this one. The rules were simple, find a wingman and hit the nearest enemy. Radio silence was not important. Find out who the senior pilot in the vicinity is and let him take over. Use individual initiative.

At 0830 that morning, Rear Admiral Chuck Patterson, U.S. Navy, had taken off from his flagship of Carrier Task Force Five in an A-6 Aircraft. Chuck Patterson was the Admiral commanding the Task force. He had under his command the carrier Midway and the carrier Nimitz, both of which were nuclear powered. Each carrier had on board about 120 aircraft of various types: three squadrons, or thirty six, F-14s; three squadrons, or thirty six, F-18s; two squadrons of A-6s; two E-2Cs, and a number of other types, such as surveillance S-3s and rescue helicopters. Patterson was flying copilot in an A-6, since he was no longer considered qualified by the Navy to be the Pilot in Command of a single seater aircraft. He was too old. It grated on him that the pilot was young enough to be his son and had 6,000 fewer hours in jet aircraft than he did. Still, it sure beat flying a desk at the Pentagon. He had a sea command and one of the best. The reason he was in the air that morning was that he had been called to a meeting at Osan Air Base by the Commander, United Nations Air Forces, Korea. One of the things that the Air Commander had done upon receiving Operational Control of the aircraft of all services was to appoint Admiral Patterson as his principle deputy.

As the flight was approaching Osan, the pilot came on the intercom and spoke to the Admiral. The A-6 is a great airplane and had been around for thirty years, but it is very noisy. It had been barred from landing at any commercial airport in the United States except for emergencies, it was so loud. In spite of what you might have seen in the movie "Flight of the Intruder," normal conversation was impossible. The pilot told the Admiral that something significant was going on and that it looked as if a major air battle was about to take place. He suggested that they return to the carrier. That would have been the smart thing to do, but Chuck's intuition said otherwise. They landed at Osan just as the control tower and adjacent buildings blew up. The base was in chaos. There was no overall control. It was what they call a Chinese Fire Drill. Every plane was doing its own thing. Chuck only hoped that everyone would respect the normal rule that a landing plane always has the right of way. They did, but just barely. Two F-15s that were taking off together missed him by no more than twenty feet. Chuck had the pilot taxi up to what was left of the control tower and leaped out. It was obvious to him that someone had to take charge, and that for better or worse, it was he.

Chuck Patterson wandered through the wreckage until he found a few people alive. He asked what had happened and was told. He knew that the first thing he had to do was find a radio that worked. A commander without communications commands nothing. A U.S. Airman told him that there were radios in the Operations building 400 yards away that had not been hit. Chuck told the Airman that he was now his aide and to follow him to the Operations building. They ran the distance in near world record time.

All good military organizations have something called "Continuity of Command." This means that when a headquarters is knocked out that there is always another one designated to take its place. It also means that when a commander is rendered incapable of continuing command, his successor in command has been previously identified. The trouble is that quite often the alternative command center and the successor commander are not in the same place. This was the case here. The alternate command center was at Camp Humphries, thirty miles south of Osan. Chuck's first move upon reaching the Operations building was to ask who they had radio contact with. An Operations building is normally not intended for combat operations. It is similar to an airport building that administratively controls the aircraft in landings, takeoffs, and departure vectors. They told him that they had contact with Camp Humphries and the carrier task force, but not with secure radios. Whatever was said could be heard by anyone. Since Chuck was going to be issuing orders instead of asking for status reports, he decided that talking in the open was better than not talking at all. He called Humphries and asked if they were capable of handling the U.S. Air Force and ROK Air Force aircraft. They said yes but that they needed orders. Chuck asked what orders they presently had and was told "Scramble Red." Chuck told them to continue until they were ordered otherwise. He then turned to an Air Force major and asked if they had any form of data linkage with Humphries where he could possibly see displays of what was going on. The major said that he didn't know but that he would get right on it.

Patterson then asked if they could patch him through on any frequency to the USS Nimitz. After a few tries they had a frequency but the carrier didn't want to talk with them because the frequency was not secure and they did not have the proper authentication codes. Patterson grabbed the mike and started one of the oddest radio dialogs ever.

"Big November, this is Chuck, put the Air Boss on. That's an order."

"Unknown station, please identify," came the response.

"November, this is Chuck and if you don't put the Air Boss on now, your ass is grass."

"Roger, wait, out."

"Chuck, this is Boss, How's your morale?"

"If my morale was any better I would be hyperventilating."

"Roger, Chuck, Go."

"Boss, this is Chuck. We got a real mess where I was going today. I am on the ground. The bad guys are all over the place. Based upon their short legs, they will be di di wa ing in about an hour. Get the Hummers up and get a picture and then go balls to the wall. I want a full court press. Show them what old blue and gold can do."

"Roger, Chuck, Understood, Anchors Aweigh."

Chuck did this because time was critical. The opportunity would be lost in an hour and it would have taken at least that long to establish secure communications. He had spoken in slang hoping that he would be identified as authentic and issued orders that only a jock would understand. The translation was that the North Koreans could not sustain their attack for too long and if the Navy got cracking right now they could catch them on the way home and hit them when they were almost out of fuel and ammunition. Air Boss was the Navy slang for the commander of the air wings on board the carriers. Patterson commanded the task force, the ship captains commanded the ships, and the Air Boss commanded the airplanes.

Patterson then turned his attention to seeing if it were possible to get another AWACS in the air. He called Kadena, which had been monitoring his frequency with interest. Kadena told him that one was being preflighted right then and should be there in a little over an hour. Kadena was worried as to who to establish communications with. Chuck instructed them to contact the alternate command post at Humphries. He then turned back to the major and asked how he was doing. The commander answered that he was not doing very good, but that he had access to a chopper and could get Patterson down to Humphries in about twenty minutes. The chopper would fly very low and should not be observed by hostile aircraft. Patterson agreed, even though he hated helicopters. As a stick and rudder man, he really did not believe that they were airworthy. The trip to Humphries was uneventful. Patterson was escorted into an underground command post that looked as if it had been designed in Hollywood. The problem was that even with all the gadgets someone has to tell you what is going on. They didn't have much information but they had the capability to when it was the appropriate time. Patterson ordered a message to all aircraft to continue individual initiative and to report in when they felt like it. He had done all that he could for the present and all he could do now was sit back and wait.

About an hour later, the preliminary results of the air battle were starting to trickle in. At the start they had about 700 aircraft other than the carriers. 100 were airborne and 600 were on the ground. Of the 600 on the ground, all but 75 had gotten in the air before the attack started. Of these, about 50 had been destroyed and the others could not get off due to mechanical problems. Of the 525 that had gotten in the air, 200 were other than fighter aircraft and had been sent south. In addition 150 more were so low on fuel and ammunition that they were sent south also. That left about 300, more or less, to fight the air battle against about 500 North Korean aircraft. The North Korean aircraft were a combination of MiG-21s, MiG-24s, MiG-25s, and MiG-29s. The U.S. and ROK fighters engaged in the air battle were primarily F-16 Falcons and F-15 Eagles. Technologically, the U.S. and ROKs had the advantage. Numerically, the North Koreans had the advantage.

The first half an hour was a standoff. The U.S. and ROK fighters managed to disrupt the North Korean formations, and after that it was one large set of dogfights. The training and the technology of the U.S. and ROK forces started to tell. Few North Korean aircraft got through to any ground targets. Most were intercepted in route. By the end of the hour the North Korean aircraft turned north, where the U.S. Navy was waiting for them. The Navy had gotten their E2-C Hawkeyes up and had a good picture of what was going on. Some 140 F-18 Hornets and F-14 Tomcats were loaded with air to air munitions and were in picture perfect formation. It was a disaster for the North Koreans. Very few made it home. One of the problems of the post combat analysis was that, between the Air Force and the Navy, a total of 900 kills were claimed, or 300 more than they probably started with. Whatever the numbers, which were argued about for years, the North Korean Air Force had ceased to exist as an effective fighting force. Patterson figured that they had shot down about 500 of the 600.

This air victory, for that is what it was, was not without cost. These were easier to count. 23 F-15s, 42 F-16s, 12 F-18s and 7 F-14s and one AWACS had been lost in air combat. In addition, another 73 aircraft of various type had been destroyed on the ground or in non-combat related accidents. One piece of good news was that they had only lost two F-117 Stealth Bombers, since these had been given priority for shelters. They had not taken to the air during the battle. That was not their job. All in all, the North Koreans had suffered about 80% casualties and the U.S. and ROKs 15%. But now North Korea, with the exception of the air defense threat, was vulnerable. The next phase would be to take out the North Korean threat, although about 25% of air resources could now be diverted to support of the ground forces. They were just in time.

By 2000, the allies were able to resume the air offensive. A careful analysis of the days activities dictated the target priorities. It was found that virtually all of the Air Force losses had been caused by air to air combat, whereas all but two of the Navy losses had been as a result of North Korean air defense. This was a direct function of where the battles had taken place. The Navy had caught the North Korean air on their way back north and followed them as far as they could. They only broke off the engagement when they started suffering unacceptable casualties. Actually, many of the Navy losses occurred after they had been recalled, but several pilots disregarded the instructions in the heat of combat. They figured that if they got one more shot they would get themselves a MiG. Some actually did but got shot down on the return flight.

The priority for the night was clear. Take out the North Korean air defense. This had been made feasible by the day's activities. Many previously unknown air defense sites had become active during the day. Their locations had been carefully noted by the replacement AWACS and by JSTARS as well as pilot after action reports. The F-117 Stealth bombers and the FB-111 Aardvarks, as they were affectionately known, were spoiling for a fight. If they did their job right tonight the air war would be virtually over. After this it would just be like the latter days of the Persian Gulf War, when they flew out unopposed, took out a target, and came home and had a beer.

But in the meantime, another war was going on, which was the ground war in the First Combined Field Army sector. As planned, the North Koreans launched their assault at 1200. It had been preceded by an eight hour artillery preparation. This preparation was a failure for several reasons.

The North Korean artillery preparation had originally been planned to last for two hours. With the change in plans necessitated by the success of the allied air assault of the previous night and the many spoiling attacks, the preparation now had to last for an additional six hours, or for a total of eight hours. Artillery commanders were in a quandary. Ammunition is very heavy and bulky and you can only carry so much along with you. You must husband its use carefully. Artillery ammunition is usually conserved by allowing so many rounds per gun per day per purpose. Because of the time delay this allocation had already been exceeded. Should they stop firing? Should they keep firing – but at a slower rate? Should they continue to fire at the same rate and hope that resupply would happen? No two commanders came to the same conclusion. The only thing in common was that they had to conserve about 40% of the ammunition for targets of opportunity after the ground assault actually started. As a result of this confusion, the pace of incoming fire diminished. This made the job of the counterbattery radars and the allied artillery much easier.

Over the last several weeks, Colonel Han had devised a way to lash the JSTARS and the counterbattery radars together. When a North Korean artillery barrage went off it gave out an identifiable radar and infrared image, which was picked up by the JSTARS. The originating coordinates were immediately flashed to the appropriate counterbattery radar. To do this had taken the emergency writing of a specialized computer program, but this was something that Han was good at. Although these coordinates were not accurate enough for return artillery fire, they allowed the counterbattery radars to be alerted and face in the right direction. This made the response time and accuracy much better. After the return fire the JSTARS observed the effect of the return fire on the target, since this also had a discernible image. The JSTARS could then tell the friendly artillery whether or not they had neutralized the target. This helped immensely in the conservation of ammunition and target selection. It was also a huge morale boost for the friendly artillerymen. Usually artillerymen never know whether their fire was effective or not. By about 1000 the pace of incoming artillery fire had almost stopped. This occurred because the North Koreans had learned to fear the JSTARS and the counterbattery radars. They did not actually know what was happening but it was obvious that the U.S. and South Koreans had come up with an effective counterbattery fire system. This was the real reason for the slack off of the fire, although all commanders said the reason was to conserve ammunition for the offensive. Later analysis showed that the allies had taken out about 40% of the North Korean artillery in the first six hours.

This was fortunate, since one of the first planes shot down by the North Korean air offensive was the JSTARS. It had stayed aloft too long. It would take six hours to get a replacement, and even that was in question. The replacement JSTARS would not be sent up until the skies were relatively clear.

The other reason for the North Korean lack of success was that both the troops and the South Korean population were prepared for the fire. They had been warned and had dug in. The actual effects were minimal and caused no panic whatsoever.

It was obvious to Pete that the North Korean attack had been delayed, but by his JSTARS information before it had been shot down and his own military intuition, he knew that it was coming soon. The best indication would be the resumption of the North Korean artillery preparation, which started at 1000. One thing that Pete noticed immediately was that the renewed artillery preparation was somewhat halfhearted. This was important, since troops have a natural tendency to keep their heads down and get under cover when undergoing an artillery barrage. By now, the South Korean troops, very few of whom had ever been in actual combat, were gaining confidence and were reoccupying their defensive positions. They were ready when the attack hit.

The North Korean plan of attack was relatively simple. They would attack with three Corps abreast with their right (south) flank anchored on Kaesong and with their left (north) flank anchored on Yonchon. The front would be about 40 miles, which was very concentrated and about half of what is normal. They wanted to achieve a quick and violent penetration. The axis of advance was Kaesong-Munson-Uijongbu in their first phase. After that their left flank Corps, which was the 820th Armored Corps, would turn to the northeast and roll up the flank of the ROK forces which had occupied Defense Line Alpha along the DMZ. The two remaining North Korean Corps would turn south and pass east of Seoul. They did not intend to take Seoul, since that could be done at leisure after they had destroyed the U.S. and ROK forces. They would be reinforced at the end of the first day by the 815th Mechanized Corps, which was en route south from Pyongyang. The 815th was considered the elite force of the DPRK Army and would exploit the penetration made by the other three Corps. It was intended that the 815th would meet head on with the ROK Capital Corps in the vicinity of Seoul, effectively wiping out further resistance. The attack plan assumed no significant U.S. ground reinforcements after the attack. They had been assured by General Li, the Chief of the North Korean Security Service, that the United States would have no stomach for a long involved counteroffensive, which required bringing over at least 500,000 troops from the United States. They were probably right in this assumption

Pete's plans were also relatively simple and straightforward. He had the advantage of knowing the enemy's plans. He had been a little hesitant at first to totally rely on what Li had told him, since there was always the possibility that Li was playing him for a fool. However, events so far were just what Li had suggested, with some exceptions. Pete understood that Li was not in complete control of events and some details were bound to be changed. But you don't change the disposition and attack plans of four

Corps overnight.

Pete's plan was to gradually allow the North Koreans to make a limited penetration, inflicting maximum casualties along the way. With his defensive scheme he would nudge the North Korean penetration more northward than they planned, keeping them out of Munson and Uijongbu. He would also get command of the ROK I Corps, which was located north of Yonchon. This Corps would be oriented to the southwest, rather than its normal northeast orientation. The ROK III Corps, which was on the I Corps east (right) flank, would take over responsibility for the I Corps zone. The North Korean plan was to hit the I Corps in the rear. Instead, they would hit them head on. The U.S. Second Infantry Division would be the delaying force against the nose of the penetration. They would be trading space for time. At the appropriate time the Division would occupy very strong defensive positions constructed at the intended limit of the North Korean penetration. They would be the "cork in the bottle."

At that time the ROK IV, VI, And VII Corps would attack north across the penetration, taking the North Koreans on their south or right flank. At the same time the newly assigned ROK I Corps would attack south to effect a link up with the ROK IV Corps, effectively sealing off the penetration and surrounding three North Korean Corps. Essential to the plan was delaying or even stopping the arrival of the North Korean 815th Mechanized Corps coming south from Pyongyang.

That was the plan. Pete knew that most plans normally don't turn out quite the way intended. Time would tell.

Pete had another advantage that is not commonly understood by those who are not military professionals. He had what are called "interior lines." Imagine the arc of a circle. If you are inside the circle and your enemy is outside the circle, you can get to a point on the arc faster than the enemy, since your distance is so much shorter. You can react faster to changing situations than the enemy. This had been clearly understood by a Confederate General in the Civil War by the name of Nathaniel Bedford Forrest. Common mythology was that Forrest was an ignorant country boy and said "Get there fustest with the mostest." Forrest was actually well educated and actually said "Get there first with the most men." Forrest knew that a critical point of the Principles of War is to be superior to the enemy at the critical point. To do this, unless you have overwhelming numerical superiority, which Pete did not, you must use what are called "economy of force" measures, that is, you weaken yourself intentionally at less critical points to be superior at the critical point. Most Generals don't have the nerve to do this and only the best do. MacArthur and Patton were masters at it. Montgomery never was.

Once the attack started, Pete had little to do. It was in the hands of his commanders now. The very worst thing a general can do is race around changing things prematurely. You must let things develop, and this is probably the hardest thing for a military leader to do. Pete had already told Sandy to stop him and talk to him whenever he had a brilliant idea. Make him think about it. Ask him if he really knew what is going on better than the commander in the field. Napoleon said that once the battle is joined, the primary task of the Commanding General is to decide when and where to commit the reserve. Pete intended following that advice.

Chapter Thirty

The Commanding General of the United States Army Second Division was ready. His mission was clear and unambiguous. He was to meet the nose of the North Korean attack and gradually delay without ever becoming completely engaged. Because he had been told about this mission over two weeks earlier, he had had sufficient time to prepare. He and his commanders had walked every inch of the terrain and had selected fighting positions. They had rehearsed several times, first in the daylight and then at night, until everyone knew what to do. He had been given priority in night vision devices and TOW missiles. He had the wherewithal, the technology, the training, and the troops. A delaying action is very difficult, since it is easy for panic to set in. By human nature, troops are more confident when attacking, and less so when going backwards. A delaying action is not a retreat. It is a planned retrograde maneuver for an express tactical purpose. On an intellectual level people understand this. On an emotional level it is tough. Only well trained and motivated troops can do it. That is why Pete had chosen the U.S. Second Infantry Division for the job. Most of the officers and NCOs and many of the troops had been in combat. This was not true for the South Koreans.

One of the first things that the Division commander had done when he was given the mission was to get out his copy of Army Field Manual 100-5 (FM 100-5), Operations. He had the old version that had been put out in the 70's and revised in the 80's. These versions had been written by some very smart officers at the U.S. Army Training and Doctrine Command at Fort Monroe, Virginia. This organization, or TRADOC as it was called, was formed in the early 70's to standardize Army doctrine and training, which prior to that had been the purview of 52 separate fiefdoms in the Army called Service Schools. The first commander of TRADOC was General William Depuy who was known to be brilliant and very hard to get along with. He did not suffer fools easily. He took on the existing establishment and won. One of his greatest accomplishments was the first version of FM 100-5. It really did tell people how to fight and win. The opening line in the manual said that it was the mission of the U.S. Army to fight outnumbered and win. The manual was copied over the years by most of the Armies of the world,

including South Korea. It was that good. In June of 1993 a new version of
FM 100-5 was published. It was garbage. The authors based their doctrine
on the experiences of the Persian Gulf War which, in reality, was an aberra-
tion. The circumstances of that war were simply not transferable to any other
possible conflict. Most smart commanders threw the new version away and
kept the old, including the commander of the Second Division. The South
Koreans had not even bothered copying the new version.

The Second Division had one other advantage. It had its own Air Force.
One of the last acts of the now dead UN Air Commander was to take the
Army Apache attack helicopters, a squadron of C-130 Spectre gunships and
the U.S. Air Force A-10 Warthog tank killer planes and put them into a joint
task force commanded by an Army Brigadier General. This force had been
placed under the command of the First Combined Field Army and further
placed under the Second Division. This arrangement infuriated the air brass
in the Pentagon but after the well known experience of the Navy with the
Secretary of Defense, they were wise enough to keep quiet. The mutual
cooperation of the Apache, the Spectres and the A-10 was a natural. It had
been experimented with by troops in the field for years with much success,
but never had either service agreed to to put its forces under the actual
operational control of the other. This was new doctrine which would be
argued about for years. The origin of the argument extended over decades.
The Army established the Army Air Service prior to World War I. During the
years between the two World Wars The Army Air Service was striving to be
an independent Air Force like the British Royal Air Force. The use of air was
was the object of a constant argument. Should it operate independently or
not? During World War II it actually operated independently, although technically it was still part of the Army. Finally, in 1947, it became a
separate service. For a number of years it was the Air Force public relations
pitch that the Air Force could win the country's wars and that all the Army
had to do was to become occupation forces after the war. Needless to say,
the Army did not agree.

Over time the Air Force became less and less interested in the direct
support of the Army and more interested in doing its own strategic thing. In
desperation, the Army started developing helicopters for ground support. By
1962, the Army had gotten far enough along this path to worry the Air Force.
Suddenly, the Air Force was saying that there was no need for the Army to
develop helicopters and that they could do ground support. The question put
to them by the Congress after the publication of the Maxwell Taylor book
"An Uncertain Trumpet" was "with what?" The Air Force did not have an
answer. After a few false starts the Air Force developed the A-10 Warthog. It
was perfect for the ground support mission. It was slow, survivable, carried

huge amounts of armaments. including a Gatling gun that fired depleted uranium rounds that could penetrate armor, and it was ugly. This hurt the Air
Forces' feelings. They wanted their planes to be beautiful.

The Army continued to develop the attack helicopter. The first was the
UH-1 Huey. This was done by taking the standard Army air ambulance and
hanging a few machine guns on it. From there they went to the AH-1G
Cobra, which was actually a Huey redesigned to be faster and carry more
sophisticated weapons. Just prior to the Persian Gulf War the Apache was
fielded. This was the best armed helicopter in the world. It had all the target
sensing devices of an Air Force fighter, it carried radar and laser target des-
ignators and many types of lethal munitions. It was the perfect tank killer. It
was just natural that the Apache, the Spectre and the A-10 should work
together. Air support of the Army had come full circle. The results would be
spectacular.

The Second Division had integrated the air task force into their plans for
the delaying action. The task force very quickly got the nickname of
"Indianhead Air' after the nickname of the Division. Indianhead Air had two
battalions, for a total of 108 Apache helicopters, one squadron of 6 Spectres
and three squadrons of A-10s for a total of 54 A-10s. The tactics for their
joint use had been developed over the years by some visionary lower ranking officers at TRADOC and Langley Air Force Base, both in Hampton,
Virginia. Indianhead Air was a perfect weapon for a delaying action. It could
attack troop formations to the rear of the front lines, it could give direct fire
support to the front lines, and, most importantly, it could cover by fire a
troop withdrawal to the next prepared defensive position. There was still
another advantage. By the scheme of maneuver developed by Pete, the North
Koreans would be enticed into a controlled penetration where both flanks of
the penetration would be held by ROK forces. This meant that the Apaches,
the Spectres and A-10s could attack targets to the rear of the
penetration without first having to fly over the North Korean air defenses
accompanying the advancing forces. They could fly around the flanks before
going in, significantly reducing exposure time.

The North Korean attack jumped off at 1230. It was a half hour late due
to coordination problems. At first the attack seemed to be going well. The
North Koreans found that resistance in the north, or left part of their zone
was less than in the south, or right part. Commanders are trained to exploit
success and the North Korean command transferred reinforcements to the
north. They did not know that they were being suckered in. The west, or left
flank, of the First Combined Field Army was occupied by the IV ROK
Corps. To its right, or north, were the VI, and then the VII ROK Corps. As
the attack started all three corps gradually wheeled clockwise, hinged on the

IV ROK Corps. They did this while fighting a delaying action. The result was that the three ROK Corps would be in prepared positions on the south, or right, flank of the North Korean attack and the I ROK Corps was on the North flank. Directly facing the attack would be the U.S. Army Second Infantry Division. The Second was spoiling for a fight. They had come to Korea in 1950 and had remained ever since. Over the years they had suffered many unpublicized casualties to action from the North Koreans. Especially galling was the clubbing to death of two Army Majors who were in charge of cutting down some trees in the DMZ in accordance with the procedures of the armistice. Both sides, upon notification of the other, were allowed to do this in order to keep good visibility.

The North Korean plan called for making a ten mile penetration by nightfall. The first two miles went easily and then they ran into the first prepared position of the Second Division and ground to a halt. In exploiting what they saw as an opportunity, they had changed to a moving formation instead of a fighting one. It would take time to change back. At the same time the artillery of the four ROK Corps, three on the south and one on the north, started hitting the penetration from three sides. The direction of the artillery fire was from ground and air observers. JSTARS had not yet returned. Right after the artillery fire finished, for awhile the Apaches, the Spectres and the A-10s came in. It is not considered smart to run your own airplanes through your own artillery fire. Instead, they entered the penetration from the north and south flanks in the vicinity of the Imjin Gang and flew east to the nose of the penetration. This caught the North Koreans by surprise, since all their weapons were oriented to the east instead of the west where the planes were coming from. This tactic would not work again, since the North Koreans would react to it. But it did cause the North Koreans to now look in four directions instead of one.

By nightfall the North Koreans had only advanced another mile. They were seven miles and six hours behind schedule and had suffered close to 20% casualties. They asked for guidance from Pyongyang and were told to continue the attack and that help was on the way.

It was eight in the evening of the 24th in the office of Sung Tae Won, President of the Democratic People's Republic of Korea. He had called in General Yi and General Li to be briefed on the days activities. Yi told him that the Americans and South Koreans had attacked the air defenses without much success although there had been damage. He told him that the North Korean air attack on South Korea had been a success and that both sides had suffered heavy casualties. So much so that the air on either side would no longer be a factor, which was to the advantage of North Korea. He expected another attack by the Americans that night on the North Korean air defense that would be equally ineffective as the first night's attack. Yi was cutting it close. He knew that his optimistic assessments would eventually be exposed and that he had at most two more days for the deception. Li agreed with the assessment of Yi.

The conversation turned to the ground attack. This was easier for Sung to understand, since lines could be drawn on a map and looked at. It was immediately apparent to Sung that the attack had not progressed as planned and he asked why. Yi had anticipated the question.

"Great Leader," said Yi, "it is true that we have not progressed as far as we thought we would. You must remember that, at your instructions, we commenced the attack at 1200 instead of daylight. So, as far as I am concerned, we are on schedule when you take into consideration the delay of the start of the attack. That part is going well. I am worried about one thing. There have been heavy casualties on both sides. The U.S. and South Koreans have committed all of their forces. We have not. The plan originally intended that the 815th Mechanized Corps be the exploiting element of the attack. You asked us to keep the Corps in place here in Pyongyang until you released it and we have done so. I would recommend to you that it is now time to commit the Corps to the battle. It is my opinion that the Corps will break the South Korean and U.S. lines and give us the victory that you have worked all your life for."

Sung thought for a moment and asked. "General Yi, if we commit the 815th now, how long will it take to enter the fight?"

"About a day and a half. You know that it is presently in defensive positions around Pyongyang. We will need to reconfigure it and move it about sixty miles. It should be ready to attack at daylight on the 26th which, in my opinion, would be the appropriate time."

"Very well. Approved. Keep me informed," said Sung, ending the meeting.

Sung did not know that he had been deceived in two ways. There was never any intention of allowing the 815th Mechanized Corps to join the battle, but the appearance that it would gave credibility to the expectation that the North Koreans would win. The cover and deception plan involving the 815th would have to take place during the night of the 25th and 26th.

At the same time that the meeting in Pyongyang was ending, Admiral Chuck Patterson, the new United Nation's Air Commander, was putting the finishing touches on the air plan for that night. The afternoon had been hectic. Using people that he could find he had put together a new Air Staff. They were all individually competent but had never worked together before. Chuck had been smart enough to resist the temptation to bring in his own Air Staff from the Nimitz. He knew that they were good and could do the job, but the effect on the ROK and U.S. officers would have been devastating. They were mad and wanted to show that they could do the job.

Chuck's first task was to get a status report on the friendly air. He needed to know what he had to work with. Fortunately, because of the specifics of the "Scramble Red" plan, the F-117 stealth bombers and the FB-111s were relatively safe. Only two F-117s and three FB-111s had been lost, all due to being caught on the ground. Since these were the planes that would be used in the early night attack on the North Korean air defenses, that problem was manageable. The sacrifice of the F-16s and the F-15s had paid off. Damage to ground facilities, fuel storage, and ammunition supplies was less than had been anticipated in the planning for the war. Chuck felt comfortable that the early night attack on the air defenses would go as planned, and in the additional six hours that he had, he would be able to reconstitute the remainder of his fighting force. Besides, as he gently but firmly told anyone who would listen, he still had the fighting airplanes of the U.S. Navy. He could not resist telling them that this is why the country needed enough carriers. He had made a few converts. After talking with the Air Boss on the Nimitz, this time over a secure net, he had ordered the Naval Air to immediately follow the F-117s and FB-111s in. Chuck himself was starting to appreciate the command and control arrangements that had been ordered by the Secretary of Defense. Under normal arrangements the Air Commander could not have ordered the Navy to do this. It is amazing what a change of perspective does to the attitude.

All the pilots and staff had been told about the ground battle going on around Kaesong and Uijongbu. They were told to avoid that battle until ordered. It was more important to neutralize the enemy air and air defense for now. After that, there would be plenty of opportunity to join the ground battle. The pilots were promised a pilot's dream: lots of ground targets to shoot at and no one to shoot back. The Navy especially looked forward to this. During the Persian Gulf War they had been effectively shut out of most of the action.

In Uijongbu, at about the same time, Pete was being briefed by his staff. The most significant problem was that the U.S. Army Second Division was under pressure. Although the delaying action was going well, its proximity made Pete uncomfortable. If the Second cracked it would be a disaster. He ordered immediate limited objective attacks from the I ROK Corps on the north flank of the penetration, and from the VII Corps on the south, to relieve the pressure. He also ordered that these two Corps extend their lines to the east to maintain contact with the Second U.S. Infantry Division. Pete was angry with himself. This was a detail that he had overlooked. He had assumed that it would be done, but it wasn't. It was his fault. He hoped that he had acted in time. It turned out that the ROKs had assumed that the Second would maintain contact with them and the Second had assumed that the ROKs would maintain the contact. By midnight the attacks had temporarily accomplished what was intended. Pressure was off the Second Division and they could now withdraw to the next prepared defensive position. But that had not solved the problem. If the North Koreans exploited the opportunity, the defensive plan might fail. Such are the vagaries of war. In every after-action report, after every battle, there is a discussion of missed opportunities. Pete remembered a seminar that he had attended while a student at the Army War College. The topic was how to define "high risk," "moderate risk," and low risk" strategies. The best answer they could come up with was who did the best with missed opportunities. It was low risk if you missed some and the enemy did not and you still won. It was high risk if you could not afford any and depended on the enemy to miss a few in order to win. It was not very scientific, but no one had been able to come up with a better definition.

Pete decided that several adjustments to his operational plan were needed. He knew that by asking the I ROK Corps and the VII ROK Corps to extend their lines to the east to make contact with the Second Division they would be stretched too thin. So he ordered the III ROK Corps to detach a Division and assign it to the I ROK Corps, with the mission of plugging the gap between the I ROK Corps and the Second Division on the north flank of the penetration. The III ROK Corps sent the 23rd Division, which was in reserve after the previous night's spoiling attack. In return, the III ROK Corps received the 11th ROK Division from the II ROK Corps, which was on its right. In effect, Pete was using an economy of force tactic by moving his center of mass to the west. He also ordered the VII ROK Corps on the south of the penetration to bring its reserve division up and fill the gap between the VII ROK Corps and the Second Division. He asked the UN Commander, General Armstrong, to send him a division from the ROK Capital Corps to reconstitute the VII Corps reserve.

At best, all of this movement would take about eight hours, which would be a very dangerous time. Pete called the Second Division Commander and appraised him of the situation and of his concerns. The commander was equally concerned. They decided that their best bet, until the new units arrived, was the use of air power. Indianhead Air would be given the mission of filling the gaps. In addition, Pete had talked to the new UN Air Commander, who told him that he could put six or seven squadrons of F-16s into the fight.

At about 2200, it was obvious that the North Koreans were making probing attacks at the flanks of the Second Division, looking for weak spots.

If they found them and were able to exploit them they could possibly bypass the Second Division on both the north and south and isolate them. At midnight the battle was joined. The shoe was on the other foot now. The North Koreans had the advantage of interior lines in the penetration.

The commander of the Second Division decided that there was something else he should do. He had established a reserve of two infantry battalions and one tank battalion, or about one third of his combat strength. He was familiar with Napoleon's maxims pertaining to the reserve, as was General Goodwin. It was now time to commit his reserve, but he had to do it in a way that violated normal and accepted doctrine. Doctrine says that the reserve should never be committed piecemeal, but in mass. Unfortunately, he had two problems, his left flank and his right flank. He knew that help would arrive in about eight hours, but he was not willing to wait. He formed two task forces from his reserve. The first was a battalion of one tank company and two infantry companies. The other was two battalions of two infantry companies and one tank battalion each. He assigned the one battalion task force to his north flank and the two battalion task force to his south flank. He did this because he knew that the North Korean's overall plan was to turn south and that this is what they would probably do. He estimated that the two task forces would be in place in less than two hours, as opposed to the arrival of the ROK divisions, which would arrive about eight hours hence. He was wrong in this. His battalions did arrive in two hours, but the ROK Divisions arrived in five. They were as aware of the urgency as was he. It was one of those few times that you are happy to be proved wrong. It also made the difference.

In solving one problem, the commander of the Division had produced another. He was now without a reserve, something that no good commander could accept. His memory took him back to Pleiku Province in 1967 when he was a junior officer in the Fourth Engineer Battalion of the Fourth U.S. Infantry Division. The Tet offensive had started and things were very confused. The Province Senior Advisor of Pleiku Province, a U.S. Army Lieutenant Colonel, had reluctantly taken command of the Province. All the Vietnamese Generals and Colonels had somehow become scarce. He was the only one left with any authority and even that was questionable. He had gone to all the headquarters around Pleiku convincing them that if they wanted to survive, they had better become infantry and fight. Most of the units in and around Pleiku were signal, transportation, administrative, medical, and logistical. It was a hard sell. But people tend to have a change of attitude when the options are fight or die. During the first day he had put together a semblance of a defense. But intelligence indicated that the NVA 94B regiment would attack Pleiku from the west that night in an area that was short on defense. The Advisor went to the Fourth Division commander and asked if he could help. The commander, after verifying that the Advisor had done everything he could, told him that all his combat units were already committed. However, it was Army doctrine that Engineers have a second mission as infantry. To his knowledge it had never been tried, but this was as good a time as any. He sent the Fourth Engineer Battalion into Pleiku, where they repelled the NVA in a fierce battle and won the Presidential Unit Citation.

The Second Division commander called the Second Engineer Battalion and gave them their new mission. The battalion commander welcomed it, although some of his troops greeted the job with mixed emotions. They would be tested and would meet the test.

Contrary to common mythology, the North Koreans do not attack in human waves blowing bugles to scare the enemy. Rather, their strategy is to probe for weak spots and envelop and bypass the enemy and get into their rear areas. The bugles used in the first Korean war were command and control signals since they didn't have radios at that time. The Second Division commander knew this very well. He fully expected the North Koreans to probe his flanks and look for the weak spots that were there by midnight. The North Koreans had identified the probability of gaps in the Second Division's flanks and had committed a division to each of them. It took them about two hours to mount the attack, which was the same amount of time that the Second Division commander had to fill the gaps.

It was a classical meeting engagement which is what happens when two opposing forces are moving to contact without either knowing where the enemy is. There are usually neither offensive nor defensive plans. This is where training, discipline, individual initiative, and practiced battle drills prevail. The North Koreans had the advantage of numbers. The Second division had the advantage of Indianhead Air and also JSTARS information, since the JSTARS had been put back into the air around midnight. Colonel Han had arranged for a JSTARS readout computer to be put into the Second Division Tactical Operations Center.

Even with these advantages it was a close fight. The North Koreans attacked vigorously without regard to losses. By now, they had realized that this was an opportunity they could not afford to lose. The combat quickly degenerated into a number of individual fights, most no larger than a U.S. platoon against a North Korean battalion. About the only thing that saved the situation from becoming a rout was the continuous airborne fire support of the Apaches, the Spectres and the A-10s. By daylight the three U.S. flank battalions had been chewed up and were almost combat ineffective. One more push by the North Koreans would have probably broken through. But at daylight they paused to regroup and rearm. They were badly chewed up too. This was just enough time for the two arriving ROK divisions to take their places on the shoulders of the penetration. This would be the limit of the North Korean advance for the remainder of the day, but everyone thought it would just be a temporary respite.

During the early morning hours meetings were taking place in Uijongbu, Camp Humphries, and Pyongyang. In each case the purpose was the same: to evaluate what had happened and to make both near term and long term plans. The best news, at least from the U.S. and ROK point of view, was that the night's air campaign against the North Korean air defenses had been successful. No one was saying that they had eliminated all of it and that there would not be future casualties due to enemy air defense, but the emphasis could now change. The UN Air Commander now ordered that 75% of available air sorties would go to ground support. This information was relayed to Pete to ask for recommendations as to how the air should be targeted.

Pete had two very important phone calls to make. The first was to the commander of United Nations Air Forces, Korea, in response to the request for his recommendations as to the allocation of air resources. He asked that the call be placed over the secure phone voice circuit. He had found that it is far better to talk to a person than to send messages that inevitably get misunderstood. Admiral Patterson came on the line.

"Good Morning, General," said the commander. "This is Chuck Patterson, Rear Admiral, U.S. Navy, the new commander of UN Air. I took command yesterday when my predecessor was unfortunately killed in the North Korean raid. Everyone down here wants to avenge his death and I think we did a little of that last night. The enemy air is just about gone and we have reduced the North Korean air defenses to a tolerable level. We will continue to pursue both, but I believe that we can now give you the air support you need."

"Thank you, Admiral." said Pete. "I knew your predecessor well and I will miss him. I am told that you have done an excellent job. I would like to commend you and all your air, and especially your naval air. This isn't the first time they have saved my ass. You asked me for my recommendations as to the use of air. I agree with you that about 25% needs to be continued on the North Korean air and air defenses. As to the remainder, I am fighting a pretty tough battle here. I think about 50% of what you have allocated to me should be in the immediate area. I have an Air Force Direct Air Support Controller team here with me that has not yet had anything meaningful to do. They are completely aware of the situation and will coordinate my use of air resources. You are authorized direct contact with them. You may assume that they are speaking for me. I understand that you have already established the necessary communications with them."

"Roger that," replied Patterson.

Pete continued. "I have about all that I can handle here. I need to keep any more North Korean reinforcements from arriving. As far as I can tell there are four North Korean Corps that are not now involved. They are the 815th Mechanized Corps, located southwest of Pyongyang, which,according to indications are getting ready to move. They are the most immediate threat. The others have not yet shown any indications of moving. They are the 9th Mechanized corps near Wonsan, the 425th Mechanized Corps near Yongbyon, and the 10th Mechanized Corps north of Hamhung. I need for you to keep them off my back. Three additional points. Keep any air attacks in the vicinity of Yongbyon away from the nuclear complex. It represents no immediate threat and we don't want to spread radioactivity. Besides I want to personally inspect the place after this is all over to assure myself of the necessity of this war. Also, I would like for you to get familiar with a plan for some feints in the vicinity of Namp'o and Pyongyang which will occur tonight. I want enough air to give the feints credibility. Finally, I believe you know about the Marine Corps landing at Wonsan scheduled for tomorrow morning. I assume you have already coordinated that air support."

Patterson replied that he understood completely and would and could comply. If he had any questions he would get back. A man of few words and lots of action. Pete liked that.

Admiral Patterson gathered his air staff together and issued his instructions. He was most appreciative that General Goodwin had told him what needed to be done but not how to do it. This is the way that real military professionals do it, as opposed to those civilian ribbon clerks and feather merchants that infest the Pentagon. He repeated what General Goodwin told him and then added his own specific guidance. "The object is to keep these four North Korean Corps away from the battle, not necessarily to attack them directly. The way we are going to do this is by interdiction. I want every bridge destroyed using precision guided munitions, and kept destroyed. I want every road junction and choke point saturated with air delivered scatterable mines. Once we have stopped them from moving, then we will directly attack them. I need somebody to brief me on the plan for the amphibious and airborne feint in the vicinity of Pyongyang. After I have heard it I will have additional orders. I want the support to the First Combined Field army to be in the air in an hour and the interdiction of the four North Korean Corps started by noon. Questions? Get cracking."

Pete's next call was to General Armstrong, the UN CINC. After a brief discussion of the last day's activities, Pete told him that he thought it was necessary to execute Operation "Toys R Us" tonight. Pete knew that the R in the name is supposed to be backwards but no one had a word processor that could print it backwards so they settled for this label. The name for the operation had come up in a discussion between Pete, General Armstrong, and General Lee Chi Na, Chairman of the ROK JCS. The topic was the amphibious and airborne feint on Pyongyang. The intent of the feint was twofold. First, they wanted to keep the 815th Mechanized Corps from entering the ground battle. More importantly, they wanted an excuse to have the 815th surround and enter Pyongyang. In the confusion Yi and Li would take over the government and depose Sung Tae Won. They believed that they had co-opted enough of the leadership of the Corps to pull it off.

In order for the feint to work it had to be credible. The United Nations did not have the forces to really make the attack nor was that necessary if the feint worked. They knew that the North Koreans still remembered the Inchon invasion of 1950 and the airborne jump of the 187th U.S. Airborne Regimental Combat Team north of Pyongyang, at Sukchon and Sunchon in October of 1950. These two assaults had broken the fighting spirit of the North Korean Army.

The idea that resulted in the name "Toys R Us" came from Lee Chi Na. Lee was an avid student of military history. He remembered that during the D-Day invasion of France in 1944, The Royal Air Force had dropped thousands of small three foot high dummies, with 10 foot diameter parachutes which they called "Rupurt" all over the invasion area to confuse the Germans as to the real location of the actual drop of the British 6th Airborne Division. At night, and from a distance, you couldn't tell the size. They just seemed farther away than they actually were. They also exploded upon impact, further confusing the enemy. For days the Germans were convinced that they were real and chased all over looking for them. The Germans finally realized what was going on. They called the dummies "Atropen Puppen." Lee said that he could do the Brits one better. Not only could he have the parachute dummies made but he could also have a fake miniature invasion fleet made. Pete and General Armstrong were intrigued but credulous. Lee said that it would be easy. People did not realize that most of the toys that were sold in Toys R Us were made in Korea. He knew that the toy manufacturers would cooperate both from patriotism and the knowledge that they would have a perfect marketing gimmick later. "We built the toys that won the war." Hence the name for the operation. Reuben Tanaka, Pete's Chief of Staff, was already coordinating the efforts of the South Korean Navy and the UN Air Command for the operation. He was starting to wonder how many other weird things he would be involved in before this war was over, and he was already planning the outline of his book.

The pace of activities on the 25th had almost settled down into a routine. As a result of the previous night's air action, the North Korean air defenses were relatively quiet. The photo reconnaissance missions flown during the day indicated that over 70% of them had been put out of action. No North Korean airplanes had risen to challenge the UN aircraft, which were now taking out the aircraft shelters and the planes contained within them, one by one, using precision guided smart bombs. The three North Korean Corps in the penetration were making frequent probing attacks along the east and south sides of the penetration looking for weak spots. It was becoming obvious that the North Korean forces had no intention of launching a large ground attack during daylight hours, due to the air supremacy of the allied air in and around the penetration. That would probably come during the night. The Direct Air Support Controller team of Pete's headquarters was coordinating the air battle with great success.

During the morning Pete had formed what was called a "Division Group." Usually when you have three divisions put together in an organization, you have them commanded by a Corps Commander and his staff, but there was neither time nor necessity for that. Instead, the U.S. Second Infantry Division was given operational control of the two ROK divisions that had arrived during the early morning hours. In effect, the Second Division now had three divisions instead of one to hold the nose of the penetration. Pete had realized that the deeper the penetration the more his forces would be stretched out, and therefore the more vulnerable. He decided that the present locations would be his final defensive position, even though the Second Division had prepared positions further to the east. Not only was that a good tactic given the situation, but it had a positive effect on the troops. Troops naturally don't like to be told to retreat. Generals may call it a planned retrograde for their memoirs but troops don't see it that way. A seemingly minor but very important manifestation of this attitude is the digging of defensive positions. Troops get very serious about digging in when they know that this is where they will fight or die. They get less enthusiastic when they know that the positions are probably going to be abandoned when the pressure builds up.

The preparations for Toys R Us were continuing. The coordination for the many activities was less than what would normally be required if these attacks were for real. They were acceptable for this operation, since mass confusion was a positive instead of a negative. It had been decided that the time for the feint would be ten PM on the 25th. This time and date were arrived at for a combination of reasons. They wanted it to be at night. They wanted to get the 815th North Korean Mechanized Corps turned back north before it had a chance to join the ground attack. It would also take that long to get all the pieces in place.

Reuben Tanaka had visited the Commander of United Nations Naval

Forces, Korea and personally briefed him on the feint and his part in it. This was the same commander who had done so well in the nuclear event two nights earlier. He wanted to talk about that, but Reuben asked that they stick to this action with a promise that he would come back later and give him the whole story. UN Naval forces would put everything available off the coast of North Korea in the vicinity of the port city of Namp'o. They were to be there by nine PM and shell the beaches around Namp'o as if it was a naval gunfire preparation for an amphibious invasion. They were authorized to shoot at any known targets as a bonus. At ten PM a battalion of U.S. Army LARK-7 Air Cushion Vehicles would approach the beaches, but not actually land. Each LARK-7, of which there were 18, would be carrying 30 fake invasion craft. These craft were about 10 feet long and were made of plastic. Plastic was chosen because it was the material most available to the toy manufacturers. Each craft was powered by a small electrical motor that ran off a battery. The battery also powered cassette tape recorders programmed with battle sounds attached to loudspeakers. The guidance system was very simple: a compass connected to the motor with the instruction to head directly east. In the front of each craft was 200 pounds of high explosive that would go off when the craft hit something. A final nicety suggested by the toy manufactures and approved by General Lee was a fireworks display that would go off as the craft were in transit to the beach. Reuben told the Naval Commander that, starting at around nine PM, the UN Air Forces would conduct an intensive bombing campaign in and around Namp'o and Pyongyang. In a real invasion this requires intensive planning and preparation. In this case it was unnecessary. To make the Admiral feel better Reuben told him that the UN Air was prohibited from attacking any thing actually at sea, although they would attack any North Korean aircraft that ventured near.

Following that conversation, Reuben flew to Camp Humphries to speak with the UN Air Commander, Admiral Patterson. While on the way, Reuben mused that the Navy seemed to be taking over the world. That was OK with him as long as they didn't take over the First Combined Field Army. He wanted that job for himself someday.

Reuben was ushered right in to the office of Admiral Chuck Patterson. After a very brief exchange of pleasantries, they got down to business. They both knew that time was of the essence. Reuben briefed Patterson on the Naval activities and requested that the Admiral establish close coordination with The Naval commander. They wanted to avoid fratricide between the two attacks, but there was always a chance that the Naval task force might need air support. Normally, the air support for an amphibious landing would be handled by the Navy from aircraft carriers under an Amphibious Task Force Commander who, by doctrine, was a Navy Admiral. In this case it wasn't a real invasion. Besides, the carriers were on the opposite side of the peninsula and there was no sense in exposing their aircraft to North Korean air defenses as they crossed the peninsula and then returned. They were also needed to support the real amphibious landing at Wonsan the next day. One more time doctrine would be ignored in the name of cooperation and common sense. It would be interesting to see how the doctrinaires rationalized this one.

They then got down to discussing the Airborne feint. Over 2,000 dummies had been delivered a week earlier to the South Korean Air Base at Kunsan, which was on the west coast of the peninsula, about 200 miles south of Seoul. Based at Kunsan were the 18 C-130 Hercules aircraft of the South Korean Air Force. The Hercules or herky-bird, as it was affectionately known, had been around for thirty years and was still the most dependable airlift airplane in the world. It was rugged and seemingly ageless. It was the perfect airplane for delivering airborne troops and equipment at relatively short distances. For this mission it had the advantage that the entire rear part of the fuselage could be opened during flight. This feature had been designed into the C-130 for the purpose of parachuting trucks and light tanks. During the week, rails had been fabricated inside the fuselage so that the dummies could be automatically dropped out of the rear hatch. Each Hercules could carry 120 dummies in four rows of 30 dummies each. As they would leave the rear of the aircraft the parachutes would be deployed by a static line attached to the airplane. The static line would also activate the explosive charge, which had a built-in 20 second delay. The 18 Hercules with 120 dummies each would approximate the numbers in a real airborne Brigade of the 82nd Airborne Division. At Pete's request, all the dummies were wearing the shoulder patch of the 82nd. One joke making the circuit was that this was the only Brigade that had never had a jump refusal from one of the paratroopers.

The C-130s would be heavily escorted. They were not dummies. Prior to the jump time, which was scheduled for ten PM, the UN Air would blast the drop zones and surrounding area just as they would in a real airborne assault. They would have the entire complement of aircraft types needed in a real airborne operation. The C-130s would each make four individual runs. They would drop a string of 30 dummies, go out to sea, come in from another direction, and drop another 30 dummies. This way the North Koreans would conclude that over 70 aircraft had dropped paratroopers. As it turned out, the North Korean spotters on the ground reported over 200 aircraft, which helped the deception immensely. Reuben had been warned by Pete that once Chuck understood the mission and told you he could do it you should back off. As the Air Force expression goes, you don't tell a guy like this how to suck eggs. Reuben left for Uijongbu. There was nothing more that he could do here.

Reuben would never write his book. On the way back to Uijongbu his UH-1 helicopter lost the tail rotor. There is no way to recover in a helicopter when the tail rotor goes. The helicopter spirals into the ground and there is nothing that you can do about it. All aboard were killed. When Pete was notified, he appointed Colonel Han as his Chief of Staff. He would grieve later. Pete estimated that he had incurred over 20,000 casualties in the last two days. The difference here was that this was a personal friend, but objectively his life counted for no more or less than any of the others. Sandy asked to be excused and went back to a corner of the underground command center where she cried for a while. Reuben Tanaka had been her closest friend in the 11th Corps Headquarters at Frankfurt and had been her surrogate father when her previous marriage fell apart. She returned a half hour later and asked Pete to forgive her weakness. Up to now it had all been symbols on a map and seemed like a large game. Now it was real. Pete hugged her and told her that it was all right. He told her of a line from Robert E. Lee that said. "It is well that war is so terrible or we would get to like it too much." Pete continued. "We fight because we must. I don't trust soldiers that actually enjoy war." Pete would demonstrate his abhorrence of unnecessary killing in less than a day. He was later able to convince the Secretary of Defense to posthumously promote Reuben Tanaka to Brigadier General – the first Japanese Jew to have a star.

The North Korean 815th Mechanized Corps was on its way to the battle area. It was estimated that it would arrive early on the morning of the 26th.

Chapter Thirty One

At 2100 on the 25th, the South Korean naval task force was four miles off the coast of North Korea, due west of Namp'o. The task force consisted of eight destroyers, seven frigates, and an assortment of smaller craft. This was not the size of force that would normally accompany an amphibious invasion and certainly would not scare a sophisticated enemy, but it was the best the South Koreans could do. They had never considered having a naval force big enough in their force structure planning for this type of operation. They were better off than the North Koreans, who only had 3 major combatant ships in their entire Navy. While the North Koreans were supposed to have around 20 submarines, there was no record of any of them, other than the Choson Victory, having ventured out to sea. One advantage was that the North Korean coastal radars had been especially targeted in the day's air campaign as part of the UN Air and UN Navy coordination. The North Koreans would certainly know that something was out there, but they would not know what and how much.

Four miles out is actually too far for accurate naval gunfire support, but that was not a real consideration. The purpose was to shell the coast and cause confusion, and hopefully, panic. For the most part the firing was ineffective from a tactical sense, but extremely effective from a strategic sense. The North Korean Navy Commander at Namp'o called Pyongyang and told them that he was under attack and that there was a possibility of an amphibious attack. He asked for help.

At 2200 the LARK-7s came roaring in from the sea. Among other things, the LARK is extremely loud, since it needs large engines to develop the air pressure to raise the craft above the surface of the water. The LARK rides on a cushion of air between the water and the craft, which is where the name Air Cushion Vehicle comes from. It can actually ride over the water, continues to ride up on the beach and go inland until obstacles of over four feet are encountered. It was not going to do that this night however.

The LARKS approached the beach in three lines of six abreast. The craft in each line were 200 yards apart. At a half mile out they discharged their cargoes of fake landing craft. In 45 minutes 540 fake landing craft were heading towards shore. Most made it, while some did not. Most of those that got to the shore exploded. It was enough to convince all but the most hard-ened and trained U.S. Marine that a major invasion was taking place, and there were no U.S. Marines on shore. The North Korean commander of Namp'o panicked and told Pyongyang that he was definitely under attack by at least a division of U.S. Marines and needed help desperately.

While this was happening, during the same time the naval preparation was taking place and the air preparation was taking place to the north and west of Pyongyang. They were attempting to give the illusion that the two attacks were coordinated, with the intent of isolating and capturing Pyongyang. The air preparation lasted for an hour and then the C-130s came in. In so far as was possible, they had been briefed on the locations of the North Korean air defense and were authorized to avoid them and any others that became active. Unlike a real airborne assault, they did not have to fly through flak to get to a predetermined target. Within reason they could devi-ate wherever they thought it necessary. There had been a long discussion about what altitude to fly at. Paratroopers like to make combat jumps at 400 feet and training jumps at 1200 feet. At 1200 feet, if something goes wrong with your main parachute there is time to use your reserve parachute. At 400 feet there is not. On the other hand, in combat you want to be in the air for as short a time as possible. At 400 feet with the T-10 parachute, the chute pops open, you make a couple of swings, and you hit the ground. It was decided to fly at 400 feet, since that cut down on exposure from air defense. No two planes flew the same flight path, so that air defense could not predict from where or when they would be coming and simplify their firing solutions.

The airborne assault of the dummies was a real mess. Dummies were scattered all over the place. Most actually landed to the west and north of Pyongyang, but some landed on the beaches, where the fake amphibious assault was taking place, and some landed in Pyongyang. But that was OK, since the intent was to give an illusion of an airborne jump and spread confusion.

There has long been an argument in the U.S. Army over the success of the 82nd and 101st Airborne Division's jump at Normandy on D-Day. Because of enemy Flak and untrained pilots of the C-47 aircraft that trans-ported them, the paratroopers landed all over the place. Very few landed where they were supposed to and units were not fully assembled until days later. However, the airborne fought wherever they landed, sometimes indi-vidually and mostly in ad hoc squad sized units. And they fully understood that their mission was to interdict the landing site and prevent the German reinforcements from reaching it. According to later captured German records, the confusion caused by the randomness of the jump accomplished exactly that. The Germans could not determine a point to attack.

Each C-130 was to make four runs. In spite of the air tactics of the C-130s, the air preparation, and the accompanying fighter aircraft, one got shot down on the first run, one on the second run, three on the third run. and two on the fourth. Of those that got shot down, the pilot's last act was to push a button that ejected all of the remaining dummies. Seven of the 18 C-130s had been lost and not all the dummies had been ejected. But not a single one of the South Korean pilots had aborted the mission. They either completed the mission or got shot down. Of the remaining 11 C-130s, all but two had damage of one degree or another. It was estimated that about 2000 dummies had been dropped. Since it was a partially moonlit night, the paratroopers could be seen from the ground.

Calls started coming in to Pyongyang that the entire 82nd Airborne Division had jumped around Pyongyang and saying that action was required immediately. The size and designation of the two assaults were not entirely accidental. Some of Li's trusted agents had been spreading rumors of just such a thing for two days.

At Eleven PM, Sung Tae Won called an emergency meeting in his private office in his palace. With the reports of the parachute jump of the 82nd Airborne Division, he did not want to be traveling around Pyongyang. He would let others do that. He asked General Yi and Li for a report on what was going on. Yi told him that there had definitely been an amphibious landing in the vicinity of Namp'o and a parachute drop near Pyongyang. At this time they did not know the size of each, but from the reports received thus far they were extensive.

Sung asked. "General Yi, what would be the purpose of these attacks and what do you recommend?"

Yi responded. "Great Leader, I see it as an attempt to capture Pyongyang and you. If they can do that, then our successful attacks in the south and the sacrifices of our Air Forces could be negated. I believe that the attacks are serious and that we must destroy them. In order to do so we will need sufficient forces. As you know, at your orders, the 815th Mechanized Corps, which is usually stationed around Pyongyang, has been ordered south to reinforce our ground attack. Our ground attack is going well and should be able to accomplish its immediate mission without the 815th. I recommend that we turn the 815th around and get it back to Pyongyang. At present it is about six to eight hours from here. The troops are familiar with the terrain and are much larger than the invasion forces. They should have no trouble defeating the enemy. I also recommend that we start moving the 9th Mechanized Corps west from Wonsan. There is very little activity going on in the eastern part of the country and the South Koreans show no stomach for action there. By moving the 9th west, we will be in a position for it to either help out in Pyongyang, should that become necessary, or send them south down the Chorwan valley, which seems to be lightly defended by the South Koreans. If they do this they could link up with our present penetration and trap the South Koreans and Americans."

Sung liked the sound of that very much and approved the moves and ordered that they take place immediately.

Yi had failed to tell him that it was important that the 815th get back around daylight, because soon after that it would become apparent that the attacks had been a ruse.

Back in the Sea of Japan, the Commander of the United States Navy Amphibious Task Force approaching Wonsan from the Sea of Japan to the east was handed a message from his Intelligence Officer.

"Are you sure? Have you verified this?" said the Commander.

"Yes sir, it is an authenticated Signals Intelligence intercept."

The Task Force Commander gathered his staff together and told them that they had a Sigint intercept that the 9th Mechanized Corps, which was expected to be their opposition tomorrow during the landing of a Marine Expeditionary Brigade, had been ordered to move west immediately. He told everyone to be wary and that this might be a trap. They should continue to assume that the 9th Mechanized Corps would still be there until proven otherwise.

By this time the United States Space Command had placed a reconnaissance satellite permanently over the Sea of Japan. The satellite was equipped with cameras and infrared detectors and a few other esoteric sensors. It had a direct data link to the ground and one of the several readout stations was in Uijongbu at Pete's headquarters. The Space Command had objected to putting the station so close to the front lines but had been ordered to do so by the Secretary of Defense. The satellite system had the capability of zooming in on selected areas upon request. Pete asked that they look at the 815th Mechanized Corps and the 9th Mechanized Corps. The satellite control officers wondered how he knew in advance what to look for. Sure enough, the 815th had stopped and was in the process of turning north and the 9th was moving west. Pete could now completely trust Li. With minor variation, things were happening just as he said they would.

Pete then got on the secure phone to General Armstrong, the UN CINC, and requested that he order the UN Air Commander that the 815th was not to be impeded in its trip north and that the 9th be allowed to go about 50 miles to the west and then be interdicted in all directions. Do as much as possible to prevent it from moving east, west, or south. North was OK. He also requested that General Armstrong order the Amphibious Task Force to not delay the landing, which was scheduled for 0600. Time was of the essence.

Their opposition was indeed moving west and that the opportunity was a temporary one. Armstrong, who was one of the few people completely briefed on Li and Pete's plan, agreed and said that it would be so ordered immediately.

Pete then issued his orders for the morning of the 26th. Since the 815th was no longer a threat, he ordered the IV ROK Corps to attack north across the base of the penetration along the Imjin and link up with the I ROK Corps on the north. All other units were to make limited attacks to keep the North Koreans from being able to shift forces. This was possible, since the North Koreans in the penetration had assumed that the 815th would protect their rear and had brought all combat units into the penetration. They had gambled and lost. Of course, they had no way of knowing that the game had been rigged.

Pete was feeling very good. The United Nations forces now had the initiative. The North Koreans were now having to react to UN moves.

The Amphibious Task Force Commander received Armstrong's message with mixed emotions. He was starting to figure out for himself what was going on. The Navy and Marine Corps were still mad that they had not been allowed to conduct a planned amphibious landing in the Persian Gulf War since it was not considered necessary for the overall land campaign because of the success and speed of the envelopment of the Army forces around the Iraqis. He did not want this operation called off too. Not only would he be on time, he intended being a little early.

The doctrine for a Navy Marine Corps amphibious landing against opposition had been developed over decades and had stood the test of time, although no one had ever been able to explain how it could work on the nuclear battlefield. In order for a landing to be successful, the assault must be concentrated in a small area, which makes for an ideal nuclear target. If it is spread out too much, it is simply not strong enough against a dug-in enemy with much more firepower. It seemed to be an unsolvable dilemma. In this case the Navy and Marine Corps had been assured that no nuclear weapons would be used. They were concerned, since everyone now knew that one nuclear weapon had already been used.

Initially the command of the landing is vested in a Navy Admiral, who is designated as Task Force Commander. The senior Marine is designated the Landing Force Commander. The Landing Force Commander takes over operational control when he is ashore with sufficient resources to fight an independent battle. At that point the Navy is then in support. The Task Force Commander had considered the orders which he had received from the UN CINC, and decided to move his operation up one hour and have the Marines come ashore at 0500. In order to do this he had cut the naval gunfire and air preparation from two hours to one. At 0400 the Task force steamed into view. The preparation started immediately, while the Marines were getting into their landing craft. At 0430 he ordered "Land the Landing Party," the traditional signal to go ashore. When the Marines hit the beaches they were unopposed and went inland quickly to establish defensive positions. They were concerned, however, for they remembered Guadalcanal from World War II very well, where the initial landing was unopposed and then all Hell broke loose.

By 1000, the entire MEB (Marine Expeditionary Brigade) was ashore. The Marines have three levels of Marine Amphibious Group Task Forces, called for short MAGTFs. The largest is the Marine Expeditionary Force, called MEF, which consists of a Marine Division, A Marine Air Wing, and a Marine Force Service Support Group, which is the logistical part of the force. The Marine Expeditionary Brigade or MEB as it is called is the next smaller size force. It consists of a Marine regiment, a Marine Air Squadron, and a logistics force. In this case, a MEB was considerd the appropriate size force, since the objective of the landing was limited. It was to take and hold Wonsan to pin down enemy forces in the area from joining the DMZ attack. Besides, a MEB was the largest size force that could be put together and transported in the limited time available, and the Marines were not going to be shut out of this war. It was a point of honor to them. They needed to constantly remind people that they exist and are good. They understood that at the end of every war the question is always asked "why do we need two Armies?" If they do not participate, the question takes on a certain validity, at least in the minds of those asking it. The Marines had no way of knowing that the war was virtually over.

At about the same time, the commander of the North Korean 9th Corps who, on orders, had moved 40 miles to the west of Wonsan, noticed something strange going on. While the UN had complete control of the air, they were not attacking him. They had knocked out all the bridges on all sides of him and had interdicted his movement with thousands of air delivered scatterable mines. Every time one of his vehicles ventured out of his present location, it was quickly destroyed by a precision guided rocket or bomb. It was if he were being given a signal that if he moved he would be destroyed, but if he stayed in place he would survive. He was exactly right in this estimate. Those were exactly the orders that the UN Air Commander had given his forces.

At two AM on the 26th Pete had gotten a secure phone call from Noonie, relaying a message from the President. The President was taking lots of heat from all sides and there was talk of impeachment over the way the war had started. The press was furious that they were not being allowed to cover the war, since Noonie had arranged with the South Koreans to keep them out. After all it was their country. Pete told Noonie that things were coming to a head and that real soon the President would have very good news to tell the American people and would be a hero. In case it didn't work out that way, the President had two very obvious scapegoats: he and Noonie. Pete told Noonie that at ten PM Washington time, or in about eight hours from now, it would be time to play the previously planned United Nations card in New York, the Headquarters of the UN. Noonie agreed and said that he would arrange for it.

Six hours later it was apparent that the pinching off of the penetration was going to be successful. Most of the fight seemed to have gone out of the North Koreans in the penetration. They had counted on the arrival of the 815th Mechanized Corps and now felt abandoned. They had been brutalized by the air attacks and the artillery from all sides and they were down to about 50% strength. Pete then issued an order to all of his subordinate commanders. "I do not want any North Korean to escape from the pocket he is in. Any attempt should be met by all the force that you can bring to bear. But as long as he remains in the pocket and attempts no aggressive action, I want to leave him alone. He has little fight left and I believe the war will be over soon. Remember that, although these people have tried to destroy South Korea for decades, they are still Koreans."

Pete knew that he had done all that he could do. From here on out the outcome was in the hands of Li Joon Duk and Yi Bong Su.

Chapter Thirty Two

The 815th Mechanized Corps was closing in on Pyongyang at 0530. The Corps commander had issued his instructions to his division commanders. He had told them that the Americans and the South Koreans had invaded the Democratic People's Republic of Korea during the night by airborne and amphibious assault. As is normal in operations such as these, things were still very confused. They would be getting contradictory requests and orders from many places and it was necessary that they pay attention only to his orders. His orders had come directly from General Yi, the Commanding General of the armed forces, which had been received by him from Sung Tae Won, the Great Leader. The orders were simple. They were to defend the Capital and Sung from the aggressors. One division would take positions to the west of Pyongyang and not allow anyone to enter or leave. This was because it was known that paratroopers of the U.S. Army 82nd Airborne Division were already in Pyongyang. The 82nd had never lost a battle. The Corps Commander stated that the Army of North Korea would have the honor of inflicting upon them their first defeat. Another division would go to the east of Pyongyang with the same mission. The 212th Mechanized Division, which had the nickname of "Sung's Own," would go directly into Pyongyang. They would secure all important government facilities, protect the senior members of the government, and root out the 82nd Airborne. The Corps commander would accompany the 212th because of the sensitivity of the mission and because of his intimate knowledge of Pyongyang. He had been raised there and had spent many years in the city as a member of the Army staff.

The 212th Division Commander was a conspirator. He agreed that the present path of Sung Tae Won was insanity. Over the last several days he had enlisted most of his regimental and battalion commanders. Those that resisted had met with unfortunate accidents and combat deaths and had been replaced with people who were reliable. The commanders of the 212th had maps identifying where the senior members of the government lived and worked. Each had been targeted by a team of trusted soldiers. The plan was simple. They would go to the location and inform the person that he was in great danger and that Sung Tae Won had ordered him to be moved and protected. It had become known that the 82nd was accompanied by a detachment of the U.S. Army Delta Force whose business, among others, was assassination. They would be taken to Army headquarters, which was completely secure, in BMD-1 armored vehicles. Sung had ordered that there would be no questions and that his orders were to be followed. Once inside the BMD-1 the official was shot. This was no time for subtleties. Later it was determined that 23 of the designated 31 senior officials had been found and killed. The remainder disappeared and were not heard from for several days, when they were tracked down and also shot for crimes against the Korean people. This operation was completed by 0730.

At 0700, Sung had ordered Li and Yi to meet with him. They agreed to meet but convinced him that Army headquarters was more secure and had all the maps and displays that were needed to understand the situation. Sung came, but was accompanied by a company of his personal guard. This had been anticipated.

Sung spoke first. "General Yi and General Li, For over a month you have been telling me how we were going to have an easy victory over the Americans and their South Korean lackeys. But now I am having to be escorted by armed troops through my own capitol because of the threat of airborne troops and we are being subjected to air raids almost continuously. Are we winning or not?"

Li replied. "Great Leader, the battle is going well for us. Listen to what we have accomplished. We have set off a nuclear device in the vicinity of Inchon and our agents tell us that there has been great damage. Only the South Korean controlled press has kept this from becoming known world wide, but it is only a matter of time until the world will know and fear us. Our attack into South Korea has achieved all of our immediate objectives. Our penetration is now just north of Uijongbu, as planned, and will soon turn south to outflank Seoul. The South Korean forces occupying the defense lines along the DMZ have already been outflanked. I will admit that I did not expect the Americans to mount an airborne and amphibious assault on Pyongyang, but with the arrival of the 815th Corps we should be able to take care of them in short order. As soon as we have done that, the 815th, together with the 9th Corps from Wonsan, will join the attack and we will achieve a breakthrough. You are correct that things have not gone exactly as we expected, but that is the nature of warfare. As long as we do not falter, we will win."

"Well spoken, Comrade General, but what is this I hear that the airborne and amphibious attacks were feints and didn't actually happen?"

"Great Leader, I have heard the same rumors. It may be true but I doubt it. We can not take a chance. As you know, the 815th has just arrived and we will know definitely one way or the other in a few short hours."

Just then the prearranged Tomahawk cruise missiles from the Aegis cruiser Bunker Hill started landing on Pyongyang. The Tomahawks had been selected for this mission for their accuracy and because the United Nations forces did not want to risk further friendly casualties. The air defenses around Pyongyang were still quite effective, since they had been placed in and around civilian facilities that the UN was trying to avoid. The targeting officers on board the Bunker Hill had been puzzled by the mission orders from the UN Air Commander. Fire about two a minute starting at 0800 and aim at open spaces near government buildings. Put two or three near but not at the Army headquarters.

At 0815 a Tomahawk hit close to the Army headquarters. Li pushed a button on a small transmitter that he had concealed on his person. A large explosion occurred in the adjacent building and all the alarms started sounding. The assumption by all was that a cruise missile had hit Army headquarters. The lights went off. At that moment Li took out his pistol and shot Sung twice in the head and once in the heart. After verifying that he was dead he reached into his pocket and took out a hand grenade and placed it next to the wall near Sung's body and pulled the pin. Li and Yi ducked around the corner and the grenade went off. They examined the wreckage. Sung's body was mangled but recognizable, but only a good autopsy could pin down the real cause of death and they had no intention of letting that happen. The damage to the wall was not quite convincing and Li took a quarter pound block of C-4 plastic explosive from his pocket, put in the detonator with a thirty second fuse and activated it. This time Li and Yi got further away. After the blast they examined the results again. It certainly appeared that Sung had been killed by the close explosion of the Tomahawk cruise missile. They called the guards and told them that the area must be surrounded and sealed off. They also called for a doctor, telling everyone that the Great Leader was wounded but still alive. The doctor, who was part of the conspiracy, arrived and immediately informed all around that the Great Leader was wounded but would probably survive, and that he needed to be taken to the hospital right away. He said that it would be at least two hours until he could make a complete report. Both Li and Yi then ordered everyone in the vicinity to not say anything until the doctor had reported. They did not want to worry the people and, of course, no enemy could kill Sung Tae Won. What they really needed was two hours to consolidate the plan. The first part of the consolidation was that elements of the 212th Division take over responsibility for the security of the Army headquarters, Presidential Palace, and the broadcasting station.

The takeover of the government buildings in Pyongyang happened swiftly and almost without incident. Over four decades the North Korean people had become so indoctrinated that the Army was the personal weapon of, first Kim Il Sung, and now Sung Tae Won that it never occurred to them not to obey. Besides, whatever possible dissent that might have occurred had been eliminated. Within two hours Li and Yi felt confident enough to take the next step. They had arranged to broadcast a message on the national radio and television network. Since this network had been informing the people of the progress of the war for the last three days, they knew that everyone would be listening, including monitors in South Korea and other parts of the world.

Li had been selected by the conspirators to be the spokesman.

"Valiant people of the Democratic People's Republic of Korea. I have the sad duty to inform you that our Great Leader, Sung Tae Won, was killed in action this morning at his place of duty during the last air raid. General Yi and I were meeting with Comrade Sung at the time and we can verify the cause of death. What is so very sad is the set of instructions that the Great Leader had given us just before his death. He had told us that Kim Il Sung had directed this war before his death and had picked Sung Tae Won to be his successor with the express promise that the war would be carried out according to his instructions. We have done that. The last part of Sung's instructions to us was that we had achieved our objectives and that it was now time to consolidate them. I believe that you need to know what the objectives were and what has been accomplished."

"We have detonated one of our many nuclear weapons on South Korea, creating great panic and destruction and proving to the world that we have matched the technology of the west and are willing to use these weapons. Our attack into South Korea has been successful and we have outflanked the South Korean and American defensive positions along the DMZ. All the militarily important terrain is now in our hands and we are on the outskirts of Seoul. Seoul can never again be defended. The 815th Mechanized Corps which came back to Pyongyang, has completely neutralized the airborne and amphibious attacks that I know you have heard about. That threat to us no longer exists. We have won.

"So, in accordance with the instructions of Comrade Sung, who received them from the Great Leader, I am offering the defeated forces of the Americans and their South Korean lackeys the following terms. It is now ten AM. I am proposing a cease fire in place at noon. We have no intention of giving up our gains. We will meet at Panmunjon to negotiate an armistice. An armistice means that neither side admits surrender, but both sides agree to stop the war. I emphasize to you again that the war is being stopped by our initiative and to our advantage. We will not sign such an agreement with either the Americans or the South Koreans, but rather with the United Nations. We will demand economic assistance. In return, we will start to allow the normalization of trade and commerce between North and South Korea.

"I have been appointed the provisional President of the Democratic People's Republic of Korea. We will have elections very soon to choose a permanent President. The Army has sworn complete loyalty to me for the present period of transition. I know that you will obey their lawful orders."

Yi told Li that he had hit just the right tone. The North Koreans would interpret the words one way and the rest of the world another.

The emergency meeting of the United Nations had been alerted and heard the speech. The British Ambassador, who was known to be very astute, turned to the U.S. Ambassador and asked, "Does that mean what I think it does?" The U.S. Ambassador nodded.

The U.S. Ambassador, who had requested the meeting, was given the floor.

"Gentlemen, you have heard the announcement of Li Joon Duk, the provisional President of North Korea. You will note that they will negotiate only with the United Nations. I have been authorized by the President of the United States and the President of South Korea to accept the offer and agree to the cease fire. I am asking you to do so. I am also asking that you appoint our Ambassador to South Korea to be the UN Ambassador to Korea. Further, I am asking you to appoint General Peter Goodwin to be the Deputy Commander in Chief of United Nations Forces, Korea. As you know, there is already a United Nations Commander in Chief. Since this war has involved only North Korea, South Korea, and the United States, all of whom have agreed, I suggest that you do not need instructions from your government. Time is critical. I need your vote immediately. The Ambassadors of France, Great Britain, and Russia immediately concurred. Only the Chinese Ambassador demurred, and then said that he would abstain. The vote was 14-0, with one abstention.

The armistice meeting took place at Panmunjon at six PM on the 26th, the same day. As opposed to the armistice of the First Korean War, as it would come to be known, this agreement would not take over two years to be finalized. It had been written by Pete and Li at their last clandestine meeting in Uijongbu and approved by the President of the United States and the President of South Korea, as well as by Li and his fellow conspirators, who now controlled North Korea. The terms of the public armistice agreement were pretty much as Li had announced on North Korean television. However, there was also a secret codicil that would be kept quiet for a while. The North Korean forces in the penetration would give up their arms and come under the protective custody of the United Nations who would guarantee their safety and care. They would be returned to North Korea in about a month. The nuclear facilities at Yongbyon would be totally open to UN inspection and all weapons grade Plutonium would be turned over to the United Nations. Both North and South Korea agreed never to develop nuclear weapons. The 9th Mechanized Corps would remain in place, but would make contact with the U.S. Marine Corps MEB at Wonsan to arrange for an eventual surrender. A commission would be appointed to start working on the eventual reunification of the two Koreas. The United Nations Commander in Chief of Korea would have two equal deputies. One would be General Lee Chi Na and the other would be General Yi Bong Su. Their task would be to gradually demobilize and reunify the two Armies to that needed for the defense of a unified nation. Although there were an infinite number of other details to be worked out, that was enough for now. The reunification of Korea and the avoidance of further war was underway. Neither Pete nor Li thought that it would be easy, but then nobody ever thought that it would be possible. At the end of the meeting Li got up and saluted Pete. Pete returned the salute and then did something he had never done before in his life. He embraced Li.

"The war is over. Now let us see if we are smart enough to win the peace."

Epilogue

The First Korean War lasted over three years and resulted in the death of an estimated two million people. Nobody could be quite sure of the number, since the Chinese and North Koreans didn't pay much attention to that sort of thing, and even if they did, they were not about to tell. The South Koreans really didn't know, since for a period of time they simply lost track as their Army fell apart. The accepted estimates were that the South Koreans lost 200,000 soldiers and 500,000 civilians, the North Koreans about the same, and the Chinese about 300,000 soldiers. The American count was more precise. The Americans had lost 54,000 battle dead, 204,000 wounded in action, and 3,100 missing in action. This missing in action figure was greater than the Vietnam War missing in action figure, though it never got the same amount of publicity.

The Second Korean War, as it would come to be known, resulted in far fewer casualties and lasted just over three days. In this war, civilian casualties were quite small, some five to ten thousand on each side. The North Koreans had about 50,000 battle dead, the South Koreans about 30,000 and the Americans close to 3,000. Most of the American dead were from the U.S. Army Second Infantry Division. The remainder were pilots. The war had destroyed the North Korean Air Force and rendered combat ineffective four of the eight North Korean Corps. The U.S. and ROK Air Force and the U.S. Navy had lost slightly less than 200 aircraft.

The difference between the two wars was that the First Korean War had resulted in a stalemate while the Second had resulted in a clear tactical victory for the South Koreans and the Americans. The problem was that the tactical victory would only be meaningful if the peace and reunification process were successful. Only time would tell, but at least the process had started out positively.

The U.S. Air Force Special Air Mission VC-135 was approaching Hawaii. This time Pete and Noonie did not have to sneak in, and they were told to bring their wives. The flight was one long party. For the first time in months Pete and Noonie were out from under extreme pressure. Jo Ann and Sandy had their husbands back. After a few too many drinks, Pete asked Noonie whether he was man enough to join the five mile high club. That got a nasty look from Sandy, and Jo Ann asked what the five mile high club was. Pete explained and Jo Ann joined in the laughter. She then surprised everyone by saying that she would be willing to join a new club at the end of every successful war and suggesting that Pete and Sandy go to the forward compartment. Sandy broke into the conversation and told Jo Ann that she had better be careful. The last time that she did it she got pregnant. Pete asked if this were true, and Sandy said yes, but that she had been waiting for the right time to tell him. She knew that if she had told him while the war was going on he probably would have made her leave and she wasn't about to leave his side. Pete was beginning to wonder just how much better life could get.

They were met at the airport by an honor guard and personally welcomed by the Commander In Chief of U.S. Forces, Pacific, commonly called CINCPAC. He was a Navy Admiral and the same one who had crossed the Secretary of Defense on the role of Naval Air. He took the trouble to tell Pete that he was now a convert to the new doctrine. After the brief ceremonies, a Presidential limousine picked up the two couples and transported them to the Hale Koa. This time the Secret Service detachment knew them by sight and did not subject them to scrutiny. As they were going from the airport to the hotel the agent in charge told them of the days activities. Upon arrival they were to meet briefly with the President. There would be no ceremony or press conference. The President wanted to keep it low key. It was important to play down the role of the United States in this affair. This is why the President had not gone to Korea. As far as the world was concerned the armistice in Korea was between the two parts of Korea and was being administered by the United Nations. For the United States to accept any of the credit would be counterproductive to the process. This meeting for the President was to simply discuss the situation with two of his senior people in Korea. A careful analysis of all the rhetoric would note that the United States was not talking in terms of North Korea, South Korea, the Democratic People's Republic of Korea, or the Republic of Korea, but simply of Korea. This was not by accident.

After the brief meeting, Noonie and Pete were challenged to a tennis match with the President and the Secretary of Defense who, they found out later, were both 4.5 players or near pro. While the tennis match was underway, the ladies were on a shopping trip with the First Lady. Later in the afternoon they would take a cruise on a catamaran around Diamond Head and back, and then have drinks and supper in the President's suite. Since this was Hawaii, dress was strictly informal. Coats and ties were forbidden and the louder the sports shirt the better. Sandy was especially grateful for the shopping trip. She needed to buy some clothes for her pregnancy.

The afternoon went wonderfully, as well it should. There were over two hundred people involved to make sure that every detail was taken care of. Pete and Noonie lost the tennis match 6-3, 4-6, 7-6 in a tie breaker. Just about right when you are playing the President, who hates to lose at anything. The catamaran cruise was superb, especially for the Noonans and the Goodwins, who had just left the very cold climate of Korea. Here it was 78 degrees, with a slight tropical breeze. In North Korea it was 10 degrees below zero.

There had been no conversation about the war the entire afternoon. That was obviously the way the President wanted it and Pete, Noonie, Jo Ann, and Sandy were most happy to oblige. They had been living the war for over two months and needed a respite. They all figured that when the President wanted to talk about it, he would, and that it would probably happen at dinner. They were right, but first the President had a surprise in store for them. After the cruise they had been told to clean up and arrive at the President's suite at seven PM. When they entered there were no servants in sight. There was a bar in the corner of the room and dinner was on a buffet table. They would serve themselves. Later on in the evening the President and the First Lady told them how much they hated State dinners and the formality of the White House. They loved to get together with friends in an informal setting.

The President apologized for ordering the dinner and hoped that they would like it. He admitted that one of his favorite foods was Polynesian from Trader Vic's. About once a month, he and the First Lady would sneak over to the Trader Vic's in the Statler Hotel across Lafayette Square from the White House, and have a meal in the kitchen where they were not observed. Honolulu had a great Trader Vic's that had catered the meal. It was on small charcoal braziers and would stay completely warm. The President first fixed the drinks and everyone relaxed. Then it was time for business. The President opened the conversation.

"I want you to tell me all about it. Every detail. I know how important it is to give someone a mission and then leave them alone, but that doesn't make it any easier. To start with tell me about the 82nd Airborne Division. The North Koreans claimed that it jumped on Pyongyang and I don't remember ever sending it to Korea."

Pete told the President and the Secretary of Defense the full story of the "Toys R Us" operation. The President was delighted. He asked the Secretary of Defense to remind him, in case he forgot, that he might want to do something about import quotas and import duties of foreign toys coming into the United States from Korea.

The conversation lasted until ten PM. Every story was topped by another. Pete told about his rides in the garbage truck and Sandy talked about

Reuben. Noonie told the story of the nuclear event and how Dr. Chan got killed. They recalled how close a thing was the "Scramble Red" of the Air Force and the execution of it by some very brave pilots. Pete told of how close the allied lines came to breaking on the first night and the heroism of the U.S. Army Second Infantry Division. There were more stories than there was time to tell. Finally, the President asked the ladies if they could be excused and the men went into the President's study.

The President spoke. "Noonie, Pete, You have done everything that I have asked of you. I am sorry that for now you can not get the recognition you deserve because success in the reunification of Korea requires that the American role be downplayed. The North Koreans and the South Koreans must see this as something that is occurring naturally, not something that has been orchestrated. But you know as well as I do that what has happened thus far is the easy part. We have nation building to do that will require knowledge of Korea and trust by all parties. I am asking you to return to Korea and finish the job. Noonie, you will be the U.S. Ambassador to South Korea and the UN Ambassador to Korea. Pete, you will be the Commander of U.S. Forces in South Korea and the United Nations Commander in Chief of all of Korea. Do you accept?" They responded. "Yes, Sir."

After the meeting with the President Sandy asked Pete what it was all about.

Pete replied. "Sandy, we are going home."

"And where is that, Pete?"

"Korea."